To Adam,

K

The Night Comes Alive

A Gothic Fantasy Novel

Copyright © 2022 by Ross Hughes

Ross C. Hughes asserts the moral right to be identified as the author of this work.

All rights reserved. This book or any portion thereof may not be reproduced or used in any manner whatsoever without the express written permission of the author except for the use of brief quotations in a book review or scholarly journal.

This book is sold subject to the condition that it shall not, by way of trade or otherwise, be lent re-sold, hired out, or otherwise circulated without the author's prior consent in any form of binding or cover other than that in which it is published and without a similar condition including this condition being imposed on the subsequent purchaser.

This book is a work of fiction. Names, characters, businesses, organizations, places, events and incidents either are the product of the author's imagination or are used fictitiously. Any resemblance to actual persons, living or dead, events, or locales is entirely coincidental.

ISBN: 9798437255254

First Printing 2022

www.rosshughes.biz

The Night Comes Alive

A Gothic Fantasy Novel

By Ross C Hughes

Cover Design by Whitney Lynn Hayes

Published 2022

Also by Ross C Hughes

A Dead Wizard's Dream, Book 1 of the Convent Series

Secrets of the Ashlands, Book 2 of the Convent Series

The Man Who Sank An Island, Book 3 of the Convent Series

Into the Madlands, Book 4 of the Convent Series

Lord of Demons, Book 5 of the Convent Series

City of Peace, Book 6 of the Convent Series

Chronicles of Maradoum Volume 1

Chronicles of Maradoum Volume 2

Chronicles of Maradoum Volume 3

Chronicles of Maradoum Volume 4

Chronicles of Maradoum Volume 5

Chronicles of Maradoum Volume 6

Dedicated to Jack Moonie RIP

Acknowledgements
Thank you to my friends and family for being there for me, to my readers for reading and to my pup, for moral support. A huge thank you to Whitney Lynn Hayes for the wonderful cover art.

Prologue
The End

I knew there was something they were not telling me. I knew it!

Royce Moors quivered with excitement, ablaze with curiosity so that his squinty little eyes popped out of his meaty head. Finally, he knew the truth. Finally, he knew that Vampyres prowled the streets of Justiqua at night.

I can barely believe it even now, as I lay my own eyes upon the proof.

He had staggered out of *The Bent Penny* tavern only a few minutes earlier, where he had been celebrating his forty second birthday with his friends. The proprietor, Ignatius Boondoggle, had waved him off, and the world had seemed warm and fuzzy thanks to the twinkling stars and the wonders of inebriation. He had begun the walk home alone, imagining the evening would be like any other, when he had spotted something that had to be seen to be believed and his night had taken a dark turn.

Now, his eyes bore witness to a grisly scene that few lived to report in a courtyard charred by an old fire, where the travertine statue of a fabled Norn wallowed in misery atop a blackened plinth in a pool of moonlight. Abandoned by the populace after the riot that had left it so scarred, the statue and courtyard were living testament to the city's violent history. Almost entirely walled off now by multi-storey tenements, shadowy and accessible only by narrow alleys, they were a faecal smear that the supposedly noble city of Justiqua wished to forget.

Many of the flagstones were cracked or missing, and the statue itself drooped piteously. Once it had depicted a Norn bestowing blessings on a young Elf. Now, the Elf was gone, smashed to pieces and strewn around the courtyard, and the Norn had no one. She stooped for no one, making it seem as though melancholy was dragging her down. Moss crawled up her body and patched her face like a beard. Her features had been chipped away, her robes were pocked and pitted, and her wings were black, as though she had given up the light of the Prophet and turned, in her sorrow, to the Nether for comfort.

Royce had no eyes for the statue that stood as a reminder to all of mankind's bestial nature, however, only for the beast beside it. This was no man, of that he was sure. He had thought it a man once, had believed Sir Alonso Gómez to be a fine man and a fine Knight. Now, he knew better. A chill wind froze his blood in his veins. As he watched the venerated Knight sink long fangs into a young raven-haired woman's neck by the ethereal light of a full moon, he knew what the man was.

A creature of the night! A Vampyre!

He could hear the nightmare sucking the beautiful girl's blood from his vantage point secreted behind a gaggle of cracked and empty barrels, even over the ubiquitous noise of the night. An owl hooted, and a plague-stricken beggar groaned. A rat scurried through a gutter close by, and the wind hissed sinister symphonies in Royce's ear, rustling the trees in the streets beyond the confines of the courtyard. The bitter stench of piss rotted the air, and horror crept up in his throat like bile. He wanted to brush his thinning ginger hair out of his face and pull at the collar of his doublet, but he dared not move. His legs were cramping beneath him from an extended period of crouching.

This is what Spot de León refused to reveal to me, what he knew all along! For thirty years, I have lived a lie! Oh, if only I had been more watchful as a child, I might have known sooner. All those years ago, in Darcuul's mansion, he knew.

Mid-meal, the Vampyre abruptly jerked up its head and sniffed like a bloodhound scenting its prey, short-cropped hair shining silver in the moonlight. Dressed in a stylish embellished black cloak over a frilly shirt and tight trousers, it was as out of place in the blackened courtyard as a rose in a pile of ashes. It hissed, shadows playing across its thin face as it scowled, and a moment later Royce jumped out of his skin as three figures clad all in black plummeted from the surrounding rooftops to land with synchronicity in the courtyard surrounding the creature of the night. One of them landed by Royce and spotted the portly, middle-aged man cowering behind the barrels. Royce cringed, for as sure as Gómez was no man, this was no man either. Though it had borrowed the shape of a man, wide black feathery wings extended from its back and a beak disfigured its face. The other two were likewise misshapen.

If I didn't know any better, I'd swear those were giant crow wings!

He almost fainted when the closest Crow spoke in a surprisingly cultured, familiar voice. "Get out of here, Royce. You're going to get yourself killed."

Royce gasped. "Spot?"

The Crow turned away from him to face the Vampyre once more. Sir Alonso Gómez dropped the body of the woman he had drained unceremoniously, and a couple of ravens squawked overhead.

"The noble *Rugadh na Marbh* have come to kill me, have they?" Sir Gómez sneered, pale face pinched in hatred. "You'll have to catch me first!"

So saying, he swept his black cloak about him and dissolved into the darkness as if he had never been.

"No problem," the Crow grunted, throwing out a hand. "Eyes! *Luz!*"

A shadow shifted, flitting across the courtyard. As the Crow let loose the last goosebump-inducing syllable, however, there was a blinding flash of light and the shadow resolved abruptly into Sir Alonso Gómez once more, who tripped and fell clumsily. Royce rubbed his eyes.

Are my eyes playing tricks on me or have I gone insane?

All his hairs stood on end, and he could feel a strange tension in the air as if before a storm. The Vampyre Knight had transformed into a shadow, and the Crow had turned him back into a man.

Magic! Unbelievable! I thought it had been wiped out! Just wait until I tell the world. My stories will be the envy of that prolific buffoon, Monty Wainwright!

"Face me, Gómez," commanded the Crow, drawing from the sheath at its hip a broadsword with a lion's head pommel whose three-foot blade glittered like starlight. "Your kind will soon be wiped from the face of Maradoum!"

The rasp of steel scattered the ravens, although Royce noted that they circled in the clear sky above so that the stars appeared to wink at him.

"Tch, very well, Crow," snarled Sir Alonso, whipping out his own rapier in the blink of an eye with little more than a faint hiss, making his feathery blonde hair bounce. "You ask for death and I shall give it. Do you have the gall to face me alone, little bird, or will you have your friends do your dirty work?"

The Crow motioned for its comrades to stay back. "It's just you and I, Gómez."

The Vampyre Knight glanced up and then grinned nastily. "No, it isn't."

"Look out!" the Crow shouted, abruptly diving to one side and rolling – just in time to avoid a swooping shadow, Royce saw, agape.

One of the other Crows reacted quickly, slashing at a diving shade with a gleaming katana, splitting the vapour and somehow forcing the shadow to coalesce into a man crying out in pain as if a spell had been broken.

More magic! Another Vampyre!

The final Crow was not so lucky. A shade descended on it from on high with the speed of a striking falcon, and it swung its broadsword high in the air. Royce was not sure exactly what happened when the shadow made contact, but he saw a spurt of blood and when the darkness drifted away, the Crow had been flattened. It lay on the floor, groaning.

"It's a trap!" the first Crow shouted in a powerful tenor, swinging its sword this way and that at the wraithlike shadows that hounded it now on every side.

Its remaining comrade was similarly beset, Royce saw, shivering with more than the cold of the night. Shadows flowed towards the Crows from all angles like inverse black ripples. Cutting down one shade and gaining space to breathe, the first Crow grabbed the medallion strung around its neck on a silver chain and brandished it, shouting, "Eyes! *Luz!*"

A blinding light flashed, and Royce knuckled his eyes, seeing colourful spots. The shadows resolved into the shapes of men, all stumbling and falling, some dressed in ornate regalia as was Gómez, some in more prosaic gear and some in steel plate armour. All bore daggers or swords, and all sprang up and set about trying to skewer the surviving Crows with fangs bared, spitting and grunting.

Royce's skin crawled. It was an eerily quiet fight, surreal in the starlight and almost silent save for the shuffle of footsteps and the flapping of wings, punctuated now and then by the occasional clang and scrape of steel on steel, which seemed overloud in the night hours.

"Finally, we have caught you in our noose!" Gómez crowed with delight, throwing wide his arms. "A thorn in our side for too long you have been, young warrior, but now it is time for you to die!"

Clouds swept over the moon, plunging the courtyard into an abyssal blackness.

When they cleared, Royce saw with hammering heart that the Crow who had spoken to him had Sir Alonso Gómez pinned to a wall with its sword through his heart. The other Crow crouched by the one who had fallen, surrounded by a carpet of corpses. Royce thought it looked like the fallen Crow was breathing. Of the shifting shadows, there was no sign.

Gómez chuckled, drooling blood. "It'll take more than that to kill me, you know!"

"I know," said the Crow. "And it'll take more than that to wipe Vampyres from the face of Maradoum. But we'll get there in the end. I would say *recce em Pacia,* but I'd rather you rot in the Nether for what you've done. *Surtur losagadh!"*

Bright white flames erupted along the length of the glinting broadsword and rapidly spread over the Vampyre's entire body, crackling and whooshing with almost enough vehemence to drown out the undead creature's shrieks of agony as it died.

A voice purred in Royce Moors' ear then, and he felt hot breath on his nape. He froze, his blood stilling in his veins.

That's the voice of Ignatius Boondoggle, the proprietor of The Bent Penny ...

"Well, well, well, what have we here, eh? A nice juicy morsel? Can't have you spying on our goings on now, can we?"

2
Smoke and Skulls

Spot de León was small, no getting around it. He had always contended with a runt-of-the-litter mentality. At the age of twelve, he was shorter than most everyone he knew, even some of those younger than him. That they had the gall to surpass him galled him. Not only was he short but he also had a purple birthmark surrounding one eye, lending him his nickname. The teasing never ended at school.

"What's the weather like down there?" they would say, sniggering.

Or "Hey, Patchy!"

Or "There goes a Pygmy, look!"

Or "Does that eye of yours even work?"

Or the constant favourite, "Oh, look, a Dwarf!"

Not here, though. Not in the streets where they played kickball. Here, his name was whispered in hushed tones by those in awe of his ball-kicking skills – or so he liked to think. He was the terror of the makeshift playground with a ball at his feet, unstoppable. Once he got the ball, it was almost a sure thing his team would score. People would cheer him on occasionally – the only instance in his life he could ever remember that happening – and he would glow on the inside, as if his heart shone like the sun.

I feel like a child in a man's world most of the time. With this fraying leather ball at my feet, though, I feel like a champion.

The wind rushed through his short-cropped mouse-brown hair as he sped past one defender, and the dingy grey alley in which they played spun around him as he pirouetted past another. Dodging defenders, he darted in and out of the thin strip of waning sunlight illuminating half the alley, half blocked out by the rows of tall terraced buildings on either side. Groans of dismay marked his passing.

His shirt and breeches billowing on his scrawny frame in the sudden gust bearing with it all the smells of the city from excrement to vomit and the ever-present fetid taint of rats, Spot hurtled down the street at full speed, a smirk spread across his pale, sharp-featured face. He hightailed it past another defender, but then disaster struck. Waste had overflowed the runnels on either side of the alley that served as gutters here in the poorer section of the city, and Spot was forced to stretch to kick the ball away from the dung before it could touch it. Then, he teetered off-balance, windmilling his arms and trying desperately not to step on the poo himself. Tumba Koum saved him by grabbing his collar and hauling him away.

Panting, Spot nodded to his friend. "Thanks!"

A grin split open Tumba's sweaty mahogany face, and he replied in a lilting accent, "The poo almost had ya!"

Spot punched his friend on the arm and turned to see that the other team had secured the ball when he had lost it and were now sprinting back down the street towards his own goal – an overturned barrel. "Quick, get after them!"

He and Tumba hared back down the street, the taste of copper coins in their mouths, their skinny legs aching. Spot had never had so much fun. The fastest among them, he managed to catch the boy with the ball and slide at him from the side feet-first to boot the ball away from him. Having seen what his friend was planning, Tumba had positioned himself on the other side, ready to receive. The ball landed at his feet, and he took off down the alley as clouds overtook the sun, casting the city in shade. Springing up, Spot came abreast of him in moments on the other side of the street. They passed the ball back and forth between them without slowing as they approached the barrel that was their opponents' goal. Tumba lured out the goal-keeper by running close and then passed to Spot, who calmly tapped it into the barrel behind the keeper's back. The friends whooped and embraced as their team cheered, and they ran back down the street to defend their own goal with their arms in the air, their fellows clapping them on the back as they went. Spot could not stop grinning.

When the opposite team came racing towards them, one of Spot's team members tackled the girl with the ball and passed to Spot. The pass was a poor one, though, and Spot could not reach it in time to prevent it from flying into a deep doorway, there to smack awake a rag-clad beggar mumbling in his dreams. The crusty old man sat bolt upright, gazing blearily about.

"Here, what's all this fuss?" he demanded, before slouching back into a sleeping position beneath his threadbare blanket.

"Hey, be careful over there!" shouted a passing grey-haired city watchman in silver-and-blue livery.

"Sorry!" said Spot as he retrieved the ball, dropped it at his feet and took off down the alley once more.

Weaving between opponents in a slaloming snake's course, he dashed toward the barrel at the far end of the alley, barely able to see where he was going in the premature twilight. Nevertheless, when faced with the last defender, he could see enough to slip the ball between the boy's legs and continue on around him while he spun in bamboozlement and the other children laughed uproariously. Aiming for a split second, Spot booted the ball and watched with satisfaction as it soared into the barrel with a clatter. He hollered for joy and threw his arms in the air once more, beginning the

The Night Comes Alive

victory walk back towards his own barrel.

On the way there, though, the last defender growled at him as he went by, "I'll get you back for that!"

Spot shook his head, trying not to let the comment spoil his mood. He knew the boy, Wally Shanks, would be smarting at the laughter coming his way. A big brutish lad with wavy blonde hair, the only way he could make himself heard was through his fists and he was not used to being the butt of jokes. Spot was thrilled to have shamed him so, and a little trepidatious.

Serves him right.

Tumba tackled a girl on the opposite team as she brought the ball back down the alley. He passed to Spot and then sprinted off down the street to be ready for a return pass. Spot ran after him more slowly, feinting this way and that before slipping past a couple of defenders trying to close him off. Then, he was running flat out down the side of the alley by the gutter, aware in his periphery that Wally Shanks was closing in on him from the side like a fleshy battering ram wrapped in striped green-and-white cloth. He urged his legs to greater and greater speed. He was past one defender, two, three. He was almost to the barrel. Wally would catch him before he got there, though, he realised glumly. He passed the ball to Tumba rather than risk taking it around Wally again.

A moment later, Wally slammed into him, throwing him bodily into the wall of the nearest building so that he slumped down into the waste-filled gutter, the wind knocked out of him. A cloud of flies buzzed around him. Gasping for breath, he regarded his dung-drenched moccasins with distaste.

"You pig-brained mongoose!" Spot snapped a little breathlessly a moment later, stepping out of the runnel and shaking off his shoes. "Look what you've done to my shoes! Father is going to kill me!"

"What are you going to do about it, Patch?" Wally snarled, stepping close and towering over Spot by head and shoulders.

I really want to blacken this bully's eye, but my father will punish me even more for a fight than for the shoes.

"Just get out of my way," he started to say when Tumba took a different tack.

Leaping on Wally's back and wrapping his skinny arm around the bigger boy's neck, he yelled, "Stay away from him, ya hear?"

Wally grunted, took a couple of steps back and then grabbed Tumba's head and mop of dark hair and flipped him over so that he landed on his back on the cobbles with a thud and a groan.

"Get off me, you dirty foreigner!" Wally spat, kicking him while he was down.

Where are the city watch when you need them?

Spot hurled himself at Wally, punching him hard in the chest. He was going to follow up the attack, but he thought he might have accidentally killed poor Wally as the boy staggered back, ashen and wheezing as if he could not breathe. Indeed, his face turned purple as a beetroot. Spot just stood and stared as the bigger boy tottered away, clutching his chest and evidently trying to withhold tears. He looked around. The other children were staring at him in amazement. He helped Tumba to his feet, noticing that the Chilpaean boy's bare feet had been splattered by gutter slime when he had been thrown down.

"Thanks, Tumba," Spot said. "That was really brave."

Tumba grinned weakly. "You're the one who got rid of him. That must have been some punch!"

"Must have been," Spot said, running a hand through his mouse-brown hair self-consciously.

"Come on," said Tumba. "Let's go clean up at my ma's. I'm guessing you don't want your father to see you in this state?"

Spot shook his head, grateful for his friend's understanding and offer of help. "No, he'd have my hide. I'm supposed to be attending a ball to celebrate the new year with him tonight."

Sunset washed over Justiqua as the two friends bade their fellows farewell and made their way to a well to wash their shoes and feet. Spot shivered as he dumped icy cold water over his moccasins, hoping they would dry fast and clean. Then, they squelched through the streets beneath a garish sky that painted the grey houses reddish gold and made the crimson roof tiles glimmer. The Church of Saint Padrice glowed in the sunset, its colourful stain glass windows casting glorious refractions of riotous light on the cobbles surrounding it. Spot ogled the ugly gargoyles hanging off its eaves as he often did. Said to be used architecturally for helping water drainage, they always seemed to him an odd choice for the ancient church. One of the oldest in Justiqua, it was said to have existed during the Time of Witches some one hundred and fifty years ago, perhaps even before. Its arched doorway, peaked tiled roof and ridged steeple were as familiar a sight to Spot by now as his father's face.

Plum radiance blazed along the horizon by the time the friends reached Tumba's little terraced house, where he lived with his mother. Delicious smoke billowed out through gaps in the ill-fitted doorway. The friends barged in on old Ursa Koum while she was smoking a baui pipe and stirring a black cauldron set into a pit in the floor in which raged a fire. She flicked a wrist when they entered, and the pipe in her hand vanished. Spot blinked.

I'm sure she must have put it down or tucked it up a sleeve ... It was still lit, though. I could see the smoke, and now I can't. There must be some explanation. My eyes must be playing tricks on me.

Ursa was the epitome of the matronly figure, Spot had always felt. Plump and cheerful and always in an apron over a forest green frock decorated with pale green flowers and cinched with a stretch of hemp, she bustled around the house with motherly energy, silver dreadlocks bouncing, ever on the lookout for something to fix or something to improve or something to do to put a smile on another person's face. Spot felt like a self-centred boor every time he saw her and wondered if she had ever had a selfish thought in her life. Her entire existence seemed to revolve around making Tumba's life as good as it could possibly be, as well as the lives of all those around her.

Renowned as a gifted botanist in the community, she occasionally helped folk out by giving them herbs to remedy their ailments as well as giving alms to the poor and homeless, though she barely held her own head above the poverty waterline. Spot had overheard some of the other Chilpaean immigrants call her Mzee. She worked as a maid, he knew. Every time he visited her single-room shack and ate her food, he felt pangs of guilt, thinking of the banquets laid out on silver dishes back home in De León mansion.

Ursa never seemed to mind, though, always saying, "Don't you worry, my dear, we have plenty!" in that wide accent of hers.

This night was no different. She invited him in warmly when she saw him, clucking like a mother hen at the sight of his waterlogged moccasins. The dark skin around her grass-green eyes crinkled as if she were smiling in secret, though.

"Sorry to intrude, ma'am," said Spot, "but I was wondering if you could help me get rid of some of this stink before I go home? Father will be furious if he sees – or smells."

"Don't call me ma'am. What happened to da two of ya, eh?" she asked fondly, approaching them to analyse the damage and shaking her head. "Your fadder need not worry so much, child. Tis only poo."

Spot chuckled at that.

"A bully called Wally shoved Spot into the gutter," Tumba explained. "So I jumped on his back, but he threw me off. That's when I got dirty, too. Then, Spot whacked him in the chest and he just ran off."

"You protected my boy?" Ursa asked, eyebrows raised. Spot nodded. "Well, tank you for dat. But you boys should not be getting into fights in da first place, ya hear? Violence never solves nutting."

Spot wanted to point out the double negative, but he understood the point and so held his tongue. She was always good to him, after all. She scrubbed their feet in a wooden basin filled with water and lavender sprigs.

Then, she scrubbed Spot's shoes and brushed them over with herbs. In the end, Spot worried she might have gone overboard. He did not want to smell like a floral arrangement. He was too grateful to complain, though.

All the while, he gawked around the room as he did every time he came, wondering how there was more to take in inside that little shack than in his home mansion. Chairs and a small pitted table creaked if you so much as looked at them. An old armchair wallowed in one corner. Hides adorned the walls, clothes were strung across the room, and vases and pots of flowers and herbs proliferated everywhere, creating a clashing kaleidoscope of colours. Strangest of all, several human skulls stared back at him eyelessly from seemingly random locations around the room, like the lintels of the narrow windows, although Spot got the ineffable impression they were part of a specific layout, a macrocosm of a shrine of some sort. He had always been too nervous to ask Ursa about them.

"Thank you, ma'am," he said, bowing to her as he left. "I really can't stay for supper, but thank you. I really must get home to my father. Goodbye. Bye, Tumba!"

Spot hurried through the darkening streets, one eye always on the great fiery eye on the horizon, drowsily lowering its lid. He hurried past numerous beggars on street corners and in doorways, many groaning in pain. He passed by a few corpses too, a ubiquitous sight in Justiqua since the plague had struck. It was generally believed to be carried by the rats, whom he saw by the swarm, though only ever at a distance thankfully. The vermin infected the city, breeding out of control and running rampant through the poorer sections where there were less guards and those who were there cared less.

The grim sights and the odious scent lessened as he passed into a richer section of the city, where his father's mansion was to be found. The houses switched from ash-grey to bone-white, and porticos and pilasters and other architectural superfluities began to appear. As the sun finally set and the world was plunged into absolute darkness, Spot slipped into De León mansion.

3
New Year Ball

"Look at the state of you! Where have you been? What have you been doing? What happened to your shoes? Why are you wet? Ugh, we have a ball to attend tonight, son!" Viscount Marcus de León barked at Spot as he squelched inside.

Gazing at the rug-laden floor of the antechamber and the small pool of water spreading from his shuffling feet, Spot muttered, "Sorry, father. I'll go and get ready."

Marcus sighed and forced a smile to crack his stern-as-granite visage, ruffling his son's hair. "There's a good lad. Just … be quick, please."

Spot nodded and hastened up the curving marble staircase to his chamber, where he rapidly ditched his dirty clothes and donned a fresh white shirt and dark breeches before slipping on a clean pair of stockings and leather shoes. Then, since winter was tightening her grip on Justiqua, he threw on an ermine fur coat, too. He was back downstairs in mere minutes, the sight of his father tapping a foot impatiently spurring him on.

"Are you ready?" asked Marcus, barely awaiting an answer before saying, "Let's go."

They took a carriage to *Pacia* Castle on the southern bluff of the island, where the Lord Protector's New Year Ball was being held. The air there had a salty tang.

I wonder if any of the children I played with today have ever been in a carriage. I doubt it. That's sad. They're no different than me, so why am I blessed with such a luxurious existence while everyone else seems to scrape for scraps? I don't understand the ways of the world.

One thing he did understand was that it was because his father was a Knight of the Order of *Pacia* – more than that, he was Viscount of the city of Justiqua, capital of the island nation of Justiqua – and therefore worthy apparently of heaps of riches and praise. Spot had been told time and again that the Knights were cleansing the world of the evils of sorcery, which sounded like a good thing, but he had overheard Ursa and others in the slums speak of the Knights as murderous bigots looking only for an excuse to put innocents to the torch. He did not know what to believe, but he did not believe his father was a murderous bigot.

I'm not even sure what a bigot is.

It seemed to boil down to a difference of country and religion; Justiquans saw the world one way, and everyone else saw it another.

I'm not sure I'll ever understand.

The streets of Justiqua rolled past in the inky blackness, lit by pools of lantern light here and there. The *Pacia* Castle complex, when they reached it, reared up in front of them like a widowed behemoth standing vigil on the edge of a cliff overlooking the Aegis Waters, the ocean south of the island of Justiqua. A squared black silhouette cut out of the starry sky, it grew the nearer they came, blotting out more and more stars as if devouring them, as if sucking them down into its infinite dark depths. Its windows glinted in the moonlight like spider eyes, some lit orange from the inside.

Spot gulped when the castle complex's pointed watchtowers and gap-toothed battlements loomed immediately before him, seeing the points of the portcullis high above his head as he traversed the threshold. It did not come crashing down on him as he feared, though, and city watchmen in silver-and-blue livery armed with pikes waved them through. Next, he had to face his greatest fear – socialising with the elite. Passing by a barracks and a wooden scaffold surrounding a cathedral-in-construction, Spot and his father strode through a corridor of city watchmen standing at attention and entered *Pacia* Castle proper, its minarets striping them with shadow as the moon broke free of the cloudbank, shedding silvery light across the city.

The light and noise spilling out of the castle's front entrance grew and grew as they neared it until Spot felt like he was suffused in all of it, saturated. People's voices grated on his ears like a chorus of crows, and he felt hot under the collar, itchy, in proximity to so many other people. Candles and candelabras glowed everywhere he looked, illuminating the grand antechamber and main hall beyond, and he pondered grumpily whether they had enough. The crimson silken hangings appeared in danger of going up in flames.

Maybe I could help them along ...

He wondered again why his father dragged him along to these events, but he knew why – because his father did not trust him to stay home alone, with only a maid who dared not say no to him. He smiled ruefully.

I caused some serious mayhem in my younger days.

Passing through a vast and airy antechamber in which languished leather couches, statues, vases of exotic plants and a few decorated marble pillars, father and son entered the main hall, which had been filled with lacquered tables and chairs for the event. On the tables were laid out banquets upon banquets, dishes upon dishes both familiar and exotic to make the mouth water, as well as jugs of water and wine to quench the thirst. Servants bustled this way and that, refilling goblets and removing empty platters. The hum and hullaballoo of overlapping conversations clawed at him, tugging him a thousand different ways at once as his brain tried to take it all in and failed.

Trying to centre himself and hear his own thoughts over the

pandemonium, Spot switched his attention to the decorations. Moonlight filtered in through the paned windows to illuminate tapestries depicting Justiqua's warlike history banding the creamy walls, showing events from the mysterious Prophet's life as well as battles undertaken in his name after his demise. Thick rugs were strewn all across the stone floor, red as the blood in the tapestries. Gold inlay decorated the ornate cornices, and Spot wondered how long Tumba and his mother could survive off the money of just those fine lines of gold.

A long time, I suspect, and yet here it's an afterthought, a trivial expense.

"Follow me, Samuel," said Viscount Marcus de León, and Spot bridled at the use of his real name, which he considered about as unique as a beggar in the big city.

Wending his way through the throng with Spot on his heels, Marcus smiled and bowed and hand-shook his way over to his clique, whom he had spotted from across the hall when they waved him over. Gazing blankly at the heels of his father's black boots, Spot resigned himself to another night of boredom, of counting the volutes on the rugs and trying not to listen to the dull drone as adults discussed politics, the economy and general hearsay about city life. He glanced around in the hopes of distraction.

The room dances to the music of cliques.

Everyone swirled into their own clique, with their own friends from their own House.

Not unlike the volutes.

Within the Order of *Pacia,* the umbrella term for the Knighthood at large, four distinct Houses also existed. Created for the apprentices to inspire competition, these Houses had spiralled out of control from there until full-grown adults attested their die-hard devotion to their particular House, some even going so far as to avow hatred for the others, even though nominally they were all of the same rank, Knights of *Pacia*. Even the Lord Protector insisted folk call him 'Sir' as he, too, was but a Knight. Spot did not fully understand the rivalry. Spot's father and his companions gave their loyalty to the House of *La Salamandra*. All the Houses' names were in old Runic, the archaic language of Justiqua.

"Greetings, my friends," Marcus cried over the hubbub, shaking hands stiffly with the men and bowing to the women.

"Marcus!" croaked the old fossil responsible for the smooth running of the city of Justiqua, Count Milus Kronvert. "So glad you could make it, my good man. Do come and join us, won't you? Oh, and you brought your handsome little boy. Isn't that delightful?"

The old man beamed at Spot with his face a foot away from the young boy's, while Spot tried to smile in return.

This knot of old men resembles a herd of shrunken elephants with their loose-hanging, wrinkly skin and overlarge ears. It's always gross old men and women who attend these parties lately.

A wave of self-loathing washed him up on a guilty shore as he recalled why that was the case. All those of fighting age had embarked on the Crusade to the south. All that was left in Justiqua were those too young to fight and those too old. Even Marcus de León was showing signs of wear and tear.

When did the crow's feet become so deeply etched around my father's eyes? When did his curly hair become so grey? He reminds me of an autumn flower just gone over.

"Did I miss anything?" Marcus asked, accepting a goblet of wine from a servant.

"Oh, no, nothing much," a woman gushed, chubby cheeks coloured from the wine. "Sir Cel Tradat has yet to make his speech, so the entertainment has yet to begin. Still, we have been here almost an hour already ... What kept you?"

Marcus sighed, cutting Spot like a razor, for the son knew why the father sighed. "Just dealing with life, Maria. Sir Gómez has not yet had a chance to make a complete fool of himself then?"

Maria tittered, covering her ruby red lips with a fat hand whose fingers appeared inextricably connected to a whole host of rings. "Not yet, but it won't be long now, that's for sure!"

Everyone laughed, and Spot rolled his eyes, wishing they could take a seat but knowing from experience that if he tried his father would insist he stand by him. His father and his friends mocked Sir Alonso Gómez every time they attended a public event, for the man regularly became too sozzled to stand up straight and had to be carried home.

Don't they ever tire of telling the same jokes?

"I certainly won't be carrying him home!" broke in a beefy man whose face was ruled by a moustache and whose jowls wobbled when he spoke. His gut strained his damask shirt and fur coat to breaking point, and his belt and trousers looked to be in danger of giving out at any second. "I wouldn't travel on foot through the city even half a mile these days. Liable to be robbed. Or murdered. There are more vagabonds than ever out there! To say nothing of the rats! It's a disgrace! A disgrace, I say!"

"It's a tough time for folk right now," Marcus agreed, adjusting his tight, buttoned olive green coat so that his neckerchief and the collar of his pale shirt could be seen. "These rising taxes are draining us all dry. If you hadn't a lot to begin with ..." He shrugged.

"Indeed, indeed!" trumpeted the moustached man. "A pox on the tax-collectors and the Crusaders responsible for them, that's what I say!

Justiqua is going to the dogs, I say, to the dogs!"

"Well then, its's up to us to save it, Horatio." Marcus raised his goblet as if at a toast.

Baron Horatio Sigwell barked with laughter. "Us? We're but a bunch of old fogeys, De León! A bunch of old fogeys! And where are all the good strong young men, I ask you? Rolling in their graves, that's where they are, wishing fruitlessly for a life they cannot live. And why? Because of these cursed Crusades!"

"Keep your voice down, Horatio," warned an old woman in a shimmering silken gown the colour of a robin's egg. "You don't want to publicly upset the Lord Protector."

"Faugh, get your hands off me, woman!" Horatio expostulated, flailing his arms though she had but touched his bicep. "I'll not be silenced by the likes of you!"

"I'm your wife," she said icily.

He did not appear put out. "Nevertheless! I am entitled to my own opinion, I'll have you know, and to voice that opinion, as loudly and vociferously as I please."

The woman, Helena, rolled her eyes. "How much wine have you drunk tonight, dear?"

"Not enough!" roared Horatio, red in the face. "Here, boy! Bring me another goblet, if you please! And even if you don't!"

"Gómez has got some competition this evening," said a man half Horatio's girth, nudging Marcus gently with his elbow.

Marcus nodded, eyeing Horatio with trepidation. "You can say that again, Giles."

He was spoken over by the boisterous Horatio, however, who had heard Sir Reginald Giles' comment and now glowered at the man, brows beetling. "What's that, you whippersnapper?"

Giles chortled, his round boyish face warm and prone to laughter. "I'm – what? – two years your junior? My hair is just as grey as yours, Horatio. We're mutton, not lamb, and we must accept it."

"Well, at least I've got hair!" Horatio shot back, running a gnarly hand through his short silver locks and pointedly eyeing Sir Giles' widow's peak, while the skinnier man only smiled sardonically and smoothed his dark brocade doublet. "You don't agree then that these taxes are extortionate and that the Crusades should have been called off a long time ago?"

Sir Giles tilted his head. "Did I not lose my barony because of those cursed taxes? Am I not of the House of *La Salamandra*, just like you? Of course I do, Horatio. But what are we to do about it? Sir Cel Tradat stoutly ignored our petition."

"We need somebody who can bend his ear," put in Maria Giles.

"As Count of Justiqua, Kronvert *should* have that capacity," grumbled Horatio, glaring after the Count, who was making the rounds.

"You would think the Lord Protector would see reason now that the city is in the grips of such a horrific plague," Marcus said, shaking his head. "He must see that we are weak without our warriors. The Babese and Kutzians despise us. The Fjellians are suspicious of us. Any of them could storm our shores, and I fear we would be subject to their whims within the year."

"Bah, they would not dare!" Horatio waved a dismissive hand. "They know we are the superior fighting force. They cannot compete with our tactics – as we showed them in the eastern Crusades!"

"And we cannot compete with their terrain," Marcus replied. "You were there, Horatio. D'you remember trying to climb all those hills and gullies in Al Kutz, besieged all the while by guerrilla fighters? Our lads in the south are likely experiencing similar problems even as we speak."

"My knees remember those hills! Well do they remember!"

"And just think of the size of Quing Tzu," added Sir Giles. "It's by far the most expansive Crusade yet. Honestly, it's no surprise they need the taxes. Can you imagine taking and holding a country so vast?"

Marcus shook his head. "It's foolishness. We cannot conquer our way to victory over people's souls. True, the pagans must be taught the way of the Prophet to save their everlasting spirits, but there are more peaceable ways to go about it. A missionary programme could be arrange to visit the country and –"

"Bah!" blurted Horatio. "Missionaries! They'll never teach the soulless to change their ways! It must be done by blood and tears, that's the only way! I say only that the Crusade should be postponed until such time as we are properly prepared for another."

"We had scarcely recouped our losses from the previous one," Sir Giles muttered. "So many of our strong young men dead in a foreign field. It breaks the heart, it truly does." More loudly, he said, "And I agree with you, De León. With Justiqua in such a state as it is, I think our strength would be best concentrated here on our own shores. The plague, the rats, the rampant poverty and the crime to which it leads ... all could be ameliorated by a stronger military presence here in the capital. The Prophet knows we don't need another riot on our hands. The criminal underworld is beginning to run this city, I see it from my mansion. The merchants are all terrified of them. I'm sure at least half are suffering from protection rackets. Have you heard bodies have been turning up in the streets with puncture marks on their necks, almost entirely drained of blood? Some theorise that people are turning to drinking blood in their starvation! I do not believe such rumours, of course, but the fact remains that Justiqua is out of control. Something must be done to restore order to our streets, and if the Crusaders do not return, I'm not sure how it's to be done. There are simply not enough soldiers or guards in the city."

Marcus nodded. "Maybe we don't need someone who can bend the Lord Protector's ear. Maybe we need a new Lord Protector."

"That's dangerous talk," said Sir Giles quietly, though he was hanging on every word.

"La Grulla, La Pantera, El Toro ... none of them want an end to the Crusades," said Marcus. "None of the other Houses. Only us. If we want change, we must effect it ourselves."

"Hear hear!" approved Horatio loudly, belching.

"What if we could alter the perceptions of one or more of the other Houses?" suggested Sir Giles. "It seems to me that may be the best way to bring an end to the wars. If we are tied up at home, divided on opinion, then surely the Crusades cannot continue."

Marcus shook his head. "It is a temporary measure at best. The Lord Protector does not want an end to the wars, so there will be no end."

"I think our best bet would be *El Toro*," continued Sir Giles, affecting not to hear De León. "They are conservatives at heart. They want only what they see as best for old Justiqua. If they can be convinced that the Crusades are ruining our economy – which they are – then perhaps they will see reason. Even if it is only temporary. It could buy us time."

"Time?" Horatio bellowed, waving his goblet and almost decking a servant. "It is not time we need! It is an end to these infernal taxes!"

"Is Sigwell Mansion suffering during these trying times?" asked a high, weedy voice. "Perhaps I could loan you a few Reales if you're in a spot of bother."

The friends of the House of *La Salamandra* spun to behold the speaker behind Horatio. Tall, thin and pale, a man with long, eerily straight bone-white hair leered at them from the front of his own clique. A blood-red doublet and breeches of the same colour clung to him.

"Oh, bog off, Rathbone!" snapped Horatio. "I need neither your pity nor your charity, so get you gone, whelp!"

"That is no way for a civilised man to speak to another," chided Baron Erlic Rathbone, raising his shaven glass-sharp chin, his unnaturally blue eyes piercing. "I merely happened to overhear your last comment, old chum."

"Uh-huh," grunted Horatio. "Well, you've heard my response, so I bid you good day, sir!"

"You know the Crusades will never come to an end, don't you?" asked one of Rathbone's companions calmly in a voice as deep as the grave, adjusting the black gloves that matched his silver-threaded black outfit and lank black hair one by one. "Not until the whole world has been saved, that is. Not until the whole world worships the Prophet."

Why is he wearing gloves?

"There are other ways to convert folk than torching their homes, Count Darcuul," Marcus said through gritted teeth, while Horatio blustered, searching for a response.

"And yet none so effective," replied Count Ivan Darcuul with a grin that split his skinny, shaven weasel face wide open and made the dimple on his chin even dimplier.

"*La Pantera* will not be happy until the world is dust and ashes!" Horatio finally boomed.

Sir Rathbone's smile was as wide as it was infuriating. "Only from the ashes can the Phoenix rise. Perhaps you have heard the old legends?"

"Oh, please, if I believed the old legends, I'd be stringing you up for witchcraft, you daft albino!"

Sir Rathbone's smile flickered this time. Staring at his face, Spot saw a muscle twitch and then it was as if he fell through a trap door and he was somehow seeing *beneath* Rathbone's face to a horrific hidden visage. Sweat broke out on his brow, and his legs turned to jelly as he beheld a chalk-white face gaunt as a skull framed by thin, patchy hair like a dying cloud, eyes with unnaturally bright blue irises popping out of sunken sockets. Rathbone's fingernails were claws as he pointed at Horatio, and Spot gasped when he spoke, disclosing a mouth entirely devoid of teeth save for four long curved fangs in place of canines, all of which overlapped his lips.

"Mind your tongue, you bloated walrus!" Sir Rathbone snapped.

Spot blinked, and the vision was gone. His view beneath the veil was replaced in an instant by the scene he expected to see. Rathbone appeared normal once more, his face – while still pallid – far less monstrous. There was no sign of the fangs. The eyes, though, were the same. He turned an apologetic smile on the staring boy, and Spot blanched, making the old Baron's brow furrow.

"You must have read the reports," Marcus put in quickly, while Horatio made disgusted noises. "Thousands of Crusaders killed, territories lost rather than gained, diseases in the ranks … We must call them home before they all get themselves killed out there! Surely you must see that?"

"And leave the land to the Tzunese?" Rathbone demanded. "Not a chance, my good sir, not a chance! We cannot simply leave them to their pagan ways. Think of their souls!"

"Bah, you don't give a rat's ass about their souls!" Horatio yelled, including the entire room in the conversation. "*La Pantera* is on the front line, stacking up the glory and riches! That's all you care about! Don't think

I haven't read the reports. Reading between the lines, I'd say it's clear the Crusaders – those that survived anyway – have been lining their pockets with all the plunder they can find!"

"And what if they have?" asked Baron Rathbone. "Just imagine when they bring all that wealth back here and the effect it will have on the economy." He grinned. "Everyone in *La Pantera* will be rich as sultans!"

"You as much as admit it, you scum!" cried Horatio, throwing his arms up in the air. "You admit they are lining their pockets!"

"I am here in Justiqua, and they are a thousand leagues away in Quing Tzu," replied Sir Rathbone off-hand. "How am I to know what they are doing?"

Horatio growled, but had no immediate response.

"And what of the plague, the poverty in the slums and the swarms of rats?" Marcus demanded. "Will glory fix those issues? Will the folk in the slums ever even see a penny made from the Crusades?"

"We do not undertake a Crusade for profit," Rathbone chastised him. "We merely recoup the cost of the undertaking."

"Of course you do," Marcus sneered.

Baron Rathbone opened his mouth to retort, but a fanfare of trumpets drowned out whatever he might have been about to say.

4
Crows and Clowns

All heads in the hall swivelled, and all eyes focussed on one old man as he doddered out from a back room and, with help from his two strapping young aides in maroon livery, tottered up onto the dais at the far end of the room to take a place at the grand mahogany table there. Armoured Knights in tabards emblazoned with the crest of *La Grulla* took up posts by his sides. Several more old men followed to take their own seats, and Spot de León recognised them as the Heads of the Houses. Spot thought it looked as though the giant fresco of the Prophet, pale, golden-haired and pointy-eared, was gazing down benevolently on them

Murmurs rippled through the hall. "It's the Lord Protector!"

"I heard he was ill."

"I heard he might not attend."

"He looks ready to collapse!"

The Lord Protector, Grandmaster of the Order of *Pacia*, Sir Theodore Cel Tradat, cleared his throat and beamed out at the congregation gathered before him. He had a grandfatherly face, broad and open, wise and friendly. His head gleamed in the candlelight where his tonsure refused to grow. Though ancient and clearly unstable, he was weighed down by some of the heaviest-looking brocade robes Spot had ever seen, rich red velvet inset with gold thread and pearls. The Heads of the Houses were similarly bedizened.

"Friends, compatriots, kinfolk," the Lord Protector said in a high hoary voice that yet carried to the far corners of the hall, "tonight we celebrate the new year!" Cheers and stomping feet rattled the rafters, and Sir Cel Tradat smiled, allowing the hullaballoo to continue for a moment before waving for silence. "Tonight, we eat, drink and make merry, knowing that we have well earned such respites after a long and arduous year. There have been many difficulties this year, and we have all had to make sacrifices for the greater good. We have all had to suck in our bellies to provide for the Crusades, so that the world may be saved from paganism. In order to provide for the Prophet's holy army, we have spent tens of thousands of Reales – and I am pleased to say it has paid off! Knight-Commander Lopez has successfully invaded Quing Tzu, established a beachhead on the coast and is using it as a staging post to launch assaults further inland!"

"He's been on the coast for years," Sir Giles muttered. "He hasn't gotten anywhere. I bet the Lord Proptector doesn't mention all the losses and defeats."

"There have been setbacks," Sir Cel Tradat continued.

"Setbacks," Sir Giles repeated sarcastically.

"But I am confident in time that the holy army will prevail over the pagans and save their souls," finished the Lord Protector. "The Prophet wills it so. The logistics of supplying armed forces so far overseas is not an easy one to overcome, and I must thank you for all the money you have raised in the past year from your own pockets. Thank you, thank you, from the bottom of my heart. It gladdens my soul to know that we have so many ardent believers here in the city, willing to lay down their lives – and Reales – for a noble cause. I am aware that you have all sacrificed, as has the city. Justiqua languishes in the grips of a plague unlike any we have seen for a generation. The rats are everywhere, carrying with them their stench. The corpse collectors are overwhelmed. We cannot dig graves fast enough. And yet we persevere. Horrible weather and freak storms have ruined the yields of some fields, resulting in fewer crops to go around. The people are hungry, starving even. More and more have been turning to crime, putting a greater and greater strain on the city watch. And yet we persevere. The construction of the new cathedral has been delayed by the loss of workers to the Crusades, as have many other construction projects and labours at large – believe me, I know. And yet we persevere. Our soldiers are stretched thin, so that we have fewer than ever to guard against the Goblins of the Archipelago. The Goblins have not attacked often of late, but when they do, we lose invaluable men every time. And yet we persevere. We have almost eradicated magic, so that no one need suffer the cruelties of sorcery, but it lingers on in the dark corners of the world. And so we persevere.

"We persevere in putting Witches and Sorcerers down wherever we find them. We persevere in curing the sick and helping the homeless and starving. We persevere in cleansing the city of the accursed rats. We persevere in our building projects and our tilling of the fields. We persevere with our Crusades. Why? Because if we do not persevere, who will? Who will save this world from itself if not us? We are Knights. Crusaders. Holy warriors pledged to the Prophet. And it is our duty – nay, our purpose – to fight back against the wrongs of the world! We fight back against the rats! We fight back against the plague! We fight back against paganism! And we will win!"

He spoke the last three words slowly and forcefully, emphasizing them with a fist banging on the table. The room erupted with cheers and applause, whistling and hooting.

Wow, that was a good speech. Even father looks inspired.

Marcus' cheeks were flushed, and he did not appear to be faking his cheering. Spot noticed Sir Alonso Gómez passed out on a couch and shook his head with a chuckle.

The Lord Protector eventually waved his arms for silence, and when it descended, he said, "I have initiated a number of public works programmes, hiring folk to help clean up the streets of rats, beggars and the corpses of our lost loved ones. Your Reales may be running a little low, thanks to this newest tax, but I assure you your souls are saved, for the Prophet cares not for materialism, only for our immortal spirits."

"To spirits!" Horatio roared, brandishing a bottle of whisky that came from Spot knew not where. He had not thought there any whisky around and could not banish a suspicion that the drunk old man had brought it in secreted beneath his robes. A wave of laughter swept through the room, and the Lord Protector's smile only broadened.

"On that note," Sir Cel Tradat continued, wheezing with laughter and raising his goblet in a toast with a wavering arm, "here's to the year 154 AC! May the Prophet watch over us all!"

"Hear hear!" cried a jumbled medley of jarring voices, making Spot wince.

The Lord Protector waved a hand – he might have spoken, but it was lost amid the rising tide of noise all around him – and a troupe of entertainers was ushered in from another of the back rooms. Jugglers, acrobats, dancers, singers and instrumentalists romped in, setting the room ablaze with song and dance. Worst of all, in Spot's mind, were the clowns.

I hate clowns!

"It's Bibaldi's Clowns!" people gushed, hands on cheeks.

Spot was petrified of clowns. Their chalked and painted faces, with rouged cheeks and overlarge lips, gave him nightmares. Every time they hooted on one of their little horns, he jumped in fright. He hid behind his father and prayed they would not spy him. He peeked out at the rest of the troubadours, however, in awe of the complex melodies they could weave together with their different instruments and voices. Lyres twanged, drums banged, trumpets honked, and flutes twittered like a host of birds at dawn, all intermingling, complementing and emphasizing one another, rather than detracting. They sang a song with which he was familiar, *The Tavern Keeper's Daughter,* and he could not resist singing along. Neither could Horatio, much to his wife's chagrin.

To everyone's surprise, a second troupe, the Hound's Fools, was brought in then, which seemed at first superfluous – until the two troupes began to sing alternating songs, clearly having choreographed the performance beforehand. While one troupe sang and played instruments, the troubadours in the other took a break. The acrobats and jugglers were given no such respite. Spot was relieved to see there were no clowns in this second troupe, and so he oriented himself to be hidden from the first, where he could better see the second, helping himself to bacon-wrapped sausages from one of the tables.

Once everyone was deep in their cups, the second troupe began to play a song more mournful than had been the wont of the evening so far, surprising Spot and a great many others. Indeed, Spot had never heard the song before in his life, while he could at least hum the tunes of most of the others. The chorus branded itself into his brain in letters of fire.

"The Lord of Crows,
Over the damned weeps,
His host of ghosts,
Rises up from the deep,
Creatures of the night,
Be afraid, be aware,
The Lord of Crows,
Over the damned weeps."

The verses put Spot in mind of a fairy tale, depicting the journey of the legendary Lord of Crows through a fantastical landscape on an epic journey to a world beyond Maradoum, where he encountered mythical beneficent beings, the *Sluagh na Marbh*, who empowered him to fight evil in his home world. He returned home and slew the blood-suckers who had kidnapped his love, thereby freeing Justiqua from evil forever and ever. Spot was enthralled, eyes fixed on the lead singer, a man in purple leggings and a doublet with a handsome, aquiline face and a mostly bald head split in two by a strip of purple-dyed hair running down the middle and continuing into a ponytail at the nape.

"Did you know you're drooling a little bit?" squeaked a feminine voice, startling Spot from his reverie.

"W-what?" he stammered, turning to see a girl his own age in a frilly magenta gown staring at him.

"You should close your mouth," she advised.

"I-I wasn't drooling," said Spot, blushing and wiping his mouth. "I was just enjoying the song."

She smiled and nodded, her elfin features brightening Spot's life. "I could tell. You were lost in it. The singer's very famous, you know. His name is Lebron DeRose."

"Oh ... I didn't know."

"I'm Aiva Thragon."

"I'm ... Samuel de León, but please, call me Spot."

"It's nice to meet you, Spot de León."

She doesn't seem put off by my birthmark.

"It's nice to meet you, Aiva. I don't recognise the name Thragon. Who are your parents?"

"Oh, they're over there," Aiva said nonchalantly, jerking a thumb over her shoulder. "My father is Baron Valdimir Thragon."

Following her vague jab, Spot laid eyes on a large group of people, none of whom he recognised. "Oh, so you're not of *La Salamandra?*"

"No," Aiva scoffed, flicking her plaited raven locks over her shoulder. "My family is of the House of *El Toro.*"

"Oh," said Spot, sagging. "Mine is of *La Salamandra.*"

"I know," she said. "My father says *La Salamandra* are a bunch of yellow-bellies, who don't want to fight in the Crusades because they're scared."

Spot bridled. "We are *not –*"

"I don't believe him, though," she continued, leaving him flustered and speechless. "I don't think you're all cowards. In fact, I think you're very smart to want to bring an end to the Crusades."

"Oh, really?"

"Yes. It seems to me they cannot continue forever." Her voice shrank. "Too many brothers and fathers have been buried already."

Spot nodded. Many boys his age at school had lost older brothers. In a flash of insight, he understood then what she meant.

"You ... lost someone?" he asked gently.

She searched his face for a moment, found only sincere sorrow, and nodded, her eyes welling. "My brother, Romero."

"I-I'm sure he was very brave," Spot said.

I don't know what to say ... I wish I had not pried.

She nodded, but said, "Why do bravery and foolishness go hand in hand so often?"

Spot blinked and spoke before he knew what he was saying. "Sometimes we must be brave for our loved ones by putting ourselves in foolish situations to keep them safe."

She stared at him for what felt like several years then, and he coloured.

"That's exactly what he would have said," she said in the end.

They resumed watching the acrobats and listening to the troubadours sing *Young Janie,* a classic, in silence. Marcus de León tapped Spot on the shoulder a while later to offer him a cup of fruit juice and a platter of beef and vegetables, and Spot turned to accept them, involuntarily locking eyes with one of the ghastly clowns at the far end of the room as he did so. Once again, he felt like a rug had been yanked out from under his feet, the wool pulled from his eyes in an instant, so that he was looking *beneath* the clown's outer visage to his secret inner mien. The red wig he wore was unchanged. Like Rathbone, though, his face was a skull with pale skin as thin as parchment stretched over it. He grinned nastily at Spot, his four long fangs shifting and scraping together where they protruded past his lips. Spot felt as though his blood had frozen in his veins, transforming him into a statue unable to tear his gaze from the clown's evil ice-blue eyes. He dropped the plate, and it shattered loudly on the stone floor. All eyes turned on Spot for a second, before everyone returned to their conversations. A servant in blue-and-yellow livery hurried over and started cleaning up the mess.

"Butter fingers," commented Marcus, before moving away.

"Yes, sorry, father," agreed Spot distractedly.

"Are you okay?" Aiva asked, seeing him staring off into the distance with his neck twisted at an uncomfortable angle.

Spot's head snapped around so fast she jumped. He blinked rapidly and his eyes unglazed, as though he had come back to reality from a deep daydream. He gazed at her open-mouthed for a second, then looked back over his shoulder, then back to her again.

"What do you see when you look at that clown?" he asked, pointing subtly.

She shrugged. "I see a clown. Face paint. Wig. Stupid painted lips. Ridiculous colourful clothing and overlarge shoes. What's to see? I've seen hundreds of them."

Spot ogled her. "You don't see anything ... unusual ... about him then?"

"No," she replied, brow furrowing as she began to suspect he was poking fun at her. "Should I?"

"I don't know," Spot murmured pensively. "I thought for a moment I saw ... I don't know. I don't see it anymore."

"Right," she said, drawing out the word sceptically. "Are you a few bananas short of a bushel, Spot de León?"

He chuckled distractedly. "Maybe. Maybe I am." He was silent for a moment, before blurting, "D'you believe in monsters?"

She tapped her dainty chin with a slim, pale finger. "Depends what you mean. There certainly *are* monsters of a sort out there in the world – my father told me so. There are Goblins in the Archipelago, Orcs in Chimanchu, Ogres in the Sultanate and some kind of creepy cat-people in Al Kutz. If you mean Dragons and their kin, my father says they have all been slain – or soon will be. If you mean the human kind of monster – a monstrous man, for example – then, yes I do."

Spot shook his head. "No, that's not what I mean. I mean ... shapeshifters ... people who can hide in plain sight with more than one face."

"Two faces?" she repeated sceptically. He nodded, and his earnest expression prevented her from teasing him. Instead, she hummed, "Hmm, I don't know. Perhaps. My father says the world is full of unsolved mysteries.

My mother says there is an explanation for everything, though. What of your parents?"

"My mother died in childbirth," said Spot, "and my father believes only in what he can see with his eyes and touch with his hands."

"I'm sorry to hear that," said Aiva quietly, wringing her hands.

"Oh, he's not all bad," replied Spot off-hand.

Aiva withered him with a glare. "I meant I'm sorry to hear about your mother."

Spot smiled awkwardly. "Oh. Thanks. I mean, I never knew her, so it's hard to miss her, and yet … sometimes …" He trailed off, staring through the fire-breathers.

His alone time with Aiva Thragon took off after that as a group of bored youths clustered around them, chatting and watching the entertainers.

On seeing Spot peering closely at the troupe, though not at the clowns, one chubby youth asked, "What's piqued your interest, Spot? Lebron DeRose was good, wasn't he?"

"Oh, sod off, Royce."

A little while later, a drunken Horatio insulted Baron Rathbone loud enough that the other could hear him and Marcus de León and the others of the House of *La Salamandra* had to drag Horatio outside to his carriage before he could be challenged to a duel, or before he challenged Rathbone himself. Spot bade farewell to Aiva and followed his father, chuckling at Baron Sigwell's incoherent spluttering and loud bouts of unaccompanied singing.

5
Rathbone Manor

The carriage ride out to the country manor of Baron Erlic Rathbone on the edge of the city of Justiqua seemed to Spot de León to take an age and a day. The city was a grandiose, sprawling mess of a place, extending for leagues, so it took a few hours to reach the manor. The white horses were lathered by the time they arrived, snorting heavily. Spot's bum was numb. He had wriggled around the entire time, trying and failing to achieve comfort.

I'm so bored!

There had been few distractions in the carriage. His father was a taciturn man at best, and trying to engage him in conversation about anything other than politics and the wellbeing of the city was akin to explaining the benefits of a hat to a dog.

There's no point in telling him about Baron Rathbone or the strange clown. It must have been a daydream. Or food poisoning.

There was nothing to be seen out of the carriage windows, save for an inky world rolling slowly by, its sounds deadened by the clattering wooden wheels on the cobbles. Rows of houses loomed in the darkness, striping his vision with shadow, like the silhouettes of the fingers of a monstrous god raking the world in anger. The pearl of the moon came and went, flirting with the thunderous clouds. A faint drizzle pursued them like a clingy lover all the way to the manor, its ardour undampened.

Spot knew they had arrived before his father announced it from the appearance of the fireflies of torchlight ahead. Darkness had swaddled them for so long by then that it felt strange to be born again to the light. Torch-bearing servants awaited them outside the manor in matching red-and-white livery, bowed to them when they alighted from the carriage and offered to escort them inside. Viscount Marcus de León graciously accepted and swaggered into the behemoth building behind a servant, eager to showcase his new mustard doublet. He even wore a small cape, purely for fashion.

There are no city watchmen to keep us safe this time, only servants loyal to Baron Rathbone.

Spot dawdled after, eyes on the faux castellation engraved on the walls, the peaked slate roof, the ornate architrave and the creaking iron weathervane in the shape of a crane. The wind howled, and the crane spun around and around, looking like it might fall off at any moment and skewer some passerby with its beak. Spot could not look away. His father shouted him, and he darted inside.

The manor put Spot in mind of the hollow of a tree, wood panelling seemingly sprouting from the walls and rug-laden floor in the foyer, sturdy rafters overhead supporting peaked ceilings. Battle tapestries marched on either side of them, depicting war and death on a grand scale. Spot shuddered at the sight of the inhuman little stick-men poised for an unfeeling skirmish. They were shown to the main hall, a large olive-carpeted stone room, where they met Baron Rathbone and the other guests, who were inspecting the archaic weapons on display with interest. Stuffed animal heads grew from the walls above the weapons as if the beasts had been subject to some horrible curse, many with associated plaques. It looked like the home of a hunter. It looked like the home of *the* hunter. Ice sculptures of swans topped a few small tables, despite the fires in the hearths. Busts were arrayed around the room atop plinths, old beardy men glaring at the revellers. Rain pattered on the narrow paned windows.

"Ugh," groaned Marcus. "I'm sure Rathbone will find an excuse to tell every living soul here about his bloody hunting trips at some point tonight. As if none of us have ever been hunting."

Spot looked up at his father, surprised.

He never normally swears. He must be uncomfortable here.

"You don't like Baron Rathbone, do you?" asked Spot quietly.

Marcus glanced down, equally surprised, a smile passing over his face. "No, I must admit I do not. Still, I am the Viscount of Justiqua. How would it look if I did not attend a gala held in honour of raising money for the Crusade?"

"The Lord Protector doesn't attend."

"Yes, well ... he *is* very old, so he is excused."

"But you don't want the Crusade."

Marcus looked around to check nobody was eavesdropping. "That's true. But the policy of the Lord Protector is to support the Crusade movement. I cannot go against him in this. It would be nigh treasonous."

"You can't have your own opinion?"

"Of course I can. And I can try to influence the Lord Protector to see my point of view. But I cannot act on that point of view. Not without consent. Understand?"

Spot shook his head. "Not really."

Marcus ruffled his son's short, umber hair. "You will one day, my son. For now, just watch and learn. Over here. I see Count Kronvert and Baron Sigwell."

Easing through the throng gathered in the hall in their finest regalia, father and son waved over the Count and Baron. "Good evening, Count, Baron!"

"Good evening, Viscount, good to see you again. You're looking well," wheezed Kronvert, before leaning so close to Spot that the young boy could smell the almost bald old man's pickled breath and see the elephantine wrinkles in his wide, wizened face. "And Samuel, my boy, so good to see you, too! My, how you've grown. You know, I've known you since you were yea high and it has been my pleasure to watch you sprout into the strong young man you've become!"

Spot tried a smile and nodded. "Thank you, Count."

The Count beamed and moved away.

"I'm surprised you came!" boomed Baron Horatio Sigwell in his signature subtle tones. "Everyone knows you hate Rathbone for the dog he is!"

"Shh! Not in his own house!" Marcus hissed.

"Boy, am I glad you're here," muttered Sir Reginald Giles, stroking his moustache. "Now there's three of us to control Sigwell."

"What's that, you mutterer?" Horatio demanded.

"Nothing, Baron," replied Sir Giles innocently. "I was just saying you're the heart of the party."

"Damn right I am," the Baron mumbled, mollified.

Marcus stifled a laugh with a cough. "Did you hear? Another body was found two nights ago with puncture marks in its neck, drained of blood. Just a husk." He shivered. "I don't know what's become of the city. The people are becoming more and more depraved every day."

"It's the hunger," Horatio said knowingly. "Malnourishment will make a man do strange things. I heard a rumour that the beggars have started eating one another."

"I heard they've started eating the rats," said Sir Giles, "and that those that do have cysts in their groin before the day is out."

Marcus sighed. "I don't know how true any of that is, but it is true that there are more and more beggars every day. These taxes are pushing the people to breaking point. They can't take it much longer. I fear there'll be a revolt before the next New Year Ball if we are not careful. Unless riches start pouring back into Justiqua from the Crusade, the aristocracy may just fall prey to the starving masses in yet another riot. Knight-Commander Lopez is bleeding us dry with nothing to show for it! Not a single victory for months!"

Sir Giles nodded glumly. "I'm surprised he hasn't been ousted from Quing Tzu entirely. His forces have suffered so many losses."

"The people will never overthrow us, no matter what Lopez does," said Horatio, waving a goblet dismissively. "The people need us! Most can neither read nor write."

"But they can farm and fight," said Marcus grimly, "and what more do they really need? The city is fast becoming a ruin scattered with half-finished buildings, ever worsening slums and abandoned houses full of criminals. The Crusades are costing us everything."

Sir Giles nodded. "I think you're right, De León. I think we need a shift in leadership if we're to surmount these obstacles."

"We cannot talk here," said Marcus lowly. "We'll discuss it in the week. I have a few supporters in *La Salamandra* and *El Toro*, but not enough. Not yet." He watched Count Kronvert's back. "The timing must be perfect."

Spot thoroughly enjoyed the plates of partridge, boar and venison that were served in the vast, portrait-dotted dining hall, hardly noticing the stiffness with which his father ate, too focussed on Horatio's gusto.

I wonder why all the portraits look exactly like Baron Erlic Rathbone? He must take after his ancestors a great deal.

After the servants had cleared away the dishes and the guests had returned to the main hall, the entertainment was ushered in.

"Ladies and gentlemen," intoned Baron Rathbone theatrically, "you may recognise the Hound's Fools from the New Year Ball. I was able to convince them to come and entertain us one more time. Please give them a warm welcome!"

Spot recognised them as the troupe without clowns and whooped in approval, while those around him applauded and cheered. The acrobats and fire-breathers came bounding out, flipping and cartwheeling, followed by the instrumentalists weaving a merry melody on their lutes, drums and trumpets. The singers came last, their voices the music's crescendo, the cherry on the cake.

Spot was awed, so enthralled he did not even notice the approach of Aiva Thragon until she said, "Amazing, aren't they?"

"Hmm, what? Oh, oh yes, they are. Good to see you again, Aiva."

"Good to see you too, Spot."

They stood in what Spot felt was a very awkward silence for some time, observing the troupe's antics.

What do I say to her? Why do I feel like a clot every time she is near?

"So," said Spot eventually, feeling like his mouth was thick with molasses, "how have you been?"

She looked at him, and he was trapped by her gaze like a fly in a web, unable to look away. "Do you really want to know?"

"Erm, yes."

She sighed, sagging like a sail on a still day. "I miss my brother. I know my father misses him terribly, too. It's been hard on him since Romero passed away, and he has been hard on me."

Spot nodded. "Parents can be terribly strict sometimes."

"That's not what I mean," she said in a small voice, so small that

Spot did not hear her over the whoosh of a man close by breathing fire and the applause it elicited.

"Did you see that?" he asked excitedly.

She nodded, though her vision was distorted by welling tears. "Yes, I saw it. Can we ... go somewhere else?"

"Yes, let's take a look around!" Spot enthused, before turning to see her watery eyes and slumping a little. "Where did you want to go?"

"I don't know ... just somewhere quiet, please."

Spot nodded. He wanted to take her hand, but felt self-conscious. So, instead he turned and walked away, looking over his shoulder every few seconds to be sure she was following. His mind raced under the pressure of pleasing her while she was in a tearful state.

Where should I take her? I don't know the manor any better than she does! I could take her outside, which would guarantee us privacy, but it would also guarantee cold and wet. I could take her upstairs, but father says never to go upstairs in another's home without invitation. So, all I can do is wander around and hope to find a quiet study or something of the kind.

So that was what he did. Sidling away from the adults while they were busy watching the acrobats and listening to the music, Spot led Aiva down various green-carpeted corridors, finding adults in every room they entered, until at last they followed their noses to the kitchens, where servants were bustling about cleaning dishes. Nipping past servants who either did not see them or did not care enough to say anything, Spot and Aiva descended a stone staircase into a torch-lit wine cellar.

"We should have a moment's privacy in here," said Spot, looking around at the dusty bottles stacked on shelves, the barrels and the sconce-set stone walls. "At least until the servants come down for more wine." He cleared his throat awkwardly. "D'you mind if I ask – why were you crying?"

"I was crying because boys never listen, Spot de León!" she snapped.

"Oh," said Spot, taken aback and immediately wishing he were elsewhere. "S-sorry."

Aiva sighed and sat on an ale barrel. "It's not your fault. I'm sorry. I just ..." Her eyes welled again, and her words were almost sobs as she continued, "I just don't have anyone to talk to about ... about my father."

"What about him?" asked Spot, sensing that he was required to do so.

He took a seat on a barrel beside her.

I can't just leave now that she's crying again. That wouldn't be right.

"He's been different since Romero's death," said Aiva. "He ... he would always beat me when I was out of line in the past, but ever since my brother's death ... he drinks from dawn till dusk and beats me at the drop of a pin. I can't be in his presence alone without him beating me." Seeing Spot searching her face, she added, "He is careful not to leave bruises where people can see them. But look at my body."

Standing, she lifted her gown, revealing her pale legs, undergarments and belly. Her stomach was purple and yellow as a peach, and Spot winced as he imagined the pain she must be in, while also feeling a twitch of the loins.

"I-I'm so sorry," he said, not sure what else to say or how he could possibly help her – although he wanted to. "I could tell my father if you like, and perhaps he could –"

Aiva shook her head, dropping her gown and plopping down on the barrel once more disconsolately. "No. There's nothing he can do. It's fine. I just ... I just wanted somebody to confide in. So ... thank you, Spot."

She touched his arm, and he flushed. "Happy to help. Anytime."

Silence swirled around them for a while then, until eventually Spot said, "It's not right, what your father does to you. It's horrible. Maybe there's some way we can –"

"Shall we try some wine?" Aiva interrupted, reaching over, taking a bottle from a shelf, blowing the dust off it and then coughing.

"I don't think I can allow that," said a faint chucking voice that seemed to come to them from far away.

A see-through silver man drifted through the wall then, floating in the air with only a smoky wisp below the waist rather than legs. He wore antique knightly armour with a sword at his waist, and his short hair was puffed up in an old-fashioned style. Spot and Aiva let out a shriek, but the ethereal moustached figure only smiled at them with a grandfatherly mien. When he spoke, his voice seemed again echoing and distant.

"I cannot in good conscience allow two so young to partake in these fermented delights," said the apparition.

"You're a g-g-g-ghost!" Spot stammered.

The ghost rolled its eyes. "Yes, I am, now stop stuttering, boy! It ill becomes you. Now, go on, scram! Get out of here. And don't tell your friends you saw a ghost. Or they'll all be coming down here, banging on the walls and wanting to see me. I'm not a performer, you know!"

Spot's brow furrowed. "Wait, why *are* you here? Who are you?"

"Oh, here we go," muttered the ghost as if fed up with proceedings. "I suppose I might as well tell you. Nobody else tolerates my tales anymore. The servants all just ignore me, if they ever notice me at all. Blind as bats, all of them." He drew himself up. "Ahem, my name is Baron Jorge Rathbone, sire of the current Baron Rathbone."

"You're Erlic Rathbone's father?" Spot repeated in amazement.

The spirit nodded. "I am ashamed to say I am. My son always had a cruel streak. As a boy, he would tear the wings off dragonflies. As a man, he … he favoured ladies of the night, if you know what I mean."

No idea.

"And when I say favoured them," the ghost went on, "I mean he … he enjoyed their pain."

"What a horrible son you have," Aiva said, her face scrunched up in disgust.

"Yes," put in Spot, pretending to understand.

The ghost hung his head. "I know. When I discovered his … tendencies, I confronted him. I told him I would no longer fund him, and I kicked him out of my home, telling him I was going to change my will so that he would be left with nothing." The wraith looked around and chuckled ruefully. "I'm sure you can guess what happened. He snuck back in and slew me before I could change the will. Everything went to him. The manor, the title, the land, the money … he got it all. And to make matters worse, he had become a creature of the night by then, so he used his supernatural powers to bind my spirit to my bones, trapping me in the astral plane for all eternity and denying me the sanctuary of *Citta Pacia*. Such spite …" He shook his head. "I am ashamed to call him my son."

"Your bones?" Spot repeated dumbly, trying to take it all in.

The phantom nodded. "Would you care to see? They are through a secret door over here. Come, just press on this rock here."

Aiva pushed the brick indicated by the ghost, and with a loud clunk and rattle, a door-shaped section of the wall began to slide sideways to reveal a musty aperture. Dust wafted out. Spot grabbed a torch from a sconce, and he and Aiva peeped inside. Aiva squealed and turned away immediately, and Spot felt green as he laid eyes on the mound of skeletons inside the secret room.

"You're not the only ghost that haunts this manor then?" asked Spot.

"No," the spirit admitted. "There are others. I'm the only one who can be bothered to manifest anymore, though. The others have pretty much given up on life – or the afterlife."

"Who are they?" Aiva whispered.

"Servants, Knights, a gardener, a cook," replied the ghost. "Whomever my son finds … distasteful."

"You said he was a creature of the night?" asked Spot.

"I did indeed. I know not exactly what he has become. I know only that he is not human anymore."

"What are you two doing down here?" asked a voice from the stairwell, and Spot and Aiva's heads snapped around to see a podgy ginger boy in a dark doublet. "Found a secret passage, did you?"

"Go away, Royce!" Spot bellowed.

Royce Moors' face fell, and he sulked off.

By the time Spot and Aiva turned back, the ghost was gone. Not sure how to close the secret door, they decided to scarper back to the gala, hearts thudding. Their eyes darted around while they sweated once they were back in the main hall, but no one seemed to have noticed their absence and they soon relaxed. They were again enraptured by the musicians, singers and dancers, particularly when one of the dancers flipped her way over to Aiva to invite her to dance with the troupe. Shyly, Aiva allowed herself to be drawn in and was soon jigging with the dancers with a sheepish expression. Spot's sides hurt from laughter. When the up-tempo song ended, the dancer led Aiva back to Spot and curtseyed to him.

He applauded her in earnest. "Bravo! Bravo!"

"My thanks, young man," grinned the dancer, a dark-skinned woman with long blue-dyed hair tied up in twin pigtails. She had a broad face, low cheekbones and a high forehead, giving her an open look. "If I am not much mistaken, you are Samuel de León, are you not?"

"I am, and whom do I have to thank for the wonderful dancing tonight?"

The woman curtseyed again, holding her multicoloured gown as she did so. "My name is Zola Igbinedion."

"Well, rarely have I seen such skill as yours, Zola," said Spot, dipping his head while Aiva scowled.

"I am sorry about Baron Sigwell," Zola said unexpectedly. "I understand you are close to him?"

Spot frowned, confused. "I am. My father is. But what do y–"

Zola nodded. "Beware the fangs that slay him. They may be closer than you think."

With that, she twirled away, leaving Spot flabbergasted.

What did she mean by that? Does she know about the folk with two faces?

"What did she say?" asked Aiva, face scrunching in perplexity. "Beware the fangs? What a strange woman."

"Yes," agreed Spot absently, "strange."

Spot's attention was drawn like iron to a lodestone towards Baron Horatio Sigwell then, who was ramping up momentum in one of his infamous rants. All eyes began to turn on the rambunctious fellow, in fact, despite the performers' best efforts.

"I know what you and all your cowardly friends of *La Salamandra* think," sneered a stout little man with a black beard, a black hat and a dapper black coat. "You think we should give up our efforts to convert the pagans. You want to abandon the Crusades!"

"Do not put words in my mouth, Reyes!" Horatio roared, red-cheeked, brandishing a goblet. "But yes, as a matter of fact, I *do* think we should put the Crusades on hold *for the time being*, until such time as we can restore Justiqua to her former glory! I'm sure those of *El Toro* can agree with me in that, at least?"

"So, why are you here?" Reyes demanded. "Why are you here in the manor of my friend, Baron Rathbone, drinking up his wine and eating up more than a fair share of his food if you believe not in his cause? In our cause? If you are not here to donate money to the cause of the Crusades, then you are not welcome, *Baron!*" He made the word sound worse than the vilest insult. "And more than this, I once more accuse you of cowardice!"

The smack as Horatio whacked the man on the cheek with one of the leather riding gloves he kept tucked into his overworked belt echoed around the main hall of Rathbone Manor for a full minute, Spot thought, heard by all, entirely unopposed in the field of sound, for not another soul made a peep for that minute. Even the music skirled to a stop.

I never realised how long a minute was until now, how it could crawl by at a snail's pace while I hold my breath and wait for the next one, just praying it will come and rescue me from the current instant.

Horatio's own booming voice shattered the spell of silence. "I challenge you, Baron Irvil Reyes, to a duel, right here, right now! Only your death will satisfy me after the craven slander you have hurled my way!"

Baron Irvil Reyes reached up and rubbed his cheek. Then, a smile slowly invaded his visage. Spot shivered at the look in his eye and thought the brown orbs looked pale blue for a heartbeat.

"I accept, Baron Sigwell," intoned Reyes ceremoniously. "We shall meet at the given hour on the field of battle outside Rathbone Manor."

"Indeed we shall!" huffed Horatio, casting aside his goblet and stamping off, trying to tuck his glove back into his belt while his sword flapped against his leg.

Viscount Marcus de León, Count Kronvert and Sir Giles dashed after him, worry written on their faces.

Spot turned to Aiva and took her hand. "I'm so sorry. I have to go."

He let go of her hand and took off after his father.

6
The Duel

Everyone gathered outside Rathbone Manor in the rain for the duel, the women watching from the sheltered wooden porch that extended all the way across the front of the sprawling residence.

Barons Horatio Sigwell and Irvil Reyes took up position ten feet apart, their shiny boots smothered in mud, hands on the swords at their waists. Regarding them beside his father in the downpour, Spot de León thought they could have been brothers. Both were paunchy fellows, Horatio the paunchiest and tallest. The Baron of *La Salamandra* was bedecked in an unsightly gold-lined purple coat that evening, emblazoned with a boar on each shoulder. His frilly mauve shirt scarcely contained his belly. Baron Reyes' frizzy grey hair, when he removed his tall hat, lay flat on the top of his head and puffed up to the sides where it had not been compressed.

I might have laughed if not for the circumstances.

"As lord of this land, I will serve as impartial judge for this duel," uttered Baron Erlic Rathbone, stepping forward, pale as a ghost in the murk, dressed head to toe in creamy garments to accentuate his bone-white hair and bloodless complexion. "Who will serve as seconds to the combatants?"

Patricidal maniac.

"I, Sir Reginald Giles, will serve as second for Baron Horatio Sigwell," said Sir Giles, looking queasy.

"I, Sir Estaban Rodriguez, will stand as second for Baron Irvil Reyes," declared a blonde, moustached man in a dark green doublet, pointy chin held high.

"I object!" barked a hoary voice, and all eyes turned as a bald old man with a frosted beard pushed to the front of the crowd. "It is nonsense to fight duels in a time of war! Put an end to this immediately, I say!"

"Respectfully, Count Laflamme, I must decline." Horatio's voice was a war drum beating an anticipatory tattoo.

"I, too, must decline." Baron Reyes' voice was an animal growl.

"Count Kronvert," Count Manuel Laflamme pleaded, "will you not put an end to this?"

"And how would you have me do that?" the old Count rasped. "Even if we could stop them – which we can't, because Rathbone's friends will prevent our interference – they would merely resume the duel at another time and another place. Best let them hash it out, old chap."

Count Laflamme stared at him dumbly, as did Marcus, Reginald and Spot.

Count Kronvert took in their expressions and shrugged. "It's true."

"If there are no other objections," Rathbone drawled, "let the duel begin!"

Reyes' sabre was out of his scabbard in the blink of an eye, while Horatio awkwardly yanked out his own longsword. Spot groaned. Reyes danced forward and Horatio tottered back, his sword swaying to and fro as if he could not hold it straight. Reyes jabbed once, twice, thrice, evidently seeking the measure of his foe. Spot thought the duel was over there and then, but somehow Horatio managed to dodder out of the way of all three stabs and even retorted with a clumsy sweeping blow that Reyes easily avoided, springing back as lightly as falling ash.

"You are old and slow, Baron," sneered Reyes, "a relic of a forgotten age. Best you move aside and let the fitter dogs run the show now."

He's the same age as Horatio. What is he talking about?

Horatio did not reply, nor did he attack. He waited, rain saturating his unruly grey hair. Reyes shuffled closer inch by inch and then, sudden as a striking cobra, he pounced. His sabre lanced through the air straight for his foe's heart. Horatio shifted sideways and parried awkwardly, sword pointed at the ground, which Spot at first thought foolish and unwieldy. Then, Horatio stumbled and all his weight came down on the sword as it plunged into the earth. Reyes staggered back and screeched like a wounded eagle, startling some of the onlookers.

Seeing their looks of confusion, perhaps, Baron Reyes screamed, "He's cut off my big toe!"

Only then did Spot, and many of the others present, realise that Horatio's sword must have caught the edge of Reyes' boot as it stabbed down, and the toe beneath. Horatio drew his sword out of the dirt and righted himself with a wobble, taking up a semblance of a fighting stance once more.

"I'll take you apart piece by piece if I have to!" Horatio blustered.

Reyes brandished his sabre, eyes glittering with hatred, blood leaking from his boot into the mud. "A lucky stroke!" he ground out. "You will not live to strike another!"

Limping forward, Reyes slashed at Horatio with venomous quickness. Horatio parried, shoved his opponent's blade away, stepped in close and punched Reyes in the face, all in the blink of an eye. As Reyes reeled from the blow, Horatio's longsword blurred out in an arc to sever his head from his shoulders. Reyes had to throw himself backwards to avoid the swing, landing on his rump in the muck with a splash. Spot gawped. He had never seen Horatio move so fast, would never have guessed him capable of such celerity. Reyes picked himself up and surveyed his besmirched wardrobe with disgust. Then, he turned his glittering eyes on Horatio.

Blue eyes. Oh no, he has blue eyes!

Reyes' blue eyes began to glow more and more brightly in Spot's perception until they engulfed his entire vision and he was falling into the pools of icy water they had become. As his vision slowly returned to something approximating normal, he felt as though he were indeed underwater, or as if the moonlight he usually saw had been bent somehow by glass or jade. He was seeing *beneath* again, to the faces hidden under those shown to the world. He quivered in fear as he glanced around and grabbed his father's hand for comfort.

The land had come alive around him, grass leering, mud chuckling hideously with air bubbles. The manor itself had come alive, swaying this way and that as it tried to peer around the people blocking its view of the duel. A thousand tarantulas made up the walls instead of bricks, and the faux castellation and architrave took on the form of demonic faces grinning at him with needle-teeth. Black bats congregated in place of tiles, and a gusty groan came from the front door as if it were a yawning maw waiting to swallow them all whole. Goosebumps crawled across Spot's skin as a waft of mustiness hit him, as of dust and death. Nightmarish creatures intermingled with common folk in the horrific field in which they all stood, rife as stars at night. Each had four curved fangs, bone-white skin and eyes of supernatural sapphire.

What is happening to me? Am I going mad? What is real and what is not? Where did these monsters come from?

Many of them Spot did not recognise. Many he did.

Baron Erlic Rathbone and his retainers had fangs to put wolves to shame. Sir Estaban Rodriguez had eyes blazing with blue. Spot's heart sank as he returned his gaze to Baron Irvil Reyes, noting the blaring blue eyes, pallid complexion and four long fangs.

There's no way Horatio can win against such a monster!

Then, he blinked and all was normal again. The grass only rustled in the whipping wind, and the mud squelched only when stepped on. The walls were just brick walls, the tiles terracotta. The manor stopped seesawing, and the door was just a door. The monsters had their human masks back on.

"You were deceiving me," Reyes spat, pointing his sabre at Baron Sigwell. "You're not as slow as you make out, old man!"

Horatio stood taller now, straight and firm. He lifted his sword higher, and it stopped trembling. "You catch on quick."

He strode forward purposefully and unleashed a flurry of furious slashes, surprising Spot again with his quickness. Horatio advanced and Reyes retreated. Swords skirled again and again as the tip of Horatio's longsword narrowly missed his enemy's throat or breast with every stroke.

Reyes backed away, parrying and dodging desperately just to stay alive with no chance for a retort. Horatio's blows were unforgiving, and whenever Reyes was forced to parry or, worse, block, the onlookers could see the effort it took to divert the hearty swings. The duel that had been taking place a moment before had changed as violently as the environs, thought Spot, glancing around nervously. Horatio had taken over, was invading Reyes' space and forcing him back step by step.

Reyes blocked an overhand blow and they locked swords, straining against one another, both evidently deciding it was time to put an end to proceedings. Horatio was spitting with effort, red in the face as he loomed over Reyes, who also looked to be struggling.

Then, Baron Reyes smiled. It was a nasty sort of smile, like the sort a spider might give a trapped fly. "You're not the only one with tricks up his sleeves!" he hissed, the sound serpentine, making Spot shiver. "You'll die for making me look the fool, *old man!*"

Though Horatio had been dominating the tussle, abruptly Reyes threw him off with as little effort as wafting away dandelion seeds. Horatio wobbled back like a drunkard, eyes wide with fear. Reyes was a storm descending upon Horatio, his sabre a thunderbolt stabbing and raking.

Managing a few lucky parries, Horatio garbled out, "He's a monster, a villain, a monster, I tell you!"

Whether because he was distracted, shouting, or because he simply could not keep up with his opponent's lightning speed, Horatio missed a parry. His arm gushed red where it was sliced open beneath his purple coat, and he inhaled sharply as he waddled back. With his sword arm injured, more and more attacks started to slip through Horatio's defence. Spot wanted to cover his eyes and hide away. It was awfully clear to him, to everyone present, that Reyes was toying with the Baron like a cat with its food. He left the sword arm alone after the initial cut, however.

To make it seem like it's still an even fight, when it's not! Not at all! No man can move that fast or be that strong! It's unnatural!

Horatio flailed to parry, but never succeeded once. Reyes' first jab took him in the shoulder, paralysing his left arm. Then, he carefully cut off a few of Horatio's fingers on the dead hand, and the Baron wheezed in agony, plum-faced, biting his lip and evidently trying not to scream. Spot thought he might vomit when he saw the Baron's fingers fall in the mud. He half-wished his father had covered his eyes, but Marcus de León made no move to do so.

I wonder if he's forgotten I'm here. He looks furious. His fists are clenched and he's pale as a ghost. Not as pale as the monsters, though. And his eyes are still green. Thank the Prophet.

Next, Baron Reyes nicked Horatio's cheek with a cheeky slash, making Baron and crowd gasp at the audacity. Reyes had risked much to humiliate his foe with such a move, for he could easily have been run through had Baron Sigwell been fast enough. Horatio was labouring now, though, on his last legs. He waved his sword at Reyes as the other danced away, but missed by a wide margin. Reyes sprang in close again to feint, and Horatio took the bait, swiping clumsily. Reyes darted around behind him and slapped him on the backside with the flat of his blade to the cheers and laughter of Baron Rathbone and his cronies. Spot noticed that those with nightmare masks all laughed, as did some of those without.

How petty we are.

Horatio stumbled, but did not fall. He spun and stabbed wildly at Reyes, who leaned aside and tripped him as he went past. This time, Horatio went down in the muck, kneeling and planting his hands to stop his face from hitting the mud. Reyes stomped on him savagely, and he tasted the dirt, face mashed into the cold slime. Rathbone and his sycophants whooped, and Marcus and those of *La Salamandra* booed. Reyes stepped back then and allowed Baron Sigwell the dignity of regaining his feet. It took him some time, and he wiped off his brow with a filthy once-purple sleeve when he was done. Spot's heart broke at the resigned look on his face. There was nothing he could do to prevent his death now. He knew it just as surely as did everyone else.

How horrible that feeling must be ...

Horatio waited for Reyes' next assault, and Spot wanted to cry out for the monster to leave him alone, but he could not move a muscle, could not wrench his eyes away. Reyes leapt in close to feint again, but Horatio did not move to counter this time. So, Reyes bounced back, perplexed, then sprang in again to slash open Baron Sigwell's dead arm.

Horatio gave a feeble roar then as his blood drained into the mud and swung his longsword half-heartedly. Reyes was behind him in a flash again, and this time his sword hummed out low, cruelly low. Spot and many of the onlookers winced as the blade sliced across the back of the heels on both feet, severing the tendons there with audible snaps. Horatio let loose a short scream to shake the sky then, and Spot jumped. The sound was almost inhuman, something of the animalistic and primal revealing itself. Horatio collapsed to his knees with a splash, and Reyes stood over him like an executioner, silhouetted against a strand of distant lightning for a heartbeat.

As Reyes moved to stand in front of him, Horatio tried one last swing of his sword, though he barely had the strength to lift it and it dragged through the mud. Reyes batted the blade aside with his own and slit Baron Sigwell's throat on the reverse. Then, to Spot's horror, he plunged his sabre into Horatio's chest, before yanking it out and allowing the Baron to slump to the ground.

Bellowing, "No! You beast!" Marcus and the others of *La Salamandra* rushed forwards.

Reyes was on his guard against them for a moment, but none of them unsheathed their swords. They had eyes only for Horatio Sigwell as they gathered around him. Spot could only see the dying Baron through a medley of jostling bodies, but he thought he saw the Baron grip Marcus de León's hand and whisper something. Spot could not hear him over the commotion.

Marcus returned to Spot's side a few minutes later, his face grave. "Baron Sigwell is dead."

"Baron Irvil Reyes has dispatched his enemy fairly," ruled Baron Rathbone, his pale face smug, "and is declared the victor. The friends of Baron Sigwell are welcome to take his body for last rites."

Glaring at Rathbone, the Knights of *La Salamandra* acquiesced, lifting Horatio's body between them and bearing it solemnly through the rain to his carriage.

The ride home was silent. Spot could think of no way to tell his father that his friend had been slain by horrors with the faces of men.

How could he believe that? How can I?

7
Words from Beyond

"Father, I need to talk to you," said Spot de León.

"Oh? What about, son?" asked Marcus de León distractedly, shuffling through a sheaf of parchments on the tamarind desk in his study.

"I don't know how to tell you this ... but I think Horatio was killed by monsters."

"You've got that right," Marcus muttered to Spot's surprise, not taking his eyes off the parchments. "Reyes, Rodriguez, Rathbone, Cel Tradat ... they're all bloody-minded monsters." He looked up from his desk then, and Spot was taken aback to see a manic gleam in his father's eye. "Death dealing should never be undertaken lightly, my son. These so-called leaders of ours seem to have forgotten that. That life is precious. All these duels, these wars, these feuds and factions ... It must come to an end. It simply must. I will make it so. D'you hear me, Prophet?" he shouted abruptly at the coffered ceiling. "I will make it so, this I vow! Always remember, Samuel, that war is never the answer. Peace is only ever a conversation away."

I'm not so sure about that.

"That's not what I meant, father," said Spot, shuffling his feet and gazing at the rug before locking eyes with his father once more. "I have been having ... strange visions of late. Visions in the daytime, in which I see people transformed into ... monsters with fangs and eyes of the bluest blue. I don't know how to explain it, but it is as though I am seeing the *real* people beneath the masks. I think they *really* are monsters, father. Unnatural monsters."

Marcus sighed. "The eyes of the bluest blue return to haunt us again, eh? I had thought that part of your life over, but I do understand. Grief affects us all in different ways, and the mind compensates however it sees fit."

"Wai – what?" spluttered Spot. "You knew about the blue eyes?"

Marcus nodded. "When you were young, you would often break out bawling and pointing at passersby, calling them monsters with fangs and eyes of the bluest blue. I had the priests of Saint Padrice bless you with holy smoke and oil, and the visions stopped after that. I thought they had stopped for good."

"*That's* why I was put through that torture?" Spot gasped, faintly remembering the horrific experience of near suffocating on smoke in a room like a furnace, being yanked out, dunked in ice cold water that near stopped his heart and then being daubed in oil so hot it had scalded the hairs from his youthful body. "I could never remember why … or even if it was really real."

Marcus nodded. "And it seemed to work. I may have to contact the priests again if the hallucinations have begun again, though."

Spot hesitated.

Maybe he's right. Maybe I am crazy.

"What if they're not hallucinations?" he asked eventually. "What if – somehow – I am seeing the truth? What if they really are monsters?"

Marcus fixed his son with a knowing look. "I forgot how long you have known Horatio. His loss must have been a blow to you, too. He was a charismatic man, always full of vim and vigour. There are no monsters, Samuel. Grief has addled your mind, that's all." He found the parchment he needed. "Now, come, we need to prepare for the funeral. We must show Baron Sigwell the proper respect, so your finest clothes, if you please. Let me know if the visions persist, and I will contact the priests if needs be."

I am not going through that torture ever again!

"Yes, father."

They were early to the funeral. Marcus just stood and stared at the headstone prepared for Horatio.

Here lies Baron Horatio Sigwell 95AC - 154AC.
Noble knight. Beloved husband. Fierce friend.
Long live La Salamandra!

Spot felt a tear make a break for it down his cheek.

A man's whole life summed up in a pithy fifteen words. Are we so little in the end?

"It makes you think," said Sir Reginald Giles, approaching from behind with his wife, both clad in spotless white funeral robes as were Spot and his father, to symbolise the purity of the soul being reborn into *Citta Pacia*, "about the fragility of this thing we call life and about the choices we all make every day. Had Horatio not argued with Reyes, would he still be alive today? Perhaps. Was it inevitable that he would one day argue and duel with Reyes? Perhaps. Who can know these things but the Prophet and the All Mother herself?"

"Good to see you, Sir Giles," offered Marcus sombrely, "though I wish the circumstances were less dire."

Sir Giles nodded. "As do I, old friend, as do I. I did not think Horato would be the first to go. The man had an iron liver. I thought he'd still be drinking when the rest of us were six feet under."

Marcus toyed with the idea of a smile at that. "He was … prolific."

"Now there's a eulogy befitting the man," said Sir Giles with a small smile of his own. *"Noble Knight. Beloved husband. Fierce friend. Prolific drinker."*

"You could call him a wine connoisseur," Marcus pointed out.

"Yes, I'm sure he would have loved that."

"He would indeed," came a voice from behind them all, making them spin to behold Lady Helena Sigwell sweeping across the cemetery towards them, her white robes only slightly stained at the hems by grass and dirt, her face hidden by a gossamer white veil. "He loved his wine. More than he loved me, I sometimes think."

"Outrageous!" Sir Giles exclaimed.

"Of course he did not love wine more than he loved you," Marcus assured her. "He was besotted with you, my dear."

She smiled wanly. "Forgive me. I loved him more dearly than I can express, and I know not how to …" Her face crumpled, and she whispered, "How to mourn."

Sir Giles' wife, Maria, enfolded the woman in a tender embrace while she wept. The other attendees arrived in dribs and drabs, a grey drizzle pouring down to match everyone's spirits, obfuscating the world in a haze. Off-duty Knights serving as guards, armed and armoured, waved the approved guests past. Spot was soon saturated through, his hair and robe clinging to him coldly. He did not move, though, just stood and waited and stared at the hole in the ground yawning open before him.

I've never been to a funeral before. Isn't it strange how we commemorate the dead? We have no notion of whether Horatio can see us from the afterlife, from Citta Pacia, *and yet we act as though we know he can. If he can, well and good. But if not, if there* is *no* Citta Pacia, *or if he simply does not have the divine vision we seem to assume he has where he can see everything and everyone no matter where they are, then ultimately we are doing this for ourselves. We are giving ourselves a sense of closure, not Horatio. When it boils down to it, we are incredibly selfish creatures. The entirety of religion could be a fiction we sell to ourselves on a daily basis just to avoid complete mental breakdown, that feeling of hopelessness that dwells inside us all when we consider the possibility of a fateless existence. Without fate, all is random. And if all is random, where is the meaning? No, no, better to make life like a story with a happy ending. It gives us a goal, a purpose. Be a good person and you can go to* Citta Pacia. *That way, we can all make it through the day.*

Spot glanced at the twenty-foot stone statue of Saint Padrice that towered over the graveyard. Though he was known to have become a pacifist when he met the Prophet, he was yet sculpted as he had been in his earlier years – a Justiquan warrior in the time before Knights, one of the first true followers of the Prophet's Way. He wore archaic armour and a peaked helmet, and his sword pointed unflinchingly at the sky.

What a strange way to depict a man of peace.

A murmur rippled through the gathered crowd of mourners, and Spot and Marcus both craned to see what was happening. Marcus's face flushed an ugly colour when he beheld a skinny man approaching flanked by two bodyguards in steel plate armour. The man wore black, as always, down to the gloves. His face was shaded by a brimmed black hat.

Count Ivan Darcuul.

"Count Darcuul." Marcus de León outpaced the others to greet the Count, who had been stalled by the funerary guards, Spot almost running to keep up with his long strides. Sir Giles and many of the other Knights, all unarmoured for the funeral, were by his side in a heartbeat. "This is a private function, and I think it fair to say that friends of Baron Sigwell's killer are not welcome at his funeral, where his widow is currently grieving. Please leave before the situation turns ugly."

"There's no need to get your hackles up, Viscount de León," replied Count Darcuul in tomb-deep tones, pale face drawn and composed. "I come in peace."

"You shouldn't have come at all, *La Pantera* scum!" snapped Sir Giles. "It is you and yours that have done this, provoking him until he lost control – as would any man of honour and dignity!"

"I did not force him to duel Baron Reyes," Darcuul shot back, a gust blowing his black hair across his visage for a moment. "I did not even attend the gala. I was busy on matters of state that evening. Baron Reyes may be a friend of mine, but that does not exclude Horatio from that title also."

"Horatio would never have counted you a friend!" Sir Giles shouted, jabbing a finger, while Marcus tried to subtly wave for him to calm down.

Darcuul frowned for the first time, pushing his hair out of his face. "And yet I would have counted him one. It is unfair to deny a man the chance to pay his respects, do you not think? I bear him no ill will."

Marcus nodded. "And yet bar you we shall. You are not welcome here, Count. You may pay your respects at another time, after the funeral."

Darcuul took a deep breath, evidently preparing for one last ditch effort. "I grew up with Horatio Sigwell. Perhaps we have not always seen eye to eye, but I have known the man almost my entire life. All I ask is the chance to show him the respect he deserves."

"Begone, Count," Marcus growled, "or it will not go well for you."

"Oh, is that right?" Darcuul snapped, grasping the filigreed hilt of the sword at his belt.

Marcus, Sir Giles and all the Knights in attendance at the funeral laid their hands on their own sword hilts and glared at the Count.

Darcuul smiled sardonically and took his hand away. "I see the city has corrupted you, as it does everyone else. You're supposed to be the good guys."

With that, he turned and walked away. A Dragon was embroidered on the back of his coat in silver thread, a lance piercing its heart.

"What was that about?" muttered Sir Giles. "Good guys? What did he mean by that?"

Marcus dismissed Count and question with a wave. "Who cares. He's gone. That's all that matters. Let's get back to the funeral."

Sir Giles nodded and then asked the question that had been burning in Spot's heart since the Baron's demise. "By the way, I never got a chance to ask you in all the commotion, what did Horatio say to you when he was dying, Marcus?"

Marcus shook his head and forced a brittle smile. "Nothing. Just nonsense."

Sir Giles nodded, deflating, and Spot knew how he felt.

The crowd resumed their places, clustered around the empty grave. A white-robed priest arrived to conduct the funeral, took his place behind a wooden lectern, looking incongruous in the middle of the grassy, tombstone-dotted field, and cleared his throat to indicate his readiness to begin. The crowd's murmur died at once and the clouded sun dipped down behind the Church of Saint Padrice, casting the ceremony in shadow. The drizzle continued unabated, a faint pattering in the back of the mind of everyone present, like the question of whether or not Horatio could really see them.

"We are gathered here today to commend the soul of Baron Horatio Sigwell to *Citta Pacia* in the presence of all those he held dear, his family and friends. We know that Baron Sigwell will be accepted to the Prophet's bosom, for he was a true and noble Knight, who served the Order of *Pacia* for forty years."

The priest droned on about the Baron's life story and legacy, while Spot wondered what the man had really left behind.

A widow and some fading memories.

Horatio's body was borne out of the Church on a litter by half a dozen priests and gently lowered into the grave with the use of ropes. Then, the priests buried him.

When the time came to sing songs of praise for the Prophet and All Mother, Spot was not in the mood. He mumbled the words until his father elbowed him and gave him a sharp look, at which point he sang a little louder. As a song ended, Spot noticed a wave of inquisition pass over the crowd as all heads turned to behold another intruder who had been barred entry by the guards.

Sir Estaban Rodriguez, Baron Reyes' second in the duel.

The Night Comes Alive

Spot recognised the man, but felt somehow compelled to remain rooted rather than to follow his father when Marcus de León set off to intercept the Knight, face plum-coloured. Sir Giles and the rest of the attendees were hot on Marcus' heels. In just a few moments, only Spot and Lady Sigwell remained standing by the fresh grave, along with a couple of ladies-in-waiting. It seemed to Spot as though he stood in the rain staring at the tombstone for aeons, but it could not have been more than a few seconds, he thought in hindsight.

Lady Helena Sigwell's dreamy voice broke his reverie, issuing through her veil as if from another word entirely, giving Spot goosebumps. "The spirit of my dead husband comes to me by the light of the moon. He told me what it is he saw. He saw the truth in the instant before he died. And he knows you have seen it, too. His last words to your father were, 'Monsters! They are the damned, Marcus!' Protect those you love, young Samuel. The Old Ones are coming. And when they get here, they will devour the world. Only the Lord of Crows can stop them now. By cleansing the city. In fire and blood." She shook her head and raised a hand to the sky. "Either way, I will not see it."

The Saint's statue's hand crumbled, and its ten-foot sword fell directly on Lady Sigwell, cleaving her in half from skull to groin and spattering her petrified ladies-in-waiting with blood. The sword sheared into the ground, its stone tip a mere foot away from Spot's feet. While the ladies-in-waiting shrieked, Spot just ogled the sword in shock, an odd ringing in his ears.

What just happened? What did she mean by all that?

His father and Sir Giles and the rest of the attendees rushed over, jabbering in grief and surprise, and Spot felt like a stuck deaf mute, unable to move, unable to hear anything but the ringing in his ears, unable to speak even when his father was clearly shouting in his face and shaking him. He barely remembered being carried to the carriage or the ride home as the sun set. He came to as his father was tucking him into bed.

"Father," he said, "the monsters are real. Horatio saw them, too. Please don't leave, father. I don't want to sleep alone tonight."

Marcus hesitated, eyes widening at mention of Horatio's last words, but then he sighed. "I don't know what Lady Sigwell said to you, but there are no monsters. I promise. I won't leave you alone. I'll stay with you tonight. Now, go to sleep, my son. You've had a trying day."

"Yes, father. Thank you."

He fell asleep to the soothing sensation of his father's hand stroking his hair.

8
Laflamme

The ceremony blew by in a blur.

That morning, he had awoken Squire Dion Laflamme III. A sword, a suit of armour and a ceremonial cloak later, he was Sir Dion Laflamme III, Knight of the Order of *Pacia*. It had always astonished him how people were apparently 'transformed' into Knights by the touch of a sword tip on their brow, how they seemingly changed overnight. And yet, now that he had been Knighted, he *did* feel transformed.

The world is my oyster and I am an oystercatcher on the wing.

People treated him differently. Men treated him with respect and women with adoration and fluttering eyelashes.

I cannot get enough of it!

Once the formal banquet held in honour of the freshly Knighted young men had ended, a stilted affair with tepid red wine and even more tepid conversation, the newly minted Knights took to the streets. Ditching their armour at their houses, they made a beeline for the more respectable taverns in one of Justiqua's more wholesome neighbourhoods, where they all lived, close to the *Pacia* Castle complex.

Once they had caused enough drunken ruckus and been kicked out of those taverns, they made for some of the seedier establishments. By then, Dion had a black eye from a brawl that he tried to cover up with his long dark hair. His frilly white shirt and cerulean coat with embroidered lapels were a little ripped, and his black breeches, stockings and polished ankle-high leather boots were stained with ale and mead.

Braving the stench of the gutters and tottering towards *The Bent Penny* in the heart of the Justiquan slums, meandering past beggars, corpses, brawls and inert rats in the streets, the trio of Knights iron-livered enough to make it this far were greeted by a bald bouncer with the mien of a berated bear and the sour-sweet smell of alcohol, vomit and baui smoke. Eyeing the swords at their hips without enthusiasm but their fine regalia with more than enough to make up for it, the bouncer waved them inside.

They stopped once past the threshold, astonished by the depths of debauchery being achieved in the room before them. Men were passed out on the bare wooden floor while their comrades stepped over them and continued to drink and talk and sing at the top of their lungs. Whores worked the inn shamelessly, sitting on customers' laps and stroking their beards.

Seems like everyone has a beard here. A dirty beard.

The Night Comes Alive

Several different gambling games were being conducted in the open on pitted wooden tables, one of which descended into a brawl even as he watched. Men and women smoked baui from pipes and leaves with impunity, and Dion was fairly certain he could hear the faint sounds coming from upstairs of the whores' completions of their contracts. He lost count of the number of laws being broken within the first few seconds. Drunk and disorderly conduct, possession of the narcotic herb baui, gambling, prostitution, aggravated assault – all were crimes punishable by time in prison. And as a Knight of *Pacia,* it was Sir Dion Laflamme's duty to bring the lawbreakers to justice.

He threw his arms wide, grinned from ear to ear and yelled in a charismatic baritone, "Hallo, *The Bent Penny!* Let's party till the sun comes up! Barman – a drink for everyone, on me!"

The roar of approval that met his words stunk of whisky and baui, and Dion breathed it in deeply, relishing the joy flooding his frame.

Or perhaps it's inebriation. Either way, I'm relishing it.

He and his friends staggered over to the bar, almost knocked over several times by meaty dockworkers clapping them heartily on the back in gratitude. He recognised only one other Knight amid the melee, Sir Alonso Gómez, and he nodded greetings to the older man, who hoisted a tankard in return.

The barman stroked his mutton chops and grinned at them like a whaler spotting a biggun, revealing several wooden teeth. "What'll it be, young fellas?"

"How's your rum, my good man?" asked Dion, leaning heavily on the bar while the room seesawed.

"Best in the city."

"Then, rum all around, if you please!"

A small, skinny rat-faced man in a mink overcoat met them at the bar while the barman rummaged around for the rum. "Well, well, well, men of taste and culture, I see," he drawled, smooth as a coat of fresh lacquer, his shaven cocoa-skinned face taut as a drum skin despite his middling age. "Welcome to *The Bent Penny.* I am the proprietor, Ignatius Boondoggle." He doffed his black brimmed hat and bowed with a flourish. "Please, see to it that you inform me and my good barman of your every need and it will be seen to. Your *every* need."

"My thanks, Ignatius," said Dion with his own wobbly bow, green eyes glazed from the liquor. "You are a true gentleman!"

"What is it that your hearts desire?" asked Ignatius, replacing his hat atop umber curls.

"Rum, baui and gambling would be a magnificent start, don't you think, chums?"

"Hear hear!"

Ignatius leaned in close to whisper conspiratorially, "I also have some wampcha procured at great expense from Quing Tzu, if you are interested?"

"How much?"

Upon hearing the outrageous price, one of the Knights shook his head and muttered, "I don't know if I can afford that. My father will kill me if I spend any more of his money."

"We're Knights now!" Dion reminded him scornfully. "We needn't spend our fathers' money anymore. We have our own significant stipends now!"

A smile spread slow as treacle across the other's pancake face. "Oh, yes, I suppose you're right!"

Several pints of ale and spirits, who knew how many baui cigars and a few dabs of wampcha later, Sir Dion Laflamme was practically comatose, olive face sagging like he'd had a stroke. It was then that he decided to take Ignatius Boondoggle up on his latest offer of companionship for the evening. Ignatius paraded a bevvy of beauties through the inn for the Knights' pleasure, and Dion picked a buxom woman with thick black hair like a mane.

"She's twice the size of you!" one of the other Knights said, laughing.

Dion smiled lopsidedly. "I love a yummy tummy."

Raucous laughter shook the rafters.

Bunny, the smiley woman in the red dress with the dead eyes he had chosen, led Dion up the rickety stairs to one of many pokey rooms, in which a dresser, a wardrobe, a small table and chair and a bed were the only ornamentation. A window let in a cool breeze and the restless sounds of the city. The world spinning woozily around him, Dion shut the door behind him, collapsed on top of Bunny and tried to rub himself turgid.

The door banged open. Bunny shoved him off violently, and he was pinned to the floor by several pairs of hands and gagged with what smelled like a well-used sock before he could say a word. Ignatius Boondoggle swept theatrically into the room, flipping a golden coin in the air and catching it again and again with one hand, while the thumb of the other was tucked into his belt. He shut the door behind him.

"Well, well, well," he drawled, "in what different circumstances we meet tonight, *good Sir Knight*. You're stuck up a creek without a paddle this time and no mistake, mate. I'm under strict orders, ya see, to turn any lonely Knights who might wander into my lowly establishment. Don't worry, we haven't forgotten about your friends. We'll get to them next. Now, I'm sure you have a great many questions like 'what's going on' and 'why are you doing this', so allow me to explain while we proceed with our little ritual. You're going to need to understand what's happening to you, after all. Before we begin, however, I must warn you not to scream or cry for help. If you do, we won't kill you, but we will hurt you. A lot. And we don't want that. We don't want to hurt you. We don't want to kill you. Just take part in our little ritual, and you'll be free to leave this place ali ... ahem, healthy and well. Understand? Good."

Dion could not move with his head pinned, could only stare like a frightened rabbit in a snare as all the trappings of civilisation fell away before his eyes, as though the world had sloughed its skin to reveal its true self. Abruptly, the starlight peeking in illuminated not a plain bedchamber but a crumbling ruin. The furniture was wrecked, the floor splintering, the mouldy grey plaster on the walls hanging off like flayed flesh. Even the ceiling beams were crooked. Worst of all, though, were the monsters. Everyone in the room, Bunny included, took on the countenances of creatures of the night. Four long, curved fangs jutted from each of their mouths, overlapping their lips, and they glared at him with brightly glowing eyes with irises the colour of lapis lazuli.

Ignatius took out a small knife and slit open his forearm from palm to elbow nook. Dion could see he had cut deep as blood welled rapidly. He had cut the artery, the Knight thought; he would bleed out in seconds. He could only gargle in protest, however, as the gag was ripped from his mouth and Ignatius held his arm above the Knight's face, allowing blood to trickle and stream down into Dion's mouth. Some of it splattered on his face, hot and sticky and smelling of iron. Dion could not even close his mouth or turn away, for his head was held firmly and a finger and thumb were jammed into his cheeks between his jaws. So, he coughed and spat out the blood for as long as he could, until too much of it was pouring into his maw and dribbling up his nostrils and he could not breathe. Finally, he swallowed, feeling tainted.

The blood did not stop coming, though, and with it Ignatius poured out the heinous explanation.

"This little ritual, ya see," he said calmly, "is an initiation, of sorts. There is a reason I chose you, young man, a reason I have been ordered by my higher-ups to target errant Knights. Particularly those of your ... abundance. It is simple really. My ... organisation, ya see, is interested in power. Absolute power. Over Justiqua and all its inhabitants. And there is no easier way to power than wealth – or having friends with wealth. That is where you come in, young Knight. We want you to be our friend. We want you to join our ... organisation and help us. In fact, we're not giving you much of a choice. You may be feeling it already. Yes? Feeling your blood stir, your heart pound and your brain become fuzzy? I thought so. Those are the symptoms. Well do I remember them from my own initiation so long ago. Death is not the end for us, ya see. Yes, you are dying, but there is no need to be afraid. Death for us is not like death for others. Death for us is a beginning, not an end, a time of transition. Once you have died and come back, you will understand."

Blackness consumed Sir Dion Laflamme, and he knew nothing but the Void.

Then, he reopened bright pale blue eyes and knew he had been transformed. He could feel it in his un-beating heart, his stilled veins, in his face and in his teeth. He licked gums where his teeth should have been and his tongue came up against four huge canines that poked out of his mouth they were so large. He was still pinned to the ground, but blood no longer rained down on him. Ignatius had stepped back and was stroking the smooth unbroken skin on the inside of his arm where he had cut himself. Though dried blood remained, Dion could see no sign of the wound. It was gone.

How did he heal so quickly?

"How do you feel, brother?" asked Ignatius, still wearing the mask of a monster.

"What have you done to me?" Dion gasped, tasting iron on his tongue.

"We have made you one of us, Dion," Ignatius said soothingly. "The rat race is over. Now, you can join us in our domination of the humans."

"I ... am not human?"

The proprietor shook his head. "The humans have many words for us. Creatures of the night, bloodsuckers, life-leeches. The one you may be most familiar with, however, is Vampyres."

"I ... am a Vampyre?"

Ignatius grinned. "Welcome, Sir Dion Laflamme, to your afterlife."

9
The Crypts

"Oh, come on!" pleaded Tumba Koum, tugging Spot's arm. "It'll be fun! It's the Day of the Dead, when ma says the fabric between the world of the living and the world of the dead frays and the living can speak to ghosts!"

"You don't actually believe that?" Spot asked, laughing off the finger of fear tracing a line up his spine.

Tumba studied his friend's face, almost as if he were disappointed. "No, of course not, but we can tell spooky stories and try to scare each other."

Spot rubbed his nape. "Are you sure you wouldn't rather go home to your ma's for a nice bowl of pumpkin soup? It's getting dark out."

"Then, we'd best go *quickly*. You're not afraid, are ya?"

Spot bristled with indignation as Tumba started squawking and flapping his arms around in his best chicken impression, pecking the air. "I am *not* afraid. In fact, I'll race you there!"

The sooner I get this over with, the sooner I can go home. I cannot let him know I'm terrified.

Water flying from his heels, Spot hightailed it up the street towards the cemetery, splashing through puddles in the pitted roads left over from the deluge earlier that day. Tumba could not keep up with him; no one could. Spot had yet to meet a faster runner. He was only breathing a little hard by the time Tumba pulled up beside him, panting, bent double with his hands on his knees.

"Stand up straight," Spot advised distantly, eyes scouring the graveyard for signs of horrors lurking in the shadows. "You'll breathe easier."

Tumba did as he advised and soon achieved a state near enough to normalcy to ask, "How do you move so fast, damn you? Your legs are a Gods-damned blur!"

"Prophet-damned blur," Spot corrected him. "You know the other kids like to beat you up for espousing such heresies."

Tumba shrugged. "I thought I was among friends."

Spot blushed. "You are. I only meant it might be good for you to get into the habit of saying it the righ- saying it our way."

Again, the look of disappointment flashed across Tumba's face, gone so fast Spot was not sure if he had imagined it.

"Let's have a look around," was all the Chilpaean youth said, before striding past Spot into the cemetery.

Spot gulped and followed him. The giant stone sword had been removed, although the gouge where it had cut into the ground near Horatio Sigwell's grave remained. The statue of Saint Padrice held a stump up to the sky now. The tombstones were gappy teeth grinning at him ominously in the patchy moonlight. The crypts at the far end of the grassy field were hulking overseers, caretakers of the dead.

I don't want to be back here, especially after both of the Sigwells' funerals. Why did I agree to this?

"So, do you know any spooky stories?" Spot asked to fill the silence previously filled only by the whistling chill wind, not because he wanted to hear one.

"I do." Tumba nodded, strolling aimlessly across the field and glancing left and right at the tombstones. "You have heard of werewolves, no doubt? They are said to have been found and slaughtered by Knights all across the world, even right here in Justiqua, no?"

Spot nodded, feeling his gut cramp up at the thought of the existence of such things. "Yes," he squeaked.

"Well, there are legends in my country of folk who can turn not into wolves under the sway of the full moon, but into bears whenever they please. You might think such creatures would be terrors, scourges of the streets, but in fact they were revered among my people, it is said. They helped to protect us when ... when bandits and such attacked. So, you see, what might at first seem terrifying can often prove not only to be harmless, but in fact to be a friend."

"It doesn't sound like they were very friendly to bandits," Spot pointed out.

Tumba waved a dismissive hand. "Bandits have it coming to them. Have you ever heard of bloodsuckers?"

"Vampyres?"

"Yes. Ma says there were legends of such creatures back home in Chilpaea, even as there are here, though of course we had a different name for them – the *Ma Ca Rong, Eaters of the Dead*. It was said they could become shadows on a whim and fly through the night sky like wraiths, though not in the daytime, for the sun burns their skin. It was said they held power over nocturnal creatures and even over the corpses of the damned, able to command them to obey their will. That they had inhuman strength and could move faster than the eye could follow. Scariest of all, it was said they had the power to charm folk so that nobody could even tell they were Vampyres at all, that they could hide among us in plain sight and we'd never even know." Spot glanced at him sharply, heart thundering. "It was said that, once upon a time, they treated we humans like cattle. They took positions of power and ensured that we bred and proliferated so that they would have a plentiful food stock. Then, they could pick us off at their leisure whilst we glutted ourselves, believing ourselves safe and cared for."

Spot shivered as someone scuffed his grave in another time. "Okay, that gave me goosebumps."

Tumba laughed and punched his friend on the arm. "You big ninny! Come on, let's check out those crypts."

"I really don't think we should," Spot whined. "I think they're private property, owned by the old aristocratic families."

"Just a peek!"

Tumba would not be dissuaded, and Spot would not let his friend go alone. So, he sloped after him, moping and dawdling his way over to the crypts. As they drew near, however, Spot caught a flicker of movement in the blackness ahead and his heart stopped. He grabbed Tumba's arm and instinctively dragged him down to the ground behind a tombstone close to a bush, hissing, "Get down! There's someone over there!"

He wasn't sure what he was more afraid of in that moment; that he had discovered a ghoul of some sort or that he himself would be discovered trespassing and his father would be informed. One, while horrific, seemed less plausible than the more mundane terrors of the other.

"Who?" whispered Tumba.

"I don't know. I just saw someone move by the crypt over there."

Darkness enclosed them, oppressive in its totality. They waited with bated breath until a break in the clouds let loose a shaft of moonlight that illuminated the crypt in front of them. Both gasped as they witnessed a shadow slip inside, leaving the engraved iron door ajar.

"Let's see who it is!" Tumba was on the move before Spot could stop him.

Spot cursed and sped after him, sticking to the shadows as much as possible. Up close, the stone sentinel yawned at him with a vast iron mouth flanked by embellished colonettes, embossed golden discs inset in the wall above serving as eyes that glared at him. Its pediment, engraved with an escutcheon featuring a rearing panther, blocked out the moon.

"Tumba, wait!" he hissed, but too late.

Tumba was already inside.

Spot hesitated on the threshold, peering thanklessly into the darkness ahead and steeling himself. Then, he plunged in.

He almost immediately tripped over Tumba, who – as it turned out – had only taken a few tentative steps. Both squawked in alarm, the sound echoing off into the distance, and batted at one another for a moment before recognition set in and they stopped, panting and holding one another's arms as if wrestling.

"Let's get out of here!" Spot breathed as quietly as he could, though vehemently. "I'm blind as a bat and we're in big trouble if we get caught!"

"We're not going to get caught," Tumba whispered. "Besides, aren't you curious? Who would come here alone at this time of night? Who would have a key to the door?"

Spot froze, Tumba's meaning immediately clear. Any aristocrat wealthy enough to afford the upkeep of such familial crypts would surely never venture here alone at night when a storm was expected. They would come in the daytime in a carriage with servants and bodyguards. Suddenly, Spot was intrigued despite himself.

Have we stumbled across a grave-robber?

"If we see who it is," he said slowly, testing out the words, "perhaps we can report them to the city watch. Or my father."

"We'd be heroes!" Tumba's quiet voice shook with excitement.

Trying to keep the enthusiasm from his own voice, Spot said in hushed tones, "Very well, we can go a little further, feeling our way along. Surely whoever is here must have brought a torch."

They crept down the unseen stairs together, hands on the walls to guide them, clutching at one another. Every clop of his shoes on the stone steps sounded like a cymbal clash in Spot's ears, every breath like the pluck of a lyre and every heartbeat a drum beat. His pulse raced, and his palms were slick. After a short while, they detected a faint orange glow ahead and quickened their pace unconsciously.

What they saw at the stairs' terminus made them halt in their tracks, agape. Hiding in the shadows just outside the firelight in the room emanating from an unseen source, they gawped at the vast long hall beneath a ribbed vault laid out before them, propped up by two rows of embellished pillars marching along its length. Spot lost count of the stone sarcophagi he could see, each with a lid sculpted into a likeness of the man or woman laid within. The far end of the hall was lost in shadow.

There must be dozens. Maybe scores. Maybe a hundred. Maybe more.

"It's bigger than I ever imagined," Spot breathed. "It must be old as time itself."

Imagining that all those within the tomb were of the same bloodline, he imagined how far back the generations laid to rest here must stretch – hundreds if not thousands of years. Since before the end of the Time of Witches. His mind boggled. Little was known of the time before the Witches' reign, save that the Sisterhood had been created by the Prophet, whom the Witches later slew with the help of the Betrayer, who was in turn betrayed.

Perhaps I can be the first to uncover the secrets of our past!

Dreams of archaeological successes flitted through his mind like birds tweeting of a famous future, and he almost smiled before he saw the figure in the flickering shadows by the right wall. The smile died on his lips. He recognised the man as Count Darcuul of the House of *La Pantera*, whom he had met at *Pacia* Castle. He could not see the man's face clearly, but the pattern embroidered in silver thread on the back of his black coat of a Dragon in flight with a lance through its heart was unmistakeable. Spot was sure it was a unique garment.

There was something disturbing about seeing the man down here in the heart of a crypt at night. Spot felt a shiver course up his spine, making his head tingle and his hands shake. The man did not appear to be doing anything sinister – he was on his knees beside a sarcophagus, seemingly paying respects – and yet Spot's instincts screamed at him to run.

It turned out they were right.

"Well, well, well," purred a voice in Spot's ear, making him jump out of his skin in fright. "What intrepid little adventurers you are."

Spot and Tumba spun in terror and, as they backed into the faint firelight, beheld the exit blocked by three men and a woman, none of whom looked familiar. Their unwashed stench spoke of the slums.

The closest man, a wiry little fellow wearing a mink fur overcoat and a black brimmed hat, sneered at them, "You shouldn't be down here, little ones. Here, Darcuul, look what I found!"

Spot's heart lurched in horror as he turned to see Count Darcuul stalking towards them, whatever curtain he usually pulled across his face drawn aside. His bright blue eyes lit up the room like baleful lanterns, his scalp could be seen past his moulting black hair, and four outsized fangs curved over his pale lips. Spot gasped, for the Count's face was just as nightmarish as had been Rathbone's, as had been the clown's. He blinked and blinked again, but the illusion did not fade this time and his knees started to knock together when he realised it was no illusion. He was seeing reality, perhaps for the first time.

A nasty smile stole across the Count's face when he locked eyes with Spot, and he said playfully in bass tones, "My, my, if it isn't young Samuel de León. What a wonderful surprise to find you down here, my boy."

"Please, sir," Spot piped in a trembling voice, "please just let us go. I'm sorry for the intrusion, really sorry, but please just let us go home."

A mock-quizzical look furrowed the Count's brow. "Oh, no, I'm afraid I can't allow that, my boy, no, no. You're here now, and here you will stay." He glanced up at the man in mink fur. "I know this may sound strange, but let's turn this one. His father could prove useful to us if … leverage … can be applied."

"What about the other one?" asked the man in mink.

The Count's eyes raked over Tumba for less than half a second, before he said, "I have no use for the other one. He would only be another mouth to feed. Dispose of him."

"What an excellent opportunity," purred the man in mink. "Dion, we've got another meal for you right here!"

The man in mink fur seized Tumba roughly.

"Tumba!" Spot cried out.

Tumba screamed and Spot tried to pry the man off his friend, but was shoved over. Looking up from the ground, Spot beheld the man in mink fur shove Tumba towards the man behind him, a tall young man with an usually sallow complexion for a Justiquan, whose garments – a frilly white shirt, dark trousers and leather boots – seemed of higher quality than the others', even if the embroidered lapels on his turquoise coat were a little frayed from use.

The man caught Tumba instinctively to stop him from slamming into him. Then, he seemed to hesitate, though, looking at the man in mink with a pleading mien.

"Get on with it, ya big –" The man in mink suddenly cocked his head, sniffed the air and growled, "Crows!"

Figures flew into the room from the torch-lit entryway, and abruptly pandemonium broke loose.

10
A Living Nightmare

Sir Dion Laflamme was living a nightmare.
I am a living nightmare!
It had been the worst week of his life by far.
He had awoken from a drunken stupor in the grotty little room in *The Bent Penny*. Thanks to his transformation, the curtains of cleanliness had long since been pulled aside. Whatever enchantment had caused him to see the room as he had first seen it was gone, and he had seen once again the mould-infested flayed walls, the broken furniture and the uneven splintering floorboards. He had groaned, praying the night before had been a dream. Then, he had noticed the bloodstains on his white shirt and blue coat.

He had reached up and felt blood crusted on his face and lips. He had felt the long, thin fangs protruding from his gummy mouth like a boar's tusks, and he had known despair. He had wanted to be sick then, but somehow he couldn't. He suspected he had vomited up his stomach's contents the night before and been left empty as an old man's dream. He had dared not leave the room, dared not confront the truth. His hangover had paralysed him, but it was as nothing to the terror that had pinioned him to the bed.

It was not a dream. It truly happened! Prophet help me, it truly happened! What have I become? What will become of my tainted soul? Will I ever make it to Citta Pacia *now, to the gates of paradise beyond death? The Prophet's Word teaches us that only those pure of heart are admitted ... And that is not me. Not anymore. Perhaps it never was.*

A few minutes later, Ignatius Boondoggle had dawdled in, swept off his hat and bowed with a wide grin affixed. Like the room, the enchantment no longer held true for Ignatius either. Dion had seen him then as he truly was; a fanged horror in a mouldy mink coat, wearing a patchy brimmed hat, glittering pale blue eyes set in a stubbly ratty face surrounded by lacklustre earthy curls. Dion wished he had had his sword, but it had been taken from him.

"Good morning, my newest recruit!" Ignatius had drawled. "And how are we feeling today? A little worse for wear, eh? I'm not surprised. You can really put it away, ya know! Haha! Ah, we had a grand time last night. A *grand* time. You may be pleased to hear your comrades escaped my attentions last night. It seems they had a change of heart when confronted with the realities of prostitution and decided to scarper off home before they further tarnished their good names. I guess they just weren't as depraved as you, eh, my young friend? Ah well, it cannot be helped. I'd have loved to turn all three of you, but presenting just you to Count Darcuul will work just as well, I think. You're the rich one, after all, aren't ya? Haha! Rich old daddy, yes?"

He had nodded as if speaking to a simpleton, and Dion had wanted to throttle him, to tear out his windpipe with his teeth. He still was not sure why he had not.

Because it's pointless. It's too late. I've already been changed.

"Yes," Ignatius had continued. "Very good, very good. Now, I'm here to introduce you to your new life – or afterlife, perhaps. I've never been very clear on how it all works. Above my pay grade, I suppose. I'm just the recruiter. Regardless of whether you're alive or dead, though, you are *different* than you were before, and I am here to help you adjust." He had beamed, as though Dion ought to be grateful. "A few key disparities exist twixt us and the living. First, we cannot die. Again. Not unless we are beheaded or burned to death. Or magicked. Besides that, we are near enough immortal. Second, we are nocturnal creatures."

He had crossed to the window and drawn back the tattered curtains with a quick motion, allowing daylight to bathe the room for but a second before he closed them again. In that second, though, Sir Dion Laflamme had screamed in agony as sunlight washed over his sallow olive skin, feeling as though a fire had been kindled in his flesh.

"Daylight cannot kill us, as some of the stories would have you believe," Ignatius had said, his voice taut with pain for a moment, "but it does greatly weaken us. By night, we are stronger and faster than any human. By day, we are weak as mewling babes, it is sad to say. So, stay out of the sun. Rest in the day. Feed at night."

Bunny had come in then, curly black hair and blue frock flouncing girlishly. She cupped her hand and whispered in Ignatius' ear for a moment, leaning on him. He nodded and they locked eyes for a moment, before kissing deeply. Then, she left and Ignatius turned back to Dion.

"Where was I?" he drawled. "Ah, yes. Number three. Third, in death, we acquire powers over all the faculties of darkness. Nocturnal creatures are ours to command. We can shift our shape into shadow and cast glamours to trick the human eye. I will teach you this, in due course. Fourth, secrecy. We must keep our existence a secret from the humans at all cost. Especially these godforsaken *Knights.*" He spat the word, before remembering his present company and adding, "No offence, but they are a pain in the ass. Any human would kill us if they could if they knew what we were, but Knights most of all. They're on the warpath for any sort of magic or unnatural creature since the Time of Witches. But I'm sure you know that already." He grinned sarcastically. "Fourth – or was it fifth? – we need not eat. We require no sustenance whatsoever – besides blood. Human blood contains all the nutrition we need, and you will find, in fact, that you desire nothing else anymore. The craving will come upon you soon, I'm sure, if it hasn't already. D'you feel your belly rumbling?"

So hungry.

Dion's gut had gurgled loudly, and Ignatius had nodded smilingly.

"Yes, I thought so," the man in mink had purred. "Well, it is gone noon. You've slept half the day away already. Just try to go back to sleep until nightfall if you can. You need to switch your sleeping habits to a day-cycle anyway. Best get in the practice sooner rather than later. I remember when I was turned …" He sighed. "Took me forever to switch my sleep cycle over. I was dead on my feet for weeks. Anywho, just stay here and we'll get you someone tasty to eat after dusk, okay? Any questions?"

Dion had had a million, but had been rendered near speechless. Only one question had forced its way up past his lips, ribbiting out into the world in desperation. "Is there any way to undo it? Is there any way to undo what has been done to me?"

Ignatius Boondoggle had studied him for a long moment then. "None," he had said, the syllable a misericorde to the Knight's heart, the coup de grâce for his hope and faith. "See you in a few hours, *good Sir Knight.*"

He had bowed with a mocking flourish and left the young Knight alone.

Dion had done what anyone would have done then. He had jumped out of the window and tried to hightail it home as fast as humanly – or inhumanly – possible. He had been prepared for the caustic sunlight this time and gritted his teeth as he burst through the curtains. As soon as the sun had hit him, though, he had hissed as excruciation boiled up in his body like lava. Falling from the second storey, he had crumpled on landing, a sore pile on the cobbled street below. The sun had blazed directly overhead. There was no escaping it, despite the terraced tenements on either side of him. He realised then he had badly mistimed his escape attempt and groaned, face-down on the cobbles so that nobody could see his fangs. He had barely been able to move a muscle, such was the wildfire coursing through his veins. Still, he had begun to crawl at a snail's pace, dragging his body slowly and agonisingly down the street while people stepped over him or walked around him, city life continuing as normal, oblivious to the horrific events of the night before. Nobody offered to help him up. He would not have offered to help him up, would have thought himself just another beggar who had thrown his life away.

I must get away from this place! I must get home!

Ignatius Boondoggle found him less than twenty yards away from

The Bent Penny, clapped him on the back and sighed. "Ah, I told you not to go out in daylight, my young friend. You'll fry. Come on, let's get you back inside, ya numpty."

Not ungently, he had dragged Dion back inside, apologising to the customers in the common room as he went and saying that the young man had had a few too many already. Once inside, he had enlisted the bouncer's help to carry Dion upstairs and put him back in his room, in bed.

"H-how could you stand the pain?" Dion had stuttered, teeth chattering.

He felt the fire slowly leaving his system as the shade took effect.

"You grow used to it, to some extent," Ignatius had replied with a shrug. "And feeding helps. Blood fuels our strength now. Once you feed, you will feel the power flow through you, I promise. It is ... intoxicating. Are you hungry?"

So hungry.

Dion's gut had garbled again, but he had shaken his head.

Ignatius had smiled knowingly. "Perhaps it's best we feed you sooner rather than later. Then, you'll truly understand what you are. With knowledge comes acceptance. With acceptance comes peace. We are not evil, ya see, you and I, Dion, no. We are merely hunters. Is the human evil for hunting the buck? Is the lion? Is the winter evil for freezing folk to death? No, of course not. Nature takes its natural course, and we are a part of nature, Dion. We are beasts, just like the humans. It is in our nature to feed on them, just as they feed on the beasts of the field. You'll come to see that we are not so different from the humans really. We kill them, but they would kill us if they knew what we were. And would they be evil for doing so? I don't think so. They'd only be following their natural instincts after all, as do we all, no matter where those instincts lead us. Ponder on that awhile. I'll be back soon."

So saying, he had departed once more.

Tired, hungover and in pain, Dion had passed out once more.

So hungry.

He had awoken to the sound of the door creaking open and stirred enough to crack open on eye and behold Ignatius Boondoggle entering, leading in a frumpy woman with a hairy wart on her cheek and cooing, "Come in here, my sweet dove. In here, we can be alone together, just you and I ..."

"What's he doing here?" the ginger-haired woman had snapped peevishly, spotting Sir Dion Laflamme sprawled on the bed.

"Oh, I didn't realise someone was in here!" Ignatius had exclaimed, feigning surprise and swiftly shifting around the woman to close the door behind her, barring the exit.

Once the door was closed, his fawning demeanour had evaporated and he had chopped the woman in the neck with the blade of his hand, knocking her out quickly and quietly. She had hit the floor with a thud.

"Eurgh!" he had exclaimed then, shivering in disgust. "I can't believe she actually fell for that. Did you see that wart? Repulsive! Anywho, look, Dion! I brought you a snack."

"A snack?"

"Yes, a snack. For you to eat. Or drink. Or consume. Whatever. Just drain her, will ya? You'll feel a lot better."

"Drain her?"

Ignatius had rolled his eyes. "Yes. Drain her dry. Suck her blood. Get your nourishment. Come on, come on, we haven't got all day!"

So hungry. I can smell her blood. I can sense it rushing through her veins, sweet and warm. I can taste it on my tongue, sweet as wine ...

Dion's stomach had betrayed him with a growl, but he had shaken his head vehemently. "No! No, I won't do it."

Ignatius had sighed. "You will eventually. You'll be too hungry not to." He had slipped a poniard from the sleeve of his mink fur coat and casually dipped it hilt-deep into the unconscious woman's neck. The movement had been so smooth and unhurried that it had taken Dion a while to comprehend that she was dead, despite the blood on the blade. "I'm going to lock you in here with her," Ignatius had drawled, wiping the knife on the woman's blue-and-white-striped smock. "You'll feed eventually." He had turned to leave and then turned back. "Oh, and don't even think about jumping out of the window again. The bouncer will see you, and we'll chase you down and break your legs to make a point if we have to. They'll heal. They'll heal quicker than they would have done when you were human. But it will still hurt. A lot. Besides, you've got nowhere to run. We know where you live, Sir Dion Laflamme. Halfway down Dirk Road in that mansion house bought for you by your father, Baron Manuel Laflamme. Oh yes, we know. There's no escaping us, Dion. This is your life now. You must learn to accept it."

So hungry.

Dion had tried to escape again that night, but the bouncer had spotted him as he fell from the window in the bright moonlight. Also a creature of the night, the bouncer had easily manhandled Dion back inside, and the Knight had realised he was weak as a new-born calf with hunger.

So hungry.

For two days, Dion had resisted the craving, praying for death's sweet relief.

On the third, he had no longer been able to resist.

He had not been sure how he could even bite anything. Ignatius' fangs looked so long that the mouth could not possibly open wide enough to admit anything between them, and his own felt just as long. When he had loomed over the dead woman, however, salivating like a starved dog, he had found that his mouth opened unreasonably wide now, snakelike, new ophidian muscles granting him previously unknown stretchiness. He had sunk his fangs into the woman's neck and known nothing then but warm, wet bliss until he came to again on the floor beside the desiccated corpse, his belly full. The taste of her blood had lingered on his tongue, and he had groaned in horror at the deliciousness of it.

What have I done? What have I become?

Ignatius Boondoggle had found him on the floor not long later, praying for death once more.

"Congratulations!" he had purred, seeing the bloodless woman. "I take it you feel better now? Wonderful, isn't it, that first feeding? Oh, I remember it fondly. A fat old man ... mmm, he was scrumptious. So ... how are you feeling, Sir Dion Laflamme? Have you come to terms with your new existence yet? You could be of great help to us, you know, our ... organisation."

"I want nothing to do with you or your organisation," Dion had croaked, voice breaking from lack of use and emotion. "Just leave me alone."

Ignatius had frowned. "Disappointing. That's not the reaction I was hoping for. Nevertheless, it is time for you to become acquainted with our little outfit, so you must come with me. Tonight, I am going to introduce you to one of the higher-ups in our organisation." He had eyed the Knight's bloodstained clothes. "I'll have some fresh garments fetched from your mansion. Wait here."

Not long later, Dion's own clothes were delivered to him, and he undressed and put them on in a daze, thinking that he would have chosen a coat with less frayed lapels.

This must be a nightmare! Prophet help me!

He had been led through the nighted streets in a trance to the cemetery, and from there into one of the crypts.

"What an excellent opportunity," purred Ignatius Boondoggle, seizing hold of the brown-skinned boy and tossing him towards the Knight. "Dion, we've got another meal for you right here!"

Now, staring into Tumba's eyes, Sir Dion Laflamme felt a wave of vertigo sweep over him as a vision of eternity spent as a monster opened out before him.

So hungry.

"Get on with it, ya big –" Ignatius began angrily before stopping, cocking his head and barking. "Crows!"

Dion barely heard him. He found that despite his omnipresent hunger, he was able to resist the urge to sink his fangs into the boy and suck out his blood.

His sweet, warm blood.

More than that, he did not want to do it. He *could* not do it. Not again.

Before he could admit this to Ignatius, however, three more horrors swooped into the underground crypt on wide black feathery wings, cawing like crows. They looked human by the light of the single, flickering torch by the entryway, besides the wings growing from their shoulder-blades and their visages, which were horribly warped into beaked nightmare fuel. To a man, they were wrapped in unreflective cloth from neck to toe, and in their hands they bore a mixture of broadswords and sabres.

"Time to die, creatures of the night!" one of them boomed in authoritative bass tones. "May the Prophet have mercy on your souls, for I shall have none!"

Dion pushed the boy, Tumba, away from him and instinctively reached for his own sword, only to remember that it had not yet been returned to him. "Boondoggle!" he yelped as he sprang behind a pillar to hide from a whistling sabre swipe aimed at him by one of the flying anomalies. "Where is my sword?"

Clutching his hat to his head and ducking just in time to avoid being beheaded by a broadsword, Boondoggle turned on him with a vicious expression, hissing like a startled cat, "No names, you fool! These are the cursed Crows, and they will kill you if they can!"

"Then, give me a weapon so I can defend myself!" Dion snapped, peeking out from behind the pillar.

"Just stay there!" Ignatius growled. "We'll deal with this. Bunny, Vazquez, you know what to do!"

Bunny and Vazquez nodded and, as one with Ignatius, melted into the darkness of the crypt. Dion blinked and rubbed his eyes, only to realise that he could still see faint outlines of them depicted in wavering shade cast by the torch. They had *become* shadows, he realised with a start, recalling then Ignatius' words – 'We can shift our shape into shadow and cast glamours to trick the human eye'.

Peering out from behind the stone pillar, he witnessed the shadows shifting as if sentient, not just flickering in the irregular light but moving in tandem, with intent. Dion blinked then and almost lost track of them; they moved fast. The next thing he knew, they were upon the Crows, blurring faster than the eye could follow. A downpour of blood splattered the wall nearby, and it took Dion a moment to replay the scene in his mind's eye and realise that one of the shadows – *Ignatius, maybe* – had carved one of the bird-men open from throat to scrote as it zipped overhead. He watched the savaged Crow squawk and crash down face-first into the flagstones, leaving a gory trail where it skidded. A heartbeat later, Bunny was crying out in pain as her forearm was slashed open to the bone.

She cannot cast the shadow spell when she is in pain!

Dion saw her coalesce from wraith-form with his own eyes, a whole woman seemingly materialising from the darkness, clutching her arm and sinking to her rump. One of the shadows came to her rescue in a flash, and though Dion could see no blade anywhere on the inky form, he heard the clash of steel and saw sparks fly as one of the Crows' broadswords clanged against a shadow sword. The skirling sound of swordplay reverberated around the tomb, echoing off the distant walls again and again as the winged figure hacked over and over at the shadow the Vampyre had become.

It seemed as though the Crow had the upper hand, as if the shadow were on the back foot, retreating. Then, however, another shadow extricated itself from the blackness behind the winged fighter and pounced. Blood jetted from the Crow's neck as a wide gouge appeared there as if by magic, and it croaked like its namesake and flopped down to the ground, wings twitching for a moment before stilling. Ignatius Boondoggle and Count Darcuul reformed from the darkness as if born from the Void. Dion glanced around and saw another dead Crow behind him, alongside the decapitated corpse of Vazquez. He had not even heard the struggle.

"Where are the children?" Ignatius demanded, suddenly remembering that two boys had been witness to the proceedings.

He cast around, but could find them nowhere.

"I think I saw them scarper when the fighting began," Bunny said through gritted teeth, still clutching her arm on the ground. "They're long gone by now."

"You led the Crows here, Ignatius!" Count Darcuul intoned in his deep-as-the-grave voice, his pale countenance composed as he smoothed his black coat and white shirt, which had somehow escaped even the faintest speck of blood. "And now the children have gotten away *because of you!*"

"That's impossible!" retorted Ignatius, waving towards his dead companion. "I had Vazquez follow us to make sure –" He stopped dead in his tracks and sighed as he realised what must have happened.

Count Darcuul nodded knowingly. "So, they followed *him* instead. Very clever of you, Ignatius. Very clever."

Ignatius scowled. "Well, what would you have me do? Have someone follow him? Have someone follow the follower? Have someone follow the follower of the follower? When does the madness end? How many precautions can I take, Darcuul? There must be limits!"

"Perhaps this *was* too obvious a meeting place," Darcuul observed.

"The Crows are all over this little cemetery like flies on shit. We'll meet elsewhere next time. For now, though, I believe you have a new recruit you wanted me to meet. I remember meeting Vazquez, so I assume it must be this quivering spineless piece of dung hiding behind the pillar here, hmm?"

Ignatius' scowl eased into a rueful expression. "Yes. He's more useful than he looks, though – or I think he could be." He dragged Dion out from behind the pillar to stand before the Count, looking at his toes like a chastised child. "Sir Dion Laflamme, may I present Count Ivan Darcuul. Count Darcuul, may I present Sir Dion Laflamme."

"Laflamme, eh?" Darcuul repeated ponderously. "You could be right, Ignatius. The Laflamme family certainly has some influence we could use. Well done, Boondoggle. A small prize, but a prize nonetheless. I take it from his expression that he has not yet come to terms with our ways?"

"He has tasted blood," Ignatius answered. "It is only a matter of time now."

"Marvellous. Well, do keep me updated on his progress and on any other promising recruits you may happen upon, won't you?"

"Of course, Count."

"For now, let us introduce our new recruit to the Old One and see what is to be done with him."

"Yes, Count. Lead the way. Bunny, get back to the tavern and heal up."

Bunny left, the blood on her red dress invisible. Count Darcuul led Dion and Ignatius all the way to the far end of the crypt, their footsteps echoing a staccato tattoo as they went. They were enshrouded in shadow before they were halfway there, but Dion found that he could see perfectly well in differing shades of grey despite the pitch blackness.

Another effect of Vampyrism.

At the back of the crypt, the Count easily slid off the heavy stone lid off a sarcophagus with a loud grating noise and lowered it gently to the floor. Dion peered into the sarcophagus and gasped when he saw a set of stone steps descending through the tomb to an unknown shadowy depth.

Count Darcuul led the way down. Ignatius gestured for Dion to go next with a wave of his hat. "After you, good Sir Knight."

Dion gulped and stepped into the sarcophagus, following the Count down into darkness.

11
The Old One

Sir Dion Laflamme was lost within seconds of entering the catacombs beneath the Darcuul family crypt.

A thousand openings yawned at him from left and right, beckoning him to oblivion, and Count Ivan Darcuul zigzagged through them seemingly at random, a pale ghost in the shades of grey which were all Dion could see, his vampyric eyes adjusting to the pitch darkness.

"Ignore the ferals if you can," Darcuul advised in a low voice. "They will attack if disturbed."

"Ferals?" whispered Dion, glancing around nervously.

"Vampyres who lost their minds when they were turned," Darcuul explained, turning to bestow a sombre look on the Knight. "Not all are as lucky as you or I when the gift of immortality is bestowed. For some, it is too much to handle. Their minds fray and tear apart, and they become little more than mindless beasts with no greater desire than to satiate their endless hunger. We keep them down here, feeding them people and scraps of meat, so that they at least serve some purpose, as guards for the Old One."

Dion gulped.

Not long later, he laid eyes on a feral for the first time. Shaped like a human, the creature was emaciated to the point that he could see its bones poking through its thin, fish-belly skin. It shuffled around in the darkness with its head hanging on its chest, its feet scraping the floor, unaware or uncaring of their presence. Most of its hair had fallen out, leaving only a patch or two here and there, and it evidently had not changed garments since it had been turned. Its old-fashioned frilly regalia was washed out and tattered, spattered in dried blood the colour of rust.

Dion let out a small gasp, and it turned toward him with a violent twitch, its glassy eyes locking onto his own. He reeled back a step unconsciously, for there was not a spark of humanity in those eyes, not an iota of compassion or intelligence. Only hunger. It groaned and drooled, and he saw that its lips and cheeks were coated in the same rust colour as its ruined doublet. It lurched towards the Vampyre Knight abruptly with a high-pitched warble, hands outstretched to grab, and Dion flinched and fumbled for the sword that was not at his hip.

Darcuul backhanded the feral to the ground before it could touch Dion and then dragged the Knight away, hissing, "I told you to ignore them. Do *not* make eye contact with them."

They encountered many more ferals in their underground journey, but Dion kept his gaze firmly fixed on the floor, following Darcuul's heels like a loyal hound while the shambling monsters moaned and shuffled all around him. He did not look up, even when they passed through a cavern where it sounded as though there might have been as many as a hundred ferals milling in aimless circles. He shivered at the thought.

Better not to look up. Better not to know.

When he and the others finally emerged from the narrow confines of the endless rough-hewn stone corridors into an empty spacious cavern, Dion breathed a sigh of relief. The oppressiveness of the close quarters and the proximity of the ferals had begun to chafe him. Water trickled down the rugged walls of the cave and dripped from a crack in the ceiling to pitter-patter on the rocky ground below. Stalactites hung down like fangs from the ceiling and jutted up from the centre of the floor, as if the whole cave were a Vampyre's maw.

"Where are we?" Dion murmured.

"We are beneath Lágrimas River," Ignatius whispered reverentially from behind him, even that faint sound echoing.

Dion shivered, imagining the tons of rock and water above him coming crashing down. He began to feel oppressed again, as if the wide walls were tightening around him like a noose. He followed Darcuul through an arch in a relatively flat grey wall running with water, a few droplets sprinkling him as he went like a macabre parody of the ritual bathing he had undertaken as a child to be inducted into the Prophet's Way.

Dipping a baby by the heel into a pool of sanctified water. What an odd ritual.

Once in the extensive cavern beyond, he looked around in confusion.
A dead end.

Horror slithered over his skin, leaving him with goosebumps.

Prophet help me, they're going to kill me down here where nobody can hear me scream or find my body!

Then, the whole cavern changed.

A ripple of light pulsed across the room, and in its wake the true cavern was revealed as the illusion peeled away. A hollow stone ring pulsing with runes spelled out in purple fire caught Dion's attention first, and his breath caught in his throat at the thought of magic being conducted here beneath the streets of Justiqua. A score or more Vampyres cluttered the cavern, chit-chatting nonchalantly with barely a glance towards the newcomers, all of them fanged horrors to give a man nightmares for the rest of this days. One, though, was the most grotesque of all.

What is that throne made of? Human skin and bones?

On the grisly throne at the far end of the cavern sat the oldest-looking creature Dion had ever laid eyes on, with grey skin that looked as though it were growing mould sagging off its scrawny humanoid frame. A ragged, filthy hide loincloth was all that preserved the unholy creature's dignity. It transfixed Dion with its glare then as he studied it, and he found to his horror he could not look away as he plummeted into the infinite depths of the hoarfrost of those four hoary blue eyes. A long sharp nose spiked out from the creature's hairless head between its deep-set eyes, and a whole host of vamypric fangs curved up and down from its slit of a maw.

When it opened its mouth, its sibilant voice slithered across the room with the strength to be heard by all, raspy and snakelike. "Fresh blood! Ss ss ss! Bring the boy to me! Ss ss ss!"

Sir Dion Laflamme was lifted off the ground by an invisible force and flung across the cavern with enough speed to give him whiplash, only to be abruptly yanked to a halt a mere foot away from the heinous creature on the throne.

"Ss ss ss!" The creature made gross sounds as it sucked in air through its slit maw, wheezing all the while. "Let me take a good look at you, boy! Ss! A wretch of a man, I see your soul, hehehe! Perfect. Ss ss ss. Perfect. You will be a malleable tool in the hands of Ra'Gthul."

"Mighty Ra'Gthul," Ignatius cooed ingratiatingly, sidling nearer, "may I present Sir Dion Laflamme, our newest recruit. As I'm sure you're aware, the Laflamme family is very wealthy and holds a lot of sway –"

"I know more about the Laflamme family than you do, whelp!" rasped Ra'Gthul. "I watched Justiqua grow from a mere fishing village to the city it is today! For half a millennium have I awaited my kin here in this cesspool world lest they need to escape their cursed war, through Witches and Knights and all manner of foes, and my memory of it all is faultless. I recall the first occurrence of the name Laflamme, though it was no ancestor of this mule. So, pray do not waste your breath or my time trying to teach me what I already know, dear Ignatius. I know the Laflamme family, and I know the perfect use for this little tool."

"What are you?" Dion squeaked, mouse-like, trying to shrivel in on himself and present as small a target as possible while he hung in mid-air.

Ra'gthul grinned. "Why, I created the first of your kind, my son. I am Ra'Gthul, the Old One, Sire of Vampyres."

12
Ma Ca Rong

Spot de León had never run so fast in his life as he did when he and Tumba Koum legged it out of the crypt. The wind chilled his face and tousled his hair, and the cemetery and the inky phantomscape of Justiqua blurred by in his periphery. He thought he could feel death breathing down his collar every step of the way, but nobody stopped them as they sped through the nighted streets at breakneck speed.

Tumba's thin, grey terraced house had never looked so appealing as it did just then, a bower in the savage stone jungle. Slipping inside, they slammed shut the door and bolted it, before leaning against it, breathing hard.

Thank the Prophet! Safety!

"What is going on?" Ursa demanded from her usual spot by the cauldron in the middle of the room, from which wafted rapturous scents.

Was she floating a foot off the ground, or am I going crazy?

"We never bolt da door unless we're asleep," said Ursa sternly, now definitely planted on the floor.

"Just ... getting ready early," panted Tumba. "We won't be going out again."

I guess he doesn't think she'll believe him if he tells her the truth. I cannot blame him. Who would believe such a tale?

Ursa frowned. "Does Spot not need to go home?"

"Actually, I was wondering if I could stay here for the night, please, Mzee Koum?" Spot said quickly to save Tumba from the necessity of lying again.

He was not lying; he truly did want to stay the night. He did not feel like walking home alone in the darkness.

Ursa smiled, her plump cheeks bunching and her eyes twinkling warmly in the candlelight. "Of course, dearie, of course you can. It's so nice to see you boys getting along. I've plenty of supper for da boat of you. Grab some bowls and let's eat."

When asked what was in the delicious broth, Ursa only shrugged and said, "Whatever I had lying around dat looked tasty."

Spooning some of the indiscriminate but tasty broth into his mouth, Spot froze when Ursa asked, "So, what have you boys been up to today? Anyting fun?"

He heard Tumba's wooden spoon clatter on the table as his friend dropped it and hastily picked it up again.

"Just ... playing kickball," Tumba said, before shovelling more food in his face.

"All day?" Ursa asked.

"Yef," said Tumba around a mouthful of food.

Ursa arched an eyebrow. "You must be exhausted. Well, eat up, eat up. Dere's plenty to go around."

Once he started to feel his belly bulge, Spot's mind returned to the horrors it had witnessed once more and he said tentatively, "Mzee Koum, Tumba was telling me a story about the ... *Ma Ca Rong*. It – it was really interesting, and I wondered if you knew any others. About them." Spot blushed, feeling like a fool, thinking she must be able to read his thoughts plain as ink on his face.

Ursa eyed him askance for a moment, during which time he thought his heart would give out in anxiety, and then she shrugged and said with a smile, "You've been telling spooky stories to commemorate da Day of da Dead, haven't you, huh?" She chuckled. "Oh, very well, I'll indulge you. Just wait until we finish supper."

Spot almost choked trying to eat as much food as possible as quickly as possible, as did Tumba. They ended up waiting for Ursa, tapping their feet or their fingers on the table top.

When she had finally finished eating and washed the wooden plates, she sat on a patchy old armchair and the two boys lay flat on the threadbare rug on the rough wooden floor, chins cupped in hands.

"Ahem," she began in her storyteller voice, brushing her silver dreadlocks out of her mahogany face, her lilting accent adding emphasis at strange moments from time to time. "Da *Ma Ca Rong* are said to be as old as time – or near to it. Stories vary on how dey came to be. Spawned from da Nedder. Sired by some ancient evil creature. Come from anudder world. Magic gone wrong. Teories vary. What da stories agree on, however, is deir reason for coming here to Maradoum. Stories say dat dey have been fighting an ageless war in anudder world – be it da Nedder, nobody knows – and dat dey keep open da portal to dis world as an escape route for deir race. Stories say if ever da *Ma Ca Rong* were to come true dis portal en masse, all life as we know it here on Maradoum would be wiped out, transformed into vampyric nightmares!"

Spot gulped, and Ursa smiled reassuringly. "It's only stories, dough, my boys."

"Well, how would you kill one," Spot asked, "if you did ever come across one?"

Ursa frowned, but replied, "One story tells of a Knight who slew one of da *Ma Ca Rong* by decapitation. Anudder tells of a wily woodcutter who lured one of da *Ma Ca Rong* into his own home and set it alight, dus killing da creature. Why, are you planning to go hunting da *Ma Ca Rong?*"

Spot tried to smile, but was afraid it came out as a grimace. "No, of course not. It's just stories, like you said."

I may have to kill them. Before they kill me.

"Mmhmm."

"I was wondering, though," Spot continued awkwardly, "how did people ever recognise them in the stories if they could use magic to mask their true appearance?"

Ursa regarded him with furrowed brow for a long moment. "Dere is one tale dat speaks of a Chilpaean magician, who sought da answer to dat very question. Nefulim da Grand, he styled himself. He captured one of da *Ma ca Rong* dat had revealed itself to him by trying to kill him and tested every teory known to rumour and gossip. Iron did not work, nor silver, nor gold, wooden stakes or garlic. Daylight hurt dem, he deduced, but it could neider kill dem nor shatter deir enchantments. In da end, he came to da conclusion dat dey must be da same as any udder magician, to some extent, in dat dey require *concentration* to cast deir deceptive spells. Distraction, he decided, was da only way to break true deir illusions. He was killed trying to prove his teory, dough. Da *Ma Ca Rong* are not to be trifled wid."

"Indeed they are not," came a severe voice from the window, where Marcus de León could be seen peering in through the rain, his curly grey hair plastered to his head. "I was worried sick waiting for you to come home, Samuel. Come now, it is time to get you to bed."

"I tought you said you wanted to stay over?" Ursa demanded, rounding on Spot. "You did not have your fadder's permission?"

Spot smiled wanly. He had known his father would come looking for him here. "I guess I must've forgot. Sorry."

Ursa threw her hands in the air in exasperation. "Oh, I'm sorry, Viscount, truly I am! I had no idea he was here widout consent, no idea! Ah, it's just like young boys, dough, eh? I didn't mean nutting by it, Viscount. I love Spot like my own son, and I would never let any harm come to him, you know dat."

"I know," replied Marcus, raising a hand to forestall more apologies. "You are not at fault here, my good lady. It is my errant son on whom my disappointment must fall. Come, Spot. *Now.*"

"Yes, father."

Spot felt safe walking home with his father, even in the dark, even in the thunder and rain. Beggars lurked in doorways, and what his father called 'ladies of the night' called to Marcus as they went. Rats scurried this way and that amid excrement and detritus in the gutters, and scrawny rag-clad figures skulked in alleys, eyeing father and son predatorily, and yet still Spot felt safe. He could see the lion's head pommel of the knightly broadsword at his father's hip glinting in the occasional shafts of moonlight, and he knew his father felt no fear.

He didn't even bring any bodyguards with him! He's so brave. I wish I could be as brave as him one day.

"Father," he began, "I don't know how to tell you this, but –"

"Where have you been, boy?" Marcus exploded. "It is the middle of the night, and Bona Dea and I have seen neither hide nor hair of you since this morning! I give you a lot of leeway, but you know you are expected home earlier than this! This sort of behaviour cannot be allowed to continue, Samuel! As long as you live under my roof, you will obey my rules. No more gallivanting around the city all day and night with the Chilpaean boy. And as for the woman ... did you know Ursa Koum was accused of baui consumption and witchcraft a few years ago? Eleven witnesses testified to her guilt, and still she got off scot-free! Some say she used witchcraft to bamboozle Kronvert, her judge. You're to stay well away from that woman, d'you hear me? I've had enough!"

"I'm sorry, father. I know it was foolish to stay out so late, but if you could just listen for a moment, I need to tell you –"

"No, I will not listen! You have some explaining to do, that is for sure, but I don't want to hear your excuses right now. I am exhausted. I just want to go home and sleep. So, not a peep out of you!"

"But –"

"Not a peep!"

I need proof. I need to find a way to make him see what I see. Then, he'll understand.

13
A Gala in a Storm

Spot de León had not yet had a chance to share his newfound knowledge of the horrific underworld of Justiqua with his father. By the time he awoke the morning after his chastisement, his father had gone out.

"Where has he gone?" Spot asked the maid, Bona Dea, a Babese woman half Ursa Koum's age and weight and looking like she was catching up.

"He don't say," Bona Dea replied in an accented voice, folding clothes. "He just ran out of the house and said not to let you go nowhere till he got home. He said you got to go to a gala with him tonight, and he don't want you dirty."

Spot stamped a foot in frustration before stomping upstairs to read one of his favourite Monty Wainwright novels, and a smile haunted Bona Dea's lips for a fleeting instant.

By the time Marcus de León returned that evening, Spot had decided that rather than telling his father about the Vampyres, the *Ma Ca Rong*, he would help his father *see* them at the gala that evening. All the usual suspects attended these galas, he knew from past experience. It was in vogue for aristocrats to put on galas to raise money for the Crusades.

If all the same people attend these parties every time, though, who's to say the money isn't just being passed around and never actually passed on to its final destination?

When his father summoned him, Spot appeared at the head of the broadening staircase promptly and descended to meet him fully attired for an evening with the socialites in an immaculate white shirt, a brown buttoned coat, dark breeches, stockings and moccasins. Dressed in a frilly shirt with a neckerchief, a long fox fur coat, khaki trousers and yellowish leather boots, his father was the apotheosis of the flamboyant fashion trends gripping Justiqua at that time, thought Spot. Together, father and son stepped into the carriage awaiting them and were soon trundling through the nighted streets once more on their way to the mansion of Viscount Vivari Levont.

The mansion's escarpment-like façade was fronted by nasty-looking grotesques leering at anyone who passed by, its ornamental architecture giving it a skeletal look in the half light, as if its bones were showing. Thunder clapped the ears and rain pelted father and son as they rushed from the carriage, through the wrought iron gate and well-tended garden to the mansion's door, which was held open for them by a privately hired guard.

Spot's chin itched where the water dripped off it by the time he was inside; the garden was extensive, rampant with statues, raised grey marble flowerbeds and weeping cherries.

As Viscount of Crossroads, perhaps the second largest city in Justiqua, second in command there only to Count Darcuul, Vivari Levont had the kind of wealth that made him disdainful of it and walked around all day with a derisive sneer permanently affixed to his thin, pasty face. Even his little moustache did not detract from the expression, rather enhancing it. As he seemingly eschewed company, his hairline eschewed his forehead, receding from it as fast as possible. An ostentatious silver cloak billowed as he walked, and his grey doublet was stitched with the crest of the House of *La Grulla*, a crane, on the breast. He met them in the portrait-lined antechamber, striding across the patterned cerulean rugs with a speed that belied his expression to grip Marcus' hand tightly with both of his own, giving it a little shake.

"Welcome, welcome, Viscount," he sneered.

He sneers every word he speaks.

"I'm delighted you were able to make it despite the storm," continued Levont. "Do come inside and dry off, won't you? Dinner will be served shortly, and after that the entertainment will begin."

"Thank you for your hospitality," said Marcus, dipping his head. "Prophet's blessings upon you, brother."

"Blessings, brother."

"Why did you call him brother?" Spot asked as they moved past.

"He is a Knight of *Pacia*," replied Marcus. "All Knights are my brothers."

"Even those of *La Pantera?*"

Marcus did not answer.

They sauntered past a marble staircase and through an arched corridor into the main hall, where broad paintings of animals and landscapes striped the stone walls and lit gilded chandeliers hung from the flat cream ceiling, despite the moonlight beaming through the arched paned windows. Silver goblets and cutlery glimmered in the candlelight, anthemions adorned the indigo rugs, and the gilded base mouldings were intricately sculpted. Fires burned in multiple hearths under ornate wooden mantelpieces lined with souvenirs from around the world, from vases painted with old pagan gods to a skeleton's hand. Gold glinted everywhere the eye looked, in people's smiles, in their clothes, on their fingers, in their hair, on their ears, in their hats, on their necks, wrists and even their noses. Spot thought again about the poverty running amok in the slums.

I wonder, how many starving people could this needless jewellery feed?

The Night Comes Alive

He had scrutinised the Viscount's face carefully and had seen no sign of anything outside the ordinary in the man's squinty little eyes. Still, he was on guard. The *Ma Ca Rong* would be here, he knew it. He scanned the faces of those present, recognising Baron Rathbone and Sir Gómez of *La Pantera,* Baron Reyes and Sir Rodriguez of *La Grulla* and Count Kronvert and Sir Giles of *La Salamandra,* as well as Baron Thragon of *El Toro* and his daughter, Aiva.

He realised he had lost his father while he had been scrutinising faces and hurried to find and catch up with him. When he did so, Marcus de León was conversing with a bloated walrus of a man squeezed into a sea-blue coat and trousers and a yellow shirt, and a bookish-looking fellow with squinty eyes and a tonsure. Two gowned women smiled woodenly behind the men – their wives, Spot presumed. Spot found his eyes drawn to the Sea Serpents drawn in silver thread on the squinty man's grey doublet.

Are they moving or am I crazy?

"And who's this here?" the walrus asked jovially, noticing Spot sidle up behind Marcus.

Marcus turned long enough to see who was behind him and then faced forward again to reply, "Count Delgado, Viscount Lamprey, this is my son, Samuel de León. Samuel, may I introduce to you Count Joaquin Delgado and Viscount Bautista Lamprey."

He waved a hand vaguely, and Spot bowed.

"I'm honoured to make your acquaintance," he said as he had been taught.

The walrus, Count Delgado, guffawed, and the bookish man, Viscount Lamprey, smiled thinly.

"The honour is all ours, I assure you, little man," chortled Delgado, holding his ample gut as if to contain the chuckles.

"Do not think to distract me with my son," said Marcus. "I have not forgotten the question to which you have given no answer."

Delgado's face fell in an instant, but he rallied and put on a smile in time to say, "Ah yes, good Sir Cel Tradat is concerned over the revenue streams. You may put his mind at ease. The recent shortages are entirely anomalous, I assure you."

"Your assurances are unfounded," returned Marcus evenly. "For almost a year, you have failed to deliver sufficient revenue, and the Lord Protector is growing concerned. He wonders if he picked the right man to appoint."

Delgado's face flushed an ugly colour for a moment, but once more he forced a friendly expression and said, "You may inform the Lord Protector there is no need to recant my title. The revenue stream will thicken, I assure you. Anomalies. It has all been anomalies."

"Are you undermanned?" Marcus asked. "Are your tax collectors insubordinate? Or is someone along the way appropriating funds for their own pockets, do you think?"

Count Delgado was about to snarl a reply when Viscount Lamprey laid a hand on his shoulder, and abruptly the Count blew out a heavy breath and said nothing, only waved for the Viscount to reply in his stead.

"We will look into the possibility, Viscount de León," Lamprey said smoothly, clasping his hands before him. "But as Count Delgado has already stated, the revenue stream has been thin on account of the hardships we have endured in the north. Bad weather, poor yields, diseases and fluxes – all leave the land wanting and, unfortunately, the coffers, too."

Marcus nodded, though he looked as though he smelled something foul. "The Lord Protector will be watching you, and if you come up short –"

"We will not," Lamprey butted in calmly.

Marcus nodded again. "Have a good evening, gentlemen. Come, Samuel."

"What was that about?" Spot asked.

"Those two are stealing cookies from the jar, I'm sure of it," Marcus answered as they wove through the throng, leaving Spot yet clueless. "Good evening, gentlemen, ladies." He greeted his fellows of *La Salamandra* with a nod.

"De León, I'm glad you could join us." Sir Reginald Giles nodded in return.

"Ah, Marcus and little Samuel!" Count Kronvert beamed at them both.

"Did you notice that Count Delgado was in attendance?" Marcus asked the Count.

"No, I cannot say I did."

"I presumed he would be here," said Marcus. "He is a known degenerate, who never misses one of Levont's galas. I spoke to him about the insufficient revenue."

"Oh, and what did he say?"

"Are you drunk?" Marcus asked abruptly.

"A little tipsy, yes," Count Kronvert replied happily.

"We must always be on guard," snapped Marcus. *"You* taught me that."

"After the Sigwells' funerals, I think we can indulge the old fellow a few drinks," intervened Sir Giles swiftly.

Marcus scowled. "We are here to convert the ideologies of the idiotic, not to join them in inebriation!"

"And because we'd be pariahs if we didn't show up and donate every once in a while," muttered Sir Giles, sipping. "The Lord Protector'd see to that."

Marcus' scowl did not move. "Yes. That, too."

Count Kronvert wandered off to make the rounds shortly thereafter, moseying around the hall with an air of superiority.

"Have you heard the reports from the south?" Marcus asked once he was gone. "Knight-Commander López has just taken another unpronounceable town, moving him one small step closer to Xi'Ping. These blasted Crusades will never end if he keeps sending back word of these pathetic small victories to rally the peoples' spirits."

Sir Giles nodded. "He has been trying to storm the capital for months. He is not within a hundred leagues of the place yet, though. Most of his steps are sideways rather than forwards."

"And he throws away the lives of good men every step of the way," added Marcus darkly. "He'll never make it to Xi'Ping, that much is clear now. The only question is – how long will we fund him to keep trying? How many more men will die in pursuit of this pointless quest?"

"Pointless?" quizzed Giles. "I thought you believed in peaceful proselytization?"

"I do," replied Marcus, "and that's exactly why this is pointless. Religions seem to flourish under our persecution, Reginald, have you never noticed that? Have we ever entirely eradicated a nation's paganism? Do not the Chilpaeans still worship their God of Blood? Do not the Freemen still worship the sea? Do not the Ishambrians and Tzunese still worship their plentiful pantheons?"

"The Babese abandoned their pagan ways and converted to the Prophet's path," Sir Giles pointed out.

Marcus pinched the bridge of his nose, gently jamming finger and thumb into his eyes as if for relief. "Very well. One nation. One nation has come around to our way of thinking by the way of the sword. But no others. It is time for the Lord Protector to see that this method of fire and rapine does not work! This is not how we will spread the Prophet's Word to the farthest corners of Maradoum, I just know it."

Sir Giles bobbed his head. "I agree. But what can we do? Sir Cel Tradat will not listen to Count Kronvert's remonstrations."

"Then, perhaps," said Marcus, steepling his fingers, "it is time for a new Count of Justiqua – one who can better serve her needs."

Sir Giles was taken aback. "If you're suggesting what I think you're suggesting, you ought to watch your tongue. Those are dangerous words. If Kronvert finds out you're planning to supplant him –"

"He will not," Marcus cut in, "because you will not tell him. Not if you want your barony restored on my ascendancy."

"Would you be able to do that?"

"I am positive I could."

"Very well," said Sir Giles, raising his silver goblet in a toast. "To the new Count of Justiqua, then."

Marcus raised his own goblet. "To the new Count of Justiqua."

A rumbling welled up from deep underground, such a noise that folk could feel it through their feet, booming in their chests like fear itself. People began to glance around in concern. Then, the ground began to move. At first, the rugs vibrated like lute strings. Then, the stone floor joined in, rattling ominously. It jiggered faster and faster as if dancing along to some music only it could hear, until it was shaking so violently that dishes and goblets began to topple off tables, clanging like chimes, while the furniture drummed against the floor. The paintings of animals and landscapes turned skew-whiff, and then some fully fell off the jiggling walls with a clatter. Barely able to stand up straight, people screamed and stamped frantically on the rugs when the chandeliers fell from the ceiling, crushing several aristocrats and setting the fabric aflame. Acrid black smoke blossomed and tainted the tongue, pervading the chamber.

Covering his mouth with his sleeve and tottering from side to side, Marcus coughed and wheezed, "It's a Prophet-damned earthquake!"

Spot hardly heard him. He had fallen through the trap door once more, only this time it seemed there was no going back.

As people began to stagger around, the chamber put on a nightmare mantle, leering at him with its malevolent stone face. The walls squirmed like bugs crawled beneath their skin. The burning rugs dragged themselves across the floor towards Spot, moaning through their holes. The tables jumped up and down like they were standing on hot coals. The silver cutlery and goblets skittered around the floor nervously, some stabbing into the animals depicted in the paintings, who promptly clutched their afflicted body parts and began to howl. Hearing a creaking and looking up, Spot wished he had not. The creamy ceiling was reaching down for him grotesquely like pouring syrup, only it receded as soon as he laid eyes on it as if embarrassed to have been caught. Despite the horror of the incident, it did not hold Spot's attention for more than a moment. He dared not take his eyes off the *Ma Ca Rong*.

Baron Rathbone and Sirs Gómez and Rodriguez had taken on the miens of monsters. Their fanged maws opened unnaturally wide as they hollered in alarm, and their bright blue eyes swept the room like unholy lanterns. Scanning the room quickly to see how many of the horrors were in attendance before the vision faded, Spot was horrified to count over a score, men and women both, among them Vivari Levont. The Viscount of Crossroads gnashed his fangs in concern as he witnessed his mansion falling apart at the seams, blue eyes wide.

Pleased with his new information, Spot blinked.

Oh no! The vision did not go away!

He blinked again and again, even tried slapping himself in the face as he stumbled about, trying to keep his balance while others toppled onto their backsides. Still, the nightmare world ensnared him. He could not look away. He could not return to the world he knew, of brightness and normalcy. He was stuck in the crazed world of the *Ma Ca Rong,* where the walls were alive and the Vampyre infestation was very real. He whimpered, afraid he would never return, that he would be trapped forever in this state.

"Where is Kronvert?" Marcus bellowed, leaning on a wall for balance.

Do not touch the walls! They are alive!

"I don't know," shouted Sir Giles from the floor, where he had fallen. "I think I saw him head for the exit!"

Spot glanced around, knees bent and arms spread wide like a sailor on deck. Sir Giles was right. People were fleeing back down the corridor and out of the mansion now, keening like Netherhounds were on their tail. Spot realised then he could no longer see Baron Reyes anywhere and assumed the man must have left. He looked for Aiva Thragon, but could see no sign of either her or her father. He prayed they had gotten to safety.

"Let's get out of here!" yelled Sir Giles, on one knee.

Spot wholeheartedly agreed.

But Marcus cried, "Wait! We have to help them put out the fires before this whole place burns down!"

Cursing him for his quick thinking and altruism, Spot knew in his heart his father was right. The desire to protect the innocent and the need to hide from the monsters warred in his mind.

I cannot fail my father.

So, he followed Marcus as the Viscount tottered towards the fires, and the people and Vampyres there helping put them out. The fire seemed to writhe and roil unnaturally high, screaming and crackling like a living thing. The rugs bubbled blackly beneath its touch. Spot caught sight of Royce Moors amid the ruckus then, who was staring aghast at something. Wondering if the boy could see what he could see, Spot followed his gaze and beheld another boy, some son of an aristocrat with whom he was not familiar, who made his blood freeze in his veins. Clad in a fur coat and a puffy white shirt, the boy was pale as snow, his eyes as blue as ice. He turned then, as if sensing the scrutiny, and locked eyes with Spot. His four long, sharp fangs gnashed together as he grinned evilly.

They can be any age, any gender! They can be anyone! They can be anywhere!

People streamed across his vision, and by the time they cleared the way, the boy was gone. Spot looked back to Royce, who met his gaze, slack-jawed. Spot turned away, not knowing how to explain any of it. He felt like he was in a dream as he strode behind his father towards the horrors, rather than away from them. Along with the rest of the humans, he started to stamp out the flames still springing up, while the Vampyres poured jugs of water on the larger conflagrations, which were swiftly growing out of control. Disparate fires met with a whoosh, forming one grand blaze. A window shattered as an uprooted tree toppled onto the mansion, and people screeched as glass showered the chamber and a cold wind howled in, more and more committing to a rapid exodus. The earth bucked, and Spot was thrown from his feet, alongside many others.

He felt strong arms catch him, but his moment of thankfulness was spoilt when he glanced over his shoulder to see who had caught him. Baron Rathbone looked down at him, fangs less than an inch from the boy's face. Spot screamed and wriggled out of the Baron's grasp, who let him go in perplexity, a baffled look on his hideous visage for a moment. Then, his eyes widened.

He knows! He knows I can see what he really is! The earthquake must have broken his concentration. Why can't everybody see it? I have to get out of here before he decides I've seen too much!

Backing away, Spot bumped into someone and spun to behold with growing horror Sir Estaban Rodriguez, Baron Reyes' second in the duel.

"Mind your step," said the Knight mildly.

Spot shrieked again when he saw the shifting fangs and inhuman eyes. He turned and ran – straight into Viscount Vivari Levont, who caught him by the arms with talons of steel and sneered down at him with fangs the size of toothpicks, eyes blazing blue balefire.

"What's the matter, Samuel?" hissed the Viscount. *"Are you scared?"*

Spot could not escape. A thin dribble of urine trickled down his leg, hot against his skin.

He was pushed into the arms of another man, and he gaped up at Sir Theodore Cel Tradat, whose brown eyes stared back at him. "Careful, boy," murmured the Lord Protector in his ear. "Forget what you saw here. No good will come of it."

He nodded to Levont, who nodded back.

Oh no, they're in league! This is a nightmare! The city is under the control of a man in the pocket of Vampyres!

Before he could beg for his life, a voice snapped, "What are you doing to my son?"

Spot sobbed in relief as he spied his father over Cel Tradat's shoulder. People poured past all around Marcus de León, and yet he stood unbudging, despite the mounting flames and the howl of the storm.

"Merely protecting him from a fall on all this glass," replied the Lord Protector, nodding to the shards on the ground before brushing Spot off as if he were dusty and then presenting him to his father.

Trembling, Spot doddered into his father's arms. "We-we have to get out of here," he managed through chittering teeth.

One look at his son's face, drained of blood, and Marcus nodded. "Let's go."

Marcus half-carried Spot out of the mansion into the thunder and rain, while the youth moaned about bugs in the walls and monsters in masks. Then, he bundled his son into the carriage and had the coachman take them home while lightning scored the sky. Behind them, Viscount Vivari Levont's mansion continued to burn.

14
The Final Solution

Sir Dion Laflamme had been sent home.

This is no escape. Ignatius knows where I live. He can find me anytime. He told me to go home and wait until he calls on me. I have no idea whether that will be in a week or a year. I cannot relax, knowing that slimy trickster could walk in at any moment and demand my servitude. And how can I refuse him? He has me by the balls.

Dion milled around the mansion his father bought for him in the heart of Justiqua aimlessly, unable to go outside during the day thanks to the burning effects of the sun. He was trying to switch his sleep cycle so that he slept through the daylight hours, but it was difficult to change the habits of a lifetime. Whenever he was awake, he didn't know what to do with himself.

Nothing seems worth my while anymore. Not even the Monty Wainwright novels I used to love. I cannot even sit still for too long without growing jittery. How can I build a life when I know my life is over?

So, he practised the skills that came with vampyrism in private and he practised duelling with his servants once he was sure he could cast a glamour to prevent them from seeing his true nature. Physical activity was the only way to keep his mind occupied, he found. In the evenings – or rather, during the time just before he slept, which was early in the morning before the sun rose – he drank himself into a stupor.

In the end, after a couple of weeks, it was not Ignatius Boondoggle who visited him, but Baron Erlic Rathbone. Hearing a knocking at the door just after dusk, Dion was surprised to hear his servants announce the Baron and hurried to welcome him in person, swaying a little with drunkenness. The Baron wore a crimson doublet, tight breeches, stockings and polished boots, while Dion wore only a puffy shirt and trews. Dion enjoyed the feel of a warm night breeze on his bare toes for a moment before a servant closed the door.

Rathbone gave him a judging look. "Clean yourself up, man. You have a visitor."

Dion scowled, smoothed down his sleep-tousled hair and straightened his slept-in shirt. "Can I help you?"

"My name is Baron Erlic Rathbone. May I come in?"

Dion glowered, but muttered, "The servants will show you to the study, Baron, and supply you with refreshments. I'll join you there once I've freshened up."

Once washed and freshly attired in a plum coat with gold-embroidered lapels and hems, a clean shirt, tight riding breeches and soft satin slippers, he found the Baron inspecting the sagging bookshelves lining the study walls.

"Fond of reading, are you?" asked Rathbone.

"They are a repository of knowledge," replied Dion stiffly. "Might I enquire as to your reason for visiting so late, Baron?"

"I came to see the newest recruit for myself," replied the Baron off-hand. "Boondoggle told me where to find you. I wanted to give you a once-over before he takes you on a job. Your first job."

Dion's blood froze in his veins. "You're ... one of them, aren't you?"

"I think you mean one of *us,*" Rathbone corrected him, turning away from the paintings to allow Dion to see his blue eyes and fangs now that they were alone. "And yes, I am. Ignatius tells me you're not too keen on our ... particular lifestyle?"

"I'm not."

"Hmm, I do understand where you're coming from, believe me," said Rathbone gently, taking a seat in the leather chair behind the cherrywood desk, leaning forward and steepling his fingers, "but here's the thing. If we suspect you're going to go and blab our secret to anyone – *anyone at all* – we're going to have to kill you, Dion. Post-haste. You do understand that, don't you? We can't have you giving the game away. So, like I said, I have come to give you a once-over. And I am not leaving until I am satisfied you will not betray us. *You* are not leaving if I am not satisfied."

Dion's mind whirred. "Why would I tell anyone your secret? It's my secret now, too."

"You promise you won't tell anyone?" Rathbone purred.

"Yes."

Rathbone blew out a sigh of relief, leaned back and clapped his hands on his knees, before rising to his feet. "Very well. I believe that solves that, then." He walked to the door, but paused before opening it. "Just remember, Dion, that should we *ever* have *any* reason to doubt you, it's not just you we'll kill. It's your entire bloodline. Well, goodnight! I'll have the servants show me out."

With that, he was gone. Dion stared at the door, shuddering as ice flowed through his arteries.

*

Sir Dion Laflamme's skin crawled uncomfortably as he walked into Reinhard Castle under an overcast sky, as if he were walking into a Dragon's maw. He tried not to stare at the armoured soldiers in the grey watchtowers and on the battlements, not wishing to invite attention. Every Knight here would slay him if they only knew the truth about him, he knew

– save for those in his own nocturnal brotherhood. He had learned enough now to cast the glamour that made him appear normal to those that perceived him, but it required never-ending concentration and he constantly worried he would cock it up.

Ignatius Boondoggle, on the other hand, swaggered in with the air of owning the place, hands on his dirty mink coat collar, black brimmed hat at a rakish angle. He waved cheerily to the Knights in the courtyard and enquired as to how he might find the dungeons. Armed with directions, he turned to Dion with a broad grin.

"Come on," he said with a jerk of the head that made his umber curls bounce.

Dion and the new bouncer for *The Bent Penny* followed him into the castle, navigated the labyrinthine corridors inside with the help of a few more pointing Knights, each encounter making Dion sweat profusely, and eventually tramped down and down long sets of stone steps until they reached the rough-hewn dungeons built into the bottom of the castle. Dripping water could be heard ominously here and there.

"Ignatius Boondoggle," Ignatius introduced himself with a bow, sweeping off his hat with a flourish when they encountered the pale and greasy dungeon guards. "Proud member of the Lord Protector's clean-up-the-city crew. I'm here to escort these prisoners to the work camps up north. Here – I have a signed document from Count Darcuul delegating the job to me."

The guard pretended to read the piece of parchment, decided it looked officious enough, fished around in his ear with a finger for a moment and then nodded. "Alright. Get 'em out of here then."

"My thanks, good man," said Ignatius, sweeping the piece of parchment back out of the man's hands as he bowed again. It had vanished by the time he stood straight once more.

"You want the chains left on 'em, right?" asked the guard as he unlocked the closest cell door in which some dozen people were crammed.

"Ooh, yes, please."

"Are you sure you've got enough men for this?" asked the guard, frowning. "I've got almost fifty prisoners here, and there's only three of you."

"Ah, that's why I brought these strapping young lads," replied Ignatius, gesturing to Dion and the bull-necked bouncer, Thiago Mandrini. "Handy with a sword to say the least. Worth at least a hundred men. Maybe two."

The guard shrugged. "Whatever you say. Just tell Darcuul I did my job."

"Of course, I'll be sure to mention you, my friend. You are doing a marvellous job here, helping clean up the city's streets. Keep it up!"

The guard brightened a little. "Oh, thanks. Will do."

Soon, Ignatius was all but skipping back out of the castle into the empty field that lay between the outpost and the tilled fields a league away. Thiago plodded ponderously after him, a morose mass of muscle clothed in a simple maroon tunic and hide trousers.

Ignatius stared south for a moment at the city of Justiqua, taking a deep breath and savouring the sight, and then he turned his gaze north. "This way, ladies and gentlemen, this way!"

Almost fifty scarecrows shambled out of the castle, seeming barely human with their pasty skin, squinty eyes, moulting hair, gaunt frames and gross cysts. In the cloudy half-light, they resembled the undead. The chains connecting them by their ankles clanked with every move.

Like a chorus of crows.

Dion shivered at the thought.

Once they were out of sight of the castle, but had not yet reached the tended fields, the prisoners decided to make a run for it. They were so weak from malnourishment and disease, however, that it was easy work for Ignatius, Dion and Thiago to smack them back in line. Dion was shocked at how easy it was. Not one of them laid a finger on him, though many tried. None of them could get very far anyway, since all were chained together and some of the prisoners were barely capable of movement. Indeed, some had died and others were forced to either carry their corpses or let them drag along on the floor behind them.

"Why are we doing this?" Dion asked Ignatius. "Are we really part of the Lord Protector's clean-up crew? Does he know about us? About our ... affliction?"

Thiago frowned at him. "It's not an affliction. It's a gift."

"Right you are, Thiago," agreed Ignatius with a grin, before turning to Dion and adding, "And no, he doesn't know ... I don't think. I don't know. They wouldn't tell me things like that. I'm pretty sure I've seen him, though, and he didn't have any fangs, so he's not one of us."

"So why *are* we doing this?"

"Because Count Darcuul has asked us to," replied Ignatius. "We're doing the city a favour really, when you think about it."

"Right," said Dion sarcastically, "because escorting beggars and criminals to work camps is noble work."

"Hehe, we're not taking them to work camps."

"We're not?"

"No."

"Well ... where are we taking them?"

"Here." Ignatius gestured to the massive hole in the grassy ground in front of them, barely visible in the early gloaming.

Dion gasped, wondering how he had missed it. He was glad Ignatius had pointed it out, otherwise he might have walked straight into it.

"What is this?" he breathed.

"A corpse pit, obviously. And we need to fill it."

"A corpse pit? You mean ... we're not taking these people to work camps because we're *killing* them? *That's* how the Lord Protector is solving the problem of beggars and criminals?"

"And overpopulation," added Ignatius, nodding.

"But that's ... that's abominable!"

Ignatius chuckled and clapped his companion's shoulder. "We *are* abominable, my boy. We do the dirty jobs others won't do. It makes for a good living, though. At least there's plenty to eat." He gestured towards the prisoners, who had overheard every word and started fleeing, albeit very slowly. "Agh, now d'you see what you've done? We're going to have to drag them further to throw them in the pit now. Ugh."

With that, Ignatius vaulted some twenty feet through the air to land on one of the prisoners and sink his fangs deep into his victim's neck while the man in question screamed. Thiago was but a step behind him.

Ignatius looked up with a bloody mouth to see that Dion had not moved and the prisoners were getting away. "Do it, Dion, or we will turn all those you know and love into creatures of the night *just like us!*"

Dion flinched as though struck. He did not doubt the Vampyre's word, though, and he could not take on both of them. And so a moment later, he too leapt high into the air and came down hard on the back of a shrunken woman, pinning her to the ground.

She looks a little like my mother.

"Please!" she shrieked. "Please let me go, I beg of you! Please!"

Her words were cut off when his fangs found her throat.

15
Ill Omens

"What d'you mean, *ill omens?*" Spot de León asked sceptically.

"You have never heard of omens?" asked Tumba Koum, round-eyed.

"I've heard of them," Spot said defensively. "I'm just ... not sure what they are."

"Omens are ... portents of things to come," said Tumba in an unusually sombre voice. "They are signs the world shows us, to help us better prepare for the future, and they are all around us ... if only we have the eyes to see."

Spot returned his gaze to the dead rats laid out in an ouroboros in the gutter and felt a shiver worm down his spine. His vision had returned to normal upon awakening after the nightmare that had been the gala at Levont's mansion, and he had not seen a creature of the night since.

Just corpses of rats and men.

"It's just a bunch of dead rats," he said uncomfortably. "Come on, let's go see if the others are playing kickball today."

Tumba shook his head as Spot walked away, looked up at the low iron clouds and said quietly, "There will be no kickball today."

He was proven right not long later when the two of them found one of their kickball companions alone in the dingy alley sandwiched between rows of terraced houses where they usually played, sitting on the step in his doorway.

"Tom!" Spot shouted when he saw him. "Where have you been? I haven't seen you in days!"

Tom looked glum, half-lidded eyes watching them as they approached from beneath a long fringe of dark hair. "I was taking care of my ma," he said in a hollow voice. "No need for that anymore, though. She passed away last night. The corpse collectors just took her this morning."

"That's awful," said Spot, not knowing what else to say. "I'm so sorry, Tom ... Where is everyone else?"

"Sick," said Tom, staring at the ground. "The plague. They'll be dead soon too, I reckon."

After commiserating with him a short while longer, Spot and Tumba made their excuses and hurriedly departed the boy's grim company.

"Omens are everywhere," said Tumba as the grey sky rumbled, "and they do not look good."

"The plague is everywhere," said Spot, eyeing a rag-clad beggar with a large cyst on his neck uneasily.

The man turned milky eyes towards them from his spot in a recessed doorway and moaned, holding out his hands for alms. Spot hurried past and glanced back to see the man being kicked into the street when the owner of the building came out. He hurriedly averted his gaze, and then wished he had not as he beheld three pale, gaunt and dirty youths strolling towards them, all bearing rusty knives.

"You lost, boys?" the leader rasped, his high voice a rockslide, his face pinched into a vicious smile beneath dirty blonde hair. "This isn't your neighbourhood, is it? I can tell. Well, maybe yours." He pointed the knife at Tumba. "But not yours." He pointed the knife at Spot. "No, you look way too rich to be from round here. Just look at them clothes, lads. You can tell this one comes from money." He stepped closer, and abruptly the rusty knife was scraping against Spot's throat. "Got any on you, mate?" the blonde youth leered. "Spare some change for us measly beggars in the slums?"

"I-I don't have any," Spot squeaked, trying not to gulp or move too much. His breath came fast, though, and his palms were clammy.

"Cough it up or I'll slit you from ear to ear," ordered the lad with the knife, pressing harder and making Spot wince.

"Orin, look out!" one of the other muggers cried out.

Orin, the blonde, looked around just in time for the dead rat Tumba had scooped up to hit him full in the face, touching his tongue where his mouth was open. While Orin spat and cursed and jumped back in disgust, Tumba yelled, "Run!"

Spot and Tumba flew back the way they had come, vaulting the beggar who had been shoved into the street and circumventing the man who was still beating him, tearing past the dead rats laid out in the symbol for infinity and sprinting on until their burning lungs gave out and they stopped and panted heavily while leaning their hands on their wobbly legs. They listened for sounds of pursuit once their breathing had calmed, but could hear none.

"I think we lost them," said Spot breathlessly, passing a pair of city watchmen who made him feel a little safer.

Tumba nodded, sucking in deep gulps of air. "I think so, too." He studied Spot's clean skin and dirt-spotted but expensive cream shirt, red coat and fine moccasins. "You know, maybe you shouldn't wear such nice gear."

Spot returned the appraisal, taking in Tumba's unwashed state, bare feet and filthy tunic and trousers. "Point taken." He looked around. "Where are we?"

"We're near the northern edge of the city, I think."

"What's that smell? I think it's coming from this direction."

"Wait, Spot! Spot! Damn." Tumba traipsed after his friend as Spot loped off, following his nose.

He found Spot standing and staring at a vast hole in the ground that had been dug outside the city limits. The hole was almost full to the brim with the bodies of men, women and children. Flies buzzed around the mound, and rats scurried about here and there.

"What is this?" Spot whispered.

Colour seemed to have been leached from the world by the cloudbank, so that everything appeared to him in shades of grey.

"A plague pit," said Tumba quietly. "This is where they bury the bodies of the plague victims. They used to take them further from the city, but now ... I guess there are simply so many dead that they cannot afford the longer journey."

"Who?"

"The corpse collectors, of course." Tumba pointed to a man upending a cartful of corpses into the pit.

"That's Tom's mother," Spot whispered, unable to take his eyes off the familiar face until flies start settling on its chubby pale cheeks. "I think I'm going to be sick."

He was not wrong.

Wiping his mouth a moment later, he gasped, "How can you be so calm?"

Tumba shrugged. "This is not the first pit I have seen."

"How many are there?"

Tumba shrugged. "Dozens. Maybe hundreds. The plague is wiping people out in their scores."

"So many," Spot breathed, awed.

"My mother says a plague just like this swept through Chilpaea when the Crusaders came," said Tumba, "almost as though your people brought it with them."

"They're your people, too," Spot pointed out. "Your father was a Justiquan Knight, just like mine."

"A Knight, yes, but not a Viscount."

"Nevertheless," Spot persevered, "you are half-Justiquan."

Tumba shook his head and looked around. "These are not my people. I am Chilpaean. That is how they will always see me, no matter what."

He's right. Even I think of him that way. I don't mean to, but ...

Aloud, Spot grudgingly admitted, "Maybe." Then, feeling guilty, he continued, "I was hoping to convince you that you're Justiquan enough to come to the Saint's Day Ball tomorrow night, though, at Count Darcuul's mansion."

Tumba's head snapped around. "Darcuul?"

"Yes. I – I need some help, Tumba. I need to find a way to prove to my father – and everyone else – that the *Ma Ca Rong* are here, among us. You're the only other one who knows."

"I think we'd be allowed in, because my father was a Knight," said Tumba slowly, thoughtfully, "but my mother and I would be looked at like rats, you know we would. We would not truly be welcome there ... But what did you have in mind?"

"I don't know," said Spot. "I've been thinking about what your mother said – about breaking their concentration in order to break their illusion. We need to find a way to thoroughly distract one of them."

"I do have one thought," said Tumba unexpectedly, indicating his eyes. "I accidentally wiped my eyes with paprika on my hands once – that's a spice from Chilpaea – and it stung like fire. I bet nobody could concentrate through pain like that. And it'd be easy. All you'd need is a little of my mother's paprika."

"That's perfect!" Spot enthused. "So, you'll come?"

"I'll talk to my mother about it."

"Oh, thank you, Tumba, you're the best! Let's go talk to her and get some of that spice!" As they began walking, Spot could not resist asking his friend a question, though he felt naïve and unworldly doing so. "Why do you say everyone would look at you and your mum like rats anyway? *I* wouldn't. Nor would my father."

Tumba sighed. "Maybe not. But others would. They see us as savages, Spot, barbaric pagans who supposedly sacrifice babies to Gods of blood and practise dark magics. They see us as ... different. And not in a good way."

"Who could believe such drivel?"

"There are those. You know, when my father fell in love with my mother and impregnated her in Chilpaea, the Heads of the Houses apparently discussed throwing him out of the Knighthood for what they saw as his treason. I was born a crime here in Justiqua, Spot. My father used to explain it to me, to make sure I understood, before ... before he died in the Crusades. He believed in the Prophet's Way, but he did not believe it was the only way. He believed in dispatching those wielding dark magics to hurt people, but not in forced conversion. That was why he answered the call of the Crusades – to protect people, not to hurt them. He explained to me, though, that not everyone thinks that way. Some – a lot of folk here in Justiqua – believe that all pagans should be wiped from the face of Maradoum if not converted, that they are no better than rats. Soulless animals to be annihilated at the whim of a better race."

"That's abhorrent!"

Tumba cocked his head. "That's what Knights are taught."

He knows I want to be a Knight. He's judging me. I don't want to hurt people either, though, or annihilate them. I want to protect them. Don't I? Do I even know why I want to be a Knight? Is it just because that's what's been expected of me my whole life?

"My father has always taught me that to be a Knight is to be virtuous, to bring peace and safety to the world," said Spot. "I have wondered, though, whether I'm getting a skewed impression. What would my mother have said?"

Tumba laid a hand on his friend's shoulder. "You and your father mean well, Spot. I know that, and it is all that can be asked of you."

16
Saint's Day

"Father, please, I beg you, don't go tonight!" pleaded Spot de León, wringing his father's hand.

"Needs must, my boy."

"But there are monsters there! I keep trying to tell you! Rathbone, Reyes, Levont, they're all –"

"Just because they are scoundrels does not make them monsters," said Marcus de León severely, snatching away his hand and adjusting his feather cap. "You will conduct yourself with aplomb and dignity tonight, as befits the occasion."

"Father, please, listen to me, I know it sounds crazy, but I saw them at Levont's mansion. We cannot go tonight! *You* cannot go tonight! *They know I know!* Please, father, stay home with me!"

"I've heard enough of this nonsense about monsters," growled Marcus, straightening his dark gold doublet. "It is time you outgrew your imagination, boy! You are almost of an age to train as a squire. I must go tonight. It is the Saint Elmo's Day Ball. It is said even Sir Cel Tradat will be there. And you *are* coming with me."

So, Spot sat now with his father in the carriage in a frilly shirt, a robin's egg coat with lapels embroidered with gold thread, dark breeches and soft moccasins on the way to the Saint Elmo's Day Ball at the city home of Count Ivan Darcuul with only one thought rattling around in his mind.

This is insane, I just know it. Nobody else saw their real faces even during the earthquake, when they all lost concentration, so why will it work now if just one of them loses composure? It's insane. And yet I have to try. I have to show my father, everybody, what they really are ... before it's too late.

The Count of Crossroads' city mansion was short of a castle in nothing but name. He had bought several blocks in the city centre and transformed them some years ago into a leviathan cathedral-castle hybrid that he dubbed his mansion. Gargoyles in the shape of monstrous panthers protruded from the sculpted façade, beneath several levels of intricately wrought grey stone balconies. Flying buttresses on either side supported the centre mass of ribbed pinnacles and spires that spiked up high into the air above a massive slate roof dark enough to match the void between stars. Pointed arches adorned the walls between embellished pilasters and tall, thin windows. The double door was of black iron patterned with signs of peace that looked a little too sharp and vicious to be earnest.

Marcus de León was surprised to run into Ursa and Tumba Koum outside Count Darcuul's mansion, while Spot was inwardly thankful that they had shown up.

I feel bad for tricking Ursa into this. She's like a mother to me, and I'd hate to see her hurt. I will not let it come to that, though. I will unmask the Ma Ca Rong, and then everyone will see them for the monsters they are and she will be safe, protected by all the Knights.

"We do not usually observe you at these events," said Marcus woodenly to Ursa, trying to make small talk.

"You do not tink anybody will object, do you?"

No, they'll just mutter about you behind your back.

"No," said Marcus, "as a Knight's widow, you have every right to be here. As does your boy. It's nice to see you again, Tumba." He gritted his teeth, evidently caught between distaste and a sense of chivalry. "May I have the pleasure of escorting you inside?"

"Of course," replied Ursa, taking the arm that was offered her.

Inside, she stuck out like a bear at a banquet of swans. The murmurs began as soon as she stepped through the threshold. In a riotous woollen gown that was a hazy mixture of green, peach, orange, pink and red, she provided a stark contrast to all the single-coloured silk garments worn by the other women, most of whom were less than half her girth. Her wooden clogs clonked on the stone floor when she missed the rich purple rugs in the foyer, while other women whispered around the room in slippers. Her silver dreadlocks were tied up and wrapped in a colourful shawl out of fashion in Justiqua. Moonlight trickled in, miserly, through tall thin windows under a vaulted ceiling, aided by the candelabras set out on small tables in their efforts to illuminate proceedings. Crimson leather couches reclined around the main hall, artfully complementing the mauve carpet, and a broad frieze of mounted Knights a-gallop bannered the walls between sconces, ornate cornices, pilasters and marble base mouldings inlaid with gold. Spot eyed the lit cressets with misgivings.

This whole place could go up in flames!

"Would you care to join my friends and I for a drink?" Marcus offered, now resigned to his lot.

"Dat would be delightful, tank you," replied Ursa graciously, allowing Marcus to lead her over to the other members of *La Salamandra*.

"I say, Marcus, bonny of you to bring a guest," said Count Kronvert in greeting, bowing to Ursa and bending to peer at Tumba. "So good to see you again, Lady Koum. And how is young Tumma?"

"It's Tumba," said Tumba, "and I'm well, thank you, Sir. How are you?"

Kronvert chuckled good-naturedly. "It's *Count* Kronvert actually,

Count of the whole city, isn't that grand? And I, too, am well, thank you for asking, young man. I can see already that you'll grow to be a polite and strapping man like your father. No better man has ever been knighted." He bowed his head for a moment, as did the others.

"Tank you, Count," said Ursa, her eyes glimmering.

"Damn fine man," added Sir Giles. "So, if you don't mind my asking, what brings you out of your hermit's life, Lady Koum?"

"I'm no lady," answered Ursa with a modest smile. "I decided it was about time my son saw how tings are done in da big city if he is ever to fly da coop one day. Da time for grieving is over. I will always miss Valentino, but he is gone and nutting will bring him back. I have my son to care for now, and he is my whole world."

The group nodded sorrowfully.

"I'm surprised to see you at one of these events, considering ..." said Sir Giles, trailing off awkwardly.

"Considering my husband was killed in da Crusades?" asked Ursa, and though she did not snap or shout, her voice was yet a whip that she wielded ferociously. "Considering your people invaded my homeland? Dis is not an event to raise money for da Crusades, dough, as I understand it, which is why I have come. Dis is merely a celebration of da first Saint, no?"

Marcus nodded. "That's true. No donations are in order this evening."

Maria Giles took over the conversation then, plying Ursa with questions about fashion and Tumba, much to the men's relief. Marcus wished that Helena Sigwell were there to join them. Spot spied Aiva Thragon across the room and waved. She waved back. He was relieved, upon looking around, to see unmoving walls and a distinct lack of monsters.

"So," said Tumba, "this is where you and you father spend your evenings, is it? In places like this?"

He swept the room with his gaze, and Spot felt embarrassed by the amount of needless opulence, even though the mansion was not his. He knew his father was more austere than Darcuul, but their own mansion was still a lavish leviathan.

I suppose I feel guilty for being a part of such a rich circle when Tumba is not. It's not my fault, though, really. We cannot help who we are born.

Spot faked a yawn. "Yes, but it's *so* boring. All these old geezers ever do is talk about wars and economics and politics. It's a sleep-fest."

"These are the men who rule the country," said Tumba quietly. "How can it possibly be boring when the most important people in the nation are discussing ways to improve the island for us all? Besides, look at all the food and drink! There's so much!"

"Yes," agreed Spot, who had not even noticed the table laid with clams, oysters and mussels, knowing the true dinner would be served a little later. "There is a lot."

Am I foolish and immature for finding these galas boring? No, Tumba just doesn't realise how tedious they can be. Anything new is interesting. He'd be bored too if he'd had to attend hundreds of them.

"Did you bring the spice?" Spot whispered, glancing around to be sure they weren't overheard.

A pudgy ginger boy in a doublet the colour of a satsuma approached. "Hello there," he said to Tumba, "I don't believe we've met. My name is Royce Moors. I –"

"Oh, go away, Royce, you dunce!"

Royce sloped off, a hurt look on his face.

"Yes, I've got it," said Tumba, dipping a hand in his trouser pocket. "Here."

He passed a handful of vermillion powder to Spot, who took it and stashed it in his own coat pocket. His nose itched as the faint scent wafted to him.

"Thanks, Tumba. You're the best."

A stir swept through the room, and heads craned to witness Sir Cel Tradat dodder into the room, flanked by armoured Knights in tabards emblazoned with the crest of *La Grulla*. The Lord Protector was garbed that night in an illustrious blue robe over a frilly red shirt, pale trousers and moccasins. Aided by two muscular squires in maroon livery, he made his way to stand by Count Darcuul in front and centre between two lit cressets. The fire played off his features, sinking his eyes even deeper than they were already sunk and making his wrinkles more defined. He looked old, stubbly and haggard. By contrast, Darcuul's handsome shaven face was only enhanced by the firelight. The apotheosis of a warrior, he was tall, broad-shouldered, slim-hipped and vain in a black coat trimmed in silver, a white shirt, black trousers, black gloves and black boots.

Futilely trying to smooth down his tonsure, which appeared to be trying to make a dash for it off his head, Sir Cel Tradat wheezed, "Welcome, one and all, to the Saint Elmo's Day Ball!" People leaned in, trying to hear the words. "A time of celebration when we remember the noble sacrifice of the first Saint, who, by the Prophet's own holy Word, 'died so that the dreams of all sentient kind could be achieved'. While we may not know exactly what this means, it has always reassured me to know that the saintly Elmo did not die in vain. He had a purpose, as do we all. That is why the Crusades are so essential. We must spread the Prophet's good Word to the farthest corners of Maradoum that the people of this world may be saved from eternal damnation, their souls rescued from the fiery pits of the Nether.

That is why our work must continue, and it is why any and all donations to the cause are more than welcome this evening.

"As you may have heard, Knight-Commander López has recently besieged and sacked the town of Sawei-fu, a mighty victory in the campaign to be sure, and a sure sign that López's acts are favoured by the All Mother herself! Quing Tzu is on her last legs, and soon her pagans will be wiped from the face of Maradoum. The Prophet is with us, ladies and gentlemen, never forget! Though freak storms have terrorised the city of late, we go on. Though vermin inundate our streets, we go on. Though the cost of living rises and more and more beggars are tossed out on their rear ends, we go on. Though plague wracks our loved ones, we go on. Because we, in this city, are a family, and we look after our own. I am pleased to say my public works programmes are finally taking effect. I have men and women cleaning up the streets every day, clearing out the rats, treating the plague victims and helping the beggars as best they can. Soon, Justiqua will be restored to her former glory – just in time to welcome the victorious Knights home from the Crusade!"

The crowd cheered.

What dream world are you living in, Cel Tradat?

"And now," continued the Lord Protector of Justiqua, breathing heavily, "a few words from our gracious host, Count Ivan Darcuul! And a round of applause for him for putting on such a magnificent ball in honour of the Saint! Bravo! Bravo!"

The crowd cheered and applauded dutifully, and the pale Count bowed.

How can he ignore me after what we went through? How can he pretend like it never happened? He knows I haven't told anyone. Or he knows no one would believe me even if I did.

"Thank you, Lord Protector," Darcuul said in a strong bass, "for the moving speech and for everything you have done and continue to do for this great country. We are all truly grateful to have such a strong and wise leader." The women *aww*ed and some of the men applauded. "As you have said, Knight-Commander López has won a mighty victory, but it is you who sent him on his divine quest. It is you who put this most holy Crusade in motion. And for that, we thank you." More applause rang out. "Tonight, though its exact date is lost to history thanks to the Time of Witches, we celebrate the first Saint, noble Elmo, who gave his life so that the Prophet could achieve his dream and create an afterlife for us all, where our souls can live on, everlasting, in paradise. We thank you, Elmo."

"We thank you, Elmo," was echoed all around the room.

"To celebrate, I have arranged a banquet the likes of which you have never seen, after which the entertainment will have you stuck in your seats. I dearly hope you all enjoy what is sure to be a wondrous evening." He raised a golden goblet inset with rubies. "To Saint Elmo, Sir Cel Tradat and Justiqua!"

"To Saint Elmo, Sir Cel Tradat and Justiqua!" the aristocrats brayed, raising their goblets and guzzling the contents.

Ew, that wine smells like vinegar.

The guests were allowed a little more chitchat, and then they were summoned into the dining hall for the evening meal. Three obscenely long glossy tables had been set out, each set with dozens of chairs arrayed across crimson rugs. Silvery moonlight beaming in through the high paned windows reflected off the silver cutlery and goblets, making Spot gawp, both at the beauty and the presumed price. Marble mouldings climbed halfway up the walls, intricately sculpted into scenes of myth, of the Prophet, All Mother, Knights, Elves and Goblins. The cornices were elaborately stylized leaves picked out in gold where pilasters met the ceiling in the corners. Between cornices and mouldings, a fresco of a hunting scene was painted on one long wall, while the others were bare but for sconces. The ceiling was flat and painted with a depiction of the creation of *Citta Pacia* – a blonde Elf standing in a beautiful meadow with paradise in a bubble growing in front of him in the sky. Spot peered closely at the picture and wrinkled his brow.

Why is paradise depicted as a castle amid a forest? It does look like a nice castle and a nice forest, to be sure, but I'm not sure that's what paradise would look like.

The feast was sumptuous. No expense had been spared in the preparation of a medley of dishes, both exotic and familiar, from ostrich and shark to boar and partridge with an assortment of fruit, vegetables, breads, wines, ales and meads. Despite his uneasiness in his current environs, Spot could not help but tuck into the meal with relish, a boy's powerful hunger pangs driving him until he felt as stuffed as the turkey of which he had eaten half. He sat back then, hands on his bloated gut, and burped contentedly. Monsters with two faces seemed as remote and impossible as fables in that moment as he basked in the warm glow of family and food. The servants cleared away the dishes once everyone had finished eating almost an hour later, Sir Theodore Cel Tradat holding up proceedings.

Then, Count Darcuul clapped his hands. "Let the entertainment begin! Bring in Bibaldi's Clowns! Feel free to return to the main hall or remain here, my friends. This section of the mansion is at your disposal."

Spot groaned, and the aristocrats cheered as the troupe performed their own fanfare and pranced into the chamber, acrobats flipping and twirling, musicians strumming and beating and blowing on their instruments, singers hitting high notes and dancers convoluting their lithe bodies into unimaginable knots. Last came the clowns, giggling and jigging, and Spot gulped as he laid eyes on their chalked faces and rouged lips, their crimson wigs and calico clothing.

I hate clowns!

The sounds of merriment suffused the mansion, and Spot could almost feel swept up in it if he avoided the sight of the clowns.

Almost.

People began to drink and smoke in earnest, their faces turning redder and redder as though they were transforming into volcanoes, their voices mounting to a deafening discordant eruption to be heard over the performers' sweet music. Spot started to feel queasy, seasick, like the mansion was as turbulent as a choppy ocean and he was at risk of drowning. The room swayed like the deck of a ship, and Spot reeled, only to find himself inadvertently locking eyes with one of the clowns. He sank into the clown's icy eyes, into a washed-out world where the blue orbs were by far the brightest colour in the room. He could not look away. The dancing clown noticed him staring and smiled and waved, its four long fangs gnashing together. Spot blanched at the sight of its skull-like face.

"Are you okay?" asked Tumba, tapping his arm.

Spot swivelled to his friend and then turned back to the clown and breathed a sigh of relief. The clown's fangs and blue eyes were gone.

Thank the Prophet. The nightmare is over ... for now.

"Yes, thank you," said Spot. "D'you see that clown over there? Does anything strike you as odd about him?"

Tumba peered at the clown in question. "No. He's doing a daft dance, if that's what you mean." He glanced around surreptitiously, before dropping his voice to a whisper. "Why? Is he one of *them?*"

Spot nodded. "I think so. Best steer clear of all the clowns."

Tumba nodded, clenching and unclenching his fists.

"There was another body found in the street with two pinprick wounds in the neck this week," murmured Marcus close by. "The city watch are at a loss to explain it. Either that or they're in the pocket of some mob running the streets."

"More likely," grunted Sir Giles. "The streets are rife with criminals these days. Can't walk two paces without running into a pickpocket, whore or thug."

True enough. Tumba and I were almost slain the other day by a group of thugs.

"Or a rat," added Marcus. "The Prophet-damned vermin are everywhere. And you can't even see them coming with the weather what it is. I'm sure it's the rats spreading this damned plague running rampant through the city. I must find a way to eradicate them. We've tried all sorts of poisons and traps, but ..."

Spot was not listening. The sound of his father talking about rats receded into the background, a mere drop of water in the sonic ocean of Bibaldi's Clowns' tunes. The musicians played the classics, time-old traditional songs that they knew would be loved by the audience rather than risking anything new or different in the vein of the Hound's Fools. The singers' voices rose and fell in melodies so well-known as to feel hollow, and Spot found he could not focus on the music.

I must find a way to enact my plan and show everyone these monsters in our midst.

Besides that, Aiva occupied a great deal of his attention.

She looks beautiful tonight in that pale green gown.

When she strode towards him, he felt like his heart was a wild horse caracoling.

"Happy Saint's Day, Spot de León," she said, one side of her pretty mouth twisting up in a smile.

"Happy Saint's Day," he replied, glad she had greeted him with something he could parrot, for he had a feeling he'd have repeated whatever she said in a daze. "Are you enjoying yourself?"

"Very much so," she replied, nodding towards Bibaldi's Clowns so that her hair, done up in a bun atop her head, bobbed. "They're amazing, aren't they? Isn't it incredible how they have honed their skills to such perfection? It must take the work of a lifetime to strum the lute with such skill, or play the drums, or blow the trumpet, or dance or sing as they do. D'you think you would ever have the patience for such honing?"

Spot considered this, finger tapping his lips. "I don't know. It is incredible, though, you're right. I find it difficult just to remember to brush my hair every day, much less train for hours on end."

She shook her head, almost as if disappointed, though her elfin face bore a wry smile. "I know what you mean. Such focus is difficult to achieve and maintain. How have you been anyway? How is your father?"

"He is well, thank you," said Spot, "as am I." He thought back to all the horrific events of the last few days. "I haven't been up to much, what about you? And how's your father?"

"He's ... well ... unfortunately. As for me, I've been stuck inside on my father's orders, as usual. I tell you, the tedium of our mansion is beginning to get under my skin. And when it's not tedium, it's ... worse." She whispered the last word, subdued, eyes downcast.

Spot laid a hand on her shoulder. "I'm sorry to hear that, Aiva, and doubly pleased that you could be here with me tonight now that I know." She smiled a small smile, and his heart performed a cartwheel. Emboldened by what he was about to attempt, Spot mustered the courage to force himself to say, "D'you think your father would mind if I called on you during the week?" He was shocked when his voice came out smooth, if a little thin.

"You want to visit?" she asked, glancing up at him wide-eyed.

"Yes."

"Oh ... very well." She brushed a lock of raven hair that had escaped her bun behind her ear, colouring. "That would be ... most pleasant."

"Then ... I shall do so."

"I look forward to it."

They stood in stilted silence then.

I wish I could hold her hand again. I don't know how I did it before, though. I can't seem to move. I'd rather fight a dozen Vampyres than have to take that risk. What if she pulls away? What if everyone sees me grab her hand and she pulls away?

He shuddered at the humiliating thought.

"Dead?" Spot's head snapped around at the sound of his father's sharp voice and he witnessed Marcus de León bellowing at Viscount Vivari Levont. "How can that be? Explain yourself, man! She was in perfect health the last time I heard from her!"

Spot was already sidling through the crowd to get closer, and so he heard Levont's quieter response. "Like I said, I am sorry to be the bearer of such ill tidings, Viscount, but I presumed you would like to know."

"How did it happen, damn your eyes?"

Levont bristled visibly, drawing himself up to say, "I will overlook the slur on account of your grief on this occasion, but please don't make a habit of it, Viscount. Your sister's husband, Baron Warf, could not pay his debts and so he took his own life. Hung himself. Your sister was left in the weeds with no husband and no money, ousted from her home. Her body was found in an alley in the middle of Crossroads a week later."

"Darcuul!" Marcus roared like a lion, and all eyes turned on him as he stormed across the room, shoving servants and aristocrats out of the way. When he finally came face to face with the host of the ball, he seized Darcuul by the coat collar and snarled, "You send your lick-boot to do your dirty work? You send your lick-boot to tell me my only sister has died before her time? What kind of a monster are you? I know full well why you had Levont tell me – to try to distance yourself from the event as much as possible. I know full well what *really* happens down in Crossroads – and don't think I don't! *You* have been buying up every plot of land around town for some grand project of yours, and every landowner who refuses to sell to you mysteriously dies or vanishes mere days later. Did you think I wouldn't pick up on the pattern? So, tell me this, Darcuul, did rich Warf *really* fail to keep up with his payments, or did you off him for his land, steal his riches and leave my sister penniless? Answer me, damn you!"

The room was very still. Even the performers had stopped performing.

All eyes were on Count Ivan Darcuul as he scowled, shoved Marcus away and shouted, "How dare you lay hands on me, you scoundrel? And how dare you accuse me of such perfidy on my own property? I am insulted and affronted! I would never stoop to such measures as you suggest! It would ill befit a man of my breeding."

"*Breeding,*" Marcus sneered. "Is that what you call it? Your family is one long line of jumped-up dogs fit only for eating the scraps off the tables of better men!"

Darcuul paled, though Spot had thought it impossible for him to become any more pallid. Then, he began to tug off one black glove, finger by finger. Arriving on the scene, Spot flung a handful of paprika in his eyes and waited with bated breath as the whole room – including his father – gasped. A caustic moment of silence was followed by the eruption of Count Darcuul's shrill screams as he began to frantically wipe his red, weeping eyes and stagger about in agony, hollering for help.

In that first moment of screaming, the Count's face flickered; and for just a second, Spot saw ice-blue eyes and fangs. The hall dimmed, and dark ichor leaked from the walls, dripping from the high, vaulted ceiling. Then, the mask was back in place, the darkness banished, and the Count looked normal again, save for his stinging eyes. Spot glanced up to see Marcus de León staring at Darcuul in horror. Then, Marcus grabbed Spot by the collar and began to haul him rapidly away and out of the mansion, ignoring all the protestors and questioners, though many tried to accost them. Pushing past them all without a word, Marcus slung Spot into their carriage and sprang in after him, pulling shut the door and shouting to the coachman to take them home.

He turned to Spot with a deadly serious expression and said lowly, "I'm sorry I doubted you, son. You were right. I saw beneath the masks tonight ... fangs and eyes of impossible blue. Those men truly *are* monsters." Spot's heart did a somersault for joy, but then it haemorrhaged when his father added, "They'll be coming for us now."

17
The Chase

Spot de León would never forget that stormy night for as long as he lived. The rain lashed down, the wind howled hungrily through the back alleys, black clouds bellowed their fury and tridents of lightning scarred the firmament as Spot and his father raced home through the inky streets of Justiqua in their carriage, wheels rattling on the cobbles. Over the sound of their own horses' hooves, Spot thought in growing horror that he could hear other hooves drumming the boulevards close by, going far faster than was warranted, as were they. Marcus de León had given the coachman no uncertain instructions to get them home as fast as possible, and the man was doing his utmost, to the extent that the squealing carriage almost capsized every time it took a sharp turn. Spot could see little out of the windows save for shifting shades of black and grey and the occasional pool of half-obfuscated lantern light, like solitary stars amid the emptiness of the night sky, as if the carriage rolled through the sky rather than the street.

It almost shook Spot out of his skin when a champing horse pulled up level to the window and a gloved hand reached out to snatch at him. His father yanked him back out of harm's way and shouted for the coachman to go faster.

"Look out, Samuel!" he said, clutching the boy. "I suspect they'll do anything to keep their secret. This could go all the way to the top … I cannot believe how many of those creatures I saw back there … Damn it! Where is the city watch?"

"I've been trying to tell you!" Spot squeaked.

"I know. And I should have listened. And for that I'm sorry. We have more pressing issues than my blindness now, however. We must get back to the mansion if we're to survive the night. My guards can protect us there."

The sound of a sword raking the wood of the carriage was unmistakeable, as was the grunt of effort preceding it.

"Those bastards are attacking us!" Marcus snarled, drawing the double-edged three-foot steel broadsword etched with his family name, which accompanied him everywhere. It hissed as it snaked free of its black lacquered scabbard, its leather-bound hilt snug in the Viscount's palm. The pommel was a snarling lion's head. "Stay away from the windows, Samuel. I'll take care of these buffoons."

With that, he slung open the door with a bang and Spot heard a neigh as a horse was presumably struck. Then, the Viscount was leaning out the door with one hand on the threshold and the other swinging the broadsword at the rainy night.

"Take that, you knaves!"

Spot heard a thump that might have been a body hitting the ground outside and then another neigh, this time more distant. Hooves were still beating a tattoo all around them, though, mounting to a horrendous crescendo. Spot gasped when Marcus suddenly scampered out of the carriage and up onto the roof surprisingly nimbly. The carriage sped up as the coachman cracked the whip and juddered as it hit a bump in the road, and Spot wondered how his father was managing to cling on. He could hear his father stomping around on top, hollering at his enemies, and occasionally the sound of steel on steel jarred him like the raucous croaks of crows. His heart stuttered and his legs felt weak at the thought of his father meeting his end on one of those pieces of steel, falling from the carriage to be left in some unknown street in the middle of the city for the rats to gnaw upon. Spot would be left entirely alone, and the thought humbled him, made him feel smaller than ever he had before.

What would I do without my father? I'd be lost and alone in the vastness of the world.

After what seemed an age of swords scraping, wheels creaking and hooves drumming, the coachman shouted, "We're nearing the mansion, Viscount!"

"Take us to the front doors," Marcus replied, sounding strained, "and tell the guards to help us slay these criminals!"

18
The Hunt

Sir Dion Laflamme had no wish to participate in the hunt.

He dawdled at the back of the pack, barely bothering to kick his horse while the others whipped theirs into frenzies in their frantic efforts to destroy the carriage's occupants. All Baron Erlic Rathbone had told him was that those inside the carriage knew their secret and therefore had to die. He squinted, trying to make out the crest emblazoned on the carriage by the meagre light of the storm and eventually recognising it as that of the De León family; two crossed swords under a roaring lion's head on a background of blue. The sounds of hooves clattering, swords scraping, horses neighing and hoarse voices yelling made Dion feel nauseous.

Or maybe it's because I haven't eaten in days. Or maybe it's because of when I did eat ...

Memories of the massacre outside Reinhard Castle threatened to swamp him, but he strangled them, reminding himself that he had done what he had done to protect his family.

He was distracted from his remembrances when Viscount Marcus de León threw open the carriage door, knocking Thiago Mandrini's horse back. Then, the Viscount was leaning out of the hurtling carriage, throwing caution to the wind as he swatted at the bull-necked bouncer of *The Bent Penny* with his broadsword gleaming in the transient flashes of lightning that were all that illuminated the scene. Thiago urged his horse closer once more, swiping at the Viscount with a slightly rusty straight sword. He missed time and again thanks to the horse's bucking rhythm, as did the Viscount, but then Thiago grew impatient and drew too close to the carriage.

Marcus de León's broadsword carved an arc like a half moon as lightning flashed, and then darkness descended. Dion waited with bated breath, and when a thunderbolt chanced again to score the sky a split second later, he witnessed Thiago's head roll clean off its shoulders, tip end over end as it plummeted, and then bounce on the cobbles. Dion was past in a heartbeat, his own mount breathing hard, craning his neck instinctively to see what had happened to the head. Thiago's dun gelding slowed in confusion without any heels in its flanks or jerks on the reins and was soon left behind. Unbelievably, the Viscount then somehow clambered up on top of the carriage while it was still racing down the street and balanced on top, swaying with the movement with his sword poised.

He swatted at any horseman that came too near, lashing out left and right at the dozen men Rathbone had been able to convince to ride at a moment's notice. Dion wished he had not been among the number, but Rathbone had met his eyes, jerked his head and ordered him to come, and Dion had followed along like a loyal hound, fear for his family driving him.

I cannot stand up to these nightmares. They are everywhere! Should I betray one of them, another will surely rip out my father's throat by the end of the week.

So, here he was, on his speckled silver gelding, once his pride and joy. Now, the horse could scarcely stand the sight of him and juddered at his touch.

I cannot blame the beast. It senses my true nature.

He heard the Viscount shout something about front doors and guards, and then the carriage was skirling round a corner, almost tipping as it did so, and De León mansion came into sight down the boulevard. The carriage squealed on, the white horses pulling it lathered and waning, while those bearing lighter burdens behind began to pull ahead. Overtaking the carriage, Rathbone and his cronies slashed viciously at the four fine white horses, bringing them down in a neighing tumble of broken bones, split skin and tangled reins, barely heard over the thunder's callous song. The carriage abruptly tipped forward, its front end hitting the cobbles, and skidded to a stop outside the mansion. Spot was thrown into the wall of the carriage, Marcus leapt clear and rolled on the cobbles before the crash, and the coachman was flung off the front seat to land face-down in the street.

Baron Erlic Rathbone manoeuvred his horse carefully so that it was standing over the man and then barked, "Vento, stomp!"

Lit by a thunderbolt scorching the sky, the horse reared with a whinny and brought its front hooves crashing down hard on the coachman's skull, which flowered with brains. Seeing that Marcus de León was trying to fight his way back to the carriage, detained by the mounted swordsmen in his path, Baron Rathbone turned his attention to the guards pouring out of the mansion's grounds. These were no Knights, though, merely warriors for hire in leather armour, and some decided they were not being paid enough to fight off trained and mounted foes and so took off down the street. Rathbone shouted for them to be let go, eyes on those who remained.

Together with a few of his fellows who had accompanied him on the hunt, Rathbone mauled the men to death in seconds. The guards' armour stood no chance against the Vampyres' strength. The fiends' swords tore through leather cuirasses as if through silk, and when the guards did manage to retaliate, their blows had no effect. One Vampyre, skewered through the belly, still slew three of the guards with whistling swipes of his sabre.

Once the guards' bodies littered the ground like detritus, Rathbone slowly dismounted his pale mare, holding Viscount Marcus de León's gaze the entire time as the storm alternately gifted and leached light from the scene. The Baron's crimson doublet was no longer the hue of fresh blood, thanks to the tempest stealing colour from the scene, but rather that of dry blood, old and crusty. Last to arrive, Sir Dion Laflamme dismounted at the back of the pack, a silent observer as the other Vampyres discarded their steeds and hurried to encircle the Viscount. They were not fast enough.

Surprisingly agile for a man of his age, Marcus sprang between two swordsmen, taking them by surprise with the boldness of the move, dodging the swipes of both and carving a red line across the chest of one that made the man screech.

A lion's roar erupted from the Viscount's maw as he dashed towards the carriage. "Run to the mansion, Samuel!"

19
A Strike from the Shadows

Spot de León heard his father's lionesque roar, threw open the door and sprang out of the carriage, having been waiting, unsure what to do. He saw the mansion at once on the other side of the wrought iron fence, lit by a thunderbolt that struck one of the trees lining the avenue, making it burst into flames with a crack and a whoosh. The crest on the gate waved to Spot encouragingly from some twenty feet away, creaking in the squall, but between it and him prowled four men in finery armed with swords. He froze.

Darting around the carriage, Marcus de León bulled into the man closest to his son, taking the man unawares and pronging him in the side as he turned. The man wheezed and collapsed as the Viscount kicked him clear of the blade, which slid free easily thanks to its wide blood groove.

"Stay by me, Samuel!" Marcus gasped when he laid eyes on his son. "I will clear the way!"

The second swordsman, Sir Estaban Rodriguez, was on him in a flash, not seen until the last second when lightning illuminated his vicious pale moustached face, blonde hair and flying sword blade. Spot screamed as he witnessed his father's blood spray through the air by the intermittent light of the tempest. Clutching his gashed shoulder, Marcus spun with the speed of a cornered animal and lashed out. Sparks flew, sizzling in the rain, as the swords scraped together time and again. Then, as soon as it had begun, it was over. Ducking a swipe, Marcus spun around Rodriguez and slashed through his spine with a nasty crunch. While the man collapsed, Marcus turned and readied for the next foe. When the man tried a series of fast chopping strikes, Marcus parried proficiently and put the tip of his broadsword through the man's ruff, making him spit up blood as he tottered and fell. The last of the four charged the Viscount, who backed away, parrying desperately, before managing to spin around the man and slice open his throat with a well-placed slash.

"Come on, Samuel!" Marcus urged, beckoning with a bloody hand. "Let's get to the mansion!"

"Look, father!" Spot breathed, pointing, moon-eyed.

Marcus squinted through the rain and inhaled sharply when he saw the bodies of the four men he had just slain rising once more, as if entirely unhurt. Each of them turned ice-blue eyes on him and snarled with four long fangs.

"You'll have to do better than that," sneered Sir Rodriguez.

"Fire or decapitation," Spot murmured.

Just then, a thunderbolt streaked across the charred firmament and Spot's eyes popped out as he witnessed Baron Erlic Rathbone materialise from the shadows by his father's side and thrust his sabre into the Viscount's belly beneath the ribs. Marcus groaned, and Spot had never heard a more awful, hollow sound. Rathbone withdrew the sword and made to strike again, but somehow Marcus managed to parry the looping overhand blow and shove the Baron away with his free hand. Then, he seized Spot by the collar and thrust him towards the mansion, so that he ran, tottering, to the gate and pushed it open with a metallic creak lost to the storm's wail. Dashing through the small but fragrant front garden to the door, Spot thumped on it.

Knowing there was no time to be lost trying to use his key, Marcus put his back to the door with Spot behind him and bellowed, "Open up, Bona Dea! It is Marcus!"

Then, he had no more breath for shouting as the four dead men were upon him once more, swords flashing in the lightning's fickle radiance. Parrying desperately, Marcus wondered why each foe seemed to have the strength of ten men. His sword-arm was tiring fast, so he felt a lifting of the heart when he heard a lifting of the latch and the door opened.

Spot darted straight in past Bona Dea, turned and yelled, "Get inside, father!"

Moored by conflict, Marcus took a few moments to parry and dodge, looking for an opportunity. Thunder crashed overhead. Only two men could attack him at once in the doorway beneath the portico, while the others crammed in behind them, but two was almost enough to overwhelm the injured Knight. Time and again, he avoided death by the narrowest of margins, only able to see their attacks coming by the flickering light of the capricious squall. Once or twice, their swords snaked past his guard altogether to further nick his flesh, wounding him in the thigh and arm. So, when the slimmest opportunity to escape presented itself, he took it.

Growing impatient, Sir Rodriguez overreached himself while slashing, incapacitating his comrade if only for the blink of an eye. Parrying the slash and seeing the other man hesitate, not wishing to hit his own comrade, Marcus acted lightning fast. Allowing Rodriguez to overreach, he whipped up his broadsword to pre-empt the second man's strike, slitting the man's face open from chin to hairline. Then, he booted Rodriguez into the second man, sending them bowling into all those behind, before springing inside.

Bona Dea slammed shut the door, locked and bolted it and turned to the Viscount. "You must let me tend to those wounds, Sir."

"No time," grunted Marcus, leaning heavily on the wall.

"Face me, De León!" Rathbone screamed outside, his weedy voice distorted by wrath. "Face me or I will burn your mansion to the ground, d'you hear me? The city watch will not be coming to save you! They serve me and mine!"

"I must go," said Marcus before anyone else could speak.

"No!" Spot and Bona Dea exclaimed as one, babbling, "You can't! You have to stay! Don't leave! Please!"

"Face me, De León, or I will kill that brat and wipe your bloodline from the face of Maradoum!"

"I must go," Marcus repeated, standing straight. "I love you, Samuel. May the Prophet always watch over you, my son. Take good care of him, Bona Dea. *Dajuan.*"

20
Here There Be Monsters

Sir Dion Laflamme could not believe his eyes when the door of the mansion opened and Viscount Marcus de León stepped out.

What are you doing, you fool? You cannot beat us! We are abominations.

"There you are," sneered Baron Erlic Rathbone, his bone-white hair blowing around his thin, bloodless face. "It is long past time we put this dance of ours to bed. I am sick of adopting a smiling mask in your presence! You saw what we truly are tonight, did you not? Thanks to your brat. Well, since we are all in the know, I think the time has come that I discard my façade!"

He let the illusion fall, and Marcus gritted his teeth as he witnessed the shift in facial features. Rathbone sprouted four long sharp fangs that curved over his lips, and his eyes iced over, while his skin seemed somehow to pale even further, while at the same time growing parchment-thin so that it barely seemed to stretch over his skull.

Marcus spoke as if in a dream. "Let my son go, Rathbone, and I will fight you."

"You don't have much choice," Rathbone jeered, "but very well. I will leave your pathetic son out of it. You and I will finish this."

"As it should be."

Marcus took up a fighting stance, knees bent, sword held in both hands. Rathbone bent his front leg expertly, descending into a fencer's preferred position. Marcus' lip curled in disdain for the technique, and Dion thought he knew what the man was thinking

That heavy broadsword could chop the thinner sabre in half if given the chance.

Rathbone's jabs were like the thunderbolts overhead, however, almost faster than the eye could follow thanks to the lightness of the weapon. Marcus took a nick to his uninjured shoulder on the very first exchange, before forcing his aching body to step up its pace in an attempt to keep up with the monster he faced. He had time only for defence as Rathbone flew at him again and again, pasty face fixed in a terrifying snarl. His broadsword whirled around and around in circles, ever parrying the sabre away from his body. As Rathbone's strikes only seemed to grow stronger, however, the margin for error decreased until the sabre was missing tender flesh by mere inches with every swing.

Dion had never doubted the outcome from the outset. Knowing the

Vampyre's superior strength, he watched Rathbone pretend to struggle to beat the Viscount in a shoving contest as their swords locked. The Baron reached out and backhanded Marcus de León hard in the face, sending him staggering. He dodged the next few attacks, slippery as an eel, and then darted in close to slit open Marcus' shin, making him cry out. Circling the Viscount with a cruel smile on his face, he parried a few blows and then nicked Marcus' cheek with a swift slash. Next, he drew blood on Marcus' belly. Then, his shoulder, arm, leg and other arm.

Just shallow cuts so that he won't bleed out – yet. Rathbone is toying with him, a cat with its food.

Rathbone overstepped himself, however. Evidently allowing his blazing wrath to overcome him and knowing his physical prowess far outweighed that of the Viscount, he abandoned finesse when Marcus stumbled and proceeded to rain down blow after heavy blow on the sagging Knight, trying to beat him down with sheer force rather than precision and skill. Marcus soon sank to one knee, unable to do anything but block. Dion winced at the sight, thinking of what his sword instructor would have said.

Don't be a fool, Dion! You're not chopping a log with an axe. You're using a sword!

It did not take long before the inevitable came to pass and Rathbone's sabre snapped in half against the thicker steel of the broadsword. Rathbone screamed in fury, gawping at his sword hilt like a buffoon. Marcus had more left in him than the Baron had given him credit for, however, and surged upright then, sinking his sword to the hilt into the Baron's chest so that it stuck out gruesomely from his back. Blood dripped onto the street along with the rain, soon washed away.

Rathbone laughed then, a horrible, high, grating sound like nails on a chalkboard.

Gurgling and drooling blood, he rasped, "You'll never know what lies off the edge of the map, De León. Here there be monsters!"

So saying, he grabbed the Viscount's arms, yanked him closer and sank his long fangs into Marcus de León's neck.

21
Bona Dea

"No!"

Witnessing his father's end from inside the mansion, watching through a thin ground floor window, Spot de León let loose a howl of anguish and tears bled from his eyes.

His father's maid, Bona Dea, was at hand to sweep him up in her arms and press him to her bosom. "There, there, child," she cooed, making soothing noises.

He clutched her thick brown arms tightly, choking on sobs.

"Samuel, oh Samuel!" called Baron Erlic Rathbone from outside in a singsong voice. "Where do you hide? I promised your father I would leave you alone ... but if I am being truthful, I have no intention of keeping that promise. Knights, knock down that door!"

Many clomping footsteps preceded a heavy hammering on the mansion's front door. Running to the door, Spot and Bona Dea stared at it as splinters sprayed from its middle, an axe blade showing through briefly before being wrenched back out.

"What are we going to do?" Spot squeaked.

"Do not worry," said Bona Dea confidently. "I will not let anything happen to you. *Dajuan.* Your father paid me well to ensure I was prepared to deal with any situation like this that may arise."

"Thank you, Bona Dea," Spot said meekly, knowing he could do nothing against a full-grown man with a sword and wondering what the maid could do.

His heart sank like a stone as he realised she was just coddling him, trying to make him feel better.

There is nothing she can do either. There is nothing anybody can do. My father is dead, and soon I will join him in Citta Pacia. *I had so much left to accomplish ...*

It did not take long for the Knights outside to bust down the door. As it hit the floor and several men in silk and satin sprang inside, Spot sent up a prayer to the Prophet to look after his soul.

"There you are!" leered Sir Estaban Rodriguez in the lead, blonde hair and moustache plastered to his face. "You're coming with us!"

"No," replied Bona Dea, "he is not. Back away, Samuel."

She and Spot backed away from the intruding Knights, through the foyer and into the main hall. The Knights prowled into the mansion like wolves, slowly, wicked grins on their faces as they beheld their prey trapped

The Night Comes Alive

before them.

"D'you think *you* can stop us?" Rodriguez drawled nonchalantly, running a pale finger along the length of his broadsword.

"With a word. *Aga'arve-muucolis!*"

Bona Dea's voice boomed out in a strange double timbre with preternatural volume as she spoke the last incomprehensible word, seeming to rock the mansion to its very foundations. Spot's ears rang, and his hairs all stood on end. The air seemed charged, as if lightning was about to strike, or had just struck. A red rope cord materialised out of thin air by the maid's side, dangling down from the ceiling. She reached out and tugged it, and the whole mansion juddered as she did so.

The men stalked forwards.

The mansion trembled again, Spot was sure of it this time. And again. And again. Soon, the constant vibrations were almost enough to throw Spot and the Knights from their feet. They tottered about like drunkards while Bona Dea stood still as a rock. The tapestries fell from the shrugging walls, and torches clattered from rattling sconces, setting the heavy curtains ablaze. Bangs sounded around the tenement as furniture toppled over. The quaking increased until Spot could see the bricks dancing in the walls. Thunder boomed. He and the Knights screamed as the rafters snapped and the ceiling caved in, the entire mansion crumbling to the ground on top of them.

Coughing, Spot surveyed the scene through a haze of rock dust, seeing great heaps of broken masonry, shattered tiles and splintered wood all around him where once had stood his father's proud mansion. Sir Rodriguez and the Knights were gone, buried beneath the rubble. None of the debris had landed within a foot of Spot and Bona Dea, however. Above them, the storm growled and bared thunderbolt teeth.

How is this possible? How are we still alive? Magic. It must be. Bona Dea is magic. But that makes no sense! Father was a Knight, sworn to dispatch magicians wherever he found them. Did he know? He must have. It must be the reason he hired her – to protect me with magic if steel should fail.

His heart swelled with love for his father, and fresh tears burned his eyes as his father's killer strode towards boy and maid over the rubble.

He must have hung back when the others charged in.

Baron Erlic Rathbone was infuriatingly free of wound or even blemish. He walked slowly now, sword in hand, picking his way carefully through the wreckage and setting off small scree slides here and there. He pointed a broadsword at them, and Spot recognised the lion's head pommel.

That's my father's sword! Curse him for taking it! How dare he taint it with his touch?

"What in the name of the All Mother happened here?" Rathbone demanded in his shrill voice, flicking his long white hair out of his face with a jerk of the neck. The roaring wind blew it back.

"You have no right to invoke the All Mother, abomination!" Bona Dea's voice rapped out, a verbal whiplash. "Begone or join your friends in death!"

"I don't know how you did this," he said slowly, "but you must be mad as a bat if you think I'm letting that boy leave here alive. Or you, for that matter."

His entire body abruptly melted into shadow, fading into the ethereal, and the shade he had become swept towards them scarily fast.

"Jin'joku!" Bona Dea snapped, and a bright greenish light flashed from her eyes for a split second.

"Argh!" Baron Rathbone rematerialised on his backside amid the wreckage, clutching his sword with one hand and his head with the other, as if he had a splitting headache. He met Bona Dea's gaze with wide eyes after a moment. "Witch! You're a Prophet-damned Witch!"

"It is you who are damned, Vampyre. Now, begone. This child is under my protection."

Scrambling to his feet, Rathbone snarled, "I'm not going anywhere! Dion, get your lazy ass over here and help me kill this sorceress!"

22
A Hammer and an Anvil

Sir Dion Laflamme had picked up a talent in life for looking busy while he was, in fact, doing nothing. So, he had loitered at the back of the mass of Vampyres pouring into De León mansion, not actually stepping foot inside himself. He had gawped, dumbfounded, when the building had tumbled down amid a boom of thunder, crushing the other creatures of the night in an instant, and when the dust had cleared to reveal young Samuel and the unknown maid still standing. When Baron Rathbone identified the dark-skinned woman as a Witch, Dion desperately hoped that he would be able to slink away without anyone noticing.

Then, he heard Rathbone call his name. "Dion, get your lazy ass over here and help me kill this sorceress!"

The Prophet pisses on me again!

A trident of lightning lit up the night, and there was no escaping Rathbone's glare. Dion made his way sullenly to stand by Rathbone's side, ornate steel longsword in hand, knowing the Vampyres would hurt his family if he did not. He and the Baron closed in on the boy and the maid warily, step by step, expecting with every second to be turned into a toad or melted from the inside.

They were almost right.

The sorceress lifted a hand, and Dion saw a flash of brilliant jade radiance. Instinctively, he leapt to one side and thus avoided the fist-sized green globule of energy sizzling through the air towards him, cast from the Witch's palm.

"What was that?" Dion squawked, jumping aside to dodge another of the energy blobs.

The Witch unleashed another and another, but the Vampyre's preternatural speed allowed him to dodge them all, bounding to and fro. Meanwhile, Rathbone circled her, snuck closer and made to pounce.

"Oh, no you don't!" the maid cried out, turning her palm on him, while her other hand held Spot protectively behind her. "Now hold still! *Ilithichikiyai!*"

A ray of tinkling blue energy with a frosty aurora beamed from her palm then, and she swept it back and forth across the length of the tumbled-down mansion as the Baron bobbed about in evasion, darting forward only to backpedal and dash side to side. Dion crept towards her then, but at a glacial rate so that he would not have to actually tangle with the terrifying woman.

When the maid had pushed Rathbone some fifteen yards back, she turned on Dion once more, shouting, *"Surtur kambala!"* and almost burning the young Vampyre Knight from existence with a fireball twice the size of his head, which he scarcely managed to dodge.

Patting out the flames that had sprung up on his sleeve, he flourished his longsword threateningly but uselessly and the Witch proceeded to blast him away with a gust of wind produced from her palm that out-wailed even the storm. Tumbling heels over head through the air, Dion landed on his face ten yards from where he had begun. Wheezing and seeing lights, he looked up with bleary eyes.

"Look out!" Spot piped in horror.

Caught up watching Dion, Bona Dea had neglected to keep an eye on Rathbone. Just as Spot yelled a warning, the Baron rematerialised from shadow form behind the maid and plunged his sword into her back, ramming it through so that it extruded from her stomach like a gruesome umbilical cord. The Witch gasped as if he she had dived into cold water and sagged off the blade to land in a crumpled pile amid the rubble.

The boy, Samuel, did not shout, cry or beg. He just backed away, ogling the Baron with wide eyes that reflected the light of the storm.

"Hold still, boy," said Rathbone in a pseudo-friendly voice. "It's time to join your father."

Dion picked himself up and dusted himself off, hoping that Rathbone would not notice. He was just about to depart the scene when he heard a beating of wings. The blood froze in his veins. He recognised that sound.

"Crows," he murmured, before yelling, "Crows! Crows! Look out!"

Limned against a bolt of lightning, a winged figure flitted down out of the stormy skies to tackle Baron Rathbone and bear him up and away from the boy. More winged figures circled the ruin like vultures, descending with every rotation until Dion could better see them whenever lightning chanced by. Just as those in the Darcuul crypt had been, these were men wrapped in unreflective cloth with wide black feathery wings extending from their shoulder blades and beaks where their noses and mouths should have been. In their hands, they bore naked blades gleaming in the flickering storm light.

The Crow that had grabbed him tried to drop Rathbone from a height to his death, but the wily Baron transformed into a shadow halfway down and wafted into the closest Crow to gut it with his shadow sword so that gizzards hailed down on the ruined mansion. The Crow cawed and dropped like a stone to smash into the street below. Rathbone dealt the killing blow to two more Crows before one managed to gash him and he was abruptly yanked from shadow form mid-air to plummet some thirty feet to the ground. He landed on his back in the debris with a thud, a clatter and a groan, and Dion winced.

That must have hurt.

To his surprise, Rathbone bounded back to his feet in an instant, spotting him and shrieking, "Get up, Dion, or you'll be slain!"

Dion realised suddenly that he was not as injured as he had thought. His new condition served to heal him remarkably rapidly whenever he did accrue a wound. Sighing reluctantly, he pushed himself to his feet, knowing the Baron was right. Either the Crows would kill him or – if he refused to fight – the Vampyres would. Picking up his sword, he squinted into the storm, searching for black wings against black clouds. He saw them only briefly, never close enough or for long enough to act. Willing the change, he morphed into shadow form, a skill he had recently acquired under Ignatius Boondoggle's rather impatient tutelage. He could see as well as ever, and his strength and speed were magnified tenfold. He tried not to think about how his clothes and weapon had transformed into shadow, too. Doing so hurt his head and tended to ruin his concentration and thus the spell. He had not yet mastered the ability of wafting up into the air like a malevolent cloud, however, so he waited on the ground for a Crow to come near enough for him to attack.

Come on then, you freaks! I'm stuck between a hammer and an anvil, living a nightmare, and I cannot die, so do your worst!

He did not have to wait long. Screeching, one of the winged figures dived down towards him sword-first. Parrying and riposting, he cut open his foe's leg as it tried to turn mid-air and fly away. Blood drizzled down on Dion alongside the rain. The beaked man squawked in pain, but gained enough altitude to escape the Vampyre Knight. Circling in the dark sky, it tugged a medallion from beneath its clothes and held it out. Goosebumps broke out on Dion's skin as the medallion lit up like a lantern.

The brightest lantern I've ever seen!

Dion was blinded in an instant. He felt like he was aflame. He blinked again and again, praying the white haze that obscured his vision would fade in time for him to defend himself against the Crows. A rill of fire burning on his back told him he might have missed his chance, and he screamed in agony, hearing flapping too late. He felt something strange inside, like a mental ligament stretching and tearing. As he slowly regained his eyesight, he realised why.

Prophet help me, I'm no longer in shadow form. The light ruined my concentration. I'm vulnerable as a naked babe out here!

The Crow above launched another assault a few moments later, flying fast at a tangent so that it did not have to slow down to swing its sword. Its swipe was harder to predict this time, but Dion threw himself out of the way at the last moment thanks to his vampyric reflexes, avoiding the broadsword by a gnat's breadth. He had no time for a return strike this time before the Crow vanished into the night.

Hearing flapping behind him, he turned too slowly to avoid the arcing blade of a second Crow and yelped as a sword tip drew a line of lava across his left arm. Grateful his spine had not been severed as had clearly been the plan, he yet could focus on nothing besides the burning pain and his burgeoning burning desire for vengeance. The Crow that had cut him was getting away. Rabid with rage, he threw his sword with all his might and watched with sadistic satisfaction as it impaled the Crow through the ribs, making the freak of nature caw and twirl down out of the firmament to crash to the ground. Running to retrieve his sword, Dion did not see the blade that took him in the back. Hissing like a snake as he felt cold steel slither through his body only to explode from his front, Dion slumped to the ground and blackness overtook him.

23
A Pyrrhic Rescue

Spot de León gawked as men with beaks and black wings came to his rescue, swooping down out of the storm as if born from it to savage his enemies. He watched Sir Dion Laflamme go down, pronged in the back, while Baron Erlic Rathbone was engaged with multiple foes at once, flitting this way and that while his broadsword flicked out left and right, letting Crow blood.

When Dion went down, however, the Crows were able to focus all their attention on the Baron and soon he was surrounded on all sides. Though his sword arm made the thunderbolts licking the sky seem like they moved through treacle, it was only a matter of time before he was overwhelmed. Spot eagerly anticipated the moment, observing with wide eyes as Rathbone laid about him with frenetic energy, desperately trying to stave off half a dozen swords at once. Soon, they began to slip past his guard, though he maintained a stoic silence even when they gashed open the milky white skin of his back and legs.

Spot did not even notice the Crow alighting behind him amid the rubble until the beaked man tapped him on the shoulder. "Ahem, are you Samuel de León?"

Spot stared at the pale man with dark hair tied back in a ponytail, slack-jawed, wondering how he could speak Traveller's Tongue with a beak. "Y-yes. Who are you?"

"Nice to meet you, Samuel," said the Crow, extending a hand. "My name is Aguilar de la Torre. It looks like we got here just in time."

"Yes, you did ... although earlier would have been better." Spot shook the hand. It was hard and calloused. "What I mean to say is ... thank you."

"You're welcome, Samuel."

"Call me Spot. Everyone does."

"Very well, Spot."

"Why *are* you here?"

"We are the *Rugadh na Marbh*, or the Crows," said Aguilar. "Vampyre-hunters."

"Rugadh na Marbh?" Spot repeated, dumbfounded but feeling as though he had heard the term somewhere before.

"Yes. I can explain more once we get you out of here. We've been watching you, Spot, and it's clear the Vampyres know you know about them. It's not safe for you here now. If you want to live, you'll come with us."

"It's up to me?"

"Of course. We will not kidnap you. If you want to die, your death will be on your own head. I offer an alternative."

Spot thought about this. "Where would we go?"

"I would take you to our headquarters in a town nearby and train you to be one of us – if the First approves. It's obvious you have a knack for spotting these dread creatures. You could be a great asset."

Before Spot could respond, the fracas snagged his attention. He had been watching Rathbone through the rain while the Crow had been speaking, waiting to see the man die with his own eyes, but the Baron had called in help and now a flock of nighthawks, owls and nightingales were pecking and tearing at the Crows, mauling them with their little beaks and talons amid a chorus of chirps and hoots almost drowned out by the tempest's dirge. He recalled what Tumba Koum had said then – 'It was said they held power over nocturnal creatures'.

"Look!" he said urgently, indicating the bloodthirsty birds.

Aguilar's wings shrank into his back as he followed Spot's finger, and his beak transformed into lips and a large, arched nose. "My fellows can deal with this mess. I need to get you out of here. Will you come with me, Spot?"

"But Rathbone's getting away!" Spot blurted, watching with feverish intensity as the Baron began to retreat away up the soaking street, yet hounded by the Crows but protected to some extent by his macabre flock.

"It is of no importance," said Aguilar. *"You* are important, Spot. More Vampyres will come. Soon. I need to know – will you come with us?"

Thunder pealed, a lightning bolt tore the sky in twain and fury crescendoed in Spot's mind as Baron Rathbone disappeared into the night, but he said, "There is nothing left for me here now."

24
The Hood

Spot de León followed the stranger into the tempestuous night, leaving his father's mansion behind, though not without a sad backwards glance. Aguilar de la Torre had a carriage secreted a few streets away. The four black horses neighed and stamped at the sight of him, and the coachman tipped his saturated hat, looking relieved to see them. Aguilar and Spot hopped in, and the carriage set off.

Spot had never been on such a long journey. He had only ever pootled around Justiqua with his father, so he felt like he was leaving his home behind when they passed the city limits and emerged into the countryside. The tall tenements seen through the windows fell away to be replaced by green fields rolling into the distance, ducking into dells and climbing to crests. Spot had never seen so much space. Had he known the word 'agoraphobia', he would have used it for how he felt – vulnerable and exposed.

The Vampyres are in Justiqua. I am getting away from them. There is nothing to fear out here.

Still, all the unfamiliarity made him itch and he found himself longing for the narrow, excrement-ridden alleys of his home. The smell of the manure spread over the fields was somehow not the same.

Where are the rats, the criminals, the beggars?

More than anything, though, he longed for his father. Playing the scene of Marcus de León's demise over and over in his mind's eye, he wept quietly for a long time, strangling the sobs in his throat, not wanting to cry openly in front of Aguilar. He eventually fell asleep on the cushioned seat as the carriage trundled past cultivated fields, the wind soughing through the wheat and barley a lullaby in his ears.

When he awoke, the peachy fuzz of dawn was growing on the sky. He glanced out of the window at the wheat fields disinterestedly.

"Take a look," Aguilar encouraged him.

He looks fresh as a daisy. I wonder if he even slept.

Confused, Spot poked his head out of the window and saw their destination ahead. A small town awaited them at the end of the paved road, its cream-brick buildings shimmering in the sunshine, distorted by the horizon into waving white flags of truce. As the carriage rolled through the unwalled town, Spot stared in astonishment at the marketplace where only a handful of people and traders had gathered to exchange goods.

It's puny compared to the marketplaces in Justiqua.

A while later, Spot gaped at the clementine-coloured church looming large on their left, where the Prophet and his disciples hung out of the facade in sculpture and stain glass windows depicting scenes of myth glittered in the morning sunshine. Bells clanged loudly in the twin steeples, sounding the hour, and Spot thought he saw one of the red tiles on the ridged roof between the bell towers slip off with the force of the tolling and shatter on the cobbled street below.

Aguilar smiled. "Here we are. It's not as old as it looks." He took a deep breath and exhaled. "Ah! The Church of Saint Elmo."

"Where are we?" Spot asked.

"This is the town of Callachia, Spot. Welcome."

"Why are we here?"

"This town is home of the headquarters of the *Rugadh na Marbh*. More specifically, the church is. It's consecrated ground, you see, where no creature of the night can tread. The deacon is a friend to our cause."

Snorting, the horses halted outside the church and the coachman hurried to open the door for his passengers. Aguilar threw it open before he could reach it and jumped out, cracking his back, looking around and waving to some of the folk on the streets. Spot alighted behind him, squinting in the morning sunshine. Despite the brightness of the day, his breath frosted in the air. The town had a remarkably still, sleepy quality to it totally anathema to the city boy.

Where are the hawkers' calls, the arguing spouses, the corpse collectors and their bells?

"Come," said Aguilar, "I'll introduce you to the deacon."

The deacon was not at all what Spot expected. Built like a boulder, the middle-aged man's cream robe was stretched across broad shoulders and over a barrel chest, hiding bulging biceps. Like a small cottage, he was thatched. His bushy brown beard split apart to disgorge a friendly smile when Aguilar pushed open the doors of the church.

"De la Torre, how in the name of the Prophet are you, m'lad?" the deacon boomed, his baritone echoing loudly.

Aguilar smiled, crow's feet around his eyes abruptly making Spot realise he could not place the man's age. His body was fit and spry, his black eyes haggard and aged.

"Surviving," he replied wryly. "Deacon, I'd like to introduce you to my young friend here, the newest addition to our unconventional family. This is Samuel de León, although he goes by Spot. Spot, this is Deacon Arturo Rambit. Don't be intimidated by his appearance. He was conscripted as a young man and rose fast through the ranks to become a Sergeant. He could not be a Knight, of course, on account of his lack of nobility, but he was well-respected. After that, he was the most famous boxer in Callachia for a while, before he stumbled across a Vampyre in the middle of the night."

Arturo Rambit had been approaching them down the aisle between the pews while Aguilar had been speaking and now added, "I barely escaped with my life. The creature gave a nasty keepsake." He unbuttoned and parted his robe to reveal five long claw marks down his abdomen. "After that, I knew unholy fiends abounded in the night and so I dedicated myself to holiness – and to slaying the foul creatures wherever I can find them!"

"How did you escape?" asked Spot, intrigued.

"I cut the Vampyre's head clean off." Spot ogled the man in awe. Arturo clapped his shovel hands. "Anyway, I expect you're eager to eat, drink and sleep, so don't let me keep the two of you! We can catch up once you're rested. Will you be in town awhile, Aguilar?"

"Yes, I think so."

"Excellent. Blessings on you both."

"Blessings, brother," replied Aguilar, gently taking Spot's arm and steering him past the mountainous man to the dais at the far end of the church, where a stone pulpit oversaw everything that transpired.

Placing his feet carefully on pressure pads, Aguilar pushed the pulpit and Spot watched in astonishment as the great scarp slowly shifted several feet to one side, rolling on rails in the floor with a high-pitched scraping sound.

Aguilar gestured to the stone staircase hidden beneath. "Down we go. Follow me."

Arturo returned then to hand them a torch he had found and lit for them, and Aguilar took it and nodded thanks. Spot followed Aguilar down the stairs and then jumped in fright when he heard the pulpit being slid back into place above them, blocking the exit.

"Don't be afraid," said Aguilar, seeing his jitters. "No harm will come to you here, I promise. These tunnels were dug by our leader, the Hood, Caróg Liath, whom you will meet shortly."

Spot was sure he had misheard.

Dug by one man? That's impossible! He must mean the man hired a whole team of diggers. That sounds more plausible.

"He dug the tunnels so that they lead straight down, so that the spell of consecration that protects the church protects us too, all the way down here," Aguilar continued as he descended the narrow stone staircase. "You might think the Prophet blessed the church, and he may have, but it was the Hood who cast the spell of consecration to keep out all creatures of the night."

Spot thought he would feel better with walls enclosing him, but the space seemed too small, constantly shrinking in on him and making him sweat.

"I should perhaps warn you," added Aguilar, "that our leader is not … human."

"Is he like you?"

"Yes and no. He is the First of us, a being from another world. A *Sluagh na Marbh*. It was he who gave us our gifts, gave us our sacred home and our reason for existence."

"From another world?"

"Yes. He says the world from which he hails is called *Nagathai*, where his kind have been battling a race known as the *Diavhal* – the true Vampyres – for centuries."

"True Vampyres? What d'you mean?"

"Well, the way Carόg Liath tells it, the *Diavhal* created the first Vampyres here on Maradoum, just as he created the first *Rugadh na Marbh* to protect us from them when their eternal war spilled over into our world."

"He created you?"

"In a sense, yes." Aguilar turned to smile at Spot, his nose casting a beak-like shadow on the wall, before he continued his descent. "I was a Knight too once, like your father. I prided myself on my vanity and put down pagans wherever I could find them." He sighed. "I am no longer proud of that time in my life. I survived the Crusade in Al Kutz and returned to my home town only to witness my wife slain before my eyes by Vampyres, who held me and forced me to watch. They would have killed me too, if not for Arturo. He showed up and fought them off. I was wounded in the fray, though. Seeing that I was bleeding to death, Arturo took me to the Church of Saint Elmo. He brought me to Carόg Liath, who saved my worthless life and gave me a new one with fresh purpose. A life lived for the innocents. The Hood bestowed gifts on me so that I do not age. I heal quickly, and I am far faster and stronger than the average man. And as you may have seen, I can hunt Vampyres from the sky like a bird of prey."

"He *gave* you those gifts?"

"He did. He is a most wise and beneficent being."

"Hmm."

Nobody gives anything away for free.

Traversing the staircase, which constantly switched back on itself, seemed to Spot to take half a lifetime. When the walls fell away, however, and Spot saw that he was descending down one wall of a vast cavern far beneath the surface of the earth, he was stunned speechless. Hundreds of feet high but no wider than the church above it, the cave seemed an impossibility to the boy, as did the weird plant life growing there. Luminous wallflowers running the gamut of colour bloomed in every cliff-like wall despite the lack of sunlight, and strange lush blue grass carpeted the floor despite the lack of water, giving off a soft glow. Spot noted a stone well in the centre then and amended his assessment.

There is water, after all.

A strange unseasonal warmth pervaded the cavern, as if the flowers gave off not only light but heat. Surrounding the well on the ground were rocky protrusions, where caves within the cave extended from the walls towards the centre like the spokes of a wheel.

Do people live down here? Does Aguilar?

A rushing shadow made him jump out of his skin then as what he took for a huge bird whooshed up past him all of a sudden, flapping enormous black wings and cawing. Heart drumming hard, he saw the creature more clearly as it performed a loop in the air before his eyes. Its head, like its wings, was black as oil, but the feathers on its body more closely resembled the colour of ash. Its scaly legs terminated in sharp black talons. It looked to Spot like a giant hooded crow, although he had no explanation for the four feathery arms.

Its grey-black beak snapped open and shut as it laid its beady black eyes on them, and it squawked in Traveller's, "Welcome home, Aguilar. Who is your friend?"

"Thank you, Caróg Liath," said Aguilar, bowing respectfully. "This is Samuel de León, although he goes by Spot."

25
Judgement

The labyrinth of caves beneath the Darcuul family crypt always creeped out Sir Dion Laflamme. His skin broke out in goosebumps as he passed the shambling ferals in the narrow confines of the rough-hewn tunnels, and he flinched every time one twitched, their heads snapping round to stare at him as he passed. He tried to puff out his chest, but the low ceilings and cramped conditions forced him to a stooped posture. Shadows jumped out at him everywhere as Ignatius Boondoggle waved his torch this way and that, sauntering through the gulf of lost souls as nonchalantly as he would through a meadow. His cane clicked and clacked as he went. When he began to whistle cheerily, Dion thought it was a bit much.

How can anyone be jolly in a place like this?

"Best hope Rathbone isn't down here, eh?" Ignatius drawled with a backward glance and a waggle of the eyebrows. "He'd pull your tongue out of your ass just to make you lick your own bunghole."

"Yes, yes," replied Dion peevishly, rubbing his belly where it still ached from having been run through by a Crow.

Evidently, the Crows had neglected to finish him off, leaving him to lie in the street until he eventually regained consciousness on a corpse collector's cart under a pile of stinking cadavers. He had screamed and kicked his way free, giving the gaping corpse collectors small heart attacks. Then, he had taken his bearings and run home, while people had gathered to ward him off with superstitious signs, pointing and shouting, "Undead! Undead!"

He had never run so fast in his life. When he got home, he had slammed the door shut behind him and leaned against it, panting.

Ignatius had been waiting for him.

"Ooh, someone's in trouble," he had cooed with a menacing smile, hands on the collar of his mink fur overcoat. "Rathbone'd have your guts for garters if he knew where you were. He's been by here once already looking for you. What happened?"

Dion had filled him in, and Ignatius had leaned back in his chair, puffing on a baui pipe that Dion would have forbidden in his house before his transformation.

Now, I have bigger fish to fry.

"Hmm," Ignatius had hummed, blowing smoke from his nostrils and tapping his lips with his pipe. "I think you'd better come with me to see the Old One. He can protect you – or at least speed up your fate should it be decided you are to die."

"D'you really think he'd decide that?" Dion had asked, wringing his hands.

"No ... Well, maybe. We'll see."

So now, Dion was traipsing through the caves behind Ignatius in a clean long grey coat and breeches, a white shirt, stockings and black boots, resigned to whatever fate awaited him.

I cannot escape – not without endangering my family. I am stuck.

They soon reached the vast cavern beneath Lágrimas River, where water drip-dropped from stalactites onto stalagmites all around them. They passed through the arch in the grey wall sheeted with a waterfall to emerge into the cavern beyond, where the mirage of the dead end promptly faded away in a revealing ripple of light. Dion found himself staring into the ancient glacial blue eyes of the Old One, Ra'Gthul, and he rapidly bowed, if for no other reason than to momentarily break eye contact. By the time he stood upright again, Ra'Gthul had thankfully shifted his transfixing gaze to Ignatius.

"Boondoggle! Ss ss ss!" rasped the sire of Vampyres in a hoary voice like the slither of a snake, evidently pleased. "What brings you to my humble abode on this particular day?"

"I've brought Sir Dion Laflamme with me," said Ignatius, "for judgement."

"For judgement, you say? Ss ss ss. What has he done?"

"Rathbone hasn't been down here to tell you about the mess he made then?" Ignatius asked. "Makes sense, I suppose. He's afraid of your judgement, too. Ahem, allow me to fill you in, mighty Ra'Ghtul." Ignatius bowed, sweeping off his hat with a flourish. "Last night, Baron Rathbone and his fellows chased down the Viscount of Justiqua and his son in plain view. Rathbone murdered the Viscount, by all accounts, but was then driven back by Crows before he could kill the son. Sir Dion here was stabbed in the back by a Crow while trying to protect Rathbone and left for dead. He awoke this morning."

Ra'Gthul frowned, his ashen skin wrinkling like old parchment. "The way you tell the story, Ignatius, noble Sir Dion Laflmme has nothing for which to atone. Save perhaps a lack of swordsmanship. Or reflexes."

"Yes, that's the way I see it, too," purred Ignatius. "It was Rathbone who organised the chase and committed the blatant murder. Dion here was just following orders. He's new to our ways, as you know."

He's trying to cover for me! Either he's grown fond of me or he really hates Rathbone.

"Ss ss ss." The Old One ran a clawed hand over its hairless head pensively, gnashing its vampyric fangs for a moment. "Thank you for bringing this to my attention, Ignatius. It would seem I need to have a word or two with Baron Rathbone." He scratched his bare bloated belly – the only part of his emaciated frame that could be considered to be even remotely bloated. He seemed to be staring off into the distance, talking to himself. "I cannot believe he would do something so foolish. He has put all my carefully laid plans at risk with his impetuosity! How am I to bring my brothers through the portal by the next full moon if he keeps drawing the Crows down on us like flies on shit? The *Sluagh must* not find us!"

Dion shifted from foot to foot uncomfortably.

He's bringing his brothers through the portal? Here? How many more of these horrors are there?

Ra'Gthul blinked then, and smiled. "I will deal with Rathbone when the time is right. You two are just in time for the feast! Join me, won't you? Ss ss ss."

Dion and Ignatius turned to behold a queue of scrawny, dirty humans being shepherded into the cavern by three unfamiliar Vampyres. The chains around the humans' ankles clanked as they shuffled along, punctuated by a whimper here and there as a Vampyre whipped one of them back into line. Judging from the range of welts and bruises, the humans had been bludgeoned into the cave. Dion counted over a score.

A score of parents torn from their children, a score of children torn from their parents. We truly are abominations.

"Please," Ra'Gthul encouraged them, "help yourselves!"

Dion could not help it. He was so tired from all the fighting and the wound. Like a man dying of thirst who lays eyes on a river, he plunged his head in and drank until he was replete.

"Now that we have eaten together," rasped the Old One, licking clean its claws, "I feel that we are bonded, you and I, Dion Laflamme."

Dion awoke from his stupor at the sound of his name, wiping blood from his lips and trying not to return the gaze of any of the dead folk scattered around the cave.

There's no way I'm going to risk correcting him for neglecting to use my official title.

"Y-yes," he stammered. "Of course, Old One … Thank you."

Ra'Gthul nodded knowingly. "You are truly one of us now. Part of my family. And that is why I feel the time has come … for you to help your family."

"What is it you require of me?" Dion asked slowly.

"I need you to make our family just a little bit bigger," explained Ra'Gthul in as pleasant a voice as he could manage, which reminded Dion of nails on a chalkboard only a little, "by combining it with yours. I need you to make Count Manuel Laflamme a part of our family, a part of *my* family. I need you to turn your father into one of us. With his influence, he could prove very useful to our cause."

"And what is our cause?"

Ra'Gthul looked surprised. "Why, the subjugation of the human race, of course, and eventually conquest of all Maradoum."

*

"I cannot do it," Dion said to Ignatius as they were making their way back up and out of the cave system, trying to wipe blood off his white shirt. "I cannot turn my father."

"You must," replied Ignatius grimly, "or one of us will."

Dion thought about this awhile, awash with horror at what his life had become. "Did Ra'Gthul really mean what he said?" he asked finally as they climbed the ancient stone stairs back into the Darcuul family crypt. "About taking over the world?"

Ignatius shrugged, lifting the stone lid of the tomb back into place. "It's above my pay-grade, but yes, I think so. What of it?"

"What of it?" repeated Dion incredulously. "Don't you care if Vampyres take over the world?"

"No. Why would I? I *am* a Vampyre."

Dion sighed, wondering if he was the sole Vampyre with a soul.

Parting ways with Ignatius Boondoggle in the cemetery, he began the long walk home in the pouring rain. He could have transformed into a shadow and flitted along the street, but he felt like savouring the walk. He needed time to think.

I cannot turn my father. There must be some way out of this!

A squawking voice and the hissing sound of a sword being unsheathed froze his blood in his veins as he was strolling along the bank of Lágrimas River, close to his mansion. "Halt, creature of the night, and face me if you dare!"

From the flapping of wings, he knew what he would see before he even turned.

He snarled up at the winged man floating in the inky night sky above him. "Leave me alone, Crow!" He heard more flapping on all sides and knew he was surrounded. "Grr! Why can't you just leave me alone?"

Ripping his sword from its scabbard, he flew at the Crow between him and his home. Steel clanged on steel as the Crow swooped down to meet him, and battle was met. Both strained against the other when they locked swords, but neither could find an advantage. Winging up and away, the Crow launched another rapid assault from the firmament, but Dion knocked aside the stabbing blade and almost took out the Crow's throat with a slash. Another Crow tackled him to the ground then, but he elbowed and punched it until it was forced to give a little ground, at which point Dion swiped with his blade, cutting it and making it hop back with a hoot like a startled bird.

Dion scrambled to his feet, only to duck a sword aimed at him from the skies, which he felt whistle inches past his head. He lashed out in return, but hit nothing as the Crow disappeared up into the black clouds above the river. He concentrated and felt his form slip into shadow, so that the cobbled street became an ethereal dream world. When next the Crows dived down upon him with blades bared, he moved to meet them with the speed of a striking cobra, his shadow form blurring as fast as the strands of lightning sparking in the sky. His shadow blade jabbed and arced through the air as light as a feather and as deadly as a snakebite, sundering one Crow from hip to hip so that it almost fell apart at the midriff, split into two pieces. Cawing like its namesake, it plummeted out of the sky and skidded along the pavement to slam into the closest wall, never to move again.

Dion flew at the next closest Crow as it drew in with a flurry of fearsome strikes, but it parried and drew back into the firmament where he could not reach it. He roared his defiance at it, but the Crow reached into a fold of the black cloth ensnaring it from neck to toe and drew out a glittering golden medallion. It squawked a word Dion did not understand then, a word that made his ears itch and his hair stand on end, and the medallion began to glow. It shone brighter and brighter until it outshone the lightning blooming behind it, until it was so blinding that Dion had to avert his eyes. Even then, it seemed to sear into him with its very brightness until he was screaming out in discomfort. He felt something pop in his mind, like a bone popping out of its socket, and he knew his spell had been ruined. He was no longer in shadow form. He was sitting on his rump in the middle of the street with his hands over his eyes, crying out in agony as the light prickled his skin like a thousand beestings.

Somehow, the light of the medallions makes me corporeal again, banishing the darkness.

The light faded, and he staggered to his feet, wondering how he had managed to hold onto his sword. His vision fuzzy, he saw a black shape swoop down towards him and swung at it clumsily. The sword sailed harmlessly through the air. He felt a rill of fire burn across his back from shoulder to opposite hip, and spun with a scream to flail his blade, but his foe had already vanished. Pain burst in the back of his legs, and he collapsed to his knees with a wail. Lightning flashed and he saw the Crows as his vision crystallized once more. They were all around him, circling, circling, growing ever closer, silhouetted against the storm. A fire plunged into his heart then, and he tumbled into the river and knew no more.

26
Imprisoned

"Samuel? Samuel de León? Is it really you?" croaked Sir Dion Laflamme, voice parched and cracking like his lips.

"Yes," said Spot de León, crossing his arms. "It's me."

"I ... I remember you," murmured Dion, fixing glassy eyes on the boy, though he could barely make him out in the darkness.

"And I you." Spot's voice was hard as flint. "You're Dion Laflamme. You helped Rathbone slay my father."

Dion nodded, barely able to do anything else while chained to the wall by his wrists and ankles. "Why are you here?"

"The *Rugadh na Marbh* thought you might open up to someone more familiar," said Spot. "It's only because of *me* that you're alive in the first place. *I* told them you seemed ... reticent. I told them you seemed reluctant to be a Vampyre ... even though you are one. I remember you hesitating when you could have killed Tumba, and I remember you hesitating when all the other Vampyres charged into my father's mansion. You're not like the others, are you?"

Dion hung his head. "No," he whispered. "I am not. I did not want to be a Vampyre, Samuel. Believe me, I did not. It's only been days since I was turned. I never wanted any of this! I wanted to be a Knight, to serve my country! I wanted to live a *good* life, to go to *Citta Pacia* when I die ... and now I'm a monster!" He broke down into sobs.

"Tell the *Rugadh na Marbh* what they need to know," said Spot, "and maybe they can help you. Their leader is a mighty magician."

"The *Rugadh na Marbh?*"

"The Crows."

Dion looked up, sniffling. "D'you really think they could help me? D'you think they could ... cure me?"

"I don't know," replied Spot, "but they're much more likely to try if you tell them what they want to know."

Dion considered this awhile. "My life has no meaning as a Vampyre. But perhaps I can find meaning in bringing down those who did this to me. What is it the Crows want to know?"

"They want to know who the Vampyres are, where they are, where their leader can be found and, most of all, what they are planning."

Dion smiled bleakly. "I think I can help with that."

27
Rugadh na Marbh

Spot de León departed the cave where Sir Dion Laflamme was chained to the wall and emerged into the larger cavern beneath the Church of Saint Elmo in Callachia, where lambent wallflowers grew sans sunlight and blue grass carpeted the floor.

Observing the *Rugadh na Marbh* gathered around the well in the middle of the cavern, while their leader, the Hood – never content to be at rest – circled in the air above them, Spot made his way over, brimming with information to share. Lilting melodies drew him in. The Crows were listening to two of their number sing a song while playing the lute and lyre.

Spot recognised the mournful song, only down in the cavern, it seemed transformed somehow – not mournful, but joyous.

"The Lord of Crows,
Over the damned weeps,
His host of ghosts,
Rises up from the deep,
Creatures of the night,
Be afraid, be aware,
The Lord of Crows,
Over the damned weeps."

"You're the singer from the Hound's Fools!" Spot blurted as the last notes lingered in the air. "Lebron DeRose, right?"

Lebron DeRose smiled, his pale face friendly, setting down the lute and flicking his purple ponytail over his shoulder as he rose. "That I am."

Spot turned to the dark-skinned woman with blue pigtails by his side. "And you're the dancer from the Fools – Zola, was it?"

Zola set down the lyre by the well, grinned and curtseyed, holding up her sea-green frock, which perfectly complemented her emerald eyes. "Zola Igbinedion. A pleasure to see you again, Samuel de León."

"Call me Spot, please."

"Very well, Spot."

"D'you not recognise us?" asked a big bald man with a black beard braided with golden rings, sporting a white vest and dark breeches.

"No, I'm sorry," said Spot. "Should I?"

"We are Hound's Fools, too," said the man, indicating himself and the dark-haired woman by his side, who smiled and bent over backwards so that she was touching the floor with both hands and feet at the same time. "I'm Mateo Blanco, world-renowned juggler, and this is Sofia Jiménez, the famous acrobat."

"A pleasure to meet you." Spot shook their hands, taking in their garish gear, particularly the purple doublet and leggings garbing DeRose and the bright pink leotard worn by Sofia. "D'you four not attract unwanted attention dressed like that?"

"Not at all," replied Lebron DeRose. "People barely even see us. They think us fools – as they are meant to – and so they let their guard down. It is a good cover for infiltrating high society as a nobody."

"Huh. I suppose I would never have guessed you were Crows."

"That is the genius of it," said Zola. "And we even tried to warn you!"

"I know," said Spot, chagrined. "You were right. The fangs *were* close. Very close ... Thank you for trying to help me anyway. How did you know Horatio would die that night?"

Zola smiled sheepishly. "A small gift for clairvoyance runs in my family. I see snatches of people's futures now and then, unbidden ... mostly their deaths."

Spot's eyebrows shot up. "Wow. Have you seen anyone else's, you know, death?" He blushed, knowing he should not have asked the question.

Zola shook her head, a grave expression on her dainty face. "Only my own, at the hands of fiends of blood and fur."

Spot blinked, slack-jawed.

How horrible!

He thought about Zola's warning again while silence formed a pall. "How did you know I would understand you about the fangs, though?"

"We have known for some time that you can see what others cannot," replied Zola seriously. "You can see beyond the veil, Spot. You can see reality for what it really is, piercing glamour. D'you know how rare that gift is?"

Spot shook his head.

"It is extremely rare in children," Zola informed him, "and unheard of in adults. Those few who do possess this ability to see almost always lose the ability as soon as they hit their teenage years for some unknown reason. Perhaps it is hormones. Perhaps it is that the mind of a child is more open to possibilities than the mind of an adult. We get so set in our ways." She smiled. "It is *you* children who remind us of life's infinite possibilities, of all life's joys."

"I'm going to lose the ability to see next year?" Spot asked, suddenly worried. "I won't be able to see who is a Vampyre and who isn't?"

"You're twelve?"

"Yes."

"Oh. Then, yes, most likely. I am sorry to spring it upon you so suddenly." Zola clutched her elbow awkwardly and bit her lip, while Spot gawped at her in disbelief and fear.

"D'you have news for us, Spot?" cawed Caróg Liath above them.

"Erm, yes," replied Spot distractedly. "Dion told me everything. The portal you seek is beneath the Darcuul family crypt, guarded by ferals and Vampyres and the Old One, Ra'Gthul. The Old One will try to bring his kin through it under the next full moon. Dion also gave me a list of names of those he knows for sure to be creatures of the night." He waved a scrap of parchment.

"So soon? Excellent work, young Spot!" Caróg Liath squawked, flapping his wings in excitement in the air above Spot de León. "This is the information we've been seeking for centuries, and it took finding you to bring it to us! At last we know who the Vampyres are and where their leader sits on the portal like a chicken incubating an egg! And just in time, too. It sounds as though we have only until the next full moon to prevent an incursion of the *Diavhal* into our realm. That gives us less than a month. We must stop more of the Old Ones from coming through at any cost. If we can reach the portal, perhaps my allies on the other side can push through and join us in this realm to help us wage our war against the darkness!"

He swooped down suddenly and snatched up in his beak what looked like a rat-caterpillar hybrid out of the grass, before tipping back his head and swallowing it whole as he soared back up into the air.

"I was wondering … is it possible to cure vampyrism?" asked Spot slowly, swallowing bile.

"No, my child," replied the *Sluagh na Marbh* gently. "There is no known way. I am sorry."

"Then … what are we going to do with Sir Dion Laflamme?"

"He could yet be useful," squawked Caróg Liath after a moment's pensiveness, "if he can lead us to the portal."

"So, you're going to the portal beneath the Darcuul family crypt?" asked Spot. "Let me come with you. I know the city, and the cemetery, and the crypts … and I can spot a Vampyre from a league away!"

The Hood cocked his head to regard the boy with one beady eye for a long moment as he hovered in place. "Hmm, no. No, no. I don't think so. Far too unsafe. You'll stay here."

"If you leave me here, I'll just sneak out and follow you back to the city anyway."

"And how would you get there? It's a long walk."

"I'd steal a horse. I saw a stable on the way here."

The *Sluagh na Marbh* cawed in frustration. "Perhaps your talents could come in useful. We do only have one shot at this. You'd have to do exactly what I say, though, *at all times*. Are we clear?"

"Crystal. Can I have a sword?"

Caróg Liath squawked again. "I suppose we'll have to give you some way to defend yourself."

"And a medallion?"

"Those are only for the *Rugadh na Marbh.*"

"Then, let me join you."

"You are too young ... yes, much too young, my boy."

"I have nothing left," said Spot in a small voice, eyes on the strange blue grass on which he stood, native to the cave beneath the church. "The Vampyres have taken everything from me ... my father, my home, even my maid ... Please, the only thing I have left is revenge. Don't take it away from me, too."

"We'll need every helping hand we can find if we're to save the world," put in Aguilar.

The Hood let loose a particularly loud screech of vexation. "Oh, very well, Spot de León. Since we're all likely to perish if the Old Ones make it through the portal under the next full moon, why not initiate you into our little family?"

Spot looked up, eyes shining with hope. "Truly?"

"If you want it, yes. You are one of us, Spot. Perhaps you always have been and were meant to be."

"I want it! More than anything."

"Think carefully, Spot. It entails a great deal. You would be ... transformed ... into one of us. A creature like Aguilar, able to morph at will into a savage winged warrior. There will be no going back should you agree to this."

Spot pondered for a while, taking in his warm alien surroundings. The wallflowers winked at him.

He took a deep breath. "I understand, and I agree."

"Then, come, and we will begin the ritual to make you truly one of us, to make you *Rugadh na Marbh.*"

28
Callachia

Spot de León wandered the cold sunlit streets of Callachia with the bodyguards appointed to him by the Hood, Caróg Liath.

Passing through the town's central marketplace, he glanced at the stalls surrounding him and then up at the men, the *Rugadh na Marbh*, one pale but tanned with short bleached blonde hair streaked with silver and a moustache, the other golden-skinned and shaven with long salt-and-pepper hair caught up in a topknot. "How did you come to be here, Fuang Shi, if you don't mind my asking? You're Tzunese, no? I'd have thought the Tzunese would hate us for what we are doing to them with the Crusades."

The man with the golden skin and the topknot, Fuang Shi, looked down sombrely and nodded. "Many of my countrymen do hate Justiquans. And with good reason. I, however, have come to learn that it is no particular race that is at fault, but all of humanity. The Tzunese are just as warlike and power-hungry as you Justiquans, only they hide it better behind civility and etiquette. As to how I came to be here, you'd have to ask Sham. I feel it is more his story than mine."

The tanned man with a shock of near-white hair, Sham Fassik, barked a laugh. "Ha! You're just too taciturn to tell a story, Fuang Shi, that's all! Never mind, I'll do the honours. Ahem. It all began with my father, who was a Knight, a Crusader who fought in Quing Tzu back in the first Crusade led in that country some forty years ago. While there, he fell in love with a Tzunese woman named Sha Ling. Against his Commander's orders, he married the woman in secret and they conceived a son – me. Fuang Shi and I were childhood friends. He lived just down the street from me. The Crusaders were sent packing by the Tzunese when I was seven years old, though, and my father got permission from the Lord Protector to bring my mother and I home with him.

"We settled here in Callachia, and I grew up to be a Knight just like my father. The underworld was revealed to me one day, however, when I was ordered by the Count of Justiqua to arrest or kill a band of Tzunese criminals who were believed to be murderous black magicians. I led a squad of Knights and we found the band hiding in an abandoned warehouse by Lágrimas River. We fell upon them with our blades and slew several, losing a few of our own in the process. Only myself and one other Knight were left alive by the time I recognised Fuang Shi from my time in Quing Tzu. I ordered a cessation of combat immediately and asked Fuang Shi what in the name of the Prophet he was doing in Justiqua and why he was murdering my countrymen. Fuang Shi gave me a most unexpected answer. He told me he was part of a secret cabal of wizards and warriors in Quing Tzu responsible for hunting down and killing legendary creatures of the night – Vampyres. He had not been killing *people,* you see. He had been killing *Vampyres.*

"Then, he told me I had been brainwashed and that I was standing next to a Vampyre even as we spoke. Fuang Shi's friend, a wizard by the name of Gyo Mo, cast a spell and suddenly I could see my fellow Knight, Sir Rale Krimbit – once a good friend of mine, or so I thought – for what he truly was. I saw the fangs, the skull and the bright blue eyes. I thought at first I had been brainwashed by Gyo Mo into seeing falsehoods, but when it became clear that I was seeing through his illusion, Sir Rale Krimbit tried his best to run me through. I barely survived. Gyo Mo did not. Fuang Shi saved me, and together we slew the monster, chopping off its head. After that, I knew I could not go back to my old life. Fuang Shi and I toured Justiqua for years, slaying Vampyres wherever we could find them, before we heard tell of other Vampyre-hunters down here in Callachia. We came a few years ago to investigate the rumours, and once here it did not take us long to find Aguilar and the Hood, thanks to our … signature lack of subtlety. Caróg Liath was kind enough to take us under his wing … and here we are. We're wanted in Justiqua. Our faces are well known in the city, so we hide out here between missions."

"Oh," said Spot. "You're not here to take care of the Vampyres in town?"

Sham chuckled. "There are no Vampyres in Callachia."

"Yes, there are," said Spot. "I saw one in the marketplace back there, hiding in the shadow of a portico."

Sham's face fell. "Are you sure, Spot?"

"Yes. I saw him plain as day."

Fuang Shi looked grave. "Where there is one, there may be more. We should investigate this."

"Now?" asked Sham. "Should we not inform the Hood?"

"They may escape if we dither," replied Fuang Shi, adjusting the katana belted to his waist by a jade sash that complimented the robe he wore.

Sham sighed and thumped his leather jerkin with a fist. "Very well. Let's head back to the market and see what we can see."

Spot looked down at the fresh black coat, trousers and boots he wore, and most of all at his white shirt.

I was hoping to keep it clean of blood for a bit longer than this.

"We may need to buy some more clothes while we're at the market."

"Good point," acceded Fuang Shi with a bow of the head.

"So, where did you see him?" asked Sham as they surveyed the marketplace a few minutes later.

Spot looked around, once more surprised by the disparity between the marketplaces he had known in the city and this paltry den of meagre meat, fish and fruit. Unlike back home, he could easily count the number of people.

"Over there."

"Hmm, let's take a circuitous route so he doesn't see us."

Spot followed Sham and Fuang Shi as they backtracked, circled around the marketplace and came at it from another street, another angle. Loitering by a corner at the edge of the market, they easily spied the man Spot had seen lurking under a portico in front of a tall beige house, one of the largest in town.

"That's Sir Hodge's house," muttered Sham Fassik. "He's a retired Knight, once a pillar of the community, now a recluse. Some say he's a cripple."

The Vampyre appeared to be on the lookout for something, sweeping the marketplace with his eyes again and again. He did not appear at all out of place in a grey waistcoat, grey breeches and a plain shirt. Indeed, he had an open friendly face and scruffy straw-like hair.

I remember what he looked like when I fell through the trap door, though. I remember the fangs and the blue eyes.

"What is he looking for?"

"The town guard," Fuang Shi replied. "See that man in the hooded poncho by the vegetable stall? He's shaking down the vendor. That's the second trader I've seen give him a bag of coins, rather than the other way around. Both times, he left with no goods and I don't think the traders were giving him change from the size of the pouches."

"Extortion, is it?" said Sham, bristling. "I'll show them extortion!"

Fuang Shi surreptitiously held him back when he would have started forward. "Wait a moment longer. Let us be sure there are no others. Spot? Spot? Are you okay, Spot?"

Spot was pale and sweaty, shivering slightly as if an ill wind had found him. "Yes, I'm okay," he said through chattering teeth as his eyes unglazed. "But you're right, Fuang Shi. The man in the poncho is a Vampyre as well."

Fuang Shi nodded. "I thought as much." A few minutes later, he said, "I'm quite sure there are only two in on this scheme. Spot?"

"Yes, I only saw two."

"Good. Then, here is what we'll do. We're going to wait them out and follow them when they leave. With luck, they'll lead us to their hideout."

They waited until the sun set, while Sham Fassik chafed with impatience.

Finally, the man under the portico moved out into the moonlight to join his comrade and both wordlessly walked away down the dusty street. Spot, Sham and Fuang Shi slipped after them, following at a distance, quiet as mice.

"Where are they going?" Fuang Shi murmured when it became clear they were leaving town.

The Vampyres soon abandoned the main road for an old overgrown trail leading into some woods, and Spot and the Crows hurried to close the distance as they disappeared into the trees lest they lose them. They almost spooked the creatures of the night then by getting too close and had to hide behind a thick clump of avocado trees to avoid notice. When the Vampyres were certain no one was in pursuit, they moved on, and Spot and the Crows pursued. Following the windy old road, its ancient slabs barely discernible beneath thick tufts of grass, the Vampyres led Spot and the Crows to a vast squared canyon. Standing on the edge and gazing down into it, the *Rugadh na Marbh* could see the Vampyres skidding down to the rubble-strewn bottom by the light of the moon.

"It's the old quarry," Sham tried to whisper, his voice too loud. "It's been abandoned since Callachia was built. They use better stone from up north now, because these beige bricks crumble too easily."

"This must be their hideout," said Fuang Shi. "Quick, we need to see where they go!"

Ignoring the thin slanting path that slalomed down in switchbacks into the quarry, the Tzunese man took the Vampyre's route, sliding down the steep cliff face and sending scree tumbling with a clatter. The Vampyres had already ducked out of sight behind a huge slab of beige rock.

"Come on, Spot!" said Sham, flinging himself after his friend.

"Prophet's piss," Spot muttered before following, skidding on his soon sore backside all the way down to the bottom, where he landed in a cloud of dust, a mound of scree and a knot of brambles.

The quarry was thickly overgrown in places with brambles, nettles, bushes and even some saplings in places. The Crows shushed him and indicated the slab of rock behind which the Vampyres had disappeared. The trio crept around it with exaggerated slowness, tiptoeing and holding their breath. On the other side, a small cave mouth was hidden behind a thick screen of brambles and nettles.

"How could they possibly have gotten in there?" asked Sham, peering in but seeing nothing by the moonlight.

"In shadow form," answered Fuang Shi.

"Ah, yes, of course." So saying, Sham started to hack his way through the living screen with his broadsword. "We'll have to go the old-fashioned way, eh?"

Once they had cleared the obstruction, they crept forward to observe that the cave behind soon shrank until it was no more than a crack in the wall through which no full grown man could fit.

"Can they really squeeze through there in shadow form?" asked Sham doubtfully.

Fuang Shi nodded. "I suspect so. We could try to widen the aperture with more men and some pickaxes, but it could bring the cave down on top of us for all I know. It would take a long time, too. Besides, the Vampyres would hear us for sure and we would lose the element of surprise."

"I can fit," offered Spot. "I could go through and see if there's anything to see, then come back and let you know."

Fuang Shi eyed him dubiously, but Sham said, "Grand idea, Spot! Grand idea! Go on then, let us know what you find!"

29
Hidden Riches

Spot de León scraped his ribs squeezing through the crack at the back of the cave. The cramped passage was longer than he had expected, so he had to stoop and shove himself through for several long minutes, choking on dust all the while. Finally, though, the way broadened enough for him to breathe and he gasped at the tableau laid out before him.

Gold gleamed everywhere by the flickering light of the torch held in one Vampyre's hand. Chests brimming with coins littered the corners, between which treasures too oddly shaped for chests had been thrown down higgledy-piggledy. Idols of the Prophet crafted of fine metals glinted alongside silver chalices, golden goblets, jade bracelets and opal-strung necklaces. Gold and silver coins were strewn about everywhere on the uneven floor, where they had evidently fallen or been tossed in the air in excitement.

It's more wealth than I've ever seen in my life! Where in the name of the Prophet did they get it all?

As they were adding their latest pouches to the pile, the straw-haired Vampyre said in a surprisingly high-pitched flute of a voice, "D'you reckon two wagons will be enough to deliver this lot to the Old One? We might need three."

"Two will do," grunted the man in the hooded mauve poncho, his tones deep and dark. "The horses will just have to work harder, that's all ... D'you smell a human?"

Spot stiffened and tried not to breathe, sliding back into the crack through which he had come.

"Their stink gets all over me," replied Straw Hair. "I swear it's all I can smell some days."

"I know what you mean," said Poncho. "The full moon cannot come fast enough. It is long past time to subjugate and eradicate the cattle of this world."

He means us, humans!

"D'you really think the Old One will be able to bring his brothers through to our world?"

"Of course. You know how powerful he is."

"I do, but ... why has he not done so before? Five hundred years he says he has been guarding the gate. Why hasn't he let them through before now?"

"It's those damned foes of his on the other side. The *Sluagh na*

Marbh, I think he called them. They're constantly attacking and distracting and interrupting any and all attempts to use the portal. As I understand it, it's not in a convenient location on the other side. The Old Ones don't have complete control of it."

"But they will by the full moon?"

"That's the plan."

"I suppose we'll see soon enough. It's only days away now."

"True. Have faith, my friend. Ra'Gthul will not let us down, and soon the world will become the feast laid at our feet that it should be."

"I'll believe it when I see it. Speaking of a feast, let's get out of here. I'm ravenous."

Hearing them, Spot squeezed through the narrow passage even faster, ignoring the many grazes he accrued in doing so.

Don't let them find me trapped in here, please!

He popped out of the far side back into the original cave like a cork from a bunghole.

Sucking in ragged breaths, he wheezed, "They're coming! They're coming!"

Sham Fassik brandished his broadsword. "Get behind me, Spot."

Fuang Shi flourished his katana in an ouroboros and grabbed the medallion strung around his neck with his off-hand. "And close your eyes."

A black cloud swept through the crack in the back of the cave, sibilant and whooshing. Spot obediently cowered behind the warriors and squeezed shut his eyes so tight that he saw colours. He saw the flash of bright light produced by the medallion even through his eyelids, as though the world burned for a split second. Then, the fire in his eyes faded and he knew the light was gone. Tentatively opening his eyes again, he beheld the two Vampyres, Straw Hair and Poncho, sprawled on their backsides on the floor, looking bamboozled. The torch burned on the ground beside them, throwing their reliefs on the rugged walls.

"Going somewhere, fellas?" asked Sham conversationally, before bringing his broadsword sweeping down two-handed in a blow that would have cloven Poncho's head in twain had it connected.

The Vampyres were unnaturally fast, though. Even as Sham and Fuang Shi's blades arced down, the creatures of the night were moving, dodging, rolling away and coming to their feet fast with swords in hand. Sham's blade clanged off rock, while Fuang Shi managed to halt his strike. In a blink, the Vampyres were the ones on the offensive, leaping, slashing and stabbing in tandem with such skill that it was clear even to Spot that the two had been fighting together for a long time. So too, however, had Sham and Fuang Shi. Backing away as if conjoined at the hips, both made sure to parry their opponents' blades away from the other whenever possible.

The Night Comes Alive

Fuang's legs shot out now and then to boot one or other Vampyre, and Sham's fist rocked Poncho's head back a couple of times when they crossed blades in a pushing contest.

The Vampyres were fast and cocksure, pirouetting and executing fancy loops and hidden jabs with their blades. Sham was put on the back foot, his heavier broadsword struggling to keep up with the sheer speed of the Vampyres' lighter curved sabres. Fuang Shi's katana blurred in the torchlight, an electric eel jolting the creatures of the night now and again, leaving red welts in its wake. He backed away with Sham, though, to prevent his friend being flanked. Sham's leather jerkin was soon crisscrossed with slash marks as the Vampyre's supernaturally fast sword snuck through his guard time and again. He could not find a spare second to retaliate no matter how hard he tried.

Poncho sprang from side to side, jumping and spinning, his sabre a steel whirlwind without cease. Sham saw it glitter in the torchlight out of the corner of his eye over and over, catching it on his own blade through thoughtless reflex, or sheer luck on occasion. Mistiming a parry, he hissed as his foe's sabre scored his thigh and staggered back. Poncho pressed forward, grinning sadistically, sweeping his sabre high and low in a blisteringly fast attack pattern that Sham could not keep up with. Sham snarled as he felt the sabre lick his left shoulder, leaving it burning.

He tried to lop off the Vampyre's head with a quick swing, but Poncho surged forward and punched him hard in the face, breaking his nose with a crack. Sham cried out in pain and anger. His vision fuzzy, his eyes watering, he stumbled back. He did not know how he managed to block the next blow, but the force of it sent him careening to the floor, his knees buckling beneath him.

Standing over him and raising his blade in both hands for the final strike, Poncho sneered, "So much for the *great* Vampyre-hunter, Sham Fassik."

Fuang Shi chopped off Poncho's left arm at the elbow, and the Vampyre screamed as his limb dropped to the floor along with his sabre and a substantial spout of blood. Straw Hair's own sabre would have taken Fuang Shi's head off then if he had not ducked, and as it was it still took a few loose hairs. Sham sprang up and severed Poncho's hooded head from his shoulders all in one smooth motion, and the neck fountained blood after the head toppled off. Even as the body collapsed, Sham was turning his attention to Straw Hair, who had had Fuang Shi on the back foot since the Tzunese man had taken a heartbeat to help his friend. Fuang Shi parried a wide swing and then shoulder-barged his foe, raining down rapid blows from all angles. Forced to defend himself from the Tzunese man, Straw Hair was easy prey for Sham's broadsword, which took him in the nape and exited through his windpipe.

"Damn it, Sham!" said Fuang Shi as the Vampyre's ichor sprayed over his face. "Watch where you're swinging!"

"It worked, didn't it?" returned Sham with a grin, wiping his wet blade on Poncho's poncho.

His nose was mangled, sticking out at an odd angle with blood gushing from both nostrils.

"Yes," said Fuang Shi stiffly, wiping his face with his robe. "It did. Come here and let me set your nose. It looks a mess."

"Wow," breathed Spot. "You two were amazing!"

Sham waved a dismissive hand. "It's all down to Fuang Shi. I'd have been dead today just as I'd have been dead a hundred times in the past if not for him. These Vampyres are damned fast, but there's no man more skilled with the blade in the world than Fuang Shi."

"I do what I can," said Fuang Shi, deadpanned.

Spot flinched as Fuang Shi set Sham's nose back into place with a sickening crack, and Sham groaned, curling in on himself.

"Don't be such a baby," said Fuang Shi. "Now, tell us, Spot, what did you see through there?"

"Money," replied Spot without thinking. "More money than I've ever seen. Hundreds and hundreds of Reales, in chests and loose on the floor."

The Tzunese man's eyebrows rose in surprise, and even Sham seemed to forget about his nose for a second.

Fuang Shi looked to Sham. "What are we to do about so much money? We can't carry it all back to town between the three of us."

"No," replied Sham thickly. "We'll have to leave it here for now and come back better prepared, with more men, and a wagon maybe. Arturo can disperse it among the townsfolk."

"The Vampyres thought they'd need two wagons," put in Spot.

"Two wagons, then," amended Sham.

"Just ... leave it here?" Fuang Shi asked disbelievingly.

"Yes, well, obviously we'll take a share for supper and a few drinks tonight," replied Sham Fassik, a grin taking form on his bloody face. "It's only fair for our troubles."

30
Bird of Prey

The wind rushed through Spot de León's short mousy hair, cupping his wings and propelling him higher, icy and refreshing. Rain pitter-pattered on his tailored leather cuirass and pinged on the hilt of the dirk strapped to his waist in a scabbard. Thunderbolts split the sky, lighting the way, and the dark clouds rumbled ominously. Flying over fields of wheat on black, feathered crow-like wings some five feet long, he let loose a wild whoop that came out of his beak as more of a squawk.

I've never felt such freedom!

Gliding close by with his ponytail streaming behind him, Aguilar chuckled. "Feels good, no?"

"It feels amazing!" Spot shouted back over the wailing wind.

He could not explain how he formed words with his new chitinous mouthpiece. When he thought about it too much, his beak gummed up.

"That's it," said Fuang Shi, banking left and right seemingly for sheer joy despite his deadpan golden face, while his topknot slowly unravelled. "Use the air currents. Very good. Come now, let's find the manor."

"I know the way!" yelled Spot. "Follow me!"

"No, Spot, stay behind us," yelled Sham Fassik, soaring alongside, his near-white tufts billowing. "You are not here to fight, only to help us recognise the Vampyres and avoid killing innocents, remember? The dirk is only a precaution."

"I remember," said Spot glumly.

The Deacon, Arturo Rambit, grinned, looking out of place outside his church, garbed all in black with feathery black wings and a beak, his thatch plastered to his broad brow. "Don't worry, my son. We all of us have our purpose."

But I want to help!

Spot thought back to the ritual that had made him into one of the *Rugadh na Marbh*.

It is all hazy now. I remember the taste of Caróg Liath's black blood, warm and bitter and heavy in my belly. I remember the spasms and the delirium of the fever as my body underwent the changes. And I remember the pain as the wings grew out of my back for the first time and my face sharpened into a long, curved beak with nares in place of nostrils. Such pain as I have never known ... But it was worth it. I have power now, the power to take my revenge. No longer am I the prey, but a bird of prey.

Along with a dozen Crows, Spot dove down on a lone beacon of radiance amid the dark wastelands of the night, the orange glow splitting into a small swarm of fireflies shining through windows as they drew closer. Little pools of light outside the windows put the boggy land on show, where elsewhere it was so dark that it seemed there might be nothing but a void. As they had planned, some alighted on the roof, some on the ground in a wide circle around the country manor of Baron Erlic Rathbone. Spot landed with a pair of *Rugadh na Marbh* in the sludge, grimacing as mud leapt up to spatter on his woollen leggings and long-sleeved tunic. Like all the Crows, he now wore black from neck to toe.

"Eurgh," he groaned.

"Hehe, it's only dirt," chuckled Mateo Blanco, the bald juggler in the Hound's Fools.

"I'm with Spot on this one," added Sofia Jiménez the acrobat with distaste, flipping her long dark locks out of her pretty face. "We could've picked a dry night for this!"

"We don't have long before the full moon," Mateo reminded her. "We need to cull the Vampyres' ranks before then, pick them apart piece by piece when they are alone. Aguilar, Sham Fassik and Fuang Shi have been on more than one assassination mission in the last week. They're going through the list of names Dion gave us one by one. We've come in greater force this time, because Baron Rathbone has so many guards and servants, many of whom are also creatures of the night, according to Dion. It might require all of us to bring him down."

Sofia nodded. "I understand. D'you really believe …?" She nodded with a distinct lack of subtlety towards Spot.

She'll believe me soon enough.

"I do," replied Mateo, his voice light, before turning serious as he spotted the flash of a medallion atop the terracotta tiled roof. "Aguilar's giving the signal. He's going in. Keep an eye out for anyone trying to escape. Spot, can you let us know if we're seeing a Vampyre or not?"

"I'll do my best," said Spot.

The trio heard nothing as they watched their fellows break into the manor through the windows, not a single shattered pane, not a single alarm raised. Their hair stood on end as they waited for their companions to be discovered.

Maybe something's gone wrong. It's been quiet too long …

Just as the thought crossed Spot's mind, pandemonium erupted. Shrieks pierced the night like crossbow bolts, jarring those listening. Shouts followed, along with a medley of crashing sounds and the clang of steel on steel.

The world changed, becoming a nightmare.

Whoever was projecting the glamour over this place is evidently distracted – or dead. Baron Rathbone presumably.

The mud bubbled, each bubble a malevolent chuckle, and started to drag Spot, Mateo and Sofia down into the dirt like quicksand. The grass laughed sibilantly, swishing this way and that as if it were one big organism, stretching out to cut at their hands as the trio tried to reach down and unstick their feet. The rain came hard and phlegmy as if giants in some unknown realm above were spitting on them. The lightning in the sky contorted into a savagely smiling face, and the black clouds lowered until it felt like they were pressing down on Spot's brow, oppressive and heavy.

Spot could swear he even heard the wind whisper, *"I'll kill you!"*

The manor warped into a mangled mutation of its former self, dark as pitch with walls writhing as if alive and each and every tile transforming into a horrific bat-like creature glued to the roof, flailing wings like a dread forest swaying in a storm. It roared at them with its maw, the double doors that served as lips banging wide open. Darkness seemed to ooze out of the manor's windows like so much ink, sinking into the ground around the manor and turning it the colour of charcoal. A waft of decay and mould reached Spot as the wind changed, and he gagged.

I cannot escape! I'm going to die here, stuck in the mud!

He had already sunk up to his navel and was rapidly sinking further now that the dirt had a hold on him. By the flashes of smiling lightning brightening the night, he witnessed the juggler and acrobat dragging themselves out of the sludge up into the air, flapping their wings frantically. That was when Spot remembered.

I have wings!

He began flapping them urgently, the sensation still strange to him, and bit by bit he began to rise. He flapped harder and accidentally mired his wings in the mud. Crying out in frustration and panic, he began to sink again. Fortunately, Mateo and Sofia were at hand. Hovering over him, they reached down to seize his hands and slowly yanked him up out of the muck with a long drawn-out squelching sound. He beat his wings to rid them of the mud and then flapped them to stay aloft.

"Thanks!" he panted as the Fools released him.

All three turned without further comment to behold the twisted manor lurching this way and that like a dog on a leash, as if trying to break free of its foundations. Screams, shouts and the skirl of sword on sword still echoed from within, heard clearly even over the roar of the rain.

"What is this dark magic?" whispered Sofia.

"Rathbone must be powerful," observed Mateo sombrely, "to so affect his surroundings. All Vampyres leak black magic into our world from the Void, according to the Hood, tainting it and turning it into … this. This is what all of Maradoum will become should the Old Ones be brought into the world."

"Then, Caróg Liath was right," said Sofia determinedly. "We must stop the Vampyres at all costs."

31
Budding Madness

People burst out of Rathbone Manor, fleeing in all directions into the rainy night, some towards carriages and some out into the fields. Spot de León observed that the carriages had grown teeth in place of doors, however, and after one man was eaten, none other dared go near the carriages – or the red-eyed, snorting horses in the stables who regarded them so maliciously. So, people fled on foot.

"Spot," shouted Mateo Blanco urgently, "which of them are Vampyres? Oh ... never mind!"

Spot glanced this way and that and realised why Mateo had abandoned his question. The Vampyres had cast aside their glamours in their panic and were showing their true faces to the night. Common folk were being guzzled down by the field in places, while the Vampyres walked freely.

"Blind them with the medallions," Mateo shouted, "and then bring them down! Let the innocents go. Spot, close your eyes, please."

Mateo and Sofia Jiménez shone their medallions down on the fleeing folk like twin suns, and Vampyres screeched as the blessed light hit their eyes, while common folk only cried out in surprise. The Crows swarmed down on the Vampyres like a flock of predatory birds, gashing them open with the steel talons of their longswords. Blood sank into the giggling ground. Spot counted only six Crows where there should have been seven in the drizzly sky, and he realised sadly that one must have already perished in the sucking muck or at the hands of the Vampyres. He waited in the sky, watching while the other *Rugadh na Marbh* took all the risk, throwing themselves fecklessly at the unnatural fanged horrors and crossing swords with their fears.

I want to help! I don't want to be afraid anymore!

By a flash of lightning, he witnessed Sofia flapping up and away from one Vampyre in the field, crying out in pain as blood dripped from her limp leg. The creature of the night shifted into shadow form to give chase, but Spot was already diving, medallion bared.

"Close your eyes!" he yelled, before whispering the word of power that activated the medallion. *"Luz!"*

Though only three letters and one syllable, it had taken him some time to master the word's pronunciation so that the medallion would respond to him. Now, he enunciated it perfectly and the medallion flared like a thousand lanterns. Spot only just remembered to close his own eyes in time and prayed Sofia was wise enough to do so. He heard a scream. He reopened his eyes a moment later, when the fire behind his eyelids faded, to see the Vampyre who had been chasing Sofia sprawled on the ground on his backside, rubbing his eyes with his sword forgotten by his side.

It worked! I can end this fight now. I can face my fears. I can help!

Spot dove down on the creature of the night like a preying falcon and slashed him as hard as he could across the neck. His arm jarred as he struck the spine, failing to sever the thick bone, and abruptly he found himself face to face with a howling, enraged Vampyre. Blood gushed and jetted from the gaping wound, the skin peeling back like red petals. The fanged horror reached out with vicious speed and snatched Spot out of the sky with his bare hands, wrenching him closer with a snarl and opening his mouth unnaturally wide. Spot kicked and punched and flapped his wings to no avail. He could not escape the Vampyre's iron grip on his sword arm and neck.

I'm going to die! He's going to suck out all my blood, and I'll be left a lifeless husk!

Mateo Blanco caromed into the Vampyre at speed from the firmament, tackling him to the ground and forcing him to release Spot, who quickly flew up out of reach of those on the ground, gasping for air and rubbing his throat. He watched in horror as the mud splashed up into the air in far greater quantities than the tackle strictly demanded, splattering down on both Mateo and the Vampyre and completely burying both. The Vampyre popped out of the muck a few moments later, only for Sofia to lop off his head in an instant. Spot and Sofia watched the chortling sludge for a short while, but Mateo did not reappear.

He's gone. He saved my life. Is it my fault he's dead? Should I have stayed out of the way? Sofia might have died without my help. I tried to do the right thing ... and still someone died. That's so cruel and unfair. What else could I have done?

Tears trickled down Sofia's dirty face alongside the rain as she said, "I have to hunt down the other Vampyres. It's what Mateo would have wanted. Stay out of harm's way, Spot, please."

Her broken voice broke his heart, as did the loss of the jovial juggler, and he nodded guiltily. "I will."

Looking around, he counted only four Crows in the sky now – Sofia Jiménez, Arturo Rambit, Lebron DeRose and Zola Igbinedion – and a wave of sorrow washed over him. The tide had turned now, though. Wherever Vampyres tried to take on shadow form to rise into the sky to give battle, they were immediately blinded by the medallions and given no choice but to remain solid. Without the edge of their arcane tricks, the horrors were at a disadvantage and they knew it. They turned tail and fled into the night, but

The Night Comes Alive

the Crows had the manor surrounded.

The *Rugadh na Marbh* fell on the Vampyres like meteors, flattening their foes with the force of their descent and severing their heads with swift swishes of their steel swords. The Vampyres relied on their supernatural speed and strength to overwhelm their victims, but the *Rugadh* were near their match thanks to the Hood. Spot saw one Vampyre impaled on Arturo's longsword, and he knew a moment's fear, thinking the deacon had made a mistake by not aiming for the neck. Expecting Arturo to be bitten and killed, Spot's eyes went wide when the Vampyre burst into white flames, becoming a living screaming torch in the space of a heartbeat. Spot was not sure in the gloom, but he thought he saw the Vampyre turn to ash and wither away into nothing. The deacon was back in the sky a moment later, circling like a vulture seeking carrion.

What in the name of the Prophet just happened?

Spot witnessed a few Vampyres disappearing into the darkness through the gaps in the net where the *Rugadh* had died, but more were those he saw taken down and beheaded, until the sodden fields were littered with the bodies of Rathbone's servants in red-and-white livery and men-at-arms in leather cuirasses. He wished he could give chase when he saw Sir Alonso Gómez running fast as a panther across the field with Sofia on his heels, his fangs and blue eyes clear in the transient light of the tempest.

I don't want to get in the way, though ...

Sofia caught Sir Gómez easily, dropped down in front of him to block his way and brandished her blade. Spot marvelled at her skill as she launched a series of stabs and cuts at the Vampyre. Gómez did not marvel. He went for the jugular. By the time Sofia hit the ground, he was already long gone, at one with the night. Spot gaped in astonished sorrow, replaying the scene over and over in his mind.

How did he kill her? He did not even attack! All he did was parry. Oh! He cut her throat even as he moved to parry her second blow. Such speed is ... inhuman. She was vivacious but moments ago ... How fleeting life is ... I wish I had helped ... I wish I knew the right thing to do ...

Lebron DeRose, Zola Igbinedion and Arturo Rambit took off in pursuit of Gómez and the others who had escaped, and Spot watched with heart-pounding trepidation as they shrank into the distance and then vanished into blackness. His skin crawled as he realised he was alone in the sky above the field outside the manor.

When have I ever been so alone in my life? In the city, there was somebody around every corner, but here ... nobody in the world can see me. Nobody in the world knows exactly where I am. I feel ... free.

Spot took a deep breath, savouring the earthy scents underlying those of death. A heartbeat passed, and the sensation of freedom fled for the hills when a screaming young girl came running out of the manor. She bolted straight into one of the monstrous carriages, and the teeth that the doors had become slammed shut behind her. Even through the downpour, he recognised her pale skin, plaited raven hair and elfin features.

Aiva! Did she not see what the carriages had become? Or was she simply too terrified to comprehend? I must save her!

Shouting, "Aiva! Aiva Thragon! It is I, Spot de León! I'm coming to rescue you!" he dove down on the carriage and landed hesitantly in the mud alongside it, ready to spring back into the air should the ground try to suck him in.

The earth held firm, and he breathed a sigh of relief. The pit-black horses in the traces stamped and harrumphed, tossing their heads and withering him with their baleful red-eyed glares. The carriage watched him shuffle closer with huge, tawny eyes, one inset in the back wall and one on the side. Its teeth gnashed together. Its wheels abruptly turned sideways, flat to the ground, and then its spokes popped out from their hubs and propped the carriage up again, serving as little legs like those of an insect.

It started to skitter away, and Spot chased after it, yelling, "Hey, come back here you!"

The traces fell away, freeing the horses from the carriage, and the beasts all turned their gruesome gazes as one on the lone boy in the field. Spot heard them coming up behind him, their hooves drumming a horrific tattoo on the earth.

What can I do? I don't want to kill the horses. They've simply been corrupted by the Vampyre's dark magics.

The first gelding to reach him shouldered him to the ground. As the rest caught up and started to stomp on him, Spot worried for a moment he would be trampled to death.

Yanking out his medallion amid grunts of pain, he held it up, closed his eyes and shouted, *"Luz!"*

The horses whinnied and turned away as one as the blinding light burned their evil eyes, galloping off to the four corners of Maradoum. Bruised and sore, Spot picked himself up and took off at a limping run after the carriage containing Aiva, which was scuttling across the field like an oversized crab.

I can hear Aiva wailing for help! I must save her!

Fortunately for him, the carriage moved at a snail's pace, its little legs moving feverishly just to move it a few yards, and so it had made little headway. Catching it, Spot summoned his courage, took his dirk in a two-handed grip and swung with all his might at the great bloodshot eye staring at him from the back of the carriage. The carriage tried to scurry out of the way, but Spot had accounted for that. His two-foot steel blade clove the eye open down the middle, unleashing a geyser of yellowish stinking ichor that made Spot wrinkle his nose. What he had not accounted for, however, were the arms. Sprouting wooden arms from the wall panelling and leaving great gaps in the slats through which Spot could see Aiva, face pale and frightened, the carriage walloped the boy with one timber arm, sending him sprawling with a yelp.

Snatching up his dropped weapon and snarling, Spot advanced on the carriage once more, ready this time for its unexpected appendages. Remembering what Fuang Shi had taught him, he carefully used his dirk to block the arms when they snapped out to smack him, moving with shocking speed. Each block mauled an arm a little more, sending splinters showering. Growing in confidence and parrying so that he was chipping away at the arms even more with each stroke, Spot eventually dismembered both arms down to the stumps. Wood chips were scattered in the grass all around him, and the carriage hissed through its vertical rows of teeth, trying once more to scuttle away.

"Oh no you don't!" Spot said firmly, darting in close and ducking down low to chop the little wooden legs out from under the carriage.

Only then did he realise his mistake.

The carriage bent down and gobbled him up, its sharp teeth raking his wings, arms, ribs, hips and legs and making him cry out in pain and terror. Inside, the carriage seemed to have been transformed into a stomach. Bright green digestive juices dripped from the ceiling and dribbled down the sides where the walls were still intact to gather in a pool on the floor, into which Spot was dumped with a groan of disgust. Sitting, frozen, on one cushioned seat was Aiva Thragon. Her mouth opened, but no words issued forth.

"Aiva!" Spot gasped, scrambling up out of the pool of reeking juices, his clothes saturated, his wings sore and tucked. "What are you doing here? Where's your father? It doesn't matter. We have to get you out of here! It's not safe!"

Aiva's face, taut and drawn, eyebrows close in consternation, abruptly relaxed into a calm smile, and Spot felt a chill seep into his bones.

"You!" she purred. "It's *you* who told the Crows where to find us, isn't it? You little shit. Just couldn't keep your Gods-damned mouth closed, eh?"

Her face transformed once more, the skin thinning and shrivelling until it barely seemed to stretch over her skull. Her teeth faded away like a mirage to be replaced by four long fangs overlapping her lips. Spot stared in horror into eyes of lapis lazuli.

She was one of them all along!

"Why didn't I ever see you?" he blurted without thinking.

Her smile became condescending. "Some of us are more talented than others at hiding our identities. I *have* been practising for three hundred years."

"You're three hundred years old? Is Valdimir even your father?"

She laughed, the once joyous tinkling sound now akin to nails on a chalkboard. "No, silly. He's not even one of us. He's just a … decent hiding place. We have his daughter, so he's clay in our moulding hands. He'll do whatever we say, including pretending I'm his daughter, though he knows not why. Those bruises I showed you? He did not give me them. I did."

Poor Valdimir.

"You must have been turned when you were young," Spot whispered, feeling a pang of pity for the girl despite everything.

Aiva nodded. "I was. As will you be. I wonder if a Crow can be turned into a Vampyre. Time to find out, I think."

She was on him in a blink, bearing him down into the goo with inhuman strength. "You could be a powerful ally to us, you know, Spot."

"Never!" he ground out through gritted teeth, wrestling her grip on his wrists.

She released one of his wrists to reach up to her face and bite her own wrist, so that blood streamed down her arm. Then, she moved her arm towards Spot's face. Frantically feeling around in the goo with his free hand, Spot cut his finger on something sharp and hissed in pain. He grabbed his dirk by the blade and rammed it tip-first into the girl's neck. She released him and gurgled blood, a shocked look on her face.

"I'm sorry," Spot whispered, before grabbing the hilt and twisting the dirk so that the girl's severed head popped off her shoulders like a dandelion.

Feeling his soul shrivel and his heart grow callouses, Spot recalled the strange rhyme children would say in a singsong manner while playing with the flowers.

Mama had a baby and her head popped off …

32
Insanity Abloom

Spot de León hacked his way clear of the carriage with a heavy heart and continued to whack at it with his dirk until it was nothing but a pile of timber, tears streaking down his face.

He flew up into the rainy sky when he was done, hoping for a better vantage point to watch for Arturo and the other Crows' return. He inhaled through his teeth as he saw a shadow streak up into the firmament after him, illuminated by a lightning whip. He returned to reality from a grief-stricken plane just in time to hear thunder crash.

The shadow was coming for him.

It must have been sneaking up on me in the darkness on the ground. What do I do? What do I do? I need help! I cannot fight this thing alone. So, do I chase after Arturo and the Fools or do I turn to those in the manor for aid? I am closer to the manor. The place may be demon-possessed, but at least I have friends there.

Split second decision made, he swivelled in the air and propelled himself with powerful strokes of his wings towards the manor before the shade could reach him.

"Help! Help!" he cried out as he soared.

The manor rushed up to meet him, the faux castellation and the architrave leering and pulling faces, the walls crawling with creepy-crawlies. The crane-shaped weathervane shrieked atop the peaked roof writhing with weird bat-like creatures, and flapped its wings with a horrible creaking rusty sound.

Spot barely had time to notice. He had never flown so fast in his life. The wind snatched at his hair, making his eyes water and numbing his face, and rain pelted him like hail, but he did not slow. He dove and swooped through the roaring doorway, feeling as though he had just been eaten for the second time that night when the doors slammed shut behind him. He dared not look back to see if the wraith was still on his tail.

I'm sure it is.

Though the manor was spacious, there was little room to manoeuvre inside with such wide wings, so he had to bank carefully through the antechamber and into the main hall. There, his eyes bugged as they drank in the tableau arrayed before them. The drapes, tapestries, rugs and tarantula-infested walls in the foyer writhed, aflame, infecting the rafters even as the boy watched, incongruous against the backdrop of the storm howling outside and the rain hammering on the window panes. The stuffed animal heads mounted on the skittering walls in the main hall howled and bleated and brayed, stags and wolves and bears crying out in pain or anger.

I cannot tell which.

The beardy busts just glared. The old-fashioned weapons on the walls spawned shadow warriors to wield them even as Spot looked on, slack-jawed. Inky blackness poured from them only to swirl mid-air and then coalesce into the ethereal forms of men with spiked or horned helmets. The shadow men then picked up the maces, flails, morningstars, glaives and claymores adorning the walls and brandished them as if they knew how to use them. Spot gulped. Lit by the rapidly growing fire, Barons Rathbone and Reyes crossed swords with Aguilar de la Torre, Sham Fassik and Fuang Shi. Several bodies were being absorbed into the olive carpet in front of Spot's eyes, half their frames sunken into the bloody fabric, some with black wings poking out.

"Help! Help!" Spot cawed, flying above the heads of his fellow Crows and continuing to circle to avoid the deadly touch of the shadow in pursuit.

The Crows seemed not to hear him, each intent on the fight at hand. Somebody did hear him, though, and wafted through the wall to investigate.

Laying eyes on the silvery, see-through figure in antique armour who floated above the ground with only an ethereal wisp below the waist, Spot searched his brain and squawked, "Jorge! Jorge Rathbone! Thank the Prophet you've come! Please, help me!"

He pirouetted though the air again and again to avoid the Vampyre on his tail.

Watching with furrowed brow, the ghost of Baron Jorge Rathbone said in a faraway voice, "Why, if it isn't Spot de León! What are you doing back here, my boy?"

"These Vampyres are trying to kill me!" Spot screeched. "Please, help!"

"I cannot interfere with mortal matters, I'm afraid," replied Jorge calmly. "I'm dead, you see." He turned his eyes on the shadow men spawned from the archaic weapons. "These, on the other hand, I think we can deal with." He threw back his head and hollered barely above a whisper, "Boys!"

Another ghost appeared next to him in similarly old-fashioned armour, covered head to toe in steel plate with a visored helm. Then, another, and another, until half a dozen of them were facing down a baker's dozen of the shadows. They drew their knightly swords with faint rasps of metal and advanced on the nefarious beings, blocking the way to the Crows' backs.

"Thanks, I guess," muttered Spot, observing the eerily quiet clash of

The Night Comes Alive

ephemeral forces.

Every ring of sword on sword or spear on axe was muffled, as if distant. Whenever one of the ghosts or shadows was dispatched, it vanished in a puff of smoke.

I wonder what happens to those that are slain ...

Spot swooped through the air unpredictably to keep the creature of the night on his heels guessing. He tried to grab his medallion, but he could not slow enough to pull it out without the Vampyre catching him and he was almost caught in the attempt.

Sham Fassik reflexively looked to see what was happening when he heard the faint sound of combat behind him, and Baron Reyes' sabre gave him a hot kiss on the shoulder as he turned, narrowly missing his neck. Sham growled and swung back to the fight, but fortunately for him, Fuang Shi had never left it. Refusing to let himself be distracted, knowing it would be the death of him, the Tzunese master swordsman had the focus of a falcon. Batting Reyes with his wings in a risky manoeuvre, he knocked the Vampyre back away from Sham to protect his friend, taking a small nick to the wing as he did so. Locking swords with Rathbone for a moment, Aguilar flicked his eyes up to see Spot and the Vampyre flying around the room. As he shoved the Baron away, though, Rathbone let fly and punched him in the face, sending him reeling back a couple of steps with a grunt.

Rathbone pressed forward with a blitzkrieg of rapid slashes, forcing Aguilar back with dazzling swordplay, but was himself then pushed back by Sham in the middle, who took a chance to lash out at the bone-haired Baron. Fuang Shi parried the blow from Reyes that would have skewered Sham's heart and retaliated with such a venomous swipe that Reyes had to leap back a moment. Suddenly, Fuang Shi was the one pressing forward with his katana tracing a glimmering silver pattern in the air so fast did it move, and Sham was free to grab the medallion strung around his neck.

He lifted it, shouted, "Eyes!" and then whispered, *"Luz!"*

Closing their eyes in the middle of a swordfight was a risk, but having a Vampyre fly around the room in shadow form was a greater one. The Crows closed their eyes, and light beamed out. A cracked wail sounded as the Vampyre in shadow form who had been chasing Spot – now wishing he had taken the chance to attack the *Rugadh* from behind – coalesced in mid-air and dropped like a rock to land on his face. Sham spun away from the conflict with the Barons and chopped off the fallen Vampyre's head in one smooth arc. He gaped at the embattled ghosts and shadow warriors for a split second. Then, he was back between Aguilar and Fuang Shi, ready to lend support to either. Fuang Shi yet had the upper hand in his duel with Reyes, so Sham turned on Rathbone and, together, he and Aguilar wove a web of steel around the Baron that he could not escape, forcing him back one step and then another while he parried and dodged desperately.

Still, Rathbone managed to snarl, "There you are, Samuel! I was wondering where you had gotten to! Found some good-for-nothing friends, did you?" He grunted as he blocked a heavy blow from Sham's broadsword. "When I get out of here, I *will* find you, wings or no wings! You hear me, Samuel? You're a dead boy walking!"

Hovering in the air behind the fracas, Spot cringed.

"Shut your damned mouth, you monster!" Sham roared, raining down sword strikes on the Baron. "Leave that boy alone!"

"*I* am Baron Rathbone! I was one of the first turned by Ra'Gthul over four hundred years ago! I have stalked the nights for centuries, petrifying men, women and children alike! I have killed more humans than the plague! Oceans of blood flow in my wake! *I* am the stuff of nightmares, the tale you tell your child to make them behave, and I will not be thwarted by a flock of stinking Crows!"

Rathbone sped up his swordplay until he was flickering in and out of shadow form every other second. It was all the *Rugadh* could do to keep his broadsword from their necks. Not one had a chance to grab their medallion, needing their spare hands for balance at all times. Darkness seemed to pulse out from the Baron like ripples in a black lake, leaching the light. Vile life manifested in the manor. Sprouting a thousand thorns, the carpet pounced on Fuang Shi and the Tzunese man had to desperately avoid Reyes' laughing sword stroke while trying to untangle himself. He eventually managed to slit open the fabric down the middle with his katana and tear it off himself with his free hand while parrying Reyes' sabre, but he was left with hundreds of little bleeding pockmarks all over his face and body.

The big hairy wriggling spiders that comprised the walls seemed to close in on the fighters until they were hissing down Sham's neck. The Vampyre-hunter kept glancing over his shoulder to check he was not about to be bitten, and Rathbone's broadsword scored him again and again as he did so, gashing open first his arm and then his chest. Sham grunted in pain, but the fire did not leave his eyes, nor did his own sword slow – even when the tarantulas began swarming over him and biting him in the back. Groaning, he tried to shrug them off. The figures portrayed on the burning tapestries of war in the foyer awoke and hopped out of their fabric. An army of tiny stick-men, some on stitched horses, hacked at Aguilar's heels with swords and axes, making him yelp in pain, before he started stomping them all to death. Even then, miniscule spears pronged his sole, making him hobble and yowl.

Hearing a faint rustling above him, Spot looked up from the insanity abloom just in time to behold another of its symptoms. The hundreds of bats that had replaced the tiles on the roof when the world had changed had somehow grown down through the ceiling as if it were porous. Spot could see them pushing their way through the elastic ceiling, black fuzz growing like mould and then extending membranous wings with vicious hooks on the end. They were no ordinary bats, though. Aside from seeming to sprout from the ceiling like plants from soil, they were monstrously large, he now saw, with bloodcurdling red eyes and great gnashing fangs. He screamed in horror.

I cannot touch the ground, or I will be eaten by the carpet and I cannot stay in the air or the bats will kill me!

He accidentally flapped too high in his panic, and the warped bats' hooks sank into his wings, snagging him so that he could not escape. He screeched as excruciation tore through him like a thunderbolt.

He flailed his dirk, screaming, "Help! Help!"

No one on the floor had the time to help him, however. The ghosts could not and were distracted by the shadow warriors, besides. The living had their own problems. Almost impossible to see or predict, Rathbone's shadow sword was a phantom menace. It was only a matter of time before it reached its goal of plunging into flesh. Sham Fassik cried out as the De León broadsword split open his thigh and blood gushed from the wound. He staggered back, relying on his comrades to protect him. Aguilar de la Torre, however, found Rathbone's shadow form boot in his face and toppled, dazed, to the ground a moment later. Fuang Shi could not intervene, for Reyes picked that moment to press the attack. Uninhibited, the shadow that was Rathbone soared up at Spot with venomous speed. It all happened so fast.

Spot barely had time to grab the medallion with fumbling fingers and shout, *"Luz!"*

Light flared, and Rathbone shrilled as he fell out of the air to land on all fours on the roiling olive carpet with a thump. The bats shrieked and released Spot, stunned by the brightness. Spot had not had time to warn the others, though, and so everyone had been blinded by the flash. He watched them all blinking and rubbing their eyes for a heartbeat that seemed like a lifetime. Sham and Aguilar were on their rear ends. Rathbone was on his knees, pawing at his eyes, sword forgotten by his side.

It's up to me. I can put an end to this here and now. All I have to do is be brave.

Dropping the dirk, he flew down and took up his father's sword, which Rathbone had dropped. It felt heavy, but somehow right in his hands. He took aim and swung with all his might at the Baron's head. His eyes widened when Rathbone caught his arm in a deathly tight grip and glared up at him. They practically popped out of his skull when Sham lopped off the Baron's arm from his position sitting on the floor. Spot did not think twice.

Putting all his power behind his father's broadsword, he cut off the Baron's head in a single swing. The severed head rolled bloodily across the floor to knock Baron Reyes' leg. Still on his feet, Reyes reflexively glanced down, and in that moment, Fuang Shi parted his head from his shoulders with one sure arc of his katana. The tarantulas stilled into wood-panelled walls, the carpet coughed up what remained of the bodies it had been digesting, and the animal heads ceased yowling. The army of stick-men disappeared only to reappear in their burning tapestries, and the bats sank back into the ceiling as if they had never been.

As blood fountained up into the air and Reyes' body collapsed, Fuang Shi turned to Spot, panting, and nodded toward the blade he held with the lion's head pommel. "Your father's sword. He would be proud, I am sure."

Spot's eyes welled.

I wish he were here. I would give anything to have him back. At least we have avenged him. The world will be a better place without Rathbone and Reyes preying on the weak and helpless. We are not done yet, though ...

He glanced down at his father's blade. He had feared the broadsword would be too weighty for him to wield, but it fit his hand like a glove.

I know it is likely because I have been transformed into one of the Rugadh na Marbh *and so my strength has been multiplied, but it feels as though the sword was meant for me. It feels like my father's hand in mine.*

Outside the manor, Spot and the others found Lebron, Zola and Arturo descending from the stormy night sky with a few of the bodies of their fallen fellows, their faces streaked with tears.

"Gómez escaped," said Arturo, his normally jovial face glum.

"Rathbone is dead," said Aguilar tiredly, "and the city a little safer. Let's bury the dead and get back to Callachia to rest. We have a great deal more to do before the full moon next week."

33
False Fools

"Are you sure this is wise, Aguilar?" asked Fuang Shi quietly.

"The time has come to abandon secrecy. The Hood agrees with me. There will be too many Vampyres gathered in one place tonight for us to miss this opportunity to cull their ranks. Whether it is wise or not, tonight we discard the shadows and take our fight into the light of day. So to speak."

Spot de León glanced up at the gibbous moon in the starry sky, shining pale light down onto the sleepy city of Justiqua and the behemoth of a mansion in the middle of it.

"It's about time!" brayed Sham Fassik, puffing out his chest. "I'm sick of skulking! I want to kick their cursed heads in, and I don't care who sees me!"

Over a score of Crows were gathered in front of Darcuul Mansion that night in the garish livery of the Hound's Fools, cloaked and sequined, many called in from elsewhere in Justiqua after the losses at Rathbone Manor a week earlier. Spot had been surprised to learn that the Crows were a phenomenon all across the island of Justiqua, even across other parts of Maradoum. Fuang Shi told him there were even Crows in Quing Tzu. Vampyres, too.

I never knew there were so many. It is strange to see them all without wings or beaks. I feel naked without mine, vulnerable.

"Secrecy has been our ally," Lebron DeRose pointed out. "This will prove the end for the Hound's Fools, you know. We'll never be hired again."

"It was only a cover for our true purpose, my love," said Zola Igbinedion, taking his hand. "Now, as Aguilar says, our time has come."

Lebron sighed and nodded. "I know. I will miss it, that is all ..."

"Unless we can break the Vampyres' concentration and ruin their glamour, the innocent Knights will attack us on sight, too, thinking we are slaughtering their fellows without provocation," said Deacon Arturo Rambit, evidently unmoved by Lebron's plight.

"Then, we must be sure to break their concentration, Darcuul above all," said Zola. She turned to Aguilar de la Torre. "You said that as soon as you engaged Rathbone in his manor, he lost his focus and the night came alive."

"That is true," agreed Aguilar, nodding and rubbing his brow. "We must pray it holds true for Darcuul, too." He took a deep breath. "There will be folk we know down there, folk we love. They will not recognise us, thanks to our masks and beaks, so we need not worry on that account. We must try to protect the innocents, of course ... but the Vampyres are the true goal. They must be eliminated at all costs, understood?"

Even at the cost of collateral damage, apparently. Surely saving lives is more important?

The group murmured agreement. Spot remained silent.

"Good," said Aguilar, drawing himself up. "Then, it is time to go. For the innocents."

"For the innocents," they echoed.

Light beamed out from the mansion's tall thin windows like breaths of flame, illuminating the panther-shaped gargoyles poking out of the façade, for a gala was being held inside. High spires loomed above them, flying buttresses resembling wings in the darkness. Privately hired armed guards in leather cuirasses eyed the Fools coldly. Spot was sweating as Aguilar knocked on the side door, though he shivered with the cold.

What if someone recognises me despite the disguise? This was a mistake! I should not have come.

He was wearing a red comical demon mask to cover his birthmark and a calico Fool's costume with a wacky hat with bells on, so that he jingled when he walked. He would have felt ridiculous if the others were not dressed similarly. He had been given two chimes to strike together, so that he would not look out of place.

A servant in black and white opened the door and regarded them snootily. "The Hound's Fools, I presume?"

"That's us," replied Aguilar jovially, jumping up and clicking his heels together.

"Hmm," the balding old squinty man hummed disapprovingly, "very well. Do come inside out of the cold. I will show you to a room where you may take refreshments. The guests will be dining soon, and once the dishes have been cleared, I will show you to the main hall."

The false troupe was taken through the servants' quarters so as not to disrupt the gala prematurely and shown to a comfy room full of couches where jugs of water and plates of dates and other fruits and bread had been laid out on small round tables lit by candles.

"Thank you," said Aguilar, bowing to the balding servant with a flourish.

The balding servant just stared at him. "Be ready in an hour." With that, he departed, shutting the door behind him.

"Well, he was a laugh riot," said Sham Fassik in his booming voice.

Aguilar chuckled, and Fuang Shi smiled thinly. Lebron and Arturo looked pale.

"Does anyone feel like eating?" enquired Zola in a meek voice.

All heads were shaken.

"Me either," said the dark-skinned dancer, flopping onto a couch. "I hate waiting."

"Well, we're here now," said Sham, spreading his arms and looking around. "Why don't we just go in there and get this over with?"

"Because we want to wait until we are better informed," answered Aguilar. "We want to use our cover to determine the Vampyres' positions before we strike. We must try to prevent them from escaping."

Sham dropped onto a couch dispiritedly. "I agree with the dancer. I hate waiting."

Fuang Shi settled on the floor in a cross-legged position and closed his eyes. "You should use this time to hone your mind."

"Why?" asked Sham, yawning. "I already honed my sword. I can't believe they didn't bring us any hooch! Just water? Faugh!"

Arturo settled on the floor by Fuang Shi. "I think I'll join you," he said, crossing his legs, resting his hands on his knees and closing his eyes.

After a while of sitting in silence, Spot asked Lebron and Zola, "How did you two first find out about Vampyres? Did you see them as children as well?"

"I did," said Lebron. "I used to see them everywhere when I was younger and living in Justiqua, just as you do. I convinced myself I was insane, though, and put aside the thought for many years. I travelled the country as a troubadour, meeting Zola here on the road, until one night we returned to the city to perform for an old friend of my father's, Sir Warrick. The Knight drugged our drinks and strung us up in the secret dungeon beneath his mansion and told me he knew that I knew what he was. He told me he had planned to kill me before I left the city all those years ago, that I had left just in time. As soon as I returned, though, he feared I would remember and told me he could not let me wander the streets knowing his secret. Zola was just in the wrong place at the wrong time. It was pure chance that the Crows were keeping a close eye on Sir Warrick, suspecting him of vampyrism. Aguilar saved Zola and I that night, slaying Warrick, and we pledged our loyalty to him when he explained his life's purpose to us." He smiled at Zola and took her hand. "We knew then that it was our purpose, too."

"Yes, we did," she said, kissing him lightly. She turned to Spot. "It was hard for me to accept that such ... demons ... are real. But I saw Sir Warrick's true face that night, and I never forgot it. It haunts me to this day."

Spot shivered as goosebumps crawled across his skin. "Wow."

The silence returned then, heavy and palpable.

Not long later, the snooty servant opened the door. "Please," he said, "follow me. It is time for the show."

Aguilar took a deep breath. "And so it is."

The servant led the false troupe along a series of mauve-carpeted, red-walled corridors lit by torches in sconces that eventually led to a small whitewashed chamber empty but for barrels and bottles.

The servant indicated a door. "The main hall, where the festivities are taking place, is just through there. Are you ready to begin?"

Aguilar looked around. "Are we ready?"

The *Rugadh na Marbh* nodded with set jaws, and Lebron and Zola started to strum their lute and lyre so that enchanting sound scales emanated through the door ahead of them to build anticipation. The servant threw open the door, and the Crows bounded out energetically to find themselves in the main hall of the manor, where marble mouldings, pilasters and ornate cornices decorated the walls alongside a long frieze of Knights astride galloping steeds, weapons in hand, all illuminated by the flickering light of cressets and candles and moonlight streaming in through the arched windows. Crimson couches lay supine here and there on the purple carpet, their leather creaking now and then. Spot well remembered the place. It had been where his father had found out about the Vampyres the night he had died.

I wish he were here.

Dozens of aristocrats sprawled on the couches, stood in familiar cliques or else milled around the room. Prancing around along with the other Crows as they had practised and clanging his chimes, while others beat drums, blew on flutes and trumpets and strummed stringed instruments, Spot gulped when he beheld a throng of familiar faces. As rehearsed, he and Aguilar started dancing around in a small circle together so that they could confer.

"I see Darcuul by the north wall, Delgado and Lamprey on couches in the middle of the room and Levont by the foyer," said Aguilar quickly. "You?"

Spot nodded, his bells jangling, and said, "Gómez, too. He's by the frieze, on the left. We mustn't let him get away after what he did to Sofia."

Aguilar bobbed his head as he danced and blew a piping melody on his flute, which Spot had been surprised to learn he could play well. Strangely, Spot found the comical blue demon mask Aguilar wore more disturbing than his beak.

I am sick of masks.

Aguilar spun away to jig with Zola and discuss with her whom she had seen that Spot might not have recognised. Between them, with the help of Sir Dion Laflamme's list of names, they hoped to identify every Vampyre at the gala before they made a move, so that they could be sure none escaped. Glancing around, Spot could not see Sir Reginald Giles or his wife, Maria, anywhere, and he prayed they had stayed home. He was confident he would not see Ursa or Tumba Koum there; they had only attended the Saint's Day Ball at his request. Normally, they had no interest in such events. He did, however, lay eyes on Count Kronvert, garbed in frilly emerald regalia. Cursing inwardly, he started to prance his way over to the old man.

Chiming his chimes and kicking his heels together, he danced around the Knights of *La Salamandra* surrounding the Count and hissed, "Count Kronvert!"

The Count peered at him curiously, his face a foot away from Spot's own.

"It's me, Spo – Samuel de León!"

All of a sudden, the Count staggered back, fear etched in his wrinkles. In that split instant, the hall darkened and a chill wind bit at Spot's hands and neck where his flesh was exposed. For just a split instant, Spot felt the familiar lurching sensation of missing a step and accidentally tripping over reality, creating a fold where he could see through the curtains of illusion that veiled his eyes. The creature that was Count Kronvert was revealed at last. Half of his face looked to have been scraped away, leaving him with ragged shreds of flesh, no left ear and a nose with a chunk missing. Skin so pale that it looked like it had never seen the sun clung to his skull, from which peered out eyes blazing with blue. Four long fangs extended from his mouth, overlapping bloodless lips.

He looks like a dead man buried in his finest gear!

Spot reeled as the fangs and blue eyes faded away, leaving Count Kronvert looking as he always had – old and frail. Spot knew that was not the case now, however. The Count might be old, but he was not frail. He possessed the strength of ten men. A flash of insight filled in some gaps for Spot then.

My father was always complaining that Kronvert never got anything done to stop the Crusades, and now I understand why. Kronvert never tried. He wants the Crusades to continue to spread his horrific disease to the far corners of Maradoum, to infect as many people with vampyrism as possible.

"You!" Spot gasped.

He knows I know!

Turning and running, he yelled, "Aguilar, now!"

This was not the plan, but he prayed Aguilar could improvise. The music skirled to a stop, and all eyes turned on Spot.

34
Flies to the Web

"Death to the Vampyres!"

Aguilar de la Torre roared the words so ferociously and loudly that it made half the Crows – including Spot de León – jump. They were so used to secrecy that it spooked them for a moment, before they remembered they were abandoning discretion that night in favour of bloodletting on a grander scale than ever before. They whipped out their weapons from beneath their cloaks, whooping and howling like wild animals to boil their blood for the fight as they threw themselves at the closest creatures of the night, targeting those they recognised from Dion's list.

The sophisticated gala was ruined in an instant as a chorus of screams and shouts erupted to replace the music. Vampyre blood soon stained the mauve rugs as the Crows fell on their foes, taking them by surprise. Severed heads rolled around the room, tripping people as they tried to escape. In a trice, the Vampyres had their own swords in hand and the clangour of steel on steel echoed around the hall. The majority of revellers flocked towards the doors, squawking in terror, silken plumage flapping. Some of the Crows had taken up prearranged positions by the doors to stop any Vampyre from escaping, though they did not halt the frightened masses.

Spot ran straight to Aguilar, who was hacking passionately at Viscount Bautista Lamprey with his curved cavalry sabre. Aguilar pulled aside his cloak even as he parried a blow from the Viscount' own sabre, so that Spot could pull out the broadsword with the lion's head pommel sheathed at his hip. It sang as it swished through the air, and Spot felt a thousand times better with it in his hands as he faced down the Vampyre horde descending upon him. While the regular folk were fleeing, the creatures of the night were turning their predatory gaze on the Fools. Spot could not even count them all before one of them was savagely stabbing at him with a longsword. He parried awkwardly, as Fuang Shi had taught him, and backpedalled rapidly. Fuang Shi had also taught him to avoid fighting wherever possible. Though imbued with the strength of the *Rugadh na Marbh,* Fuang Shi had told him, he was yet a prepubescent boy who was no match for an ancient Vampyre in one on one combat.

Fuang Shi and Sham Fassik were by his sides in a blink, having been ordered to keep him safe by Aguilar – though not at the cost of their own lives. Fuang Shi dispatched the Vampyre hounding the boy with a swift slash to the neck, and Spot grimaced as the severed head bounced bloodily towards him to roll to a stop with blue eyes transfixing him. Sham had somehow found time to rip off his calico tunic, silly hat and comical mask, and now wide black wings extended from his back and a beak burst from his face. The Vampyres bared their teeth as they realised the Fools were their hated enemies, their nemeses, the Crows. They dared not discard their own masks, however, nor take on shadow form while common folk yet lingered in the hall, all jammed in the doorway trying to escape. Many could not get past a fight that had broken out in the threshold to the foyer between Lebron DeRose, Zola Igbinedion and Sir Alonso Gómez and Count Kronvert, who had been trying to sneak out with the crowd. The frightened partygoers dared not go back further into the main hall to find a side door on account of all the death dealing in the room, and they could not escape. So, they stood and quivered like mice about to be fed to a snake.

Aguilar, Arturo and several Crows had made a beeline for Darcuul as soon as the ruse was up, but Viscount Lamprey and multitudinous Vampyre Knights had stepped in to intervene and now the *Rugadh* were bogged down in swordplay, trying frantically to finish off their foes before the Count of Crossroads could get away. A dozen Crows and Vampyres were slaughtered in the first few seconds of the fracas, their blood staining the purple carpet crimson. Arturo hammered at his enemies with powerful strokes of his longsword, knocking them back despite their supernatural strength and speed and then cleaving off their heads with wrathful roars. Stuck fighting two foes at once, Aguilar spun and leapt, pirouetting and lashing out again and again crosswise at the Vampyres' necks to the symphony of steel on steel. Locking swords with and shoving aside Viscount Lamprey with a display of strength, he unleashed a blistering series of slashes at the second Vampyre, finally batting aside the dark creature's longsword with his sabre and decapitating it on the reverse stroke.

Panting, saturated in blood and trembling with rage, he pointed his sabre at Lamprey and the remaining Vampyres. "Vengeance will be mine for every innocent you have slain!"

Spot recalled how Aguilar had become a Crow.

He is thinking of his wife.

Backing away from his own foes in another quarter of the room, Sham Fassik bumped into Spot, reminding the boy of more pressing concerns – namely, Count Joaquin Delgado and his companions, who were trying their best to turn Sham and Fuang Shi into mincemeat. Leaning out from behind Sham, Spot jabbed a Vampyre in the shin with the tip of his broadsword, eliciting a yowl. Sham promptly cut off the creature's head, spattering Spot with hot blood.

"Stay behind me!" roared Sham, arcing his heavy broadsword through the air to bring it slamming down on Count Delgado's sabre with a loud clang.

The bulky Vampyre's knees almost buckled under the force of the blow, but he rallied and served up a salvo of surprisingly speedy slashes that Sham could not keep up with, leaving the Crow with score marks on both arms. Squatting under a sword swipe, spinning and tripping his own foe with an extended leg, Fuang Shi lopped off the Count's arm even as he straightened, making him yowl. Delgado tried to turn and run, but Sham's sword caught him in the neck and his head rolled free. Fuang Shi slew the finely dressed Vampyre he had tripped with a swift slash of his katana before it could rise.

Count Kronvert escaped from his duel with Lebron and Zola long enough to witness Fuang Shi and Sham ripping the heads off two more of his fellows, and he panicked. Spot saw it in his eyes. He lurched back into the room and, with savage slashes, cut down all but one of the mewling aristocrats who stood there, too afraid to move. Then, he grabbed hold of the one quivering old woman in a silk gown who remained, who was too frightened even to scream. She just whimpered. Holding her in front of him, with his back to the room, so that she was between him and Lebron and Zola, he pressed his curved three-foot steel sabre to her neck.

"Now there's no more witnesses! Let me pass or the old broad gets it!" he wheezed vehemently at the Crows blocking the door.

Seeing the woman's predicament, Lebron and Zola stepped back from their ongoing skirmish with Sir Gómez as one. Sir Gómez grinned wolfishly and vanished out of the door in a blink, fleeing into the night. Count Kronvert was making his way towards the door, pushing the grey-haired woman in front of him, when he suddenly grunted and his arm fell off, the sabre it held clattering to the floor. He glanced in shock to his right, where stood Spot de León, holding a broadsword wetted by the old Count of Justiqua's blood.

"You!" hissed Kronvert, his fanged ragged face darkening as he stepped towards the boy to shred him to pieces with his bare hand.

His head hit the floor before he could take a second step, parted from his shoulders by Lebron DeRose's longsword. The old woman shrieked. Lebron looked at her for a moment, then waved towards the door. The woman darted out of it without a further word. Lowering his blade, Spot stared at the white shirt wrapped around the Count's body, once immaculately white, now pink and turning redder by the second. He looked around the room as if in a trance. Blood flecked the horsemen frieze, seeped into the carpet and stained the marble moulding.

Then, it started to ooze from the walls. Spot felt a hot drip on his brow and looked up to behold dark gummy ichor slowly dripping from the vaulted ceiling as if seeping through gauze. Spot gasped – and then spat in disgust as blood dripped in his mouth. He ran back to Sham and Fuang Shi.

The walls and ceiling bled more and more, turning redder and redder until they were pocked with huge vermillion blemishes that spread and spread like inkblots. Darcuul laughed uproariously, and all eyes turned on the Count of Crossroads as the moonlight beaming in through the windows was dimmed by the blood trickling down the panes. In unspoken accord, all the combatants took a step back and ceased their swordplay to gawp at their surroundings, even the creatures of the night.

"Flies to the web and I am the spider," purred Darcuul, his voice cutting easily through the bubbling silence.

As he finished speaking, howling nightmares made of blood and fur burst out of the walls, looking like giant blood-drenched bats with eyes of fire, the snouts of wolves and two enormously long, thin arms with multiple segments that ended in huge hands with seven fingers, each as long and sharp as a cavalry sabre. Like the bats on the roof of Rathbone Manor, however, the monsters seemed attached to the wall at the midriff, unable to fully step into this realm, as if they had been born from the bloody walls themselves. Stood too close to the walls by the doorway to the foyer, Lebron DeRose and Zola Igbinedion were snatched up by the snarling ghouls and yanked back into the bloody wall with splashes. The ghouls that had taken them reappeared a few moments later, hanging out of the walls, but Lebron and Zola were never seen again. Several more Crows succumbed to the nightmares' claws, before the rest wised up.

No! Zola!

He recalled her words then about foreseeing her own death – 'at the hands of fiends of blood and fur'. He shivered, as if passing through a ghost. He would never forget the frightened look on the woman's face as she was yanked into death's gulf. He thought of all she had done for him, warning him and protecting him.

I will miss her.

Stood further from the walls in the middle of the room, Aguilar de la Torre, Arturo Rambit, Sham Fassik, Fuang Shi and Spot de León flinched and cried out in horror as their friends were torn from existence. Then, they had no more time for mourning, only for self-preservation, as the bloody ghouls in the walls roared with high-pitched rasps and stretched out their unnaturally long, thin, dripping red arms to try to snag and claw the Crows. At the same time, the Vampyres hurled themselves remorselessly upon their nemeses once more. And all the while, Darcuul laughed darkly.

Parrying claws and swords frantically and backing into one another, so that they fought back to back, Aguilar, Arturo, Sham and Fuang Shi fought for their lives on every front, with Spot sandwiched between them. They swiftly tried to reorient themselves so that they could escape the clutches of the ghouls, but the Vampyres were just as swift to cut them off.

The Crows found that they could not entirely get away from the clawed fiends hanging out of the long wall that had once borne the frieze of armed men astride galloping steeds, and so Fuang Shi and Sham Fassik were caught facing the ghouls while Aguilar and Arturo battled the Vampyres on the other side.

Fuang Shi and Sham hacked ferociously at the sabre-like fingers of the fiends at first, but found to their horror that their swords found no purchase, swishing through the monsters as if through nothing but blood and leaving no mark, dent or wound of any kind. The nightmares did not seem slowed or injured, only enraged. Their howls grew louder, raking at the Crows' ears even as their sharp fingers raked at flesh. When the ghouls managed to land a blow, on the other hand, their claws were corporeal as scythes, gashing open Sham's shoulder with the ease of razor sharp steel and making him moan in agony. Realising their inability to hurt the monsters, or even block their attacks, Sham and Fuang Shi began a dangerous dance with the ghouls, dodging from side to side, ducking and whirling to avoid the snatching claws.

Aguilar and Arturo crossed blades with the Vampyres again and again, sweat pouring down their faces and their breath coming ragged. Both fighting more than one foe at once, they could find little time for retaliation amid all the parrying. When some of the Vampyres clocked that the witnesses were dead or gone and started to shift into shadow form, the Crows knew pangs of real concern. The shadow swords were almost impossible to see, harder still to block. Nevertheless, the ring of steel on steel continued to sound out as they continued their fight against the phantom blades, their reflexes and knowledge of attack patterns keeping them a hair's breadth from death. Both hissed or grunted now and then when one of the wraith sabres snuck past their guard and gouged their flesh, Aguilar taking a wound to the thigh while Arturo's spare arm hung limp thanks to a deep cut.

Seeing the plight his comrades suffered, Spot whipped out his medallion and shouted, "Mind your eyes! *Luz!*"

The Crows closed their eyes, but so too did the Vampyres, having wised to the trick. The shadows were banished, and the creatures of the night were forced to assume corporeal form once more, but though this left some of them dazed and vulnerable, those who had not transformed into shadows barely hesitated, continuing to cleave at the Crows even with their eyes closed and then reopening them as soon as the flash faded, just as did the *Rugadh*. So, Aguilar and Arturo had no chance to smite down their discombobulated enemies, although they were grateful not to have to battle shades. Spot looked to and fro. Neither Sham and Fuang Shi nor Aguilar and Arturo were making any headway.

We're going to die if I don't do something!

Leaning out from behind the Crows, Spot hurled his broadsword like a javelin at the closest Vampyre. The blade took Viscount Lamprey in the cheek, knocking his head back and making him wail in agony. His outcry was cut short when Aguilar's sabre cut off his head. The thrown De León broadsword clattered away and knocked over a cresset set on a wrought iron pedestal. The pedestal hit the stone floor with a loud clang, and the blazing-oil-filled cresset rolled into the drapes by a window, setting the thick mauve material and the carpet ablaze instantly. The bloody ghoul in the wall closest to the fire screamed shrilly as the blaze mounted, throwing up its arms in dismay and wailing. As the conflagration grew, it withdrew completely into the wall.

Seeing this from the corner of his eye, Fuang Shi yelled, "Fire hurts them! *Surtur losagadh!"*

Ancient words of power taught to him by the Hood rolled off the Tzunese man's tongue, giving Spot goosebumps and making his hair stand on end. As the last syllable slipped from his lips, his katana spontaneously combusted. Bright white flames licked along the length of the blade and yet did no harm to Fuang Shi's hands, which were protected by a bronze disc in place of a crossguard. Sham copied him, muttering the same words and wreathing his own broadsword in pure white fire. Then, the two slashed as one at the grabbing vermillion arms of one of the eerie wall-demons and the ghoul howled as several of its long, sharp fingers were lopped off. The severed digits disappeared with a sizzle, flashing bright red and then going up in smoke.

"It works!" trumpeted Sham, swinging again and making the ghoul shriek as he scored its arm.

The fire was spreading fast, eating up the drapes and the carpet in its quest to devour all life. In seconds, it was at the Vampyres' backs, breathing its hot breath down their necks and making them sweat and glance nervously over their shoulders. More than one lost his head that way to the Crows' blades. Soon, the fracas was on equal footing. Then, as if stuffed with straw, one of the Vampyres went up in flames with a whoosh. He screamed shrilly as his flesh blackened and withered away in the fire far faster than did his silken garments. Staggering about, he flailed his arms madly and infected two more Vampyres with the blaze. They went up like dry tinder. In heartbeats, nothing was left of the three creatures of the night but charred smoking corpses amid the growing conflagration. The few surviving Vampyres tried to turn and run before the flames reached them, but Aguilar and Arturo scythed them down from behind, hamstringing them to cripple them and then severing their heads. Only a handful made it out past the shrieking ghouls who were slowly withdrawing into the walls as the fire proliferated.

Aguilar met Darcuul's eyes. On the far side of the room, on the other side of the fire, the Count was standing and staring with bugging eyes at the Crows, a vein throbbing in his forehead, his wrath palpable. Aguilar took a step towards him, but his arm was seized by Arturo.

"We have to get out of here before we all burn!" yelled the deacon, and Aguilar reluctantly saw sense.

Allowing the clergyman to drag him towards the exit, he shouted over his shoulder, "Sham! Fuang Shi! We have to get out of here now! Don't forget Spot!"

Sham and Fuang Shi, who had started sprinting at the suggestion of departure, sheepishly checked to see if Spot was with them. He was. Together, they ran the gauntlet between a raging fire and a wall full of howling ghouls with hammering hearts and screams on their lips, arms and legs pumping, breath coming ragged. Slipping past the last of the snatching bloody ghouls in the wall and bursting out of the burning mansion a few seconds later, Spot felt a cool wave of relief wash over him. Together with Sham and Fuang Shi, he skidded to a stop beside Aguilar and Arturo outside in the street, hands on his knees, gulping in lungfuls of the cold night air and watching his breath curl like smoke.

"D'you think Darcuul died in there?" panted Sham Fassik, gazing back at the burning mansion, whose fire-lit door resembled an entryway to the Nether.

"I don't know," replied Fuang Shi between breaths. "He'll be dead or long gone by now, though."

"Come on," gasped Aguilar, "we have to move before we're discovered!"

"Where are we going?" asked Spot, taking off his demon mask and calico costume so that his beak and wings could grow, while the others did the same.

They could hear the city watch's horns in the distance, drawing nearer.

"Back to Callachia. Home."

35
Night of the Full Moon

The full moon was upon them.

Aguilar de la Torre had wanted to strike sooner, to take out the Old One before he had a chance to open the portal to *Nagathai*. Caróg Liath had insisted they wait until the night of the full moon, however, knowing that most every Vampyre in the city would congregate in the catacombs beneath the crypts for the occasion, giving the Crows and the *Sluagh na Marbh* the opportunity to wipe them out once and for all.

Spot de León was not sure he saw the logic.

It seems risky to leave it until the last minute. What if something goes wrong? Our world could be inundated with Old Ones spreading vampyrism wherever they go. We must not allow that portal to open.

The Crows had pulled out all the stops, recalling every Crow within travellable distance. Spot had gawped to see so many in the cave beneath the Church of Saint Elmo. More than thirty of them had turned up over the course of a few days before the full moon, men and women from all corners of Justiqua and even a pirate from Swash Isle who had happened to be in the harbour.

Spot had chatted with the pirate for a while in the cave, eyes shining at the notion of life as a buccaneer. The Freeman, Sandy Locks – a nickname, the bearded buccaneer explained, given to him by his piratical fellows on account of his long feathery sand-coloured hair – had been happy to regale the boy with tall tales of his time at sea, and Spot had soaked them in like a sponge, picturing in his head fleeing the Quing Tzu armada, naval battles with rival pirates and close encounters with Sea Serpents in the Silent Straits.

If so much as half of his stories are true, he has led a thrilling life!

Spot had even convinced the Hood to allow Sir Dion Laflamme to join them, after spending a little time with the chained up Vampyre and seeing that he was not like his kin. Hearing his story, Spot could not help but feel sorry for the Count's son.

He is a victim, not a predator. I believe he truly wants to help us.

Still, they had blindfolded him when they took him out of the cave and had not removed the blindfold until they were well away from Callachia. Escorted by two *Rugadh,* he would meet them at the cemetery to guide them to the portal.

Now, as Spot soared through a storm above the nighted spires of the city with the Crows, he gazed down into the streets by the light of flickering thunderbolts, wondering if Dion would attempt to flee, or whether he would show up to help them. Seen from a distance, the hole in the city where his father's mansion had fallen down made his heart pang.

I wish he were here. I wish Bona Dea was alive. I wish ... I wish I had never seen a Vampyre.

He felt a sense of camaraderie he had never before known with the Crows, though. Like a flock, they flew through the storm together, as one with the night, garbed in black cloth from neck to toe.

Of all the people in the world, these few understand what I am going through. They are my brothers and sisters, and I would give my life for them, as they would for me.

"There's the Church of Saint Padrice, and the cemetery," Aguilar shouted over the roar of the rain, pointing, and Spot peered down into the stone jungle, lit here and there by little pools of lantern light.

Before he could even make out the church clearly in the murk, the Crows came under attack. One of them screeched as it was borne out of the sky by a shadow, almost impossible to see in the inky firmament thanks to thick black clouds shielding the moon and stars. The rest of the Crows drew their swords with a synchronised skirl and turned toward the noise, only for another of their number to be slain from behind.

"Form a sphere and drive them off!" Aguilar barked, sabre at the ready.

Lightning branched through the storm, and Spot saw by its transient radiance that shadows were pinwheeling around them in numbers that made his heart pound. He brandished his broadsword, glancing left and right to make sure Sham Fassik and Fuang Shi were covering his flanks. As always, they were by his sides. Shadow blades came at them from the night, as if the darkness had come alive and decided to blot out all of life's light. Steel clanged on unseen steel as the *Rugadh na Marbh* desperately defended themselves, squinting into the tempest to make out their ethereal attackers.

"Look out!" Sham cried, flinging himself in front of Spot to block a blade from slitting the boy's throat, only to then be gashed on his left arm as he raised it to block another blow from the left.

Sham hissed through gritted teeth as hot blood welled and turned on the shade that had cut him, swiping his broadsword back and forth vengefully in an ouroboros that had the Vampyre backing away. The shadow that Sham had blocked with his blade swooped in close then, and Spot glimpsed death in its murky form. Fuang Shi's katana flashed across his eyes to divert the shadow's next blow with a clang, and Spot breathed a sigh of relief.

I barely even saw it coming. I would have been dead several times over if not for Sham and Fuang Shi.

The Night Comes Alive

As Fuang Shi forced the shadow blade up and away, Spot stabbed out, feeling his broadsword sink into something. With a gasp of pain, the Vampyre rematerialised in mid-air, its concentration broken, the broadsword in its gut. Spot withdrew the weapon, and the Vampyre wailed as it plummeted into the abyssal city, vanishing from sight once more.

Spot nodded breathlessly to Fuang Shi, and the Tzunese warrior nodded back. Sham finally dispatched the horror that had spilled his blood with a well-placed slash to the neck, and then he and Fuang Shi started to fly in circles around Spot in wordless accord, so that they could better protect him from all angles and so that they were not bogged down in one spot by multiple enemies. Their strategy threw their enemies into disarray. At first, the Vampyres thought they could easily flit in to kill the boy and strike the older Crows down from behind. One after another, they dove into the gap only to learn that Sham and Fuang Shi were moving too fast to allow any gap in reality. One after another was scythed down before it could strike a blow, and Spot gaped to witness Vampyres coalescing from the night in mid-air, most with their heads lopped off, to fall to their deaths on the streets far below.

How do Sham and Fuang Shi even know where their heads are?

Spot tried to help once and almost accidentally pronged Fuang Shi on his blade, who gave him a severe look. After that, he just waited, hovering with his father's broadsword at the ready should he be needed. He glanced over his shoulder to see that the other Crows had found their footing, too. Though some had fallen, most had now taken up positions that allowed them to protect themselves from all angles, forming a rough sphere. They had to space themselves far enough apart to flap their wings and swing their swords, but close enough to defend one another, striking a balance between offence and defence. Shadows speared at the sphere again and again, seeking to puncture it, only to be rebuffed by cold steel at their throats.

I swear Sham and Fuang Shi have slain a dozen between them ... Just how many Vampyres are in this cursed city?

All at once, the shadows vanished as fast as they had appeared and the Crows were alone in the sky, panting and looking at one another with crazed expressions slowly fading.

"Where did they go?" panted Arturo Rambit.

"To the crypt," Aguilar answered with surety, breathing laboured. "They'll be waiting for us. They know we're coming."

"So much for the element of surprise," muttered Sham, gasping in great lungfuls that made his barrel chest rhythmically swell and recede.

"Surprise or no," said Aguilar, "we go."

Sham nodded. "Right behind you, chief."

"Till death or victory," added Fuang Shi, a single bead of sweat rolling down his golden face.

"On me!" cried Aguilar, raising his sword and diving towards the light of the church.

Streaking past the tiled roof and ridged steeple of the church and the handless statue of Saint Padrice, the Crows flapped their wings to slow their descent and alighted gently on the grass in the cemetery amid the headstones. The Darcuul family crypt reared up out of the gloom before them, colonettes supporting the pediment where a stylized panther reared. The crypt's engraved iron maw yawned ajar, and it stared at them with golden discs for eyes. Spot thought he saw a shadow dart inside. Thunder rumbled, the rain pitter-pattered on their heads, and lightning scarred the sky. It was quiet.

Too quiet.

"Look who it is," Sham said wryly, and Spot spun to see Sir Dion Laflamme picking his way through the tombstones, accompanied by two *Rugadh na Marbh*. "Took you long enough to get here!"

One of the Crows, Sandy Locks, grunted. "We hid when the Vampyres started showing up at dusk and waited for you. I have to say ... there were a *lot* of them. The Hood said not to let any harm come to this swine." He gestured to Dion. "On account of we need him to find the portal."

"You hid?" Sham asked incredulously.

"You did well," Aguilar assured them, seeing them bristle. "Dion must be protected. Apparently, it's a labyrinth down there and we need a guide."

Last on the ground was the Hood, alighting with a whumph, having been given the signal that it was safe to land. The Father of Crows dwarfed his children as a man does a child, waddling like a bird on the ground in an ungainly fashion that spoke of his preference for flight.

"Astath lith!" whispered Caróg Liath, and a glowing crow the size of Spot's head swam into existence by the Hood's side.

It looks like it's made of pure sunlight!

"Follow me, my children," said the Hood, flourishing twin curved steel cavalry sabres, "and tonight we will save Justiqua – and the world – from the Vampyres and the Old One's schemes."

He was the first through the threshold, ducking and tucking his wings in order to fit. The golden crow flitted through after him, overtaking him and soaring on ahead. Aguilar was next, knees bent, sabre pointed into the darkness with his spare hand outstretched for balance. Arturo was on his heels, longsword held upright in both hands, face grim. Sandy Locks moseyed in next, seeming at ease with his thumb hooked in his belt and his cutlass held loosely. Sham and Fuang Shi motioned for Spot to wait until a few more Crows had entered, and then the three of them followed while yet more of the *Rugadh* brought up the rear. Spot shivered as he crossed the threshold, feeling a chill deeper than any frost seep into his bones. The only light was that cast by the glowing crow as they crept down the straight narrow stairs. Spot's heart thudded in his breast, and he wiped his clammy palm on his thigh.

I can tell they're all trying to be quiet, but we sound as loud as a fanfare to me!

The stairs opened out onto a long vault filled with stone sarcophagi sculpted with likenesses of the dead, whose end they could not see. What they could see was the small battalion of Vampyres awaiting them in full suits of steel plate armour complete with visored helmets and plain surcoats, blades bared. Fronting them was a small, cocoa-skinned man in a mink overcoat, who grinned and doffed his black brimmed hat at the sight of them, performing an elegant bow.

"Well, well, well," he drawled in a voice smoother than syrup, clacking his cane on the ground, "what do we have here? My, my, you're a big birdie, aren't you? And who is that I spy behind you? Do mine eyes deceive me, or is that good Sir Knight Dion Laflamme you have with you? Remarkable! I was wondering where he had toddled off to."

It's the Vampyre who was here before, when Tumba and I came!

"Get out of our way, Ignatius," said Sir Dion Laflamme, stepping forward. "We're going to put a stop to the Old One and his insane plans. You won't be able to stand against us."

"Oh, won't I?" purred Ignatius Boondoggle, replacing his hat atop his head at a rakish angle. "The Old One cannot be stopped, Dion. You should know that better than anybody. He *will* bring through his army of Old Ones, and they *will* subjugate Maradoum. It's not too late to change sides, you know, be on the winning team ... ?"

He raised his eyebrows questioningly.

Will Dion betray us? Surely he has more to gain by doing so than by remaining with us? His life? Riches? Power? He could have it all with the Vampyres. If he stands against them, he has nothing. Nothing but the knowledge that he is doing the right thing.

Dion gulped and shook his head. "I've made my choice. I'm an abomination who deserves to die ... and so are you. So are we all."

36
Risen from the Grave

Spot de León watched in horror as Ignatius Boondoggle scowled and his face fell away to reveal his true visage.

He gnashed his four long fangs and stared at them with chips of ice for eyes. "Fine, cast your life away, you fool. The Old One will bathe in your blood!"

So saying, he backed away, letting the armoured men take the vanguard. The stone arches crisscrossing the ceiling, the ribs comprising the ribbed vault, drooped down as if they were made of molasses, only to rise again, still attached to the ceiling by their tails, while their heads bared snakelike fangs and hissed venomously with grey forked tongues flickering in and out. The Vampyres paced forward as one, shoulder to shoulder, obviously trained Knights from their armour and coordination. The snakes ignored them, weaving through the air above their heads towards the *Rugadh na Marbh.*

"Strike down these creatures of darkness, my children!" cawed Caróg Liath, extending an arm and watching with satisfaction as the glowing crow he had manifested soared with blinding speed straight through the head of one of the Vampyre Knights, puncturing both helmet and skull easily to explode out of his nape in a spray of gore.

As the Vampyre hit the floor with a clang, his fellows let loose a roar of anger and charged, throwing their line into disarray. The shining crow took out another of them before they could reach the *Rugadh,* spearing straight through his face. Then, they were upon the Crows, slashing and stabbing, and the Hood was forced to divert his attention to the stone snakes lest he accidentally injure an ally. He directed the golden crow to start snipping the snakes off at their bases, only to discover to his horror that they slithered on even once on the ground. More than one Crow felt the bite of a giant sculpted snake and succumbed to their writhing coils.

Aguilar's sabre fanned out to divert two swords at once, and his blade clanged against a helmet on the reverse stroke, sending one Vampyre reeling into another. Arturo batted aside a longsword with his own and shouldered his foe to the ground before beheading a snake as it lunged for him. When one Vampyre swung for his neck, Sandy Locks sprang in unexpectedly close, inside his reach, and punched him repeatedly in the face with the cupping bronze handguard of his cutlass, not stopping until he tumbled over backwards, blood spraying from his mangled visor. Sandy had to backpedal rapidly then, however, to avoid stone snake fangs snapping

The Night Comes Alive

shut on his skull. Sham Fassik's broadsword hummed out to block a blow from on high and then arced down low to sweep the monster's legs out from under it, gonging against greaves. Fuang Shi leapt high and kicked one opponent in the face before his sword got anywhere near the Tzunese warrior. He parried a sword swipe in mid-air, dodged a striking snake and kicked again upon landing, laying a second foe flat.

Sir Dion Laflamme crossed swords with a tall Knight, but Caróg Liath took out his foe with a single swipe of a sabre before they could clash blades again, shouting, "Stay back, Laflamme! We need you to find our path!"

Thus incapacitating some of their foes, the Crows were left with only half the force on their feet and ready to fight. Steel clashed in earnest then, as the Crows sought killing blows. Sandy Locks swayed this way and that like a palm in a storm to avoid the lethal swings of an enemy's heavy broadsword and then rammed his cutlass deep into the Vampyre's unprotected armpit when he raised his blade high for a downward chop. A snake latched onto Sandy's shoulder with its teeth, and he hollered in agony, yanking his cutlass out of his groaning foe and then beheading both snake and Vampyre with two swift slashes. Once slain, the snake's head fell from his shoulder, leaving a bloody wound showing through the ripped cloth.

Aguilar parried until an opportunity arose and then whipped his sabre straight through his bulky foe's neck in the gap between breastplate and helmet. The head clattered to the floor, the body a moment later. From behind the corpse sprang a serpent, which sank stone fangs into Aguilar's spare arm when he used it as a shield. Grunting, Aguilar severed its head with his blade, jarring his arm as he did so, for cleaving stone with steel was no easy task. Arturo carefully aimed a parry to hit a Vampyre's hand instead of his sword, so that it lopped the appendage clean off. The Vampyre's sword bounced loudly on the ground. Still, he tried to block Arturo's hefty wallops with his vambrace, falling to his knees after a few blows, but the deacon soon swatted the arm aside and clove deep into the neck. He could not get the angle to take the head clean off in one sweep, though, so he had to swing again before it parted ways with the shoulders. When two snakes dove toward him, he dropped his sword, seized their heads, one in each hand, and smashed them together. Together, they fell to the floor as mere masonry. He scooped up his sword a heartbeat later, just in time to parry a Vampyre's blow.

Fuang Shi dodged the Knights' slow broadswords and the snakes seeking his blood, slippery as a weasel, and his katana sang through their throats like a hissing dirge, barely scraping their armour. Sham, on the other hand, soon grew frustrated with seeking the precise strike to the neck required to chop off his enemy's head, his sword clanging against armour time and again. So, before long, he opted for a different tactic and brought his broadsword hammering down with a roar on the Knight's flat-topped helmet to stave in his skull. The sword rose and fell, rose and fell. Blood fountained out of the bent helmet, and the Vampyre gurgled and collapsed. Its pulped face stared sightlessly out of the mangled keyhole-shaped gap. Sham took the same approach with the snakes, pulverising them with the force of his blows. The creatures of the night did not shift into shadow form, opting to allow their armour to protect them.

As strong as steel plate is, though, there is a chink in any suit of armour.

The Vampyres were slowed by their armour, while the Crows were the epitome of agility. There was not a lot of room to manoeuvre in the hall, especially with so many clustered together, but the *Rugadh* used their wings to their advantage to buffet the Knights with blasts of air and aid the speed of their movement, so that they could dart in for an attack and slip back out of reach before the Knights could respond. Some Knights began to wise to the tactic and hack at the wings, tucking their chins and trusting to their armour to protect them. It was too little too late, though. By the time those on the floor, who had been wriggling around like upturned turtles, had regained their feet, those who had remained standing had been hacked down almost to a man and the Crows were able to turn their ferocity on those now rising.

They fell upon the creatures of the night savagely, and many were decapitated before they could find their feet. Heads rolled this way and that like a macabre game of kickball. Though several Crows met their end, soon the bloodstained stone floor was littered with the bodies of Vampyre Knights and not one was left standing. Panting, the Crows advanced towards the far end of the hall, where they could make out smoke rising from a lit baui pipe that briefly illuminated the ratty face of Ignatius Boondoggle now and again as he inhaled.

As the golden crow cast its radiance on the Vampyre, Caróg Liath whispered, "Wait! Look!"

The Crows saw then that darkness was pouring forth from the bottom of Ignatius' cane, tendrils of oily smoke like a hundred tentacles swarming across the floor and up into each and every sarcophagus in the room.

I think I even see a few stretching back outside ... What dark magic is this?

"Hehehe," Ignatius chuckled. "You think you have won, but the truth is that was only the first line of defence. The weakest of us, most incapable of even achieving shadow form. Far greater perils await you should you trespass further, Crows. Far greater." He locked eyes with Dion.

The Night Comes Alive

"D'you know how old I am, boy? I've lived lifetime after lifetime, and I am more powerful than you can possibly imagine. You should have stayed home, Crows, or hid away in a dark hole in a remote corner of the world where we could not find you. Now, there is no hope for any of you."

He rapped his cane on the floor, and the tendrils of darkness pulsated and thrummed and then vanished. The stone lids of the sarcophagi started to slide off the tombs of their own accord, and soulless drums sounded as they hit the floor one after another in a bone-chilling melody.

"You may have heard stories of what we *creatures of the night* can do," said Ignatius, "but it is time now for you to witness with your own eyes the true extent of our power."

A chorus of guttural moans echoed around the hall as the dead began to awaken from their eternal sleep and unearth themselves from their tombs. Most were so ancient as to be nothing more than skeletons, some with shreds of rotting flesh still attached, while some were still decomposing, flaking like lepers with tatters of mouldy clothing hanging off them. None had eyes, and yet all directed their skulls towards the *Rugadh na Marbh* as one.

Having turned away from Ignatius to behold the nightmare unfold, the Crows spun back to him when his voice floated to them, but he was nowhere to be seen. "Darcuul asked me to save this as a last resort, not wishing to sully his ancestors' memories, but I will stop at nothing to prevent you from reaching the Old One. This is your tomb now, Crows. Time to clip those wings!"

Spot gasped and pointed, "Look!"

More of the dead were staggering down the stairs from outside to join those who had risen from the sarcophagi. These newcomers were just as skeletal, but also covered in dirt.

They rose from the graves outside! There is no escape now. There must be hundreds of corpses in the cemetery!

"Form a circle and fight them off!" barked Aguilar. "We cannot go back, so we stand our ground!"

The Crows gathered into a loose circle bristling with blades. Aguilar groaned as he saw that many of the men had been interred with their knightly swords and now wielded them loosely in vapid grips. They were clumsy and slow when they swung at him, but he knew they could bog him down with sheer numbers if he allowed himself to be cornered. Popping the skulls of those who were unarmed with swift slashes of his sabre in puffs of bone splinters and white powder, he then easily sidestepped the first few swipes of the dead sword-wielders, his own sword wreaking havoc among them and leaving them nothing but groaning piles of bones. Unless their skulls were shattered, he noticed, they continued to live and moan. When a knot of sword-wielders came for him, he was glad to have Arturo by his side.

Arturo slammed into the dead like a battering ram before they could even swing their rusty weapons, muscles bulging, sword held two-handed, mowing them down like a farmer in a wheat field. He ploughed on into them, shouldering and elbowing, shoving and punching and swinging his longsword one-handed as if it were a hatchet, hacking down the skeletons two at a time such was the force of his swings. Bones clattered to the ground around him, and he would have pressed on if not for Aguilar shouting for him to stay close. A quick glance over his shoulder told him Sandy Locks was in trouble, so he backtracked hastily. He barely made it back to the circle, surrounded on all sides, and took a few gashes along the way. Stuck facing too many sword-wielders, Sandy could not parry them all at once, especially since they staggered their attacks. Rusty swords started to slip past his guard and cleave open his flesh, making him yelp. His own cutlass snapped back, severing a spine and leaving a skull rolling on the floor before twirling into a parry and from there into a ribcage, shattering it like kindling. A nick to the wing forced him back, hissing. He buffeted the dead back with a beat of his sore wings and then retreated behind Sham and Fuang Shi for a moment to catch his breath.

The two took his place without a moment's hesitation, spreading out to cover the lost ground. Sham's broadsword hummed and Fuang Shi's katana whistled through the air into the rotting bones of the risen dead. Sham rampaged through those that came at him, heavy broadsword making easy work of the brittle bones. The dead were slow enough that he disregarded their ancient swords, relying on his speed to overcome them. He soon realised his mistake when his feet were surrounded by severed skulls snapping at his toes and he was forced to stamp on them while also defending himself from the archaic blades of those still standing. One such sword slid past his own, pronging him in the side and making him grunt. He backhanded the skeleton away, and as its blade tore loose of his flesh, he pulverised its skull with a downward chop.

Fuang Shi's katana whirred in a blisteringly fast attack pattern that decimated any foe that stood before him. The problem was that several foes stood before him at all times. Spot winced to watch as the master swordsman's skill was undone time and again by sheer numbers. He lopped off three skeletons' skulls with as many blows and downed two with kicks only for another to gash him in the back. He spun with venomous speed and slit the skull open through its nasal cavity, but Spot could tell from his laboured breathing that he was hurting. Sir Dion Laflamme fought by his side, feet planted, longsword sweeping back and forth to sunder corpse after corpse. Spot blinked as he suddenly leapt several yards, blurring through the air faster than the eye could follow and leaving half a dozen decapitated dead in his wake.

Hmm, his vampyric powers could prove helpful to us.

Watching from the safety of the centre of the circle alongside Carόg Liath, Spot knew he would never forget the grisly faces of the dead men and women with flesh still attached. Their saggy grey skin peeled and flaked away before his eyes like a leper's, their empty eyeholes writhing with maggots. He gagged as the Hood's golden crow punched through the faces of several carcasses and a fetid gust wafted straight into Spot's mouth, making his eyes water. Despite the *Sluagh na Marbh's* arcane tricks, the Crows could not put the dead back in their graves fast enough, it was clear to see.

Sooner or later, numbers will tell and we will be overwhelmed.

"We don't have time for this!" shouted Dion, windmilling his sword through a stack of dead men. "I can take you to the entrance to the catacombs. It's narrow. It'll funnel them, so that they can't attack more than two abreast. A few strong fighters can hold them back while the rest of us press on."

Aguilar blocked a rusty sword and hesitated, knowing it was likely a death sentence for those left behind to protect their backs.

"We *must* stop Ra'Gthul!" insisted Dion.

Aguilar nodded once, abruptly, and swept the legs out from under the dead man he faced with a kick. He beheaded the corpse with a single slash and then assigned three men and one woman to the task of staying behind. As the dead closed in on them slowly, shuffling and stumbling with little coordination, Dion led the Crows to the sarcophagus that served as an entryway to the catacombs, cutting his way past a few cadavers in his path. The sculpted lid had already been removed, so the Crows poured down after Dion, Carόg Liath having to duck and tuck his wings in tight and squeeze his bulk through. Aguilar clapped those destined to remain on the shoulder and offered a few words of encouragement, and then he was gone and the four Crows were alone with the horde of the dead.

How difficult it must be to order people into dangerous situations, knowing they'll never make it out.

37
Ferals

Grunts, cracks and the occasional clangour of steel on stone followed Spot de León, Sir Dion Laflamme and the Crows as they went. Dion led the way down the stairs and into a rugged rocky passageway with openings branching off in both directions at frequent intervals. Hesitating occasionally, Dion led them through the maze, turning this way and that, while Aguilar brought up the rear. After a short while of silent padding, they heard a growl to curdle the blood and froze, glancing left and right.

"A feral," muttered Dion. "With luck, we can slip past it unnoticed. If we run into any of them, do *not* make eye contact."

Fast thudding footsteps that matched the rhythm of their hearts forewarned them of an attack.

"Oh no," moaned Dion. "They must be able to smell your blood!"

An instant later, a howling feral burst out of a side tunnel and threw itself on Dion, biting and clawing. Clad in old-fashioned tattered breeches and high stockings, it had no shoes and only a strip of white linen remained of its shirt, wrapped around its gaunt frame. Its ribs showed vividly through its thin, fish-belly skin, patches of dark hair covered its scalp, and drool hung from the sharp tips of its fangs. Its blue eyes blazed with unholy fire, staring out of a sunken face ravaged by endless hunger. The Vampyre Knight impaled it on his blade, but the feral did not care, continuing to savage him as best it could in its efforts to reach the living.

"Protect the Vampyre!" squawked the Hood, wondering what the world had come to that he should ever say such words.

"Get its head! Get its head!" Dion shrieked, and Sham Fassik obliged.

Placing a boot on the corpse and withdrawing his sword, Dion groaned as he felt the pain of his wounds seep into him. Bite marks adorned his shoulders, having torn through his long grey coat and white shirt, and his arms bore claw marks where his sleeves were shredded.

"They will have heard that," he croaked, terror etched into his visage. "Run!"

He took off, but did not get far. As he had predicted, ferals began to boil up out of each and every side tunnel as if growing out of the ground, howling and hurling themselves without fear of pain or death onto the *Rugadh na Marbh*. Dion was forced to stand his ground as the bony fiends blocked his way, his longsword penduluming across the passage to paint the rocky walls with their blood. Practised at the art of Vampyre slaying, the

Crows were careful to aim for the neck, but it was not easy when the creatures moved around erratically with no discernible coordination, twitching their heads this way and that. They clung like limpets when they got close enough, latching on with fangs and claws and gurgling as they started to suck out the Crows' lifeblood.

"Defend the Hood!" Aguilar barked, watching out of the corner of his eye as Crows leapt to follow his orders, surrounding their leader on all sides in a ring of blades flashing in the golden crow's radiance as they scythed down their unearthly foes.

The Hood watched as his warriors rebuffed the ferals, unable to help without hurting his own. Aguilar's sabre slashed back and forth, cutting into necks wherever possible and ribboning chests and faces where he missed. One such maimed feral with its skull staved in dragged itself feebly along the ground to grab the Crow's leg and sink its teeth into his calf. Letting out a cry, Aguilar was forced to ignore the pain until he had pushed away the closest foe, using his sword like a staff. Then, he lashed out vengefully at the creature of the night chewing on his leg and watched in satisfaction as its skull burst apart in a shower of blood and brains. The momentary distraction cost him dearly, however, for he was borne to the ground by a feral in ruined purple velvet a heartbeat later.

Stuck staving off his own foes, Arturo witnessed his friend's plight in his peripheral vision. Roaring like a bear with a thorn in its paw, he sped up his swordplay and flung himself at the ferals to create some space, mighty blows of his broadsword sundering the creatures from ear to ear. Then, he backpedalled quickly, booted the feral off his friend, smacked away a bald feral in a frilly shirt and watched with relief as Aguilar sprang to his feet just in time to fend off the Vampyres once more as they came hurtling forward, baying for blood, their animalistic shrieks echoing off the uneven walls. After that, he had no more time to worry about Aguilar as he was bogged down in ferals, two seeming to appear for every one he smote down like the heads of the mythical Hydra. His brawny arms were soon coated to the elbows in gore.

He let loose so much of the fluid, in fact, that Sham Fassik, by his side, slipped on the stuff and let out an "Oof!" as he landed, winded, on the rugged floor with a thump. Feet carefully planted, Fuang Shi stood over his friend, katana windmilling this way and that to savage any feral that came too close to either himself, his fallen friend or young Spot de León, who hid behind him. Despite his skills, the ferals poured out of every opening around him – and there were many – and he knew it was only a matter of time before he was overwhelmed.

"Get up, Sham!" he snapped. "I need you!"

Scrabbling in the expanding pool of blood, slipping and sliding,

Sham struggled to scramble to his feet. Eventually, he used his broadsword as a cane and levered himself upright, only to be knocked down again immediately by a white-haired shrunken feral in a ragged blue cloak that slipped past Fuang Shi's guard. The feral clawed at his face, and Sham cried out as its sharp fingers raked over his eyes. He seized its wrists and it bit his shoulder, but he managed to throw it off him with a grunt. Fortunately, the teeth hadn't managed to penetrate his leather jerkin.

As the ferals' numbers swelled, Fuang Shi was thrown aside, Sham was trampled, and Spot lashed out at a Vampyre in a ripped shirt only to be bowled over and tossed into a side passage to bump into Sir Dion Laflamme, who had suffered a similar fate.

They heard Caróg Liath squawk, "We must keep moving! Follow me!" and then, slack-jawed, they witnessed him pelting past their field of vision, running up the tunnel perpendicular to their own and belching bolts of fire to clear the way.

Any feral caught in the blast was turned to ash in an instant, so that a path opened up. Crows sprinted alongside their leader, protecting his flanks, and some managed to follow in his wake. For those too far behind, however, bogged down in enemies or too slow to react, there was no hope. Spot and Dion watched as their immediate enemies were incinerated and then observed the straggling Crows trying to catch up with the Hood. The ferals had been pushed back for a brief moment, but now they gushed from almost every opening like a flood, blocking off the *Rugadh* who had been left behind and isolating them.

"Run!" Dion advised quietly, seeing that their tunnel was empty and turning away from the screeches of the ferals and the screams of the dying Crows.

"We should help them!" Spot hissed, but the golden crow's light faded away rapidly and was soon gone, leaving only darkness.

"We can't! There's too many of them. Come with me, before we die, too. We can't help them!"

Spot turned away from the death wails, tears in his eyes. "I know …"

38
Home

Sir Dion Laflamme glanced sidelong at Spot de León, seeing him clearly despite the blackness that engulfed them.

I haven't eaten in days ... I can practically taste the boy's blood ... So hungry ...

"Why are you doing this?" Spot asked softly.

Dion shot him a wild look, half-crazed, half-pleading, glad the boy could not see him in the darkness. He would be blind as a bat without the light of the Hood's ethereal golden crow, Dion knew.

I am a shell of my former self, an abomination with no future. I have days-old stubble growing on my cheeks, whiskers on my chin. I am as gaunt and pale as a corpse. My eyes are sunken deep in my skull. My shirt, coat and breeches are torn all over from the fight with the ferals, and from my capture. My wounds have healed remarkably rapidly, though, thanks to my affliction.

"They wanted me to ... turn my father," Dion croaked, looking away. "I ... cannot do that. I *will* not do that to him. He does not deserve to ... to become like me. A monster to plague the nightmares of young children, a cautionary tale. My father is a good man. I ... am not. Maybe I got what I deserved, but ... I will not let my fate define me. My choices define me. And I choose to fight against vampyrism rather than succumb to it."

"You *are* a good man, Dion."

Dion shook his head, and tears glistened in his eyes. "No, I'm not. But I'm doing my best. If I can get you and your friends to that portal, I will have done all I can to redeem myself. After that ... I can do no more."

Reminded of his friends, Spot asked, "Should we turn back and follow after the Hood? Perhaps the way is clear by now if all the ferals pursued him."

Dion pointed his sword ahead. "Let's see where this leads first. There must be a reason it's empty."

"Perhaps it's simply a dead end."

"Perhaps."

They padded cautiously along the eerily empty tunnel, which unexpectedly sloped upwards as they went. Dion led the way with Spot holding a fistful of the back of his ruined coat. Despite his ability to see in the dark, the utter blackness and isolation weighed on the Vampyre Knight, heavy and oppressive. His breathing grew louder and louder as it stifled him, smothering as a pillow pressed over his face. He started to hyperventilate, gasping for breath, and bumped into a wall, seeking an exit where there was none to be found. He whimpered.

What if I never get out of this cursed place? What if I'm trapped down here until the ferals find me? Will anybody ever find my corpse? Will anybody even notice I am missing? Will anybody care?

"Shh!" Spot hissed at him.

Dion took a few deep calming breaths, and his heart calmed from its butterfly-wing palpitations to a mere rapid hammering. His breathing slowed a little, though he could still feel every single muscle in his body clenched to breaking point.

I'm gripping the sword hilt so tight that I'm surprised it hasn't shattered in my hand.

"D'you see that or am I hallucinating?" Spot asked after a while.

"I see it." A light beckoned at the end of the tunnel ahead of them, a soft golden glow. "Let's check it out."

They crept forward until they reached the end of the tunnel, where Dion motioned for them to lie flat so that they could crawl forward and peek over the edge, for the light emanated from below them. He inhaled sharply through his nose as he realised that their tunnel had led them to a ledge overlooking the Old One's cavern, some twenty feet above it. It was empty, but Dion knew that was only an illusion projected by the Old One. The light was coming from a passage below them. Even as he stared, the Hood came charging into the cavern from the passage, belching fire and mauling ferals with his sabres, followed by an ethereal golden crow and a swathe of black-clad *Rugadh na Marbh* scything down the creatures of the night with their blades as they went. Caróg Liath unleashed a squawk unlike any Dion had ever heard, visible to the eyes as a shockwave like a ripple in the air. The whole cavern shook and seemed to bend in on itself, and then the illusion shattered. A ripple of light flowed over the cavern, disgorging in its wake the truth.

Spot gasped. The cave was suddenly brimming with horrors. Unseen, Dion snarled down at Ra'Gthul, sat at the back of the spacious cavern atop his grisly throne of skin and bones, surrounded by a plethora of blue-eyed Vampyres dressed as if for a gala with some noticeable exceptions. Dion scowled down at Ignatius Boondoggle in his mink overcoat and Count Darcuul in his typical silver-threaded black outfit.

Is that Bibaldi and his Clowns? What in the blazes are they doing here?

By the face-painted, calico-clad clowns was the stone ring inset with glyphs of pulsing purple fire. The sneering look on the Old One's face made Dion's fangs itch, and the Vampyre Knight noticed that, rather than his usual loincloth, Ra'Gthul sported this night a long gold-and-crimson coat over a frilly shirt, tight breeches and snakeskin boots. The gems inset in the hilt of the ornate scimitar belted at his waist in a red leather scabbard glimmered in the rune-light.

While his *Rugadh na Marbh* protected him from the ferals chasing them from the tunnel, the Hood cawed, "Ra'Gthul, you fiend! Long has it been since we met! For five hundred years have I sought you after our duel left me half-dead, and at long last I have found you!"

Ra'Gthul's four blue eyes blazed. "Caróg Liath … It took you long enough. A long time you have waited and a long way you have come just to die, my old enemy. Ss ss ss. You were never supposed to make it through the portal. *I* was sent here to conquer this world. You and the *Sluagh na Marbh* ruined everything when you attacked! Ss ss ss. None of my brothers made it through after me – only you! Why is that? For five hundred years, I have awaited word from my kin, spreading my power across this world. Ss ss ss. Why have none of my brethren joined me?"

"You know why," the Hood answered smugly. "Because the *Sluagh* are guarding the portal, protecting this world and all others from your foul kind. *I* was sent here to put an end to your nefarious schemes, and my brethren will welcome me home as a hero when I bring them your head!"

"You're too late. The ritual is complete. I have finally made contact with my brothers," Ra'gthul snarled. "They will be joining us this very night – as I presume you know – and there is nothing you can do to stop it! Ss ss ss. Just as when we last fought, you are too weak to prevail, *Hood!*"

"We will see about that!" trumpeted Caróg Liath, hopping forward and belching flames at the Vampyres twixt him and the Old One.

The creatures of the night closest to him keened as they went up in flames, and the rest brandished their swords in readiness, snarling and spitting. The stench of burning flesh pervaded the cavern, acrid and bitter. Black smoke rose from the bodies when they collapsed.

"Attack, my *Rugadh!*" shrieked Caróg Liath. "Attack!"

Hard-pressed to both protect the Hood from the ferals at his back and assist in his offence against the smarter Vampyres in front, the Crows tried their best to obey but were spread thin, their numbers depleted. As they spread out to cover more ground and more foes, they left gaps in their defence and began to drop like flies, their death cries echoing off the high ceiling and rugged walls.

Caróg Liath seemed not to notice, only kept cawing, "Onwards, my children! Onwards! We must defeat the darkness! Fight on! Fight on!"

Despite a lack of aid from the *Rugadh*, the Hood managed to massacre his way through the vampyric horde, buffeting with his wings and burping up streams of fire to incinerate his foes while the ethereal golden crow he had summoned speared straight through the Vampyres' skulls, popping them like seed pods. He scarcely needed the twin sabres in his hands, though they snapped out now and again to parry a blow or sever a head in the blink of an eye. Faster than Dion would have believed possible, Caróg Liath stood before the throne of the Old One and reared back to spew a sustained river of flames from his beak. Ra'Gthul was upright in a blink, bony claw outstretched, alien words of power slithering over his tongue and making Dion's skin crawl. Fire as blue as his eyes blazed from his hand to clash with the Hood's orange inferno in mid-air with a clap like thunder. As the two elemental forces vied against one another, roaring and spitting sparks, the cave sweltered. Dion started to sweat and saw several Crows below sag and succumb to the heat and the ferals' unceasing onslaught.

    Caróg Liath overpowered Ra'Gthul, and his stream of fire threw the Old One to the ground with a screech. The *Sluagh na Marbh* pounced some ten yards onto the *Diavhal*, missing splitting his enemy open by inches as Ra'Gthul rolled aside and sprang upright, backing away for a momentary reprieve. Darkness swelled around the Old One and propelled him up into the air like a cloud that could bear his weight, speeding him away his foe. Caróg Liath would give him no reprieve, however. Taking to the air, he flailed his sabres at the Father of Vampyres in a complex steel web that left Ra'Gthul panting and bloodied. The Old One quickly learned the rhythm of the attack pattern, however, and broke it up with swift jarring strokes of his own wide-bladed three-foot steel scimitar, gashing the *Sluagh na Marbh* open across his feathery breast and making him screak in pain.

    Blue flames roaring from his palm, his scimitar hacking and jabbing, Ra'Gthul flew around and around the room, trying to wear down his enemy. Caróg Liath chased him every step of the way with his own geyser of fire, his sabres singing out time and again to miss the Old One by a hair's breadth. Ra'Gthul lingered too long in one spot, spewing a cerulean conflagration, and when he tried to flee the Hood's retort, he found his way blocked by a roaring wall of flames. Cornered, he had no time to adjust and flee before Caróg Liath hit him like a comet, bearing him into the wall and making the whole cave shudder before swatting aside his scimitar and savaging him with his sabres. Split open and bleeding, the Old One slumped to the ground with a groan.

    Caróg Liath lowered himself to the ground and stood over the Father of Vampyres. "At last, I can go home."

    As the Hood raised his blades to strike the final blow, however, the ground shook violently and the portal pulsed with purple light. Blinded and staggered, Caróg Liath shaded his eyes to peer into the portal. Up above him on the ledge, Dion did the same. What he saw made his heart sink lower than the sea floor. Two bony figures in hide boots, garish stockings, puffy breeches, wide belts, flamboyant shirts and spiky brightly-coloured coats that made them look like sea urchins were sauntering out of the portal, each with four eyes bluer than blue and maws full of long, overlapping fangs. The taller had a pointed cranium topped with a dusting of hair and a pointed white goatee, giving his head an ovoid appearance. The shorter had a broader visage augmented by prominent cheekbones and wide lips. A wispy white beard cascaded down from his chin like a thin waterfall, and the light of the purple runes reflected off his bald pate.

"My brothers," Ra'Gthul whispered, "have arrived!"

More Old Ones! We're doomed!

Caróg Liath cursed and threw himself at the newcomers blades first, cawing in outrage. Splitting up and dodging his gouts of flame and swipes of his sabres, however, the two Old Ones took to the air on clouds of darkness just as had Ra'Gthul and caught the Hood between them in a trap of enchantments. Searing cerulean fireballs spattered on the cave walls all around Caróg Liath as he dodged this way and that frantically, flying up and down and round and round in intricate evasive manoeuvers. Eventually, though, he began to tire and slow, and they caught him. Ra'Gthul took him by surprise by regaining his feet and sending his own blue blaze up to join the rest. The Hood banked late and cawed in pain and fury as the fire scorched his wing and he caromed out of the air to hit the rocky floor hard and skid to a halt close to the portal. The few surviving Crows still battling the Vampyres and ferals wailed at the sight of their leader torn from the air.

Throwing his arms up into the air, Ra'Gthul spun away to bask in his sycophants' cheers – only they were too busy fighting for their lives against the surviving Crows. He shrugged off the lack of applause and turned back to finish off his old enemy. To his surprise, the Hood blurred past him in a sudden flurry of flapping wings before he could strike and he howled in anger as he saw his enemy's goal.

"Stay away from that portal!" he shrieked, tossing blue wildfire after him.

Caróg Liath was too fast, though.

Just before he passed through the shimmering hollow stone ring etched with pulsating purple runes, he squawked, "If I cannot defeat you, I will destroy the portal from the other side! Damn this world! We will forget about it – and you – forever!"

"You cannot do that!" Ra'Gthul shrieked. "You'll never be able to return, and we'll never be able to go home! We'll be cut off from *Nagathai* forever!"

It was too late. The Father of Crows was gone.

39
For the Innocents

Spot de León could not believe his eyes nor his ears.

Caróg Liath is gone. He was sent by his godlike people to protect our world, but he gave up and abandoned us to the Old Ones. We are alone against their unholy might. Night will fall over all of Maradoum.

Then, he spotted Arturo decapitating a feral below him and remembered when he had first met the man. After hearing of his first encounter with a Vampyre, he had asked, 'How did you escape?'

Arturo had responded, 'I cut the Vampyre's head clean off.'

Perhaps it's not so dreadful, after all. He did that even before imbued with power by the Hood. All we need to do is cut off their heads. There is always a light at the end of the tunnel.

He recalled then the warmth he had felt with the Crows and during evenings alone with his father in his youth. His own thought rotated in his mind like a mantra.

There is always a light at the end of the tunnel.

The Crows were sagging like windless sails, their strength abandoning them much as had their leader as they began to wonder who they were fighting for and how they could possibly win against such dark magics as the Vampyres possessed without the Hood. Medallions flashed time and again to prevent the creatures of the night from taking on shadow form, but even without that advantage, the Vampyres were gradually culling the Crows like a pack of wolves who have cornered a herd of deer. The only advantage the *Rugadh* had over their nemeses was their ability to fly, and those that could took to the air to use that advantage. Many could not risk taking off, however, without exposing themselves to their enemies' blades, and once their companions started rising up in a panic, they were often left vulnerable to attacks from behind and stabbed in the back within seconds.

The pirate, Sandy Locks, floated above the fanged fiends, flapping his wings and flashing his medallion. His cutlass hummed out time and again in a downward arc to lop the heads off the well-dressed Vampyres clustered beneath him, more often than not meeting a blade before it could meet flesh. Frustrated by the blocking swords, he buffeted the horrors beneath him with his wings, knocking them all back a pace so that he could swoop down and take advantage of their discombobulation. It was still a risky manoeuvre, though. The Vampyres recovered fast and many of them took swipes at him as he arced back up into the air, leaving behind a fountaining neck stump.

As he was almost clear of them, one of them snipped the tip of his left wing and he cried out in agony. Spot winced at the sight. Sandy banked hard and landed in a clear space close to the Old Ones, who had gathered together at the back of the cave by the throne to whisper conspiratorially with the Vampyre there in a thick mink fur coat.

Who is that? Why isn't he fighting? What's he talking to the Old Ones about?

Spot's eyes flicked back to Sandy, who was swarmed as soon as he landed by Vampyres in silk and satin. He beheaded two of them in quick succession, and then the rest were upon him. He went down in a dog-pile for a moment, and Spot was sure he had died, but then he emerged, tossing horrors off him and roaring like a wildcat. His broad cutlass swept left and right, sowing mayhem wherever it strode, and geysers of blood shot up into the air like little fireworks. Still, Spot was sure not all of the blood coating him was the Vampyres'. His left arm hung limp, and his sandy hair was matted to his head.

"Come on then!" he bellowed at the creatures of the night, voice cracking, hacking them down one by one.

Spot's heart panged.

He knows he does not have long to live. I can see it in his eyes and hear it in his voice. His spirit is broken.

Spot's heart went out most, however, to his protectors, Sham Fassik and Fuang Shi, who were stuck battling Bibaldi and his Clowns, the troubadours whom Spot had first seen perform at *Pacia* Castle. Spot shivered as he laid eyes on the clowns with their garish face paint, ridiculous red lips, ginger wigs, curly toed shoes and gaudy getups.

They are the stuff of nightmare!

Sweat poured down Sham's tan face as he windmilled his broadsword to keep the clowns at bay, feet planted and hair plastered to his brow, eyebrows bunched, teeth gritted and bared. The clowns came at him in numbers, giggling, with steel sabres in hand.

I wonder if one of the aristocratic Vampyres supplied the blades.

Wherever they came from, they looked plenty sharp as they painted red welts on Sham's frame, crisscrossing him with bleeding wounds. Sham swung low and tripped a couple, before chopping the head off one and booting the other in the face to keep him down while he turned his attention to the others. By his side, Fuang Shi's katana shimmered through the air so fast that Spot could not follow it with his eye, and yet the Tzunese warrior too was taking wounds. Red blossomed on his frame here and there even as he severed the necks of several clowns one after another, breezing around them like a ghost, scarcely needing to block or parry – until he ran into Bibaldi.

The troupe leader was bedecked like his clowns in overlarge shoes with curly toes, calico dungarees over a flamboyant shirt and a ginger wig. His chalked face popped with the colour of his rouged cheeks and wide, painted lips, and a blue brow marked him apart from the rest. He looked older than the rest, too, though it was hard to tell under all the face paint. His slim rapier was a thunderbolt jabbing at Fuang Shi over and over, so fast each thrust was like a mirage. Spot could almost believe his eyes had tricked him and Bibaldi had not moved at all, save for the blood oozing from Fuang Shi's several puncture wounds. The Tzunese warrior's katana flicked out to bat away the rapier just in time again and again as he backed away, trying to find some space to manoeuvre. Bibaldi and the Clowns hounded him relentlessly, giggling sinisterly, shuffling forward like expert fencers and pressing him with a medley of lunges and cuts.

Bibaldi and some of the others took on the mantle of the night, shifting into shadow form and lancing ethereal swords at the Crow. Fuang Shi danced back and forth, pirouetting and ducking and swaying to evade as many attacks as possible while he fished inside the black cloth that enwrapped him for his medallion. Spot was on the verge of pulling out his own when Fuang Shi found it, held it up and pronounced the word of power to make it flash. Bibaldi and the others were thrown from the shadow realm back to reality, some to land on their rear ends. These Fuang Shi put down first. Then, Bibaldi and the rest were coming for him again, baying for his blood, needling him with rapiers and sabres.

Though taking his own wounds from the crazed troubadours, Sham witnessed his friend's plight out of the corner of his eye and threw himself into the midst of the clowns with sword swinging. Sabres and rapiers pinged as they snapped against the thicker steel of the broadsword in his hands, and he laid about him like a bull in a china shop, flattening Vampyres left and right with wild meaty blows. Chuckling maniacally as his fellows were vanquished, Bibaldi took off his wig, revealing a tonsure nearing baldness, and tossed it into Sham's face. Blinded, Sham stepped back and snatched at the wig, only to feel Bibaldi's rapier sink into his side. He hissed through gritted teeth, sweat pouring down his tan face, and tossed the wig aside. His sword seemed twice as heavy in his hands, but he raised it over his head and brought it cleaving down on the clowns surrounding him again and again. The blade rose and fell, rose and fell, and blood washed the cave, arcing up in the air like a grisly rainbow.

With Sham shearing through the clowns, Fuang Shi could turn his full attention to Bibaldi. His katana glimmered in the purple rune light as it swept around and around in parrying circles that soon unbalanced the troupe leader, staggering him. Bibaldi's rapier whistled as it sailed out of his hand when he was disarmed.

The Night Comes Alive

Bibaldi held up pleading hands. "Please, good sir, don't kill me! I'll do anything! I'll tell you anything you want to know! I-I'll turn on the other Vampyres. I'll give you gold, women ... men, girls, boys ... whatever you want! Just please spare me!"

Seeing a clown coming at him in his periphery, Fuang Shi spared a split second to slash open Bibaldi's face before turning to the new threat. After he had gutted and beheaded the clown, he cut off Bibaldi's howls with a well-placed gash to the neck that sent his head rolling. A feral in a holey mauve robe cross-hatched with slash marks shoved his way past the Crows behind Fuang Shi then and pounced on the golden-skinned man's back, sinking its teeth into his collar. Fuang Shi cried out in agony and tried to throw off the feral, but it clung to him with its claws like a cat to wool. He could not reach it with his katana, and Sham could not help, weighed down by his own wounds and the enemies arrayed before him.

A lack of coordination and morale is killing the Crows. I have to do something. I have to remind them what they're fighting for – not for the Hood, but for all of Maradoum.

Aguilar de la Torre yet breathed, too. He had not taken to the air like some of his brethren, but appeared to be attempting to organise a defence on the ground. His calls were half-hearted, though, and Spot thought his sabre whined through the air with less than its usual venom. Managing to dispatch one finely dressed Vampyre with a lacklustre slash to the neck that left the head hanging by a flap of skin, Aguilar came face to face with Count Ivan Darcuul.

The Count grinned maliciously, scraping his long fangs together, thin nostrils flaring in his weasel face and blue eyes blazing. Spot did not hear what he said to Aguilar over the inarticulate shouts and clangour of swords echoing off the cave walls. They clashed blades. Immediately, Aguilar was on the back foot, looking haggard and wan as he desperately parried Darcuul's lightning fast assault. The Count shifted into shadow, and Aguilar could not even see the phantom blade as it sought him out. He sprang to and fro, trying to dodge, and grunted in rage more than pain when he felt the Count's sabre nick his hip and then his ribs. Fortunately, a nearby Crow brandished his medallion and a bright white light forced Darcuul to rematerialise.

The Vampyre reeled back drunkenly as he became whole, and Aguilar sought to use the moment to his advantage – only to have his sabre parried and his cheek cut open as he yanked his head back to avoid a lethal riposte. Darcuul came on. Aguilar backed away fast, tried to plant his feet and had his thigh slit open for his troubles. He backed away. When Darcuul attacked again, he did not plant his feet. He parried and managed to slip outside the Count's guard, spun around him and slashed him across the back. He had been moving too fast to aim carefully for the neck, but Darcuul growled as he felt steel grind against his shoulder blades.

Aguilar kicked him in the hip as he spun, making him stumble back, and served up a salvo of wickedly fast strikes, all aimed to take Darcuul's head from his shoulders. The Count parried desperately as Aguilar's sabre scythed towards him from all sides, swatting it away left and right barely a hair's breadth from his skin while he tried to regain his balance. He could not find time to parry one blow as his weight came down on an uneven patch of ground, and so he ducked. His yowl of agony as Aguilar's sabre carved open his forehead echoed around the cavern. He flailed his sabre wildly to keep the Crow at bay while he found his feet and wiped his head with his forearm, smearing his face with blood. Glaring at Aguilar with ichor dripping down his nose, he leapt high into the air and brought his sabre cleaving down hard on the Crow. Aguilar danced aside, but Darcuul was not done. As soon as he landed, he whacked away Aguilar's slash with venom and launched his own series of thrusts, high and low, jumping and ducking. He caught Aguilar with a spinning kick to the face and then lanced his sabre deep into the Crow's side when Aguilar stumbled back.

Aguilar cried out and windmilled his sabre to keep Darcuul away, but the Count charged in, swept aside the Crow's sword and shoulder-barged him before slicing open his chest. The Crow staggered back, but rallied and propelled himself forward with his wings, teeth gritted, sabre swiping. Darcuul batted aside the slash contemptuously and tripped the Crow by hooking a leg behind his ankle and clotheslining him. Spot saw him laugh and his gut tightened. His chest cramped, and he felt lightning in his lungs when Darcuul's sabre rammed down into Aguilar's belly. He clearly heard the Crow's screech of agony even over the ruckus as the Count twisted the blade.

"No!" Spot wailed, standing without thinking. "Aguilar!"

Dion hissed and tried to pull the boy back down, but the damage was done. Necks craned, and all eyes in the cave turned towards the boy up on the ledge above them for a split second – even the ferals', even the Old Ones'.

"My brothers," Spot felt the words well up in him and let them flow out with his tears, his small voice reverberating around the cave, "our leader may be gone, but our *purpose* remains! For the innocents!"

"For the innocents!" Aguilar sat up and jabbed his sabre into Darcuul's exposed flank below his ribs, and the Count yowled and stabbed Aguilar in the heart, withdrawing his blade in a spurt of blood.

Spot would never forget the almost peaceful expression on Aguilar's face as his head bounced off the cave floor. With bored expressions, the Old Ones flicked their wrists and sent bolts of blue fire searing up towards the boy on the ledge. Spot threw himself flat beside Dion and covered his head with his hands, feeling the fire whoosh past so close that it burned the hairs from the skin on one arm. The tunnel shook as the fire crashed into the ceiling with a roar. Spot heard a stomach-wrenching crack above him and glanced up to see a fissure winding its way through the trembling rock above his head. Just before the ceiling caved in, Dion grabbed Spot and threw him off the ledge down into the cavern below. Yelping, Spot slowed his fall by flapping his wings, but still landed hard on the cave floor. Loose rocks rained down on him, knocking him flat and leaving him dazed and sore. He looked up and saw through bleary eyes that the ledge was covered in rubble. The tunnel was sealed. Dion was gone.

Spot thought back to what he had said when the boy had called him a good man – 'No, I'm not. But I'm doing my best. If I can get you and your friends to that portal, I will have done all I can to redeem myself. After that ... I can do no more.'

He did what he set out to do, and he could not live with himself any longer. Thank you, Sir Dion Laflamme, for saving my life. I pray you find the rest you deserve in the Prophet's paradise. Recce em Pacia.

Witnessing Aguilar's death out of the corner of his eye, Arturo hollered his wrath and turned from the ferals he had been fighting to bull towards Darcuul at speed, shoulders lowered. Fortunately, the flow of ferals from the tunnel at their backs was lessening, so Sandy Locks and his few surviving companions managed to take up the slack as Arturo slammed into Darcuul sword first, driving him back a step despite his vampyric strength. Clutching his side, blood trickling from the wound on his forehead into his unnaturally bright blue eyes, the Count parried and blocked as fast as he could, backing away towards the throne. Arturo chased him every step of the way, not letting up, his longsword acquiring notch after notch as he hammered it down on the Vampyre's sabre.

Darcuul's sabre snapped with a ping, and the Count howled as Arturo's longsword lodged itself firmly in his collarbone. Placing a boot on his foe's chest, Arturo ripped out the sword and cut off the Count's head with a single swing. He roared at the headless corpse, venting his rage at the loss of his friend. The Old Ones took notice of him then, and though Spot called out a warning, Arturo was engulfed head to toe in a blue blaze. An ashen statue in his likeness remained for a heartbeat after the fire winked out, having devoured every last inch of flesh, and then it crumbled to the ground.

The Old Ones turned their sapphire eyes on Spot, and the blood froze in the boy's veins. His mind went slack, and his chest ached. One of the Old Ones beckoned with a claw of a finger, and Spot found himself rising into the air against his volition, being drawn towards the ancient

Fathers of Vampyres like iron to a lodestone. Sham Fassik and Fuang Shi cried out in horror, but could do nothing to help Spot. If they turned away, the ferals and Vampyres they battled would rip them to pieces. Spot stopped, suspended in mid-air, less than a foot from the Old Ones. He could see the blood caked around their maws and smell their rotten breath.

I cannot move a muscle! What sorcery is this?

"Who are you, boy?" one of them asked, his voice the ring of a chisel on a tombstone.

"This, Frha'Gwa, my old friend," rasped Ra'Gthul, "is Samuel de León, although he goes by Spot, according to my informant, Aiva. Ss ss ss."

Spot's gut clenched.

Aiva. That lying murderess!

Ra'Gthul grinned at the scowl on the boy's face. "Had you going, did she, boy? Ss ss ss. Ah, to be young and in love."

"You know this boy?" asked the other Old One in tones silkier than a spider web.

Ra'Gthul nodded. "He's been a real thorn in my side, I can tell you, Mha'Grith. He sees straight through our glamours for some reason. Ss ss ss. He's known about us for months, maybe years."

Mha'Grith sniffed. "Then, he has seen too much and must die."

"Put da boy down!" a woman's voice cut through the melee, reverberating off the walls with such power that the Crows and Vampyres all ceased fighting for a moment just to see who it was.

Ursa Koum?

40
Were-bear

Mzee Ursa Koum stepped into the ghoulish purple light cast by the pulsing runes etched into the portal. She wore an apron over a forest green frock decorated with pale green flowers and cinched with a stretch of hemp, and her silver dreadlocks hung loose around her pudgy dark-skinned face. Her eyes were alight with a green fire Spot de León had never seen.

What in the name of the Prophet is she doing here? Is that a bear?

What looked to be a grizzly bear padded out of the shadows to stand by her side, reaching her chest even on four legs.

"Who in the Void are you?" demanded Frha'Gwa.

"My name is Ursa Koum, and –"

"Oh, who cares?" said Mha'Grith sibilantly. "Our brethren will be ready to come through the portal any second now."

Spot felt a jolt as fear clamped its icy hand around his heart.

More are coming! We must stop them!

Mha'Grith waved a pale hand. "Kill her."

The Vampyres and ferals surged towards Ursa, but the roaring grizzly moved with surprising speed to intercept them, its paws pounding the floor and then carving tracks across the chest of the first feral within range. Its jaws snapped shut on the skull of the second. It tore through the creatures of the night like a hurricane, leaving a pile of groaning broken bones and sundered flesh in its wake. The Crows joined in, and the vampyric force was abruptly broken, the last few fiends surrounded with nowhere to go. The Vampyres screeched and fought in a frenzy to escape, but their doom was writ in their blazing blue eyes.

"My name is Ursa Koum," Ursa repeated, her voice booming now with supernatural volume, "and I am telling you for da last time. Put da boy down, and you may live."

The Old Ones regarded her with interest now.

"Who are you to threaten us so?" purred Ra'Gthul.

"Dat boy is like a son to me," said Ursa, "and I'll be damned if I let him get eaten by a bunch of filty stinking Vampyres."

"You needn't worry, woman," said Mha'Grith maliciously. "We're not going to kill the boy. We're going to make him one of us."

Ursa's eyes widened, and her hand shot out. "Over my dead body! *Sit'eshu zam'beamber!*"

A lot happened at once then. The rock wall behind the Old Ones seemed to grow stone arms, and as if those arms were anacondas, they wrapped themselves tightly around all three of the ancient Vampyres from another world, immobilising them. Free from combat with the last of the ferals and Vampyres thanks to Sandy Locks and the grizzly, Sham Fassik and Fuang Shi hurtled towards the Old Ones. Sham Fassik sent Mha'Grith's severed head tumbling through the air with a swing of his broadsword, and Fuang Shi took care of Frha'gwa with a single stroke of his katana. Instinctively reaching for a new spell to confound the sorceress, Ra'Gthul let go of the spell holding Spot prisoner. Free of the enchantment, Spot fell to the floor, landed agilely on his feet, crossed the distance between him and Ra'Gthul in a single bound and plunged his father's broadsword into the Old One's chest.

Ra'Gthul laughed a horrible bubbling laugh and drooled blood. "I am immortal, you fool!"

"Everything dies!" Spot growled, before incanting the words of power taught to him by Caróg Liath, before the Hood had enchanted his father's sword. *"Surtur losagadh!"*

The last Old One shrieked as the sword burst into flames and he was engulfed in a white inferno. He went up like a scarecrow, and within seconds all that was left was ash. The stone ring etched with pulsing purple runes shattered and crumbled to the floor with a clatter, the violet light winking out.

"We did it," Spot said to the absolute darkness.

"That we did," came the tired voice of Fuang Shi.

"I don't know how," said Sham Fassik. "And what happened to the portal?"

"Caróg Liath must have made good on his word," said Fuang Shi, "and closed the portal from the other side."

The ground shook and the rock overhead rumbled ominously.

A glowing ethereal green bear the size of a fist lit up the darkness, gambolling around in the air above Ursa Koum's head. By her side was Tumba Koum, dressed in a dirty white shirt and breeches with no shoes. There was no sign of the grizzly bear. Scattered all around the blood-splattered cavern were the bodies of Vampyres and ferals, Crows and Old Ones. The stench of death hung heavy in the air.

"Tumba?" asked Spot incredulously. "That bear was ... *you? You're a were-bear?*"

Tumba smiled sheepishly and spread his hands. "I tried to tell you."

Ursa stroked Spot's birthmark and beak. "What have dey done to you, my boy? We tought you had been lost forever when news of your fadder's murder reached our ears."

Spot tried to smile, but could not with a beak. "I'm fine, Ursa, don't worry. These kind folk have been taking care of me and helping me avenge my father's death."

The words ring hollow, much like the sensation inside. Where is the high of victory? Nothing will repair the damage done. Nothing will bring him back.

"I'm sorry you had to go true dat," said Ursa quietly. "You can tell me all about your adventures later. For now, we should really get out of here before dis whole cave system – and da Lágrimas – comes down on top of us. Come along, boys."

Spot and Tumba dutifully fell into line as she marched back the way she had come, back into the stalagmite- and stalactite-littered cavern whose ceiling dripped with runoff from Lágrimas River. Waterfalls sheeted the walls, spraying off smoothed rocks into the air. Sham Fassik, Fuang Shi and Sandy Locks, the only surviving Crows, hurried to keep up, limping and hobbling and cursing under their breath.

"Excuse me, ma'am," panted Sandy, "I mean no disrespect, but … well … who in the blazes are ya?"

"I'm no ma'am," said Ursa. "I am a friend of Spot's."

The Crows eyed Spot in surprise.

"It pays to have friend in high places, I guess," muttered Sham with a weary smile. "I'm just grateful you showed up when you did. Thank you, Ursa."

"We owe you our lives," added Fuang Shi, wincing as he bowed.

"You're welcome," replied Ursa, waving for them to keep moving. "Aldough what you were tinking taking a boy into battle I'll never know."

"Why *did* you show up when you did?" asked Spot, quickening his pace to walk by her side and gazing up at her. "How did you even know where we were? How did you make it through the labyrinth and find us?"

"I have known about da *Ma Ca Rong* for some time," replied Ursa, "and I do my best to keep a surreptitious eye on deir comings and goings. So, when a boatload of dem started showing up around Saint Padrice Church just before da full moon, I watched vigilantly. I saw you and da Crows come down out of da sky and go into da crypt, and I followed you. I wasn't sure I could trust da Crows until I saw dem fighting da Vampyres." She cocked her head and glanced down at him. "As for making it true da labyrinth, I just followed da bodies."

"Well, thank you," said Spot. "However you found us, I'm glad you did. You too, Tumba. Thank you."

Tumba smiled sheepishly. "You're welcome."

"I still can't believe you're a were-bear."

Together, the six of them – four Crows, a sorceress and a were-bear – shuffled through the cave. Phantom sounds plagued their ears as they imagined the noises for which they were listening so hard, making them skittish. It was silent, save for the distant scuffle of ferals now and again and the constant creaking of the rock above their heads. A sound like a biscuit snapping in half, magnified many times over, echoed around the cave, and they all jumped. A heartbeat later, icy water gushed out of the new crack splitting apart the ceiling, drenching the group. Yelping in shock and dismay, Spot and the others ran, splashing around. Before they could reach the far side of the cave, the ceiling gave way and, with a thunderous roar, the Lágrimas came crashing down on them, flooding the catacombs.

41
What Now?

Spluttering and gasping for breath, Spot de León climbed out of the tomb back into the Darcuul family crypt some time later, dripping wet. He had been swept around and around the catacombs by the river for what felt like a lifetime, suffocating and bouncing off the rugged walls. He had pulled himself up onto rocky ledges a few times, but each time had nowhere to go save for back into the water. Finally, by luck, he had managed to pull himself up onto a ledge where he could reach the tunnel leading back up to the crypt.

Wiping umber hair from his face, he looked around. The bodies of the four Crows left behind were sprawled at the foot of the tomb, mauled almost beyond recognition. Around them was heaped a pile of skeletons, rotting corpses and severed heads. There was no sign of the Vampyre in the mink overcoat or of any upright undead warriors. A sound at Spot's back startled him, and he sprang into the air like a cat, before turning with his heart in his mouth to see Ursa Koum's sodden dreadlocked head poking up out of the tomb connected to the catacombs. Tumba appeared alongside her, both breathing heavily.

"Ursa! Tumba!" Spot sobbed in relief, hurrying to hug them as they stepped out of the tomb and having to wait until they had cleared the pile of corpses.

When he finally took them in his arms, they felt like home.

That smell ... of smoke and spice ... ah, bliss.

Sham Fassik, Fuang Shi and Sandy Locks emerged from the tomb while they were embracing, saturated and panting. Spot hugged them, too.

They stink of sweat, but I don't care.

"Well," said Ursa when they had regained their breath, "da Old Ones are gone. Da Vampyres are slain, da city saved. What will you do now, Spot? You're welcome to come home wid me and live wid Tumba and I."

Spot looked from her to the Crows and back again. "I'm sorry, ma'am. I love you both like my family, but ... we didn't get them all. Sir Gómez got away, and ..."

Ursa nodded. "I understand. Well, you'll always have a home wid us. We're family."

"I'll miss you, brother," said Tumba, offering his hand.

Spot grasped it tight and drew his friend in for a hug. "I'll miss you, too, brother."

"Will you be able to get home safely?" Sham asked. "The city watch might be out there investigating the ruckus."

Ursa sniffed. "I doubt it. I'm convinced dey were paid off by da *Ma Ca Rong* to stay away from suspicious activity here at da cemetery, radder dan investigate it. I should be fine. Besides, I can protect myself."

"I saw that," said Sham with a wry smile.

"You take good care of dat boy, you hear?" Ursa said, a warning in her voice.

Sham Fassik, Fuang Shi and Sandy Locks nodded. "We will, ma'am."

Ursa shook her head. "Come on, Tumba. Let's get you home."

"But I'm not tired!" Tumba protested.

Ursa cuffed him lightly. "It's hours past your bedtime, and you know it."

The sound of Tumba whining accompanied mother and son as they made their way out of the crypt.

Once they were gone, Spot turned to the Crows. They looked at one another.

"What now, Lord of Crows?" asked Sham with a wry smile.

Spot took a deep breath. "The Lord Protector was in on this. We are not finished yet. Not until every Vampyre has been wiped from the face of Maradoum. For the innocents."

Coming soon ... Chronicles of Maradoum Volume 7

If you enjoyed the book, a review on Amazon, Goodreads or Bookbub would go a long way to showing your appreciation and would in turn be much appreciated. Thanks for reading!

Follow my Facebook page: Ross Hughes, Author
Or visit www.rosshughes.biz

Printed in Poland
by Amazon Fulfillment
Poland Sp. z o.o., Wrocław